KEPT IN THE DARK

A KIDNAPPING ROMANCE

L.M. WHITELEY

CONTENT WARNING

This book is a dark romance intended for mature audiences with an antihero who does bad things and a heroine who falls for him anyway. It contains themes and scenes that may be distressing to some readers, including:

Kidnapping
Explicit sexual content
Graphic violence done to and by main characters
Gun and knife-related violence
Death, murder and organized crime
Torture
Dynamics of dubious consent
Discussions of past childhood abuse and trauma
Mention of sexual assault of off-page victims
Mention of underage off-page victims

Your mental health matters. Reader discretion is advised.

DEDICATION

To BookTok and those horny little smut Facebook groups. I see you.

To anyone paying close enough attention to catch the italics easter egg...

And, to *you*. I had to get it right.

Russian Phrases and Explanations

Bratva — A Russian crime syndicate, similar to the Italian Mafia

Pahkan — the head of a Bratva

Bratok — a soldier in a Bratva

Mudak — Idiot/Asshole

Pozvol'te mne uvidet' nekotoryye dokumenty, udostoveryayushchiye lichnost — Let me see some identification documents

Med — honey, as in the food

So mnoy ty v bezopasnosti. YA vsegda budu tebya zashchishchat'. Tebe bol'she nikogda nichego ne pridetsya boyat'sya — With me you are safe. I will always protect you. You will never have to be afraid of anything again.

Koz'ye yaichko — Goat testicle (Russian insult, akin to calling someone an asshole)

YA revnuyu k lune, potomu chto ty smotrish' na neye. — I am jealous of the moon because you look at her.

Tvoye telo prekrasno, ono gotovitsya ko mne. Ty tak khorosho menya primesh'. — Your body is perfect, making itself ready for me. You will take me so well.

Ty zhenshchina, kotoraya smogla ukrotit' monstra. — You are a woman who could tame the monster

Zlaya zhenshchina — Wicked woman

Vse, chem ya yavlyayus', prinadlezhit tebe, i ty dlya menya vse — Everything I am is yours and you are everything to me

1

DIMITRI

———◆———

An American, an Englishman, and a Russian walk into a bar

The noise of the late-night talk show coming from the TV over the bar competes with the low chatter and whatever rock music is softly playing—James knows the song, I am sure, since it sounds distinctly American. The dim lights make the dingy place seem more intimate, transforming stained wooden paneling and aged fixtures into a place that the few remaining patrons might call their favorite dive bar.

It is late, but everyone left has the look of someone who makes a habit of being kicked out at closing—the bartenders busy cleaning glasses, the trio of drunk girls, an old man with a beer belly three seats over, the couple on a date that seems to be going very well, and the middle-aged man in a rumpled suit sitting in the darkest, furthest corner of the room in a booth by himself, hunched over a half-empty glass of clear alcohol.

From this seat, I can see everything, which is the reason I chose it. The mirror-backed shelves lined with bottles reflect the movements behind me and everyone who enters and exits through the heavy wooden door.

A flash of red catches my eye in that mirror, and I glance up to find a pale brunette woman in a skin-tight dress, headed straight for me like I am her mission. From the angle of her approach and the way her eyes are locked on my back, I know she has not really seen my face.

She fluffs her hair and exaggerates her hip movements into a seductive saunter. Her two friends at the table nearby are obvious as they look on, their faces a mixture of awe and envy. She is the sacrificial lamb, either the bravest of the group, or she has something to prove to them.

"Hi," the woman purrs at me from my right. My good side, if I have one.

In another life, I would have enjoyed her obvious interest and confidence. I would have let her talk to me and admired her pretty face. She is not the sort of woman I prefer—too thin and short for my tastes, dainty in a way that makes me feel too large in my own skin—but even so, she is very attractive and I would have gone with her to her home and taken from her body what was being freely offered.

Another time, when I was another man.

"No," I reply. I admire her courage in coming to speak to me, but she should have set her mark on someone else.

I remain perfectly still, as I have no wish to intimidate this woman who is less than half my size—they tend to get wide-eyed and teary about it, and I end up kicked out of a bar for doing nothing.

I have no wish to be kicked out of this bar, though my contact is late.

"What?" The woman's mask of self-assurance slips, but she recovers after a second. Her eyes are a touch glassy from the alcohol. "You don't even know what I was going to say."

"I am meeting someone."

"I'd be better company," she slurs in a low voice, shifting her body forward so her breasts brush my arm.

"Not interested." I jerk away from her touch.

"You sure—"

I sigh. Rudeness often accomplishes more than words, and she has not taken the first two rejections. From behind, she saw only my size, my muscles, the width of my shoulders, perhaps my expensive watch, and thought I would make a fine conquest.

So, I turn.

Now she sees more. She sees *me*—the jagged, pinched skin, the promise of violence in my cold eyes that normal people simply do not have. Her eyes widen, taking in the scars that bisect and ruin my once-handsome face, and they dilate as her lust becomes edged with something else that she may mistake for excitement. But it is not excitement. It is fear.

It is a natural human response to a threatening presence. Fight or flight. Deep down, she knows she should run from the predator, and her anxiety tastes acrid; burning and stinging in my nostrils.

"Go away," I growl.

She scoffs, a frown knitting her brow, but it feels much more performative than genuine as relief glimmers across her face, mingling with the false outrage. She did not mean to rouse a monster, and she is grateful for the out, even if she pretends not to be for the sake of her wounded pride.

"Asshole," she spits, nearly tripping over herself as she turns to retreat.

Correct. I am an asshole. I do not waste my time with honeyed words and games of pretend anymore, because one night is not worth the effort. I am tired of ignoring their fear and being careful. It is much easier to be alone.

The audio device in my left ear crackles. I always keep the communication piece for James in my left ear and Wesley in my right, a habit I now have no reason to break. *"Damn, D. That was cold. Sounded like she would've happily kept you company while you waited."*

I sigh at the almost taunting Southern lilt. "We have a job to do." My lips barely move, and my voice is so low that only the high-tech devices in my ears, which pick up on vibrations in my skull, would be able to transmit the sound.

James scoffs. *"Yeah... and? There's this little thing called 'having a life.' You could've taken her number and called her later when we weren't working."*

"I have a life," I mutter defensively.

"Sharpening knives and going to bed at 10 PM isn't what Mac means. You live like a monk," Wesley returns evenly. His British accent rounds his vowels and drops his R's, yet somehow sounds very close to James's Southern drawl to my ears.

"Mudak," I mutter, knowing they know this one in Russian. I find myself using it often.

"I know I'm an idiot, but all I'm sayin' is... Wouldn't kill you to get your dick wet."

I make a dismissive noise and spin the beer bottle in my hand. "Women are a distraction."

"You want to turn up the volume on Big D's mic, Wes? I can barely hear him. There's some idiot playing guitar in the apartment below me."

"You know, you'd hear much better if you ever stopped talking."

"You can't see it, so just know that I'm flipping you the bird right now."

I know it is an idiom, but I also know that James is on a rooftop somewhere nearby and has access to pigeons, so I will not guess what he means. English sayings are ridiculous. And what makes it worse is that even though it is the primary language of both Wesley and James's home countries, sometimes even they do not understand one another.

Every time we are together, it strikes me as the setup of one of those jokes with a punchline that is a pun. Though ours would not have a funny or witty end.

An American, an Englishman, and a Russian walk into a bar... and kill everyone inside.

However, I have no intention of killing anyone tonight. Tonight is simply an exchange of goods for services. Such a simple transaction would hardly justify the presence of my entire team, if not for the fact that I am meeting one of James's contacts, Felix—who, according to James, is "a bit of a loose cannon."

At times, I almost forget what my life used to be like before. I used to walk into situations like this blind, with my senses sharp and the taste of bitter adrenaline in the back of my throat. Now, I have Wesley hacking traffic cameras and monitoring the streets and James watching my back from 500 meters away through the scope of his rifle.

I much prefer the way we do things now. I have not been shot in several months.

We are a good team because we each play to our strengths. Wesley spends little time in the thick of the violence; his weapons are a computer mouse and keyboard. James occasionally steps out from behind his gun, but he is best suited as our backup from a distance. Conversely, I am not able to hack security cameras or make a kill shot with a ranged weapon—my place is as the man on the ground, dealing more closely and directly with targets. This is why I prefer knives.

"Harsh," the male bartender remarks, eyeing the small, brunette woman walking away with curiosity as he wipes the glass in his hand with a cloth. "But fair, I 'spose. You've got a 'don't fuck with me' thing going for you."

I ignore his judgment and lift my warm, half-empty beer. "I will take a fresh one." It serves a dual purpose: to drive up my bill so he will leave me alone, and it renews my reason for being here.

I feel the glares of female solidarity boring holes into my back as the woman rejoins her group. She needs something else to focus on; the sooner she gets over this slight, the better. They are attracting attention, and consequently, so am I.

In a practiced motion, he swaps my drink for a newly opened bottle. When he straightens, I see that he is a good-looking man. He is tall—though half a foot shorter than me, that still puts him over six feet—with dark hair and eyes that are set in a brown complexion. He is Hispanic, given the shape of his features. The same desire for danger that attracted the brunette woman to me will be satisfied by the tattoos on display beneath his rolled-up shirtsleeves.

"You should give her your phone number," I encourage.

"You think?" His eyes cut down the length of the bar, assessing. "Nah, not really my type. *Flaca.*"

I quirk a brow.

"Too skinny," he explains, flashing a grin that reveals a gold tooth in the back of his mouth. "I've always said, I like my women like I like my cars—sleek curves. Redheaded, too, if I can get 'em."

At that, I scoff. "Women should have curves, *da*, but cars should have headroom. And trunk space."

I do not expect the hoot of laughter, so when he tilts back his head to put his whole body into it, it surprises me. He whips the white towel off his shoulder and slaps it against the edge of the bar.

"I'm stealing that one." He crosses his arms and leans back against the table behind him, holding all the unused, clean beer glasses. "Russian, am I right?"

I incline my head.

"I heard talk of a Russian a few months back involved in some shit with that asshole Rossi who got offed. Big fucker, they said he was, like you. Deadly, too. Good with knives. Goes by *the Ghost*. Know him?"

The ease of a casual, friendly conversation falls away in an instant, and my whole body tenses. I narrow my eyes at him. "Felix."

"One and only," he confirms. His eyes shine with the mirth of a trickster—pleased by my surprised reaction to a well-executed ruse.

"*I fucking* knew *I recognized that voice!*" James interjects, sounding vindicated.

Personally, I do not think he gets to consider that a win, due to the fact that he did not fucking warn me about it.

"Why didn't you say anything?" Wesley fires back, as if he can read my mind. *"You knew we were going in blind since I couldn't find a photo of him anywhere."*

"I wasn't sure. I can't see him; the angle of the window blocks that side of the bar."

I simmer in anger, and Felix watches with a cool sort of interest meant to disguise unease.

Instinctively, I know the test is not quite over. He wants to see how I will react. I swallow the irritation and force out a calm question. "Why not introduce yourself sooner?"

Predictably, his attention is on the marred skin around the scar that twists up the corner of my mouth and disappears into my hairline through my temple. I have grown used to the surprise, the poorly veiled horror as people imagine what might have happened to me.

"Maybe I wanted to get the measure of the biggest, meanest motherfucker I've ever seen before sticking my neck out."

It was a clever move on his part, I must begrudgingly admit. My physical size—height and build—and scar are excellent for intimidation, and I use them to my advantage whenever possible. Men will agree to less favorable deals and do more to keep me happy if they are afraid.

But Felix's trick broke the illusion and forced me to interact with him first as a civilian instead of a hitman—I am no longer the aloof, dangerous, vaguely threatening presence, I am the man with whom he found common ground over a preference for large women. Additionally, because I am still here half an hour after our agreed time, he knows I want what he has badly enough to wait for it.

My hand curls into a fist, pulling at the healing scabs on my knuckles. I do not mind being bested by a worthy adversary, as it is often the only way to improve, but I rarely suffer having my time wasted.

Still, he owes me a payment. I can swallow down my frustration for now.

He is still waiting for my reaction, tense and ready to move quickly in case I become disagreeable. When I turn my head, he flinches—the smallest show of fear. I pretend not to see it as I glance around to take in all the potential witnesses and exits.

My size also makes me memorable. I cannot afford to leave witnesses.

"If I had known it was you, I would not have choked down two bottles of this American-made piss." I gesture at the beer.

He laughs, and the tension of the moment disappears. "Hey Vi, take over for me, will ya?" Felix asks a small woman wearing a half-apron at the end of the bar. She nods without looking up from whatever she is doing on her phone. "Let's step into my office. Tip your bartender, huh?" he says with a wink, as if he has not been acting as my bartender.

I exhale heavily and reach into my wallet. I toss a folded $20 to cover my tab and stand. To my surprise, he pushes through the metal door with a handwritten piece of paper taped to it declaring it an "Exit to Alley."

His office indeed.

The night air is cool but moist, and it lessens the city stink that drifts around me. There are no signs of life except for a far-off police siren and the sound of some nocturnal creature rifling through the garbage nearby. The rest of this derelict neighborhood is full of condemned homes, trash, and broken chain-link fences. A few two-story buildings flank the alley, casting dark shadows beyond the flickering light of a single bulb overhead that illuminates the path to the dumpster.

In some ways, this was the ideal location for our meeting. It is a shitty bar on the "wrong side of town." The people who live here look out for only themselves. It makes them wary of strangers and mind their own business. Still, cities such as this do not ever fully sleep, so my eyes dart around for movement or onlookers.

Felix settles against the crumbling brick siding, leaning against one shoulder. He crosses his arms. "Apologies for the stunt in there, but you can't be too careful when your sniper buddy says he's sending in *the*

Russian. I've known Mackenzie for years, and I know how he is. He's full of shit and hot air, but he knows people. Understands 'em."

"And what did he tell you about me?" I ask, lifting a brow.

"Nothing!" James protests. At the same time, Felix flashes me that gold tooth while he shakes his head and says, "Nothing. That's the problem. Anyone else he'd say, 'he's good people,' or 'watch your back,' or 'he acts tough, but he does pottery,' or some shit, like I give a fuck. But you? *Nada.*" He cocks his head. "So, me? I had to wonder, is it because he doesn't know you, or because he knows you too well?"

I mirror Felix's relaxed posture, settling against the door in case anyone inside thinks to join us. He is baiting me, and I will not rise to it. "If you want information about James, ask him yourself. If you want information about me, that is too bad for you."

After a few seconds, Felix cracks that knowing little smile. "Where is Mac tonight, anyway?" He cranes his neck, looking down the length of the alley. His eyes lift to the rooftops of the buildings flanking the alley, scanning and settling on the one due east. He waves.

"Tell him he's way off," James grumbles.

He is not, and I will not.

Tucking his arm back into the space on the inside of his elbow, Felix grins. "Anyway, we didn't come out here to talk about our mutuals. How's my witness?" He glances down at my scabbed, bruised knuckles. "Still feeling chatty?"

"I find that it is difficult to speak without teeth," I answer vaguely.

His smile turns dark, mirthless. "The literal approach. I like it. All right, *Ghost.* I'm a man who pays his debts." He reaches into the pocket of his black half-apron, produces a card of thick white paper, and holds it out to me. The reds and oranges of his ink flash in the light, a dance of color among the gray and darkness.

The wedding invitation feels expensive, with textured paper and gold leaf lettering. I suppose that is fitting, as it is a golden ticket to the event.

All our research indicates this wedding will be crawling with security, and anyone without an invitation will be turned away.

"You're Lev Petrov for the night, in case you were wondering. The barcode at the bottom will tell them who the invite belongs to when they read it. Might want to get a fake ID made up, just in case."

"Who is Lev Petrov?"

"Someone who's not going to that wedding anymore, that's for sure," Felix chuckles.

I burn to ask how he managed to get this, but I know he would not reveal this information to me. I tuck it into the back pocket of my pants, taking care not to crease it as I slide it in, and nod my thanks. "So, we are done here, *da*?"

"Square as a WASP," he replies.

I scowl. Does that word not mean what I think it means? His tone says yes, but I do not know what is square-shaped about a stinging insect. My face must betray my confusion.

"Square like uncool... White Anglo-Saxon Protestant..." he says, lifting his brows in a way I recognize—it means there is a joke I am missing. "I'm sensing this is a bit of a lost cause. Never mind. Yeah, we're good. Might call you back if Johnson buys some dentures and testifies anyway, but I'll know way before that happens."

I jerk my chin. "Then we are done."

"Pleasure doin' business, Dimitri. Feel free to give me a shout in the future if you need anything, and I'd be happy to set up another trade like this—I've got plenty that needs doing, and it's always nice to find a guy willing to get his hands dirty."

Now that I have met Felix, I understand why James was willing to utilize his services. In our industry, a man is only as good as his word, and trust is hard to come by since loyalty is too easily purchased. Felix is well-connected, discreet, and efficient. James still owes the man a favor for cleaning a crime scene for him when we were pursuing another hit months ago.

Personally, I believe a man should clean up his own messes, and the thought of owing someone a near-limitless favor makes my skin itch.

With a grunt of acknowledgment, I push off the door and head west out of the alley, towards the side street where Wesley's van is parked.

"Hope you get your guy," Felix calls at my retreating form, proving once again that he knows more than he should.

The white van with the faded Bugs-B-Gon decal blends in well with the scenery. The street is mostly deserted, and the van is parallel parked next to a fire hydrant, wearing a chipped yellow boot on its tire. On my way to the side with the sliding door, I bend down and unlock the boot to toss it into its spot in the back corner of the van.

I knock twice, and Wesley's pale face appears in the opening a second later. As I climb in, he settles back onto his wheeled stool and scoots away to give me enough room to sit on an overturned crate while we wait for James. The wall of monitors on his right flicker as the screens change and cycle through the various views he finds useful—traffic cameras from nearby intersections, weather updates, police emergency call logs, surveillance photos, and mugshots of the man we have been tasked to kill...

How he can so easily access restricted information is not my concern, though it is very impressive.

Before I accidentally crush it, I retrieve the invitation from my back pocket and hand it to Wesley. He peruses it, whistling his approval. "This is quite posh," he remarks. "Come have a look, Mac."

"On my way, Short Round."

I believe it references something from popular culture, but even after hearing it for months, the nickname rubs against me the incorrect way. It strikes me as strangely rude and inaccurate, which are not things I typically associate with James.

Wesley is neither short—though the shortest of us, he still stands over six feet—nor round. His frame has picked up plenty of bulk since we started training together, especially impressive considering the fact that he is chained behind a screen 80% of the time. One of the British flags amid the incongruous pattern of bright tattoos lining his arms appears distorted with the new width of his bicep in a way that gives me some private amusement.

A few seconds later, James opens the van door, slides the black case containing his gun under the desk, and turns over a bucket to sit on. He kicks me as he stretches out his long legs, shooting me an apologetic look before nearly tilting over in an effort to stretch out in what little space remains.

Once he is settled, he jokes, "Well, this is fuckin' cozy. I gotta tell Eleanor to stop feeding you guys."

Wesley exhales a laugh, but I purse my lips.

"So, we've got our in?" James asks. With a look at Wesley, he holds out his hand expectantly. Wesley flicks the invitation towards him, and he catches it midair between his thumb and index finger. "Viktor and Katerina Volkevich invite you to the wedding of their son, Matthew. Nice of them."

As one, we all turn to look at the face staring from the mugshot on Wesley's screen. I do not know him personally, but we share the same wide brow, thin lips, high cheekbones, and a rounded tip to our noses—Slavic features. Mine are far more severe and angular, and far less balanced, thanks to the long, twisted scar.

When our handler, a man who goes by the moniker *the General*, sent us the email with a picture and the name of our next hit, I was more than wary. Viktor Volkevich is the head of one of the local Russian *Bratva* crime syndicates operating out of Ulysses, New Jersey. It is no small matter to kill their leader, as proven by the near-obscene amount of money in the offer.

"I am still not convinced we should do this," I decide, crossing my arms. Now that we have the invitation, all I can see are flaws in the plan.

"Russian mafia boss fits the criteria to a T," James argues. "And what about all that shit Wes found in his search history? He's a fucked-up fucker, D."

I nearly roll my eyes. His criteria—his newly discovered moral compass, courtesy of a woman he has known for less than a year. Ridiculous. We are hitmen, not vigilante heroes. "Yes, he is a bad man who does bad things. This is not the source of my trouble."

"What's the issue?" Wesley asks.

"A *Bratva* is like a sewer full of rats. Kill one, and the others will feast on its corpse and make more rats. It is not like killing a businessman or a billionaire—they are isolated, lonely at the top. In a *Bratva*, there are cousins, sons, brothers, and a council of men who would step in and take Viktor's place as soon as his body hit the floor. Killing the leader will create instability for a time, but it will not destroy the organization. And besides, he will be protected all evening. I will be lucky if he even takes a piss alone."

"Dimitri has a point," Wesley says. "Normally we try to take down the whole lot, but three versus an inexhaustible supply of men, guns, and money? Not sure I like those odds."

"Well, that's what this is for, right?" James asks, flicking the edge of the invitation and leaving a small dent in the cardstock. "Recon. We can start building our files on the top brass in the Volkevich family. Then, we'll start picking 'em off."

I scratch through my short hair at the thick scar. Pick them off? He always thinks like a sniper. "So, the plan is that I will get in, find the *Bratva* men among the hundreds of other guests to take discreet photos, perhaps kill the most protected of them all at his own son's wedding, and get out without being seen?"

"Sounds like fun, huh?" James's grin will not be deterred.

I cut Wesley a look. He smirks, then shrugs. "We've done more with less."

They both look to me, knowing that I will make the final decision because I will assume most of the risk. "Very well," I agree.

"Suit up, gents. We're crashing a wedding."

2

NICOLE

Nothing makes you feel quite as alone as the celebration of someone else's love.

"You know you make me wanna... SHOUT!"

It's hard not to smile as I watch a white-haired woman wave her spindly arms into the air half a beat behind everyone else. She doesn't seem to notice or care, with her eyes closed and a huge, cheesy grin on her face. When she wobbles a bit, unsteady on her half-inch heels, her husband is right behind her with an assist.

I take a long swallow through the slim black straw to finish my Diet Coke and rattle the ice as I set it down. I resume picking at the vanilla buttercream, carefully scraping the icing off the cake into a pile to ration it perfectly with each bite.

At least Jenny has great taste in cake, even if she has terrible taste in dresses.

I know everyone says it, but this is a truly awful bridesmaid dress. It's the most I've ever spent on a single item of clothing, and I'm certainly never going to wear it again, so that's money down the drain that could have been better spent on several sets of very comfortable scrubs.

It's shiny silk, and the cut is fine, skimming over tummy bulges and bumps with a bit of Spanx magic. But whereas the ruching on the side gives the other bridesmaids, like size-zero Olivia and runner's-body Heather, a delicate hourglass shape, it makes my plentiful hips and breasts look more like a 24-hourglass. And this dark camel color is doing *nothing* for me. Between the naturally light brown shade of my skin and sun-bleached caramel highlights in my hair, I'm all one color. I feel like a baked potato.

It's a look, just not a great one.

We look good standing next to Jenny, though, which is really all that matters at the end of the day, I suppose. She chose tans and beiges as accent colors. And her skin tone is of the pale Eastern European variety, not half-Black like mine, so it doesn't give the same monotone vibe.

I wish I hadn't let myself be guilt-tripped into being a bridesmaid. Especially because I can't even remember if we're third cousins or second cousins once removed. I was a last-minute fill-in for a college friend who needed surgery—gotta keep those wedding parties perfectly balanced, and Matt has more family and "like a brother to me" friends than any man I've ever met.

One of whom is a complete douchebag.

Okay, time to press reset. I'm coming dangerously close to feeling sorry for myself.

Everything about this wedding has been perfect and beautiful and *expensive*. It's by far the biggest wedding I've ever been to, with 700-something guests, but somehow there's enough room for everyone. The sprawling estate is a super cool historical building with rolling hills, a pond and manicured gardens with a giant maze made of meticulously trimmed 10-foot hedges. We're on the outskirts of the small city of Ulysses, New Jersey, and at enough of an elevation that the city skyline is visible in the distance.

The ceremony was brief, and they couldn't have asked for better weather or a more picture-perfect backdrop than the peachy clouds of a clear fall sky.

For dinner, we moved into the ballroom, which is decorated from floor to ceiling with florals and twinkling lights that cast a warm glow. The food was great. The cake is delicious. And I may not be taking advantage of the open bar, but it *is* open, so there are quite a few sloppy drunks on the dance floor having a good time.

If my feet weren't killing me, I'd be on the dance floor too, because the band is great. A little bit ago, they threw open the balcony doors, letting in a cool breeze that's heavy with the sweet scent of roses and verbena.

It's fucking magical.

The table jostles, making the abandoned glasses clink together as my cousin Emma collapses into the chair next to me. The movement of air rustles a few of the tendrils the hairstylist had left out of my up-do to frame my face. Luckily, it's a cool night, and they're more wispy than frizzy. For now.

She reaches across me to grab an abandoned glass and starts drinking deeply from someone else's water. It's her first family event where she's legally allowed to drink, and her cheeks are flushed with it.

After a few gulps that leave her gasping for breath, she whines, "Nicole! Why aren't you dancing?"

I look pointedly down at the stilettos we both had to buy. Honestly, it's just more evidence that I was an afterthought bridesmaid. Jenny said she wanted everyone to wear the same shoes for uniformity, but changed her mind when the photographer pointed out that one girl towering over everyone else at 6'4" ruined the lines of the bridesmaid photos. Shoe uniformity wasn't quite so important then, and I had to stand barefoot in the wet grass.

"I don't know how you're dancing in these," I explain. "I can barely walk."

"Take them off," Emma suggests breezily, dabbing at the sweat on her upper lip with a linen napkin and assessing how much makeup transferred from the act. "No one will care."

Just as she makes the suggestion, a shattering noise draws every pair of eyes in a large radius towards the dance floor. Just like everyone else, we crane our necks to see who did it, and I spot a sheepish middle-aged man stooping over and piling the bigger pieces of glass into his cupped hand.

"That's the second time, and the music just started," I point out dryly. Alcohol plus dancing makes for slippery fingers and a sticky floor.

"Point taken," she winces. There's a flash of the black light that turns her teeth otherworldly white. "You may need to be on standby."

She's probably right. A few more drinks and no one's going to remember how much glass is on the floor until they're limping away, leaving a trail of bloody footprints. That's what you get when you're the nurse in the family—the expectation to handle any medical issues that crop up.

"Let's hope it doesn't come to that." Sensing Emma is settling in for a bit of a break, I angle myself in the seat towards her. "I feel like it's been so long since we've caught up. How's life? Things are going well with Natalie if she's your date, I assume."

"She's getting us drinks. Things are going so well," she replies with a dreamy look in her girlfriend's direction. "We're looking for apartments."

"That's exciting!" I say, mustering up some enthusiasm for her, since she seems so happy.

But internally... oof.

Living together is rough. Maybe it's different with another girl, but I've lived with guys before. Once the honeymoon phase wears off, you're left with a lot of strange, random *boy* stuff and a roommate whose definition of a clean toilet is nowhere near the same as yours.

"And did you get that nurse aide job at Mercy Grace?"

Emma nods wordlessly, selecting another water glass to steal. "Thanks again for writing that rec for me. The head of the ER was on the panel for my interview. He said he remembered you."

I'm surprised. I was only there for a year-long contract that I chose not to extend because New York City was too big for me. "No problem at all.

And if you ever decide to move to one of the other places I've contracted at, let me know. I've got you covered coast to coast."

Travel nursing is a sweet gig—good pay, good hours, interesting new places. Between my willingness to work unusual shifts and all the extra certifications like wound care, life support and trauma, I'm an attractive candidate and I never have trouble finding a new contract when I inevitably get that familiar itch to move. My resume is a laundry list that reads like American Airlines' domestic flight offerings.

Another grin splits her face. "Will do. You're back here now, right?"

"I rolled in earlier this week and jumped right in at St. Luke's. I gave myself zero wiggle room and had to haul ass driving up from Charlotte," I remark dryly. "The U-Haul is still in the driveway of my new rental row home—I've been sleeping on an air mattress and living out of a rolling suitcase. I have so much unpacking to do, but I've got the next four days off—I can get it all done, but it won't be fun."

"Ohhh... Is that why you're not drinking? My mom thought you were pregnant," she giggles.

A sour flash of nerves flares low in my stomach like it always does at the reminder of where other people think I should be at my age—of where *I* thought I'd be. By 31, most people I know are married, have a house, maybe a baby already or one on the way... I don't even have a dog.

I should get a dog.

"Yeah, unpacking while hungover is not fun."

A man sways close as he walks by our table, drawing both of our eyes and making me tense until I realize it's not Kyle, my "date." He's not really—he's just the douchebag who walked with me down the aisle.

The stranger brushes Emma's shoulder with the back of his hand, and she flinches, then drops her gaze, clearly uncomfortable.

"You okay?" I ask, shifting closer.

"Yeah, fine..." she says as he passes by, glancing around almost furtively. "Okay, I wasn't going to say anything because my mom told me I'm being ridiculous, but have you noticed that some people here are kind of... um...”

“Scary?” I supply.

Her eyes go wide. “Oh my God, yes! So it’s not just me. Okay, so the guy Nat was sitting next to during the ceremony gave off seriously bad vibes, and he was talking on the phone in another language the whole time apparently, even when Jenny was walking down the aisle. Fucking rude, right?”

The difference between the sides of the aisle had been noticeable. My extended family cleans up well, but we don’t know many people who wear Armani suits or gold rings on every finger. And there’s more than one Rolls-Royce parked in the lot.

She leans closer, lowering her voice conspiratorially. “Do you think the rumors are true?”

“What rumors?”

“That Matt’s family has ties to the Russian mob. That’s what my dad said. Or, they don’t call them mobs, do they?” she continues, distracted now as she whips her phone out of her wristlet, pulls up a browser, and types in her request. “I forget what he called it... brat-something. Bratwurst?”

“That’s a sausage.”

“*Bratvas*,” she says triumphantly, turning her phone around to show me the Wikipedia page.

I grab it from her hand and scan through the first couple of paragraphs. “Organized crime... dissolution of the Soviet Union... Known for illegal sales of weapons and drugs, money laundering, prostitution, and human trafficking... This says they were a huge threat in the 90s. You weren’t even alive then.”

“Yeah, whatever,” she shoots back, plucking her phone out of my hands. “It says that as of a few years ago, the FBI classified *Bratvas* as a ‘criminal superpower.’ There are a ton of branches... it’s like families in the Italian Mafia. And they're not just in Russia; they're all over the world, apparently. So, Matt's family could *totally* have *Bratva* ties."

I'm about to wave off her concern when I notice someone's head turn as she says the word *Bratva*. Honestly, you really never know. I've seen enough gang violence victims in inner-city hospitals to know better than to write off organized crime as a possibility anywhere.

I lean in, keeping an eye on the man whose attention we seem to have caught. "Wikipedia maybe isn't the best source for this kind of thing, huh?"

"True," she says slowly. The music dies, and the band announces their next number, causing Emma to perk up. "Ooh! This is me and Nat's song! Come dance!"

"Maybe later. Have fun." I wave her off as she whirls onto the dance floor and tugs her girlfriend out of the line for the bar.

I watch them, smiling. After a moment, the table shakes again, but this time I have to swallow down my irritation at who fills the seat next to me.

I have to admit that Kyle is a handsome guy in his dark suit and contrasting tie that sets off his light eyes. He has slicked back his light brown hair, which makes his forehead look higher and somehow creates the illusion that he's taller. He's in good shape, and a bit shorter than me, even when I'm not wearing these ridiculous heels.

At first, I was honestly a little flattered when it seemed like he was seeking me out—offering to get me a drink at cocktail hour, sitting next to me at dinner, finding me in the hallway on my way back from the bathroom. But he hasn't made a ton of effort to actually talk to me, and every time I try to make polite conversation, his eyes scan the crowd like he's searching for a better option, or he doesn't care about what I have to say.

I've decided he's the kind of guy who pretends to be taller than he actually is on a dating app, and his *About Me* bio says, "just ask lol."

I don't mind a short king, but in my experience, if they lie about it, it means they're self-conscious. And who has time for boring men with fragile egos?

At an even six feet tall myself, I have always been several inches taller than every man who lists his height as six-foot in his profile. Funny how that works.

Growing up, I felt monstrous, unfeminine, even goofy around my friends, who giggled with each other about the boys they crushed on, who could pick them up and carry them around. And as I grew and didn't stop, I resigned myself to never feeling—to never being—a small girl.

But I don't need to be; I am more than just my body. And I know that the only way to live in it is to do so unapologetically.

"Bet it looks like fuckin' zebra stripes when they scissor," Kyle jokes, eyes on my cousin and her dark-skinned girlfriend as they laugh and twist around each other, dancing together.

"Excuse me?" I demand.

He rolls his eyes. "It was just a joke; loosen up. Here," he says, holding out a drink and shaking it until I reach for it.

I try not to frown at it or him. Earlier, when he asked if I wanted anything, I said no. It's a clear liquid, and if it weren't for the tiny bubbles, it could just be water. "What is it?"

"Vodka soda. Girls drink those, right?" he asks, leaning back on the chair and throwing his arm over the back of mine. His leg knocks into me, jostling me and making me spill some of the drink I didn't want.

I place the glass on the table and grab my napkin. "I'm not much of a straight vodka/flavorless mixer kind of girl."

"Maybe you should be," he counters, letting his eyes drop as I pat at the small wet mark on my dress.

This time, I do frown—what does *that* mean?—but when I glance up, the look on his face is odd, hard to put into words. Not anything so extreme as disgust or desire, but somewhere in the realm of making an assessment, like he's trying to decide what he wants to do. The closest comparison I can come up with is the look on someone's face at the end of a date before they pop the "wanna come back to my place" question.

When he sees that I've caught him, he wipes the expression clean and offers his charming smile—all teeth and lips. "What do you do again?"

We already talked about this. I know he's an insurance adjuster, and he hates it. "I'm a travel nurse, mostly working in ERs."

"Oh, sick. And you live around here? You said you're new to the area, right?"

"Yeah."

"So... you're all alone?" he asks, and there's a strange glint in his eye. "You need someone to show you around?"

"Um... no. I have some family nearby," I say, just so he doesn't think I'm sad and alone. I might as well be, because I don't really plan on hitting any of them up just because of something as tenuous as a distant family tie, but he doesn't need to know that.

He nods, but looks distracted again. "Right. So. You wanna dance?"

"No," I say, leaning away as he sways into my space.

"Wanna go up to my room?" he forges on in a much lower voice, placing his hand on my thigh.

"Hey, Kyle, my man!" a passing bro exclaims.

Kyle straightens, looking startled, and immediately removes his hand and moves to the far edge of his seat. "G-Town," he shouts back with a loud laugh, pointing with finger guns.

"G-Town, down to clown!"

While they go back and forth, singing the song of their people, I stare down at the place on my leg where his hand was, settling into a serious case of the ick.

The way he pulled back... it was like he didn't want to get caught by his friend making a move on me.

Maybe that's not what it was. Maybe I'm jaded. But I've worked in healthcare for nearly a decade, and it's been whittling away at my faith in humanity for a while.

Regardless, any guy who doesn't want to be seen showing interest in me isn't worth my time.

He does nothing to disprove the assumption, either, as he waits until his friend is out of sight before leaning back to me and waggling his eyebrows. "So? What do you say? I'll give you a key, you can meet me up there in, like, 10 minutes?" He reaches into his pocket and holds the electronic room card up between his index and middle fingers.

So we won't be seen together. Called it.

I'm locked in indecision. The word "no" really ought to be a complete sentence, but he seems like the kind of guy who'd hurl appearance-based insults if you denied him, even if you did it gently. And I'm already in such a weird mood, I know it would probably ruin my night. I don't want to give him that power.

Before I can decide on what to say, he tosses down the room key, and it clangs against the plate. "Meet you up there. I gotta go take a leak," he says, and leaves.

While I stare at the room key mutinously and contemplate tossing it into the fountain, the music shifts into a slow song, and everyone starts clapping. When I look around, I see why.

Jenny and Matt had their first dance already, but you'd think they were the only two people in the room with the way they're locked in on each other. He's whispering in her ear and gently running his hands up and down her bare arms, and she's pressed so close to him that his legs are lost, swallowed in her voluminous tulle skirt. They're smiling soft, private smiles at each other.

My breath catches.

And there it is, the real reason for my bad mood amidst this beautiful night and wonderful occasion—loneliness. And fuck Kyle, this isn't about him. It's an ache in the center of my chest, full of ugly emotions that I've been trying to ignore all night, like spite and frustration and sadness.

I'm used to feeling lonely because of my lifestyle and having to constantly start over, but this runs deeper. There's a difference between being lonely and feeling alone.

And nothing makes you feel quite so *alone* as the celebration of someone else's love.

I... need some air.

I stand, wobbling a little and unsteady in my heels, and head for the terrace that leads down to the formal garden area. As I descend to the gravel path lined with rose bushes and boxwood, I catch sight of shadows and shapes moving around in the lingering twilight—occasional flashes of silk in the up-lit corners of the garden and giggling lovers stealing moments. With no real destination in mind, I follow the path shakily, letting it lead me around the house towards an overlook with a bench.

The perfect spot for a solo pity party.

By the time I reach my destination, the blisters on my pinky toes have broken, and I'm gritting my teeth against the pain. Gratefully, I sink onto the stone bench, facing the break in the trees to admire the view as I remove my shoes.

When you move around as much as I do, some aspects of the cities start to blur together. But there's one thing everywhere has in common, and that's the brief time in the pastels of twilight on a clear fall evening when everything looks perfect from afar. In the purples and pinks of the sunset bleeding into the dull blue-black of night, the cityscape of Ulysses is thrown into brilliant relief. It's too far to see, but I know the facades of the buildings are dark, setting off the few lights shining from windows of apartments and office buildings where some people haven't ended their day yet.

There's something sad and lonely, yet strangely comforting about how full the world is of places I'll never go, and people I'll never meet doing work I'll never know about. Everywhere around me, people are going on with their own small lives in complete parallel, and as ignorant of my existence as I am of theirs. I'm like a secret observer.

I'm shaken from my reverie by the sound of gravel crunching underfoot. I glance over to the right, expecting to find someone out for a smoke or wandering and texting, then do a double-take.

Being a tall girl myself, I tend to notice the heads that stand above others in a room. So I don't know how I missed him before, because this guy would be a head *and* shoulders above the crowd. He's not lanky, the way some very tall men are; he's bulky. Buff. And he's wearing that suit like he's doing it a favor. It clings to a broad chest and thick arms, tapering down and following the line of his waist so perfectly that there's no way it isn't custom. The thickest, roundest ass I've ever seen peeks at me from under the split of his jacket.

And the way he moves... You'd expect a guy his size to be stiff, or hold himself the way bodybuilders do when their lats are so big that their arms angle slightly away from their body, even at rest. Not this guy. He's almost graceful, gliding down the walkway that splits and leads one way towards the tall hedge maze or the other, in my direction.

He reaches the end of the path and pauses long enough that I get a view of his profile and see a flash of a long, thick white scar that cuts up his cheek at a steep angle before it disappears into his short-cropped, dark hair.

I can't help but stare, intrigued even more by what seems like a weighty secret.

Whoever he is, he's seen some shit. No one who's got a scar that deep in a place that obvious lives a soft life behind a desk.

Bratva. The word comes to me, swift and unbidden.

Is he one of them? He certainly looks like a man who's acquainted with violence.

When his head comes back around towards me, I look away so he won't see that I've been gawking, transfixed, like some kind of lunatic.

I try to focus on the scenery in front of me. The colors of the sunset are all but gone now, and I wonder how long it will be until I can see the city's night lights.

Crunch, crunch, crunch.

It's getting louder. Too loud. I can't ignore it anymore.

I glance up, heart racing for some odd reason, and see exactly what I expected, hoped for, and feared at the same time. The huge, scarred man is standing at the edge of my bench, eyes hooded from the tilt of his head, and he's focused right on... *me.*

"May I join you?"

3

DIMITRI

Chivalry ain't dead; it's just... rough around the edges.

The security here is so intense that it would be obvious to anyone paying attention that this is not a typical wedding. The grounds have an iron fence encircling the perimeter to limit access, and the estate house has an alarm system, with magnetic cards to swipe at every door. Prior to entry, security checked ladies' purses, and men had to open their coats to show they were not carrying. Our invitations were scanned, collected, and deposited into a locked case. Cameras point at the grounds from every corner of the building. Armed guards are posted in doorways, at key points on the grounds, and mill about among the guests.

Only important people with something to protect take this many precautions—the very wealthy, celebrities, politicians, and in this case, *Bratva Pakhans.*

It was a simple matter to identify the leader of this *Bratva*; he has been surrounded by sycophants and sentinels all evening.

But that is fine. My goal tonight need not be to kill a middle-aged man. Thanks to Wesley's creativity and technological know-how, I have been taking photos by pressing the button wired to the back of my cufflink. The wire runs through my jacket arm, up to the camera in my breast pocket disguised in the pocket square, and there is a wireless transmitter stitched into the fabric of the hem.

I know I do not blend particularly well into a crowd, but it is a large wedding. We all assumed Felix's invitation would buy me entrance, and my accent and fluency in Russian would afford me credibility.

But despite my efforts to blend in, I am being followed.

If I had to guess, the man on my tail is likely a *bratok*, a specialized soldier. It is a relatively low-ranking position, but with a singular, important purpose—to protect the *Pakhan*, even at the cost of your own life.

My heart races, adrenaline surging and infusing my limbs with strength. It will be no simple matter to hide his body; I must be vigilant and efficient. If I can manage it bloodlessly, perhaps I can make it look like he passed out from too much drink.

"I need somewhere private to handle my tail," I say, keeping my voice low. The man has followed me through the manor, across the dance floor, and outside into the gardens.

Wesley mans the screens as usual; however, tonight the van has been stripped of its decal—no one would wish to see an exterminator at a wedding venue. He is in charge of ensuring that no one will ever know I was here. Instead of being saved to a secure cloud location, the footage from the cameras is being routed through Wesley's laptop and deleted. Tomorrow, Volkevich's security team will find nothing saved in the 12 hours after the event began.

"There's a blind spot by the corner of the house that I can't see in any of my feeds," Wesley informs me. *"If you're quick and discreet, you shouldn't have any witnesses. He's about 20 yards behind you."*

I head in the direction that Wesley recommends, keeping my pace slow and purposeful, as if I am strolling and blithely unaware of my shadow. I make it to the end of the path and make a show of looking both ways...

Fuck. Of course the only convenient blind spot on the property is occupied by a woman sitting on a bench, stargazing.

I realize I have only an instant to choose my next move. If I ask for more assistance from Wesley, the guard might be close enough to overhear. If I keep running, he will catch up with me and it is equally likely that he would kick me out as it is that he would force me at gunpoint to a holding cell on the property where I would be questioned and quietly disposed of for daring to crash a *Bratva* wedding. I may have an invitation and a matching ID, but I do not look much like the man actually invited.

However, there is no better cover at a wedding than having a date. The woman on the bench is alone. If I join her and act correctly, it should appear as if we are lovers meeting to the *bratok*. I am not what people would consider charismatic, but I can usually speak with a woman without frightening her. When I want to.

And now that I have seen this woman, I find I want to. I like the look of her very much. As my father would have said, she would not blow away in a Moscow winter.

She turns with a curious expression when she hears my feet against the small stones, and our eyes meet. The world narrows, tunneling my focus for a breathtaking instant.

Her stare is pure amber—a honeyed color that makes the air between us taste sweeter.

Her dress leaves little of her shape to the imagination. It clings to wide hips, cups large breasts, and ripples against a thick waist. Her hair is tied up, long and wild, with golden-brown curls spiraling out around her head. As she tilts her head, I am drawn to the soft curve of her jaw that flows into a graceful line down her neck. The oval shape of her face is common in my country and considered desirable, though her darker coloring would be unique among people as pale as the snow they live in.

"May I join you?" I rasp.

I watch with fascination as the goosebumps rise on her upper arms and spread down the deep V pointing to her cleavage like an arrow. "If you'd like." She shifts her body to the very edge of the bench to make room for me.

Unbuttoning the single hold of my suit jacket, I take the spot next to her. She is obviously very tall for a woman—the top of her head is level with my mouth—and I catch a whiff of something mouthwatering and feminine as the breeze drifts between us.

"Thank you," I say, because I can think of nothing else.

"No problem."

"What brings you out here?"

"I'm hiding from my date. You?"

Her voice wraps around me. It is deeper than most women's and some men's, and the low register is calm and soothing.

I angle myself closer, so our legs nearly touch, then let my eyes drop to her full lips. She tracks the movement, follows my lead, and shamelessly looks her fill. Her eyes on me feel like a gentle caress.

For the first time in a long time, I am unsettled as I wait for the judgment of another person. Will she see the darkness in me? Will the twisted scar repulse her? Why does the thought of her rejection make my chest burn with the echoes of years of ignored anger?

Her eyes flick across my face, spending no more time on the scar than any other feature, then travel the length of my torso and down my legs, quietly measuring, assessing, and—fuck me—liking what she sees. The pink tip of her tongue darts out to wet her bottom lip before she takes that lip between her teeth, and I nearly groan aloud. Triumph and satisfaction swell in my veins at the tentative interest and curiosity.

"I came to admire the view," I say, remaining focused on her.

Her eyes widen, and her chest expands at the lower edge of my vision. I have to fight not to watch it swell and contract.

"Was that a line?" she asks almost breathlessly, and her eyes are smiling.

I cock my head. "A line of what?"

She stares for a second, transparently deciding whether or not to believe my ignorance, and decides that my accent is thick enough to absolve me of suspicion. "Never mind. It *is* a beautiful night." She returns her attention to the overlook, allowing me the opportunity to take in her strong profile.

"What has your date done to deserve such scorn?" I ask.

She laughs once, almost a self-deprecating noise. "Does it matter?"

"Perhaps I would like to know so that I do not repeat the same mistake."

"Wait, what's... happening? Is Big D... flirting?" James's half-formed questions ring in one ear.

"So much for being on the job," Wesley quips. *"I think he must have taken your advice about having a life to heart, Mac."*

They are buzzing in my ears so loud that I nearly miss her sharp intake of breath at my statement. It could mean many things. Is she nervous? Excited?

"Um... unless you plan on generally being an asshole, I don't think you have anything to worry about."

The accusation from the woman at the bar the other night echoes in my memory. She called me an asshole, too. "I would never plan this—it happens naturally."

She laughs. The husky sound punches me in the gut, then shoots down my spine and tingles at the base. I never expect anyone to laugh at the things I say. James and Wesley sometimes do, though it is more a shared, private amusement at my cost. This is nothing like that—this is her enjoyment of a clever turn of phrase, and it makes me feel... curiously warm.

I follow the movement of her fingers hungrily as she holds out her hand at chest height. "I'm Nicole."

"D-Lev," I remember almost too late.

Fuck. I almost gave her my real name. I am clearly too distracted to be here with her, but now that I am, I cannot pull myself away.

Her hand in mine is warm, dry, and calloused, and her handshake is firm. When we touch, her fingers brush the scabs on my knuckles, and her eyes drop to the nearly healed skin before she lets go.

"Lev," she repeats the name.

"Nicole," I say, enjoying the flavor of hers.

"What happened to your hand, Lev?"

A deep grumble escapes my chest at the sound of the wrong name in her musical voice. Jealously, I do not want to hear her speak another man's name. I want to know what she looks like wrapping her lips around *my* name. I want to hear her scream it in ecstasy.

She misinterprets the noise for something else, because she hurries to explain herself, "Not to be nosy... I'm an ER nurse. It's hard-wired in me to ask."

"I got into a fight."

Her eyes flick back down, but her posture does not change. A small, secret smile of what might be amusement curls at the edges of her mouth. She is not easily rattled by violence, then. This is good. "You must have won."

"You could say that. What gave it away?"

"Your hand is torn up, but your face is good. I mean... it hasn't been hit," she corrects needlessly. "Obviously, you were the one landing the hits."

"Perhaps the fight was a bit one-sided," I allow, thinking of how Felix's witness was tied to a chair for most of it.

Her lips twitch. "I'm not surprised. It's probably hard to find another person big enough for you to pick on someone your own size."

"*Da*," I agree.

Most people are afraid, intimidated or in awe of my height and frame. She pokes fun at it. And this is why I like large women.

"*Da*," she repeats, tasting the word in a way that drags my eyes back to her mouth with a fresh hunger. "I like the accent. I'm guessing Russian, given the rest of the guest list."

"*Da*," I say again, reveling in the little shiver that crawls across her skin.

"All the way from Russia. What are you doing in New Jersey? Other than *admiring the view* with a stranger."

As she speaks, I watch her lips, admiring their fullness. I do not realize at first that she has teased me until they tip up at the corners in an expectant smile. "It is not my usual way," I reply. "You must be an exception."

"Nice. Now call her an exceptional woman," James offers.

"Shh, let him work," Wesley chides.

Fuck. I had forgotten about my gallery of nuts. Their commentary snaps me out of the spell created by the moonlight and an unexpected encounter with temptation.

Right. My cover. The job. Viktor Volkevich.

This woman is not for me—our flirtations are not a private, shared moment. I should ensure the *bratok* has left and return to the house. I still have photographs to take.

But then she says, "An exception. I like that. Does that make me special, or lucky?" and I know I will not be leaving her side anytime soon.

"That depends on your perspective. Do you normally consider yourself special or lucky to be followed into a dark garden by a stranger?"

Her laugh is breathless; her stare is a challenge. "*That* depends on the stranger's intentions. I'll admit I have my doubts about yours."

"You are questioning my intentions?"

"Well, you did follow a stranger into a dark garden," she says in a delightfully throaty, teasing way. "But I suppose they could be good. Pure, even."

I let her see as my eyes forge a slow path up and down her body, feeling my own tighten in response. "They are not."

"D, are you flirting or threatening her?"

"I think this is him flirting," Wesley chimes in, his voice thick with restrained laughter. *"I suddenly understand the self-imposed celibacy."*

"Yeah, this is hard to listen to," James agrees, his amusement also plain. *"Stick to killing people, big guy."*

I nearly growl in frustration—they are breaking my concentration—but a startled laugh slips from her lips and her eyes widen, as if she cannot quite believe I am coming on with her, or perhaps that I am being so obvious about my desire. But her disbelief is not a joke, like theirs.

A noise catches my attention. My training kicks in, and I tense and shift away from her to turn in my seat towards the potential threat, only to realize it is a couple, drunkenly stumbling towards the maze. Drunk in a maze? What a terrible idea. I hate mazes.

"Right. Anyway..." The soft dejection in her voice makes me frown as I spin to face her again. Her eyes are averted now as she reaches for the shoes on the ground by her feet. She stands, depriving me of her honeyed stare, moving quickly into the grass and putting distance between us. "I'm going to head back in. It was... I was going to say that it's nice to meet you, but I'm not sure there's anything *nice* about you, is there?"

"No," I agree, standing. "All the same, I will walk you."

Her brows shoot up as she swallows the rest of her sentence, her jaw falling slightly open as she tilts her head up. "Really?"

"How else am I to prove my intentions to you?"

Her eyes dart across my face, searching it. Her pupils are quite large, but not with fear. With curiosity. With desire. I realize she *is* interested. She was trying to leave for some reason other than indifference. I see the hesitancy, just as clearly as I see the want and something deeper and guarded.

After a moment, she makes a pleased little *hmm* noise, and her lips twitch slightly. "I suppose it's only fair to give you a second chance, but

I warn you—it's probably a lost cause. You make a pretty strong first impression."

"You strike me as a woman who likes things strong."

"Jesus," she murmurs with another small laugh that zings right through me. "Now *that* was a line."

"Perhaps."

"Well… you're not wrong," she muses. I see her visually measuring the width of the bicep closest to her, so I flex for effect, and because it pleases me to watch her eyes widen slightly.

"God, I wish I had popcorn."

"The wild assassin is a dangerous animal, and its courting practices are as extraordinary to witness as they are befuddling," Wesley adds in a strange voice, as if he is narrating an animal documentary.

I place a hand on her lower back, and she stiffens against it briefly, then relaxes. Satisfaction thrums in my veins.

Only my feet make noise against the stones as we walk back towards the gardens; she sticks to the grass. More couples have wandered onto the terrace for some respite and fresh air, and I am almost disappointed that we are no longer alone.

She pauses, pushing back against my hand, and I look down at her curiously. Is she having second thoughts?

Sensing my question, she lifts her arm, and the shoes sway back and forth as they dangle from her finger by the strap. "I'm not sure if it's better to wear these or not. I took them off because my feet hurt, but the grass ends here, and those rocks look pointy."

"D, get down on your knee and help her with her shoe. She'll eat it up."

"What?" Wesley asks.

"Just trust me; get down and put on her shoe for her. All those little buckles and shit? When they've got those long nails, it's hard for them. Show her chivalry ain't dead; it's just… rough around the edges."

Oh, now James wants to help?

I consider the idea for a second, then realize I like this advice. It will allow me to touch her somewhere more intimate—an ankle, the arch of her foot, a calf. I want that very much. Both my hands flex, full of sudden anxious energy to have her weight and warmth against my palms once more.

"You should wear them. Here, allow me."

I hold out my hand expectantly, and with a curious cock of her head, she hands over the shoes. In a fluid motion, I drop to one knee, lean down, and gently grip her lower leg. She has good, strong muscles in her calves, and I cannot help but run my thumb across the smoothness of her skin.

She lets out a soft noise of surprise. "Oh!"

Looking slightly bewildered, and glancing around to see if anyone is watching, she allows me to guide her leg up and place it gently on my knee. The motion parts her skirt at the deep slit on the side, and I get more than a flash of golden skin. The head of my cock pulses.

"I'm not very good on heels because I don't usually wear them," she explains distractedly as her hypnotized stare tracks my movements.

Frowning at the broken skin on her smallest toe, I wrap the straps around her foot, then ankle, tying a bow when I run out of ribbon length. I am careful not to tie it too tightly. Her attempt to balance and not lean too hard on me fails as she switches to the other foot and must now stand only on her toes. Her hands press into my shoulders, and it fills me with enormous gratification as she gives me more and more of her weight, trusting me to support her.

This side is the one with the slit, and I push the dress over her thigh to reveal the entire length of her leg. The silky material cascades, swishing into place and remaining there.

"Give her a compliment, but don't be creepy. Something not about her body."

Perhaps James does know what he is doing.

"I like this dress," I murmur, as I slide my hand from ankle to knee, then back down her calf to rest around her heel.

"I'm... coming around to it." Goosebumps rise on her flesh from my touch. I exhale noisily, wishing to run my tongue along their texture.

I take as much care with this shoe, wrapping and then tying neatly, wanting to draw out the anticipation for as long as possible. When finished, I stand, brushing off the knee that was in the grass, and replace my hand on her lower back. "Ready?"

"Definitely," she croaks, then clears her throat of the desire making it raw. "Th-thanks for doing that. No one's ever... that was... um, thanks."

There is a loud hollering in my left ear. *"See? She can't even think straight. I fuckin' told you so!"*

"That was smoothly done, Dimitri. I'm impressed."

"Is she hot? Can you see her, Wes? She sounds hot—"

There is no real cause for it, but anger rises swiftly in my throat, and I tap the comms in each ear in turn, severing the connections. I will open the lines again with just a touch if anything comes up, but some things are best done alone, without a devil whispering in each ear.

I do not want James and Wesley to listen to us anymore, to know more about her, or to be there as she gives in to me. That passion is for *me.* Her hunger is *mine.* She stirs something deep and primal that has been lying dormant in my chest—jealousy, possessiveness, the urge to take and hide her away, because no one fucking *looks at* what is mine.

Perhaps James had a point. There is such a thing as *after hours.* This job will be over soon enough—perhaps I can convince her to give me her phone number.

"Shall we?"

4

NICOLE

⚫

When you meet a Russian guy, don't assume he's in the mafia.

The music from the wedding sounds much louder as we get closer to the estate house. The party is still going strong, and there's some kind of call-and-response happening right now on the dance floor that I have no interest in being a part of. I dread the noise and the crowd, like it's going to break the spell I feel like I'm under.

I'm honestly not sure what to do with all six-foot-freaking-eight of the guy ushering me around the fountain. I'm actually getting a little flustered because I'm so unused to having to crane my neck this much, *especially* once I put my heels back on. The sheer size of him is making me feel some kind of way, and it's more than his height. I got a good feel when he let me use him for balance, and his shoulders are almost unbelievably wide, and so firm even under layers of fabric. I don't think my fingers would meet if I tried to circle his bicep with both hands. His neck is thick, and even his Adam's apple is a prominent bulge that feels oppressively masculine.

I'm not used to feeling small around anyone. Frankly, it's a new feeling. And frankly, I like it more than I'd ever admit out loud.

His face suits his powerful frame. The shadow of stubble growing in, and his thick brows are dark, as is his short hair. White, straight teeth set behind thin lips give him a severe air that's undercut by a slightly rounded nose. He's got that big, old, deep scar that throws off the balance of his features, but it's not enough to distract from the cut line of his jaw, high cheekbones, and slightly hollowed cheeks.

He's not handsome exactly, but his face is so interesting. Interesting things are always the most fun to look at.

But I can understand why he holds himself like he keeps expecting to find me staring. I'm a nurse—I've seen scars—and honestly, they just make him feel more... raw. They fit him because *he's* fucking intense.

I like to give people the benefit of the doubt, even as I assess them for potential concealed weapons in the ER. But he's intimidating. I'm intimidated, even if I'm doing a B+ job of not showing it.

Some people just have an intensity about them. From years of working in a super high-pressure job, I like to think I'm fairly immune to it, but Lev is on a different level entirely. He feels *dangerous*, and I've never thought that of someone before with such certainty.

Not that I think he wants to hurt me... in a way I don't want, anyway. It's kind of thrilling just being near him.

If it were just one thing—the height, or the quick, dark humor, or the sheer size of him—maybe I could deal. But then he had to have all this predatory charm on top of it? And he's pointing it directly at me?

I mean, he got down on his knees and went all Cinderella's prince on me! And maybe it says something about me that I noticed, but he also tied them *perfectly*—they both have the same tension, which is tight enough so they stay on my feet, but loose enough not to cut off any more of my poor pinky toes' circulation. Makes me wonder what else he knows how to tie up perfectly, since he's clearly got some experience...

Heat flashes in my belly, gathering between my legs in a thoroughly distracting kind of way.

We walk along in silence, and I grasp for something to say to break it. Normally, I'm good at this kind of thing. I have plenty of practice. I may not like small talk—who does, really?—but you can't succeed in a public-facing job without some skill in it. And it makes for a more enjoyable first date, since the part where you're unraveling the mysteries of a new person is usually the most fun.

I'm curiously tongue-tied now. A dozen questions make it almost all the way to my lips, but I can't quite bring myself to ask them until I know my voice won't break. My body is practically shaking with nervous energy at his light, guiding, almost possessive touch on my lower back. My heart is racing with how close we just were.

And then there's the million-dollar question: how much do I really want to know?

My conversation with Emma echoes in my head again. Russian *Bratva*. It can't be just a coincidence that he's got such a thick Russian accent. Is he one of them? He definitely looks and feels the part.

And what if he is? I desperately want to invite him back to my place, but... beyond the fact that our combined weight would probably pop my air mattress, I'm not even sure if I could really do it.

Could I sleep with a man in the mob? What are the implications, even if it is just one night?

I don't want to get whacked for giving a bad blowjob.

But what if he's not? I'll have made all these assumptions, made up this totally far-fetched scenario in my head, and it will be mortifying. It's much more likely he isn't. And then I'll have missed out on what is sure to be the wildest of rides.

Occam's razor, right? Doctors love that saying. When you hear hoofbeats, don't assume zebras. When you meet a Russian guy, don't assume he's in the mafia. Emma's wild imagination just planted an idea in my head, and I need to let it go.

"How do you know Matt and Jenny?" I ask, nearly wincing at how it comes out all high-pitched and full of forced brightness.

"Business," he replies curtly. "And you?"

Okay... not really helping dispel the mafia associations...

"Jenny's a distant cousin."

"Tell me, Nicole..."

I love the way he says my name, pronouncing it like *Nee-cole*, with a kind of softness in his accent. "Yes?"

"What would you say if I asked—Felix?"

We've arrived at the top of the stairs, and he straightens like someone poured ice water down the back of his jacket. He scowls, eyes fixed on something—or, more likely, some*one* named Felix—inside, and takes a half-step away from me.

I feel the loss of the warmth of his hand on my back immediately, and a chill shudders through me. "Lev?" I ask.

The glance he shoots me is one of confusion, then hesitation and apology. "I have to..." he doesn't finish the statement as he starts moving. Then, as if remembering he was in the middle of talking to me, he turns back. "Excuse me. I have just seen someone I must speak with. I will find you later, Nicole."

Then he's just... gone. It's amazing how such a large man can move so quickly and quietly.

Disappointment swells, hot and sharp. Over before it began, and here I am, left holding up all those hopes.

Should I wait for him to find me? The pessimist inside of me assumes he won't, and that I'll be stuck waiting here like a silly, hopeful fool for hours. The optimist wants to give him a chance—so, *so* badly.

What was he going to ask me to tell him? I think I owe it to myself to find out.

Maybe I can ask Jenny or Matt for more information about him. Or is that a stalker-y thing to do? The guest list is so big; I wonder if Matt's even the one who invited him, or if he's a friend of the family.

Damn, I hope he's not someone else's date.

"Oh, Nicole! I'm so glad I found you!"

I can tell it's my great-aunt Margaret from the scent of the powdery perfume that envelops me as her soft, round arms come around me from the side. I try not to stiffen, but being touched unexpectedly isn't my thing. "Hi Aunt Margaret, good to see you."

"You too, dear!" she cries over the music. The beads on her dress clack together as she moves, sparkling in the light, and the silver tone matches her steel gray curls. "Where is that mother of yours?"

I shrug. "Greece, I think. She and Steve and the kids have had this big Euro-trip in the works for a while." And my mother is not one to prioritize her old family over her new one.

"Why aren't you with them?" she asks, aghast. "Didn't you want to go to Greece?"

So badly. But I'll get myself there one day—no reason to tag along on a family vacation where I'm not wanted. "I have work," I lie.

"Oh," she nods, like she understands my struggle, and brightens just as quickly. "Speaking of which, I was hoping you could take a look at this cyst I have."

Without waiting for my answer, she leans forward and tilts her neck. The papery skin succumbs to gravity and dangles around the front of her throat. There is indeed a pencil-eraser-sized lump on the back of her shoulder that's rubbing raw from the neckline of her beaded dress.

"I've had it for a few months now. I'm just not sure why it keeps coming back after I drain it... and the smell—"

I clear my throat. Being a nurse is a minefield sometimes. "I can't be sure without properly inspecting it, and I don't have any gloves or anything, so I wouldn't want to do it here. I recommend finding a dermatologist. It would help put your mind at ease to have a doctor look," I say, my party line.

She purses her lips in chagrin and shakes her head, a motion which doesn't even budge the steely gray pin curls. No one enjoys being told they should see a doctor when they were hoping to get free medical advice. "I suppose. Do you know a good doctor?"

"I believe that St. Luke's has a few on staff, if you wanted to come in," I say, doubling down on what I know she thinks is unhelpful advice.

"That's in the city?"

"Fifth and Vine."

Her nose curls as I name an area of the city she's likely scandalized just to think about. "No, that's... that's all right. I'll ask my family doctor for a referral."

"I think that would be best," I say, donning my best neutral face. "Would you excuse me? I need to find my purse."

Before she can think of another ailment to solicit my opinion on, I scoot away.

I find my table and circle it once. I thought I left my bag next to my plate, but all I see is Kyle's room key, several half-empty water glasses, and some crumbs of cake. It's not on the floor either. A mild panic builds in my gut—it's a clutch, so most of what's in there is, like, lipstick and some cash in case I needed it for the bar, but it's also got some stuff that's harder to replace, like my glasses, my personal phone, and the work phone they just gave me at St. Luke's. I only brought it tonight to build the habit of bringing it with me everywhere—my manager is going to be pissed if I've lost it after two days.

This event has more security than the White House, and people are dripping in diamonds; who would steal a purse?

Maybe a server saw it sitting here and swiped it for safekeeping, or maybe someone dropped it off with coat check...

"Oh, Nicooole."

I can barely hear it over the pounding bass of the band's latest banger, but it still sends a chill down my spine. I spin, cringing at the childish call that drags my name into multiple unnecessary syllables. Kyle is standing by the wall, holding up my purse. When we make eye contact, he waves the beaded bag at me, like he wants to make sure that I know he has it.

And then what does that asshole do? He fucking runs.

He hugs the wall, skirting around the dance floor, and darts out towards the gardens where I just was.

"What the hell?!" I cry out, barely able to believe what just happened.

Did a grown man just steal my purse and run like he wants me to chase him? What kind of moron thinks the best way to get a girl's attention is to steal her fucking purse and run? Is this grade school?

A few people around me shoot me strange looks at my outburst, so I grit my teeth and follow him back out onto the veranda.

"What the actual fuck," I grumble, staggering on my heels as I follow him through the garden. I miss Lev's steadying hand—the gravel was so much easier to navigate when I knew he'd catch me if I stepped wrong in my heel.

Kyle stays within sight until I hobble to the edge of the path, then darts through a line of trees. Almost like... fuck. Is he headed for that hedge maze?

"Kyle!" I yell, glancing around as I do. A couple kissing on a bench turn at the sound of my voice, so I lower it when I call out again, "This isn't funny or cute. Give it back!"

"Come and get me, Nicole!"

He sounds deranged—there's an edge to his voice that's so excited it borders on sexual.

Oh, gross.

Look, I'm not one to yuck someone's yum, but I am *not* a willing participant in whatever kink this is.

I make it through the line of trees, and he's waiting for me at the entrance of the maze, leaning into a bush and fanning himself with my bag. He cackles at the sight of me and spins away, disappearing behind greenery and darkness.

"Come on, Kyle, don't do this. Please, just give it back."

As he laughs again, I realize I'm not making this any better for myself. He wants my frustration, my reticence, my desperation. I'm playing right into whatever weird bullying fantasy he's acting out right now.

The entrance to the hedge maze looms in front of me. I don't know what kind of bush/tree/shrub things these are, but they must be 10 feet tall, and they're so densely packed I can't see through them. My Labyrinth-loving heart would be thrilled, if not for the ridiculous, annoying context. And I'd really prefer to be doing this with some light other than just the moon...

I open my mouth to call out for him again, but stop as I hear a commotion on my right. A group of guys is headed this way, laughing and chatting. One of them is the dude Kyle knew earlier, and I can feel his horrible eyes on me. They feel like mockery.

I hate this. I hate being out here with judgmental voyeurs, and I really, *really* don't want to go in there.

A maze. At night. Alone. What happens when I catch up with him? Is he just going to give it back without some kind of altercation? Probably not. But otherwise, how am I going to get my phone?

Stepping just inside so I'm out of sight of Kyle's friends, who appear to be about to start peeing in the bushes, I bend down and untie the careful knots Lev made. The grass is soft underfoot, and if I need to run after this complete asshole, there's no way I'll manage in four-inch heels that keep sinking into the soft earth. I hook the straps in the crook of my index finger and head into the maze after Kyle.

$$5$$

DIMITRI

⚊◈⚊

It is important to know that a man you have killed is truly dead.

"Fuck," I curse, checking the last stall in the bathroom and finding it empty. "He must have slipped out the window."

"You're sure it was Felix?" James presses.

"I am sure. He was at the bar, speaking with a man—5'10", brown hair slicked back, Caucasian. They parted ways before I could get close enough to hear anything or discover who the other man was."

"I don't like it," James decides with a sigh. *"He didn't tell either of us he was going to be at the wedding, too, which feels pretty fuckin' intentional."*

"I agree," Wesley echoes. *"We've got plenty of photos, and I've already started running them through my database for matches in the system—that's enough to get started. It was well worth the cost of admission, I'd say."*

"Cut our losses?" James suggests.

"Perhaps that is for the best," I muse.

As a general rule, it is best to err on the side of caution when faced with too many unknowns. Since I do not know why Felix is here, it would be unwise to follow through with the hit. We will take the information I gathered and assassinate Viktor Volkevich another time, when there is no one around to link me to the crime.

And in the meantime, I wish to know what Felix is up to.

"Keep watch for him in the security cameras, Wesley."

"I will, but I haven't spotted him so far. My guess is he knows where they are and he's avoiding them."

I move towards the frosted window in this bathroom, which appears to be painted shut. It lifts with very little force, and the screen is missing, so I know this is how Felix escaped. Did he see me and run?

I peer out, looking for signs of the man himself or any potential witnesses, and find only vacant darkness. Assessing the size of the window against my bulk, I shake my head. This will be tight.

The squeeze is uncomfortable, but I make it through the window and drop only a few feet, landing on a small stretch of grass out behind the kitchen, where the workers have littered the ground with cigarette butts. I can still smell smoke in the air, so I am very fortunate that the area is empty now.

As part of our prep work, we reviewed blueprints and took note of the position of the guards. I know that the best exit point is through that maze of greenery. There is a fence and a single isolated guard that separate the property from the wooded area beyond. My car is parked and waiting for me in the neighborhood that sits on the other side of the trees.

I start circling the house, heading back towards the gardens, but a voice nearly causes me to stumble.

"Sir?"

Fuck!

"Wesley?" I hiss. I do not risk looking over my shoulder, but the voice was close—no more than 10 meters away.

"Erm... let me find you... Bollocks. Same guard as earlier. I think he saw you closing the window from the outside."

Which will appear very suspicious to him. If he has not already, this will cause him to report me to his superiors. I have no choice now but to dispose of him. Leaving him alive would be a risk too great.

"Anything you can do so he cannot call for backup?" I murmur as the man approaches from behind.

"Let me just…" There is a pregnant pause, and I can barely make out the sound of Wesley's fingers clacking against the keys of his laptop. *"All right, you've got 60 seconds of outage in the area, and the cameras in the rear are off. They've likely already noticed the cameras and are trying to get them back online. Be quick."*

I will never know how he does what he does, but I cannot dwell on it.

"Excuse me, Sir."

Instead of turning, I pick up my pace and head for a line of tall, pointy trees several meters away, just outside the circle of floodlights. They have grown closely enough together that they should hide us from anyone else that might come outside.

I collect a knife from the belt I wear that lays flat against my lower abdominals.

"Sir!"

When I break through to the other side, I have only seconds to scan the grounds to assess my options. It is wilder back here, less meticulously kept by gardeners. All around me there are thick, old trees—some with branches hanging low to the ground. I head towards one, thinking the branches might offer some additional protection or screening.

I can hear the man pursuing me as his pace quickens. He clearly finds my behavior or appearance suspicious to have followed me this far, but the chances that he would attack a guest on nothing more than suspicion are low. Especially without the backup he is certainly trying to call for.

No violence at a wedding. It is a *Bratva* rule, a gentleman's agreement, though I would not expect anyone charged with protecting his *Pakhan* to follow that particular rule. I saw the piece in the guard's waistband, but I doubt he would risk the noise, even with the music so loud. His orders are likely to detain and question. So it is not a surprise when he calls to me again.

"Hey! Sir, I need you to stop right there."

I pause, but do not turn around. Instead, I grip the handle of my knife tighter.

"*Pozvol'te mne uvidet' nekotoryye dokumenty, udostoveryayushchiye lichnost*—" he says, switching to Russian to demand identification.

When I feel a hand fall on my shoulder, I move. I drop away from his grip, spin and slash outwards, but I underestimated the size of him. We are well-matched, he was prepared for my attack, and clearly very well trained. He knocks the knife from my hand. As it falls in the tall grass several meters away with a soft thud, lost, I curse at my folly. To allow my weapon to be parted from me... that is the move of an amateur.

The *bratok* takes full advantage, delivering a forceful punch to my stomach as I fail to protect an opening. While I move away to recover, he roars and charges me. I brace myself, but the impact rattles my teeth. He forces me back a few steps, and I get two good hits to his kidneys, but we are locked in a stalemate—a wrestling match of equal strength. He pushes, I push back, and no one gains anything.

Until I lift my knee. He brings his legs together to protect his most delicate area, sending me a look of betrayal that I would use any available advantage. But the concept of honor and fairness is strange to me when a single blow can determine the outcome of a fight to the death. What use does a dead man have for honor?

I pull away, move my body behind his and bring my arm down around his neck. I squeeze, cradling his throat in the crook of my elbow. His arms flail, scrambling for the gun at his waist, and I grab the tie he wears. I spin the tail around towards me, tighten the knot, and push it against the back of his thick neck as I step back towards the low branch behind me.

Holding the tie, I flip over the branch and use his body as a counterweight. His choking noises are loud, and his heels pound and scratch the ground as he attempts to get them under himself. For the span of a few heartbeats, he struggles in vain, and I grit my teeth against the effort it takes to hold the tie. Then, he slows. Eventually, he stills, and his dead weight tugs at the silk.

I release my hold, and the man's body collapses and hits the ground with a thump. My chest expands uncomfortably as I try to get in enough oxygen, caving in at the bottom of each release. After a moment to catch my breath, I pick myself up and duck under the branch to look for a pulse. I always check twice. It is important to know that a man you have killed is truly dead.

The tie is the only thing with any evidence—fingerprints—so I unknot it to take it, along with the contents of his pockets. I leave the gun. Someone will come looking eventually, but by the time they find him back here, I will be long gone.

I have to cross back through the line of pointy trees and climb over a row of rose bushes that mark the boundary of the patio to get to the garden. Then, I make my way quickly and inconspicuously across the yard, back towards the tall maze.

Three men are pissing in the bushes as I pass. One is singing loudly and poorly, and the other two are laughing about the couple they just saw disappearing into the hedge maze. I pass them, ignoring their drunken chatter, but a familiar name catches my attention.

"You think Kyle's really gonna fuck her? Wawazhername? *Nicole*?" the one on the right slurs.

"No, no, no. Shut up, listen. Kyle knows what's up. I'm betting she's a huge slut," the other says with a loud laugh. "Girls like her… I'm tellin' ya, they give the best head. We should try to go catch him railing her, maybe he'll share. Really mess with the—"

Compelled by something unnamed, I redirect myself. Before he can finish his sentence, I grab his shoulder to hold him steady and punch the man in the back of the head. He pitches forward, going down and getting tangled in the piss-soaked bush.

"Hey, what the fuck, man?!" cries one of his pals. The other is still singing.

I grab him by the front of his shirt as he scrambles to cover his balls. "Where is she?" I demand.

His eyes widen in panic. "M-maze," he mumbles, pointing.

I release him. While he tries to tuck his cock away, he gets an elbow to the nose and a fist in his stomach. He windmills his arms, falling back against the last man, whose singing cuts off abruptly as they go down in a heap.

They scramble together, but the blow to his overfilled stomach is too much, and the second man vomits all over the first as he attempts to extricate himself from the thorns and dead flowers. The singing man has passed out, evidently needing no better excuse than simply being horizontal.

The rage making my fists shake tempts me to do more—a well-placed kick to shatter a kneecap or a sharp punch to the throat to collapse a trachea. These idiots may be angry, but they are easily beaten. A concussion and a ruptured spleen are enough to make them cover their balls and run, abandoning their fallen comrade.

I head into the maze, feeling my anger slowly drain and my pulse calm.

"Erm... What was that all about?"

I shake out my hand as I try to think of a suitable excuse other than that I wanted to. My hand hurts, my knuckles are split open again, but that felt good—so good, in fact, I think I will do the same thing to this *Kyle* when I find him. He must be the date she spoke of. The one she was avoiding. The asshole.

"I am clearing the way through the maze."

"Sure," James returns, sounding wholly unconvinced.

"I'll watch to make sure they don't report Dimitri to security," Wesley offers. *"If they do..."*

We will have other problems. Three more body-sized problems.

Fuck.

That was foolish of me. Depending on who finds that *bratok's* body, the police may become involved. Wedding guests will be questioned. And now three men will recall the large, scarred man who attacked them unprovoked.

Still, I feel no remorse. Instead, I feel as if I have wrought a suitable punishment for their thoughtless insults, unearned superiority and the crime of being very, very annoying.

Since I am going in blind, and I need to focus, I temporarily mute the lines. There is little chance we will be completely alone in here, since the maze is quite large, but my first few turns leading me deeper reveal nothing more than grass and leaves rustling in a too-quiet corridor.

Nicole's voice sounds distant, so I know she is deeper in the maze. "This is so fucking lame, Kyle! I don't want to play whatever messed-up game this is. I want to go home. Please," she adds after a moment.

Her tone catches my attention—sad, tired, embarrassed.

My jaw clenches.

Kyle's answer is in an eerie, strange tone. "Don't worry, Nicole, I'll make sure you get taken care of..."

A very ominous answer that makes me pick up my pace. My next turn leads me down a dead end. Another turn twists me back around the wrong way.

Fuck! I hate mazes!

6

NICOLE

I'm generally against spooky shit.

The shadows have shadows.

Just when I think my eyes have adjusted, I find a darker darkness. The light breeze is right on the cusp of cold, and it rattles the leaves together around me, making it hard to tell if any of the noises I'm hearing are natural or human-made. It's freaking me out. I'm freaking *myself* out. My heart rate is elevated, and it feels like I can't quite get a full breath in. I wish I'd brought my inhaler.

Not that it would matter, because it would be in my purse.

The one Kyle currently has.

Fuck that guy!

It's only after I start stumbling around in the dark that I realize most women probably wouldn't follow a man they didn't know or like into a maze at night, even if he had their phone. Now, if it were Lev doing this? Not that he would, but... Yeah... I'd probably just let him have the purse. I'm not chasing down nearly seven feet of scarred muscle mass for something replaceable.

But I'm not afraid of Kyle—he's the whole box of tools, but I could take him. We're honestly pretty evenly matched, physically speaking; I might even have an inch or two on him. Plus, based on the erratic way he's acting, I think he might be on drugs of some kind. I'm used to dealing with unpredictable behavior.

It's times like these that make me realize I've lived my life with a certain amount of tall-girl privilege. Female friends have pointed out to me before that I do things they routinely avoid, like walking home from the bar down a dark alley, traveling alone, and meeting up with strangers from the internet. I guess I'm not as worried about being physically overpowered or targeted for violence because of my looks. There's a real irony in the proportionality of size and social invisibility for women.

But I suppose that means that sometimes I take that lack of attention for granted. Like now, for example—I never would have imagined myself in this situation. It's not like I'm overly scared of the dark, but... this shit is spooky. I'm generally against spooky shit. That, and it kind of feels like the setup of some terrible prank from one of my high school nightmares, where the lights come on and I'm in my underwear or covered in a bucket of blood.

When I round a corner and nearly collide with a trio of women—one leading the way resolutely, and the other two complaining and giggling behind her—I nearly shriek. The girl in the lead gives me a weird look, and I wave my apology and keep going. I'm tempted to ask her if she saw Kyle, but I chicken out. It's sort of embarrassing to admit I'm chasing someone, and asking someone for directions in a maze is like the definition of pointless.

"Kyle?" I ask the darkness as soon as the girls disappear around the hedge behind me.

The darkness doesn't respond.

Hot tears of frustration prickle in my eyes. My high school nightmare comparison from earlier was apt. It's been over a decade, but some scars never quite heal right, and bullying during our formative years happens to be one.

But I'm not that awkward, unsure-of-herself girl. I'm a grown woman. And I'm fucking pissed.

"Nicooooole," Kyle sings again.

The wind carries his voice through the corridors of the maze, and wraps around me like a wet blanket, making me shiver. I spin, trying to figure out where the sound came from. He's everywhere and nowhere.

"Fuck this. I'm leaving," I grind out. "I'm going to report my purse as stolen and let the authorities deal with you."

"Don't be like that, Nicole."

I gasp and whirl. How is he right behind me? How did he get so close without me hearing? I stumble back a step in surprise. "Kyle?! What the fuck?"

He doesn't answer, just charges forward, invading my space with a crazy, intense look in his eye. I suddenly wish I were wearing my heels again for the height advantage.

He reaches for me, and I shift away from his grabby hands. "Stop! What are you doing? Don't touch me!"

But I'm suddenly cornered, backed up against a wall of greenery that only bends slightly against my weight. I shove at his shoulders, bringing up my knee to wedge between our bodies. Sharp branches press into my back, snagging threads in my dress and pricking, poking, and scraping bare skin wherever they meet.

The press of his body against mine makes me go rigid in repulsion. He's stronger than I expected, and he stinks of booze and... blood? Is that blood on his shirt?

"Stop! Leave me alone!" I yell and pull back my arm to take a swing.

I'm not a particularly violent person, but the thumping noise of my shoes hitting him in the forehead is very satisfying. I hit him again, trying to use one of the pointed heels as a sharp edge. I catch him in the corner of the eye with it, and he reels, clutching the area and swearing.

"Ah! Fuck! You bitch!" he growls, lunging at me again, and wrestling the only weapon I've got from my grip. I scream, and he scrambles, trying to get control over the situation again. "Shhh! Shut up! Shut the fuck up!"

"Hel—" my cry for help is muffled as his hand comes up and shoves something inside my mouth.

As I react to the unexpected intrusion with panic and disgust—choking, then trying to spit it back out—Kyle presses his hand hard against my lips.

Then, there's an unmistakable sound.

I shouldn't know what that sound is—it's not exactly common in my real life—but I've consumed enough action movies and media. It's the click of a gun cocking. I feel cold metal pressed to my temple, and all the fight dies out of me at once, replaced with icy fear.

Fuck. Fuck!

"Swallow it, bitch," he hisses into my face. Blood rolls down from the corner of his eye, but it just enhances the look of mania. "Swallow it or I'll fucking shoot you."

It's hard, whatever it is in my mouth. I barely have time to feel it out with my tongue before he presses the gun harder against my skull. I whimper, feeling a hot tear scald down my cheek. Fighting the urge to bite down on something that's on the verge of being too big to swallow, I tip my head back and feel it disappear down my throat. I gag. It doesn't go down easy, and it hurts, and I have to swallow a few more times to clear it from where it feels stuck at the bottom of my esophagus.

What the fuck was that?

His laugh is gleeful and unhinged. "Good. Open up and show me you swallowed it. Open your fucking mouth, bitch. Okay, good... you got any final prayers, now's the time—"

"Let her go!" roars a distinct voice—a deeper, darker one. One that sounds like a threat and my salvation.

7

Dimitri

No good will come of this, only more problems.

If he does not let her go, I will kill him. And maybe if he does.

Based on what I heard, I expect to see her on her knees when I come around the corner of the maze, and the thought makes me see red.

The relief is acute, but brief, when instead I find her upright, sandwiched between Kyle and the thick bushes, one of his hands pressed tightly over her mouth and the other holding a gun at her temple. I step in without thinking, growl an order without considering any consequences—my only thoughts are wordless ones of sharp urgency and fury.

"Let her go!"

With a start, he swings around. He points the gun at me before I see his face, and the threat of being shot is all it takes for me to bring my arm up to let my knife fly.

Too late, I see the slicked-back hair. Too late, I realize that this is the man who was talking to Felix at the bar.

At the very last second, I try to adjust the trajectory of my throw from one that will kill to one that will incapacitate. I need to question him—to know what business Felix had here tonight. With a fleshy *pop*, my knife lodges in the lower portion of his stomach, somewhere halfway between the center of his chest, where I first aimed, and his thigh, the target I tried adjusting to.

He makes a choked noise and stares down at the knife in disbelief. Eyes wide with shock and fury, he points the gun at me again. I duck back behind the hedge for cover, but not before a shot goes off. It is dark, and his aim is poor, but a white-hot, searing pain lances me in my side.

Fuck! He just shot me!

Fuck! A gun just went off at a wedding!

He fires again and again in my general direction until all that remains is the empty click of a gun out of bullets. I emerge, ready to face off, but he is already disappearing behind another hedgerow. Those final shots were a distraction to cover his own escape.

Tonight was a bad night. So many mistakes.

But none of that feels very important at this exact moment. As Nicole scrambles to her feet, I go to her and scan her for injuries with a kind of indescribable mania I have never before felt. The beat of my own heart is so loud in my ears that it blocks all other sound, calming only when I verify that the spray of blood across her dress likely belonged to Kyle. There is no damage to her.

Instructions to retrace her steps out of here are ready on my tongue, only to wither and die at the sound of a series of unmistakable bangs. We both freeze.

Gunshots. Two, then three in answer.

Unless he had another gun stashed somewhere, I know Kyle is not part of it, though the shooting is loud enough that it must be close. The exchange of fire continues for several long seconds, and then the chaos begins.

Distant sounds fill the night air—screams, breaking glass, crashing furniture, and the noise of feet pounding against stone and bodies falling as a crazed, terrified crowd moves erratically to run for cover or hide. Nicole takes a half step towards me, eyes wide with fear.

All at once, my priorities shift from *slip out unnoticed* to *protect Nicole*. She moves *towards* me for safety. She just saw me throw a knife at and possibly fatally wound a man, but in this moment, she believes I will protect her. And in this moment, I want to be the man she thinks I am.

So, I will.

"Stay with me," I say, grabbing her arm before she can wander in the wrong direction. She is shaking in my grip, and I want to soothe her, but there are more pressing matters. I reopen the communication channel. "What is happening?"

"I don't know!" she cries softly in response, thinking that I was asking her.

Wesley's voice enters my right ear, calm, steady, and factual. *"I can't see where the shots came from, but every guard in this place is heading for the house or the maze. This is your only chance before they block off every exit. Get out of there* now!"

When another shot goes off, Nicole whimpers and shifts so close to me that our bodies are pressed together.

Now is not the time to notice how well she fits against me—how solid and tall she is, like she would not bend or break in my grip. Soft, warm skin, rounded curves...

Not the fucking time!

"Nicole, listen to me. I will lead you out, but I need both hands. Stay close and try to move quickly and silently."

Eyes wet and round, like shining coins at the bottom of a pool, she nods. Another round of gunshots that sounds even closer intensifies her shaking.

"Can you do this?"

"Yes! Let's go already!" she hisses.

In a very counterproductive response, I nearly falter in my step. Her composure is unexpected. I expected her to be crying and making noise and unable to think rationally—how most regular people react to terrifying situations. I do not know if she is hiding it, or if fear does not rule her as it would others, but I have seen seasoned *Bratva* men freeze when faced with the pressure we are under. I am impressed. And relieved.

I pull out my phone to consult the map of the maze, stow it, and head for the exit. The need to reach back and hold her hand is a physical pull that takes some effort to ignore. Instead, I fill my hands with knives.

I have to trust that she will stay behind me—if I look back, I cannot protect our front.

Before we round the first turn, I hear a strangled noise of relief and turn in time to see her bend down and pick something up. "My purse," she whispers, tucking it under her arm.

Good. Better not to leave behind evidence that we were here.

Our progress is slow as I guide us carefully through the maze, staying low and moving with purpose, so I am not terribly surprised that we do not encounter Kyle on the way out. We pass a couple cowering in a corner and a man trying to conceal himself at the base of the bushes, but I ignore them. I sense her brief hesitation, wanting to help, but ultimately deciding to follow me instead.

She has good self-preservation instincts. I approve.

When we reach the back exit of the maze, I hold up a hand to stop her so I can check if we are clear to run for the wooded area. We are. The line of trees is only 10 meters away, and the grassy stretch of lawn is empty of people as far as I can see. There was a guard by the gate all night, but he must have responded to the gunshots. Luck is with us. Finally.

I slide one knife back into my belt, freeing up my non-dominant hand to reach for her.

"Now, we run."

She takes my hand; I grip hers tightly, and we move.

We hurry across the grass towards the gate. She is able to keep up behind me, but breathing hard at my pace, so I refuse to let go when her hand twists in mine, seeking freedom. She slows further when we reach the new-growth forest falling into dormancy for the winter. I realize she is not wearing shoes as she hisses in pain and stumbles along—each gentle, muffled gasp is a shard of ice through my gut. But I cannot pick her up; it would make us a slower, larger target to hit in case we are being pursued.

Emerging on the other side of the wooded area, we are suddenly back in suburban civilization. The road where I parked is deserted at this hour, and I guide her through people's lawns so we are outside the range of the street lamps placed at intervals on the sidewalk.

I unlock the SUV with my key in the door instead of the button, so there is no flash of the headlights to give anyone a warning of where we are before we can drive away.

Opening the passenger door, I usher her into the space. "Get in."

Cornered, her eyes dart around past me, into the looming darkness. I cannot be sure what that wild look means, but she has three seconds to decide to fight me or run. It will not matter if she does either, because she is getting in the car. I would prefer not to have to carry and throw her in—I have a feeling she would kick and scratch.

The thought is more arousing than it ought to be.

She makes a brief second of terrified eye contact, then spins and grabs the internal handle to pull herself into the front seat. I have to applaud her survival instinct yet again—she has clearly judged that I am her best chance out of this situation. I close her door, then trot around to the other side and get behind the wheel.

"Where are we going?" she asks, reaching back for the seatbelt as I start the car.

"Away," I reply. I have no further plans at the moment.

I pull out into the street as quickly as the speed limit permits. The dashboard clock says 12:35 AM, but local law enforcement is still a concern. Even once I am far enough from the crime scene, it is still a Saturday night and they are waiting for drunk drivers in the shadows of side streets. Speeding is an easy reason to give them to stop me, and we cannot afford that.

The street lamps flash through the darkness of the car, periodically illuminating both of us, and the coppery scent of my blood fills the air, nauseating me—likely due to the loss of so much of it.

Nicole shivers, then physically shies away as I lean forward to turn on the heat. "Are we going to the police?" she asks, voice small.

I can tell that she already knows she will not receive the answer she wants to hear. So why ask? I cut her a look that hopefully conveys my frustration with her inane question, and she nods, dejected. "Okay, no police."

Silence hangs between us, feeling more and more intentional as we pass beyond the limits of the Ulysses suburbs. New Jersey is a curious landscape of beachfront areas, agriculture, forests and metropolitan hubs. The shift from urban landscape to highway in the middle of the forest is abrupt.

The more distance we get, the less certain I am about what to do. The stupidity of the decisions I made in the heat of the moment is slowly crystallizing.

For the first time that I can remember in a long time, I left witnesses.

Depending on how quickly he can get medical care, Kyle may survive. A knife to most places in the abdomen is a slow death of leaking fluids that can be remedied with prompt attention.

Still, there are two possible outcomes—either I killed Kyle, or I did not. In the first scenario, Nicole watched me kill him, so I cannot simply allow her to walk free. In the second, I saved her from an attack, but Kyle becomes my loose end. He might be Felix's man. Or, there is always a chance he says the wrong thing to the wrong person and they identify me as a person of interest when Viktor Volkevich ends up dead.

Plan for the worst, hope for the best. I need to lie low until I can discover whether Kyle is alive.

But what do I do with Nicole?

I cannot believe that I brought her with me. I cannot believe I did not just leave her in that maze. I cannot believe I am considering continuing to protect her.

It is tempting to blame her for my mistakes—she is the exact sort of distraction I try to avoid—but it is not her fault. It is mine. The only good that comes of a mistake is the opportunity to learn from it, and I cannot do that if I do not accept responsibility.

That does not change the fact that she remains a problem for me now.

There is one way I normally deal with problems. A knife to the throat or a bullet to the brain are both merciful deaths—quick but messy.

That particular line of thought terminates at a single, inconvenient conclusion: I will not kill this woman.

The reasons I should far outnumber the arguments in her favor. But somehow, she has become... *important* to me. Her innocence will make her difficult to deal with, as will the fact that she is clearly very smart. But I am drawn to her—why else would I have acted so rashly?—and even worse still, I think I might *like* her.

No good will come of this, only more problems. I know this.

"Thank you for doing that, Lev. For getting us out of that maze. For saving me. That was... um, thank you."

At her wavering voice, I brace myself for tears. In my experience, women always cry eventually. But when I glance over, I see she is staring at her knees and rubbing the center of her chest absently. When she realizes I am looking, she stops abruptly and twists her hands together in her lap, like she has been caught at something.

"Why did you do it?" she asks after a moment, when it becomes clear I will not respond to her softly spoken, heartfelt thanks.

"What?"

"Save me. It would have been easier for you to get out alone. Why save a person who's basically a stranger?"

I let out a longer sigh than I mean to, but it is a damn good question. "I do not know," I admit through my teeth.

I do not have the energy to try to handle her emotions for her—I can barely handle my own—and there is too much fog in my brain to think of a better excuse. The pain in my side is subsiding, but it is still somewhat distracting.

Interestingly, the terrible answer makes her relax a fraction. The shift in her body language is minute, no more than a slight rounding of her shoulders and a loosening of her jaw. I do not understand this response, and it makes me scowl.

She is... so calm. Perhaps I was too hasty to assume she is innocent—the only people this calm in the middle of this much danger are used to it because *they* are dangerous people. Innocents always lament their terrible luck. They demand to be returned to the safety of their homes. They cower, make threats, and sometimes get violent in self-defense. Nicole does none of that; she sits silently with a distant look and pensive frown.

"I hope everyone's okay. Do you know what happened?" she asks after a moment. "Like, who was shooting?"

"Why have you not asked me to take you home?" I fire back, answering her question with my own.

"I... what if..." she sucks in a breath and it breaks in the back of her throat, a sound similar to a choked sob. "I'm scared that Kyle knows where I live."

All the muscles in my arms tense at the same time, making my shoulders bunch and my jaw flex. The leather covering the steering wheel squeaks under the force of my grip.

He did something to her—something to make her so afraid she would not go home for fear that he might be there. If I ever see him again, I will ensure his death is slow.

"If he is alive, he could easily find out," I caution her.

The deepening of her anxious frown makes me feel strangely churlish, but it does no good to ignore the truth when the stakes are this high.

She pulls her lower lip into her mouth and chews at the inside of it. "*If?*" she repeats. "Do you think you killed him?"

Either she is an exceptional actress, or her response is genuine. It would be difficult for anyone hardened by the life we lead to recreate the mixture of tentative hope and guilt in her expression.

"I do not know." I wish I could stop saying that.

What do I do?

Why is it so difficult to think?

Probably the bullet wound.

I need to get us somewhere safe. But I cannot bring her to the house, or I would put Wesley, James and Eleanor at risk. I do not know this woman. I do not know what kind of threat she might pose or how erratically she might act if *she* feels threatened...

"Hey, Lev?"

"What?" I snap, irrationally angry at the wrong name on her lips again.

"It smells very strongly of blood in here. I thought maybe it was from what I got on me, but... Are you bleeding?"

Oh. "*Da.*"

"Do you know where? Or what caused it?"

"I was shot."

She inhales sharply, though not emphatically enough to be a gasp, and begins looking around at the passing scenery. "We need to stop. Is there a gas station or something up ahead?"

"We are not stopping for a graze; it is not bleeding very much."

"Even a graze can trigger shock," she admonishes. "You shouldn't be driving."

I refuse to respond to that ridiculous statement with anything more than a scoff.

As if I do not know my body well enough to know that I am in control of my faculties. I have been shot many times. I know the signs of shock well, and I am not exhibiting any. On the occasions when a bullet has hit me somewhere closer to something vital, it has triggered a kind of small panic, but I am usually able to ride it out.

"Please, Lev. If you pass out from blood loss, you might crash the car and kill us both." After a few more seconds of silence, she makes a frustrated noise. "At least answer my screening questions?"

"Fine."

It is an odd thing to watch such a shift in a person, but I feel as if I am witnessing a transformation. Gone is the frightened, worried creature, and in her place is someone very much in control, competent, and who knows exactly how to handle a medical emergency.

A golden woman in a golden dress with a low voice so calming that it could put me to sleep.

"How's your heart rate? Is your breathing normal? Any feelings of weakness or fatigue? Pain anywhere other than the area of the wound, like the chest or abdominal region? Dizziness?"

As I answer her questions in turn, she clicks on the light over our heads and examines my lips and fingernails for any discoloration. She watches my chest rise and fall with a clinical focus, then places her freezing cold fingertips on my wrist.

When I remove my hand from the steering wheel, she pulls back with a small scowl. "Let me check—"

I crank the heat, then place my hand face up across the center console, wordlessly submitting to her demands and making it easier for her to take my pulse. "Just get it over with," I grumble.

Her cool fingers find my pulse again, and she grips my much larger hand, holding it still with both of hers, one cradled around the back of it. I resist the urge to flex against her hold, just to see what she would do. Her touch is firm, but she uses light pressure. She treats me so... gently.

When we make eye contact this time, I freeze.

I had nearly forgotten, since so much of our time together has been in dim or nonexistent lighting where it is difficult to discern the color of things. Now, even with pupils large from lingering adrenaline, her eyes shine. They are the color I believe Americans would call *hazel*—almost a light tan, much like the rest of her coloring.

She is truly golden, like honey.

Her dress flashes as her chest rises and falls, and I follow the motion hungrily. She swallows, and my eyes are drawn to the up and down movement of her throat. The line from her ear down to her shoulder is long and elegant and completely bare of jewelry. I can see a vein thrumming against her skin—what would her fluttering pulse feel like under my palm, or my lips?

The car swerves, and I jerk my hand away to right us on the road.

This is... unsettling. I am unsettled.

And aroused. I have never wanted to have a woman as badly as I want this one, right now. Perhaps it is the adrenaline still coursing through my veins from the fight and the injury—an ancient instinct to fuck or kill. Whatever the reason, this is terrible fucking timing. I need what blood I have left in my head, not my cock.

I shift in my seat to adjust the hardening length discreetly, but there is only so far for me to go, even in an SUV with ample head space.

Fuck. This is going to be a long ride. But in the short term, there are things I must take care of.

"May I have your phone?"

After a second of hesitation and a hard look, she snaps open the small purse wedged between her leg and the center console and hands me her thin device. I roll down the window wordlessly and toss it out.

"Hey! What the fuck, Lev? You can't just—"

"You can be tracked with your phone," I explain gruffly, thinking of how simple it would be for Wesley or, I imagine, Felix. "If Kyle can find where you live, he can find you with that just as easily. We need to hide until we are out of imminent danger. And call me Dimitri."

8

NICOLE

Trust him, but try to stay a step ahead of him.

I wasn't scared of Kyle, and I should have been.

He didn't really give me a reason to be scared, though. He was just being a complete dick right up until he pulled a gun on me.

Lev—*Dimitri,* on the other hand... I sneak a glance his way. His brows are snapped together, pinching his face into an intense, angry look. The shiny white facial scar is prominent, even in the low light, and whereas before it gave him an ominous air, now it's downright menacing.

He looks like his baseline emotion is simmering anger. But that's just how his face is, I think? Either way, despite looking like the muscles required to smile are all paralyzed, he's like Lake fucking Placid. Sure movements, even breathing, flat voice. Not an ounce of fear. His heart rate was a cool 65 bpm when I took it moments ago.

That's not normal.

So, I *know* I should be scared of Dimitri.

I watched him do something impossible. He was standing 20 feet away; it was dark, and someone had a gun pointed at him, but he threw that knife, and it went right into Kyle's stomach. With the pointy end.

Maybe an argument could be made for some of it being due to luck, but I don't think that's it either. Who throws a knife unless they're sure it'll hit? Who even carries knives anyway? It's got to be easier to use a gun.

So, it's not just skill; it's expertise. Which means he's done it before. A lot.

Which means he's a killer.

With a growing sense of unease, I watch him out of the corner of my eye as the flickering light of a gas station illuminates half our bodies through the windows. Both hands are on the wheel, but his posture is relaxed in his seat, and he's taking up what feels like more than half of the front of the cab.

Briefly, I consider making him pull over, or grabbing for the wheel and crashing us into one of the ditches on either side of this back country road. Even in my own brain, that scenario doesn't play out in my favor. He's too big, too quick, too... much.

Can't say I'm as big of a fan of our size discrepancy anymore.

The word surfaces at the edge of my awareness again—*Bratva*. It's feeling even more likely that Dimitri is part of the Russian mob, now that I know what he can do. Is Kyle one of them, too?

What if Dimitri's in league with Kyle and I just... got into his car? What if I just helped kidnap myself?

Okay. No. They're not working together—Dimitri threw a knife at Kyle. But that doesn't mean he's not after whatever it is Kyle shoved into my mouth and made me swallow.

I flinch at the memory of the sharp edges scraping the inside of my esophagus. I didn't get a good look or have time to really feel it out, but I know it had long, flat edges with sharp corners like it was rectangular. Small, but almost too big to swallow. And it tasted like latex.

I don't know what it is, but I have a few guesses, and I hate all of them.

Drugs are my primary concern.

Because of the drug problems in some of the inner-city areas I've worked, I'm more familiar than I would like to be with some of the drug trafficking practices used by gangs. Mules sometimes swallow bags wrapped in balloons or condoms, and sometimes they rupture in the stomach, causing an overdose and inevitably killing the unfortunate carrier. Years ago, one of the coroner's assistants at the hospital where I was working in Miami was shot when two guys broke into the morgue, cut open one of the bodies, and grabbed the rest of the drugs in her stomach.

And that's when I learned that a dead body is sometimes used as a suitcase. Morbid, sure, but convenient for bad guys who are desensitized to the morbidity of it anyway, I suppose.

It's entirely possible that Kyle planned to use that gun he had aimed at my head once the goods were safely tucked away inside me.

I'm going to be sick.

Too bad it won't help expel whatever the fuck is in my stomach. If it is drugs, a forcible expulsion coupled with those sharp corners might rupture the bag. I'm not sure how much liquid fentanyl it would take to kill me, but I *am* sure I don't want to find out.

"What did he make you swallow?" Dimitri asks, like he can hear my thoughts. Or maybe it's that I can't stop rubbing my chest where it feels like it's still lodged.

The blood drains from my face. Given when he'd shown up in the maze, I wasn't sure if Dimitri had heard Kyle force the thing down my throat or not. "I don't know," I say. It's an honest answer, but it's also a stalling tactic until I'm more sure of his involvement—or lack thereof. "He didn't say."

"A pill?"

He's so gruff, and the depth of his voice sends more shivers up my spine that dissolve in the warmth of the dry heat blasting towards me. My nipples prickle from the contrasting temperature sensations, and it makes me shiver harder. I cross my arms to hide it and sink lower into my seat.

"I don't know," I repeat, softer this time, a little unnerved by Dimitri's sudden shift away from stoic and silent to caring about my welfare.

I'm not sure I trust it. I'm not sure I trust *him*.

But what choice do I have?

I still have the old-ass cell phone they gave me at the hospital—thank God I didn't give Dimitri both when he asked—but I don't have any money, and I'd be too scared to leave a digital footprint that Kyle could use to find me. If he's alive, I can't go home. And after Dimitri's reaction, I'm afraid to go to the police. Mafia men pretty famously have cops "in their pockets." I don't really know anyone locally other than extended family, and I don't think it's a good idea to bring this shit to them. They wouldn't know what to do either, so I'd only be putting more innocent people in danger.

So, I'm fucked. I don't have anywhere to go.

Then again, everything is still in the U-Haul. That piece of shit landlord would probably keep my deposit, but $2500 isn't worth my life. I could break my lease, get in the van, and pick a city at random, somewhere far away from Ulysses. Start over. Again.

I'm good at it by now.

Though that's assuming Dimitri even plans to let me go.

If Kyle's alive, he'll come after what he made me swallow and probably kill me. If Kyle's dead, I'm an accessory, and I'm in a car headed for God-knows-where with his murderer.

A murderer who saved me, who hasn't threatened me with violence once, and who—despite the fear coiled low in my belly—I don't actually think wants to hurt me.

Generally speaking, I've learned to trust my intuition. It took a while to get here, but I have a finely tuned gut instinct from a decade of seeing and treating all the worst kinds of people in the ER. And right now, my instincts are telling me that despite all evidence to the contrary, Dimitri isn't my worst option. I'm also oddly comforted by the fact that some of the questions he's asked made me feel like he doesn't trust me either, like when he demanded to know why I wasn't asking to go home.

Plus, if it is drugs, it might rupture inside of me. I need someone nearby who can drive me to the hospital in case I overdose. Bonus if he's calm in an emergency.

"A sedative would have affected you by now," Dimitri continues, almost to himself, still puzzling out the mystery in my gut.

"No... it was, um... hard. Maybe about this big?" I hold up two fingers about an inch apart. "Kind of sharp. And based on how Kyle was acting in that maze, I think he might have been on something."

His eyes cut to me briefly, like the rush of honesty is unexpected.

"I get that we're, like, on the run, but can we stop somewhere for Narcan? Just in case it's drugs and I need to prevent an OD."

"I have some in my first-aid kit."

I feel my brows lift in surprise. "Because you've got the best-stocked first aid kit in existence or something?"

This time, when he looks at me, it's the same look he gave me when I asked if we were going to the police. *Don't ask dumb questions you won't like the answer to, Nicole.*

So, I turn my attention back outside.

We've been in the car for roughly an hour so far, and I don't recognize these rural roads. The further we get from the estate, the more it feels like being able to take a deeper breath, but the air is thinning—the relief of a satisfying lung fill, countered by the panic of not getting enough oxygen from it.

"Where are we going?" I ask to distract myself. My voice is low enough to almost be drowned out by the road noise, but somehow still much too loud in the thick quiet of the cab. But that could just be the break-ing-the-silence effect.

Screaming it at him might feel a little more cathartic.

"A safe house."

The distinct lack of details is intentional, I think. He doesn't really plan on answering my question. Still, I have to try. So I ask, "Where is it? How far?"

"A safe house is only safe if no one knows where it is," he counters.

What an infuriating non-answer, even if I begrudgingly have to admit that it makes some sense. Or, it's self-consistent, anyway. But who am I going to tell? And how would I? As far as he knows, he threw away my only phone.

Okay, so he's not being super forthcoming, and that benefit of the doubt is stretching a little thin.

Exhaustion hits me, and I slump in my seat. The thin material of my dress doesn't do much in the way of warmth—I'm freezing and my coat is miles behind us, abandoned in a closet at the estate. My back is covered in tiny cuts that sting when they touch the leather seats. My feet are numb with cold right now, but I know they're bruised and bloody from our jaunt through the woods. These contacts are getting really scratchy, but I need to wash my hands before I touch my eyes to take them out.

To put it mildly, I'm in rough shape.

I let out a long breath that I know sounds tired. Reaching up, I remove the bobby pins from my up-do so my hair can act as a curtain. Then, I lean against the headrest, turn my face towards the window, and close my eyes.

Silence falls for a while.

"Nicole?" He's checking to see if I'm asleep.

Maybe it's good if he thinks I'm asleep. I'll have a slight advantage against an attack if he thinks I don't see it coming.

I don't reply, and he mutters something to himself in a language I don't recognize. Must be Russian. The lilting cadence and smooth tone are almost calming, though I doubt he means it to be, considering nothing he's said since we got into the car has been remotely reassuring. He's clearly not trying to coddle me.

He starts moving, shifting back and forth in his seat, and it takes a lot of willpower not to sneak a peek to see what he's doing. After a moment and a frustrated grunt, he unbuckles his seatbelt and resumes wiggling around with a bit more freedom. It clicks back into place, and a second later I feel a heavy warmth draped on the shoulder closest to him. I remain stock-still as he reaches over with his enormous wingspan and adjusts the other side of his suit jacket to cover as much of my torso as possible.

The scent of him invades my senses as I nearly cry from relief at the overwhelming warmth of his lingering body heat in the wool jacket. I inhale through my nose slowly and deeply, and fill my lungs with him. It's clean, but salty and a little sour. It's sweat after being at the beach. It's showering without body wash and letting yourself air dry. It's musky and masculine and human and so, so appealing.

I don't have the energy to try to tamp down on the gratitude and longing I feel. It's been a horrific night, and all I want to do is soak up this kindness. Lulled by the white noise from the road, the darkness, the warmth, and the manufactured feeling of safety by being surrounded by so much of him, I do exactly what I shouldn't. I fall asleep.

9

DIMITRI

———◆○◆———

Beds are for sleeping.

One of the interesting things about this part of the Northeast US is the redundancy of its infrastructure. There are always a dozen routes that will take you where you want to go. You can choose to avoid highways and tolls—and toll cameras—and you will still arrive at your final destination. Perhaps a few hours delayed, but it can be done. In a straight shot, I could be at the marina in just under two hours from the estate where the wedding was held, but I know that realistically it will take me four.

The rest of the drive is quiet and almost peaceful, and Nicole remains asleep for its entirety, snoring softly.

It is still pitch black when we finally arrive at the parking lot, but light will break before too long. I am greeted by the sight of crowded rows of gently rocking boats in the pale moonlight. The dock hosts over a dozen, but it is a simple thing to pick mine out of the crowd of gleaming white yachts because it is the smallest, and the only one made mostly of wood.

I come as often as I can to perform maintenance on the houseboat *Luna,* so I know that the batteries and gas tank are full and it is stocked with enough food to last two people several days on rationed calories. That should purchase us enough time for my team to find out what happened at the wedding.

I unbuckle myself and twist in my seat to face Nicole. When she fell asleep, I was grateful for the respite from her tense energy and my body's inappropriate reactions. Now, looking at her, I expect to feel irritated—she is an inconvenient reminder of the mistakes I made tonight—but I feel only a strange sort of tenderness. I stare for a while, taking full advantage of a stolen moment.

In sleep, her brow that was previously pinched in concern has smoothed. The brackets around her mouth and at the edges of her eyes are gone. Her shoulders move gently with the rhythm of her breath instead of bunching near her ears. She is at peace.

She is so... soft. Serene. Like a watercolor painting with rounded shapes and soothing colors. Looking at her makes me feel pleasant, calm, as if her peace flows into me—or perhaps I am stealing it.

But waking her is necessary. We cannot stay in this car, even to rest for a moment. We need to be on that boat before the sun rises.

Why does the thought of robbing her of her peace make my stomach drop?

I could try to lift her, to carry her to the boat, but the additional hours of losing blood and of being awake and alert have taken their toll. Without this wound, I could manage. But now... if she were to wake up confused and become alarmed, she would fight me, and I would likely drop her.

Unacceptable. She may not be fragile—in a way that is very pleasing to me—but she is precious cargo.

"Nicole," I say, lifting my voice.

Her only response is a deep inhale and adjusting her head against the seat. I reach over and place my hand on her thigh. The fabric of her dress prevents skin-on-skin contact, but I can feel the warmth of her. I swallow down the urge to ball the silk in my hand and draw it slowly across her bare knee.

I jostle her leg. "Nicole, wake up."

With a gasp, she jerks awake, her movements impeded by the seatbelt across her chest. She stares down at it, blinking away the sleep from her eyes, then looks around, out the windows, and finally to me.

Honey. Pure, flowing honey. Sweet amber liquid.

"Dimitri?" Her voice is hoarse from a sleep-dried throat. I know it is what she would sound like, waking up beside me after a long, *vigorous* night.

Fuck. A jolt of pure energy leaves me stricken and cursing myself. All it took to forget the effect that her eyes on my face and my name on her lips has on me was hiding her body under my coat for a brief ride in the car.

While I am recovering, she asks, "Where are we?"

I unclick my belt and reach for the door handle. "Come."

The air here is more humid and stickier with salt, and the scent of the ocean is all at once fresh, fishy, and rotten in this protected part of the bay. The gentle sound of waves lapping against the shore is a familiar melody that reminds me of the freedom and solitude of being on the open water.

I grab my go bag from the trunk, circle back to the front, and hold out my hand to her.

Whether it is due to lingering fear that she will not cooperate, or that it calms me to hold on to her, I cannot say, but pleasure thrums in my veins when she takes my hand for support as she slides out of her seat. As I lock the car, she stops, looking around with a pensive frown.

"What's next in this getaway—a train and a plane?" she grumbles, dropping my hand and wiping at the smudges of black makeup underneath her eyes.

"You do not like boats?" I guess.

"I'm not a strong swimmer."

"That is what the boat is for."

There is a thick second of tension as she assesses me with a small scowl, but it dissolves when her lips twitch at the corners and she spins my jacket on her shoulders to wear it more correctly. "Just tell me you've got life jackets, and spare me the dad jokes this time."

"My father never made that joke," I protest, frowning.

We stare at each other for a second, and I sense this was another idiom that I did not catch. She tries not to smile, lips clamping down around it, and I relent. At least it appears to amuse her, if not me. "I have life jackets."

She takes my offered hand again.

We approach the last row of docked boats—me with relief, her with her head down as she chooses each step across the weathered wood dock in her bare feet—and I am pleased to find my boat just as I last left it.

The *Luna* is mostly wood, with some fiberglass concessions to the corrosive nature of seawater. It is very much a houseboat designed for one person, and that person really ought to be about half a foot shorter than me. But Nicole and I should manage for a little while—long enough to get answers to some lingering questions.

I climb the ladder up onto the open deck, help her, then duck down into the top part of the interior cabin. The wheel and navigation equipment encased in polished brass sit behind the captain's chair, opposite a seating area built into the wood-paneled walls. There is a kitchen along the back wall, which is a generous name for what is really no more than a sink, hot plate and unplugged refrigerator.

She says nothing as I lead her down to the sleeping cabin, which sits just below the waterline. Half is storage for important things—pump, batteries, anchor—and half is the bedroom, which is filled nearly entirely by a foam bed built into the three walls. Off to the side, there is a small bathroom with a sink, toilet, and a tub/shower with an upright seat. There is just enough space for both of us to stand together next to the bed, though I am hunched forward.

The *Luna* has everything I have ever required, but with Nicole here, taking it all in with silent judgment, it suddenly feels curiously lacking.

"You can sleep here." I gesture to the mattress, unloading my keys and wallet from my pocket onto one of the shelves built into the wooden wall. I keep my phone, and I will sleep with my knives as I normally do.

She sits, bouncing and making a face at the distinct odor of mildew rising from the old bed covering. Cleaning and airing everything out would normally be my first order of business. My priorities are different this time.

She removes my jacket. "Where are you going to sleep?"

"Here," I say, jerking my chin at the bed, then crossing to the closet and toeing off one of my shoes.

She starts to rise, then thinks better of it, shifting further back to stake her claim in a way that nearly makes me smile. "Can't you be a gentleman and take that couch up in that cabin up there?"

"I am not a gentleman, and it is my bed," I point out reasonably.

"But it's like, a queen at best," she argues, a twinge of desperation on her tongue. "We'll... be on top of each other."

I shrug as though the knowledge does not affect me, but a pounding sensation starts in my head and slowly works its way down my body. "If we were on top of each other, we would not be sleeping."

"Kind of my point," she grumbles. "You know what I mean."

"My safe house, my bed. If you do not wish to sleep next to me, you may sleep on the floor. But you may not sleep up on the couch, where you can easily be seen through the windows."

It is a bluff, one I hope she does not call. I will not allow her to sleep so close to the exit or out of my sight.

She worries at her bottom lip in indecision, and my hand flexes as I stop myself from grabbing her to put it between *my* teeth instead.

"I'm not sure how my back would handle a night sleeping on the floor."

I nod. I am in excellent physical shape, and my back could handle it, but I will not tell her this. She will be sleeping in this bed, and I am more eager than I care to admit to have her soft warmth pressed against me.

Her eyes cut to me, flashing first with curiosity, and then suspicion. "Just sleeping, right? No funny business."

There is nothing funny about this raging need to be inside of her, but I understand this saying well enough.

Her reticence is ridiculous, as if there is something particularly arousing about lying next to each other. If I wanted to have her, I would do it on every vaguely flat surface in this safe house, not just the bed. Beds are for sleeping.

"It has been a trying night. We are both exhausted."

That at least she can agree with. She nods, eyes drooping, then scoots up the mattress. She settles flat on her back, wedged up against the polished pine paneling with her knees slightly bent, and I am pleased I do not need to tell her she will be the one against the wall. She is stiff and still as she listens to me move through the room, changing from the dress pants into something more comfortable. This shirt is a loss, and I can tell the material has fused to the wound. At least that means it has clotted, and I can deal with it later.

After I flick the light off, I move to settle next to her. I lay back slowly, rubbing my eyes and then scratching my scar through my hair. Shoulder to shoulder without enough room between us for a single piece of paper, I am nearly hanging off the side of the bed, and I know she is squished against the wall. This position will not hold. She will turn in her sleep, and the instant she does, I will too. My entire body is tense in anticipation.

The silence does not last much longer than a moment or two. I can practically feel the fact that her eyes are wide open. "So... we're safe?"

"For now."

"And what's the plan?"

"The plan is to sleep."

"I mean after that."

I sigh and stretch my free-hanging left arm under my head, seeking a comfortable enough position until I can roll to my side and curl around her softness. "I am working on it."

"Yeah, okay... fair enough. I guess we're both pretty exhausted." As if to prove her point, her voice rounds into a yawn on the last words.

She lies still for a moment, then shifts around, moving her hands from her sides to rest on her stomach, then back to her sides. She shimmies higher onto the pillow, then reaches back to beat at another lump.

"Nicole, go to sleep," I grit out.

"I'm sorry! I'm uncomfortable. Aren't you uncomfortable?" she whispers, exasperated.

"Yes." I feel her vindication at that, so I slyly add, "I normally sleep nude."

She makes a huffing exhale through her nose, and it makes me smile into the darkness above us. "Go to sleep, Dimitri," she says tartly.

10

NICOLE

⁕

The embodiment of violence.

As the sleep fog gradually lifts, I lie still and relaxed with my eyes closed until one thing—one remembered, urgent thing—shakes me fully awake.

Dimitri.

Dimitri is in this bed with me.

Even though I was on my back when I closed my eyes, I never fall asleep and wake up in the same position. I'm a toss-and-turner, and I always end up on my side. So it's not really a surprise to wake up with the wood-paneled wall about an inch from my nose, but I genuinely also expect to find a thick arm around my waist and a burning body pressed into mine from behind. There's a fluttering deep in my lower stomach at the thought.

One bed.

I don't have much time for reading, but I know what a trope is.

So when I give my torso an experimental shift and there's enough freedom of movement that I can feel cool air behind me, relief and disappointment rise simultaneously to swirl together in a confusing mishmash that makes me shake my head at myself as I roll onto my back to sit up.

What's wrong with me? It's *good* that he didn't take advantage of me in my sleep. Why does it feel like a rejection? I can't possibly be silly enough to be disappointed that he did what I asked him to and kept it PG.

Well, I can, but I shouldn't be.

With a deep sigh, I swing my legs off the bed. I hiss as the bottoms of my feet touch the polished wood floor, reminding me of all the sharp sticks and rocks I found during our trek through the woods. The satin fabric of my dress winds between my legs, creating static sparks against the blanket that cause an eruption of full-body goosebumps. They worsen as the chill of the room settles against my bare skin.

The only illumination is coming from the cabin above—spilling down the small staircase and through the open door—and it's got a filtered, gray quality to it. Though the dim light casts the room in shadows of varying darkness, it's enough to see that I'm in here alone. The emptiness is acute.

I grab the small beaded bag that contains my glasses and contraband cell phone, and wrap my arms around myself as I hobble across the room towards the light switch. Unprepared for the sudden rocking motion of the boat, I nearly fall into the wall as the door swings open. I grip the banister with my free hand and lean forward enough to see up into the top part of the boat.

Everything is wood and brass, creating a distinctly old-timey vibe. Vintage lanterns sway from hooks in the ceiling, and the steering wheel has spokes with rounded knobs. I half expect to see a ruffled, tri-corner captain's hat.

This place is... uh... rustic. Charming? Cozy?

"Ah!" I hear, followed by a string of angry-sounding Russian.

"Dimitri?" I ask, knocking on what I now know is the bathroom door—you can just tell when someone's voice is echoing off hard surfaces like tile, glass, and porcelain. "Everything okay?"

"Da." It's curt.

Go away, Mom.

Okaaay. I turn away from the bathroom. I have to pee, but I'm also thirsty, so I move upstairs. The tiny kitchen area is directly to the right, and I make a beeline right for the sink. I let the water run long enough to confirm it looks and smells clean, then wash my hands obsessively and drink directly from the faucet.

Hands now clean, I remove my contacts, toss them in the trash, and place my glasses on my face, sighing in relief as the world comes back into focus and the sandpaper feeling from blinking dissipates.

I need some food and a shower, not necessarily in that order. I don't love the idea of putting dirty underwear back on, so maybe I should wash them and hang them to dry before I do anything else... but first, maybe a little more natural light would be good. The cabin could do with being aired out...

I turn to the windows, only to freeze.

All I see is water.

What the fuck? Where's the dock? Where are all the other boats? Where's the land?

Panic squeezes in my chest.

I storm back down the stairs as the boat rocks again, bouncing off the walls on both sides in my uncoordinated urgency. I knock on the bathroom door. "Dimitri?"

"What?" His tone is even more curt this time, if possible, and I grimace.

"Where are we?"

"How would you like me to answer that? Five klicks northeast of the marina you do not know the location of?" His words are mocking, but his tone is more factual and angry than derisive.

With a stifled sigh, I rub my eyes. Frustrating as it is, he's not technically wrong—that wasn't the question I wanted answered, anyway. "I mean," I grit out, "I thought we were staying in the marina."

"I never said this."

The infuriated noise *almost* slips out this time. "*Why* aren't we in the marina?"

"Open water is safer."

Ugh. Fine. I sort of suspected there was a reason we went to a houseboat and not a motel or something, even though I don't like that he obviously moved us while I was sleeping.

"I need to use the bathroom," I mutter, just a little petulantly.

I'm not expecting the door to open immediately. And I'm really not expecting to be confronted by a thoroughly pissed-off expression and a long expanse of naked torso. Dimitri is holding a large pad of gauze to his side with one hand, his elbow awkwardly angled backwards.

My eyes drop. I can't help it. He has dark, curly chest hair that covers sculpted pecs and trails down his abs. They aren't super defined, but they are pronounced, and covered in a layer of protective fat that I know means his strength is functional and not vanity.

It's clear that he's a warrior. He's been through—*holy shit*—a lot. His torso and arms are littered with scars of various ages. There are more long slashes, like the one on his face, some circular masses that must be old bullet wounds, and one spray of tiny punctures on his stomach that makes me wince because it must have come from a shotgun. It couldn't have been fun to dig out all that shot. There are also several small, thin slivers in key places, like near his kidneys, that make me think he was shanked.

Did he do time?

My suspicion grows when I see the crude stick and poke prison-style tattoo on his right pec, a series of tally marks. I'm not sure what 12 means to him. The number of times he's been incarcerated? The number of people he's slept with? The number of people he's killed?

I'm not sure I want to know.

I glance up, realize I've been gawking for a solid few seconds, and proceed to make it worse by being totally unable to look away from his face. He's too tall to stand upright down here, so his ducked head casts his face in some shadow, but it's not enough to hide him.

In dim lighting and at night, his dark features were stark, almost sharp. Now, I realize he's not handsome, exactly—not classically, anyway, with that scar and permanent scowl—despite the angularity around the corners of his jaw. But he's all power and strength, and there's something magnetic about that.

The fury creasing his face melts into mild irritation under my curious exploration. He's watching me absorb his features, tense and wary. There's an expectation of rejection in his look that I'm not sure he's aware of, and it squeezes my heart.

But those eyes... For the first time since we've met, there's finally enough light to really see them. I feel like I'm falling into the coldest, lightest, bluest sky. They're ice chips. Frozen rivers in winter. Frankly, they're as eerie as they are beautiful and make me feel like he's got built-in x-ray vision.

They fit him, because they make my stomach flop—and not in a 100% pleasant way.

He's the embodiment of violence.

I swallow and take a deep breath. *Focus, Nicole.* He's injured, so I should help—he'll be a lot more useful to me if he doesn't bleed out or get an infection and die. It's not like I know how to drive a boat. And in that vein, I can make myself useful to him. Who would hurt the person giving them medical care?

"Do you want me to take a look at that?"

His jaw clenches as he assesses me. Can he see through my words to the underlying intent?

"I have a bunch of certifications for wound care—I can even do stitches, if you need them," I offer. Geez, what is this, a job interview?

"Why would you do this for me?"

Just like in the car, his suspicion is strangely soothing. It makes me feel more like we're in this together; he's not stealing me away on a boat to chop me into little pieces and toss me in the water for the sharks.

"You saved me first," I shrug. "One good turn deserves another."

He searches my face for something. I'm not sure if he finds what he's looking for, but he nods after a moment. "Very well. But only because I cannot reach it properly."

Despite his obvious reticence, it still feels like a win. I'll take it.

"Um, first, could I…" I gesture to the toilet.

With a glance over his shoulder, he silently collects the first aid kit that was spread out over the sink counter and squeezes past me. So focused on the impending relief, I realize embarrassingly late that I need to move out of his way, and he brushes my shoulder with his chest. Cheeks heating, I shut the door.

When I emerge, I see he has moved aside the musty covers and is sitting on the edge of the bed, leaning away from the bandage against his side that stays stuck even though he's using both hands to type on his phone. His black sweatpants are slung low to give me access, and the angle calls some muscles to the surface of his skin that I've only seen in my anatomy diagrams.

I watch as he continues tapping on the screen, silently waiting until he finishes his message. It makes me think of the beaded bag still sitting upstairs by the sink. I need to hide my work phone somewhere. There's very little chance Kyle could track me using a decade-old, shared hospital cell phone that isn't registered to me, but just in case, I'll keep it turned off.

Seeing that I'm ready, he pockets his cell phone, twists his torso, and leans on his hand, and I have to steel myself as my stomach flutters in response to the overtly sexual picture it paints.

I'm a nurse; he's a patient.

But even if he'd come into the hospital off the street and we'd never met before, I don't know that I would have been able to keep from staring at the pale expanse of skin on display. Maybe it wouldn't have been professional of me, but I would have looked. And appreciated the view.

I sit facing him. Then, I snap on a pair of disposable gloves from the kit and gently remove the pad he had pressed to his side.

It's like a bucket of cold water being thrown all over my interested perusal of his body.

I can't believe he was sitting up and moving around normally.

He's got a gash about four inches long just below his hipbone, and it's inflamed, oozing, and looks deeper than the butterfly bandages in his first aid kit can handle.

"You really should consider going to a hospital," I murmur, getting a full view of the damage.

"Out of the question," he snaps, predictably.

I look around with a grimace at the space. "This environment isn't clean, and this kit doesn't have a face mask. You're going to get an infection. You need stitches, something to control the pain, antibiotics—"

"It is not so deep. The bullet did not penetrate far into the subcutaneous tissue."

I'm a little surprised at his use of a word I wasn't sure regular people knew, then I remember he isn't a regular person. He must have learned it the hard way. "Even so—"

"There is a threaded needle here. The kit has disinfectant and antibiotics"—right, because it's the best-stocked first aid kit in the whole fucking world—"and you said you can do stitches, *da*?"

"What about pain meds? It's going to *hurt,* and if you flinch—"

His face is stony. "I will not flinch."

"Okay, but *I* might, sewing someone without so much as a local anesthetic."

"Enough, Nicole. Do it or give me the needle. I did not ask for your help."

I bite my lip, looking down at the redness of his skin again. Deep down, I knew some of those scars were the result of self-inflicted stitches.

Oh well. It's his staph infection; all I can do is my best.

"Fine."

I fish around in the kit to find the sterile packages. After cleaning the area with saline, I see the wound is still bleeding sluggishly, so I apply pressure with a gauze pad.

As I press, I try to avoid his gaze, since this is the closest we've been—while conscious, anyway. And the way I'm facing him, sitting with my knees splayed and effectively straddling him, is remarkably intimate. My silky dress, now dirty with God knows what and wrinkled beyond what even a dry cleaning could fix, pools in the triangular space between my thighs and reveals the total naked length of my left leg.

Well, whatever. If he gets a flash of nude shapewear, I'm sure it'll be the highlight of his day. The Spanx are wildly uncomfortable, tight, and I sorely wish I could take them off, along with the boob tape that's been stuck on for so long that it has probably fused to my skin. But there are more pressing matters, and being around him without underwear... well, I might as well be stark naked.

My face feels hot under his intense stare, but I try to ignore it as I check the cleaned wound area. "It's not as deep as I thought. You'll have another scar for your collection, and it needs, like, 15 stitches, but you were lucky."

"I was caught off guard," he corrects stiffly, lifting a brow at me.

I narrow my eyes, but choose not to ask a question I don't want the answer to. I hope he's not blaming *me* for this mess. "Lean back for me, so I can have a better angle."

He does, and I gather my supplies and readjust myself over him, pretending not to notice as his muscles stretch and lengthen, giving him a new, different kind of definition. He digs one elbow into the mattress and props his head on a fist so he can see what I'm doing, a posture that's almost casual.

I watch him like a hawk as I apply antiseptic spray and then iodine, but true to his word, he's totally immobile, barely reacting to what I know stings like the devil—just a slight bob of his Adam's apple. While that dries, I unwrap the needle and place my hands gently on his skin, probing the area lightly. He doesn't jump or react in any way, and I allow myself to hope that he really will not flinch when I start sewing him back together.

"This is really going to hurt," I warn again, when everything is in place and I've got the curved needle between my gloved fingers.

"Just do it. I am ready."

For once, I really do believe that.

He's still as I begin, barely breathing. His muscles spasm under my hand when I get the needle in, but I know that's involuntary. The scar on his face pulls, deepening into a line that slashes through his pained grimace, and he lets out a shaky breath through his teeth.

"You good?"

"*Da.*"

Stitching falls into a rhythm after the initial stick, and now is when I would normally start asking a patient questions, like what happened. For insurance purposes, sure, but also because it helps put them at ease sometimes to tell the story. Kind of unnecessary this time, since I saw it happen.

But talking during this kind of thing helps—I've been told my voice is soothing—and patients don't seem to care what I say. So, I created a habit of saying everything I'm thinking out loud.

"If I had a nickel for every time someone attacked me... well, I'd only have three nickels, but it's not great that it's happened at all, you know? You'd probably have a whole dollar or two, though—"

"Who attacked you?" His brows snap together.

I'm not expecting to be interrupted, so I startle. "What?"

"I assume once was Kyle, last night. Who were the others?" he asks, voice strained. Probably from the pain.

Not sure why he cares, I shrug. "Both times were years ago—earlier in my career." I shift forward so he can see the scar above my elbow, then move my hair aside to show the other at the nape of my neck. "This guy half my size came at me with a stolen scalpel in Portland, and a woman tried to jump me for some pain meds in Austin. It happens more often than you think. I've gotten a lot better at anticipating patients' moves."

I concentrate hard for a second, pausing in my stream-of-consciousness while I tie off a stitch, then glance up for his reaction since he said nothing. He's staring at me through heavy-lidded eyes.

Bedroom eyes.

"You are taking this all very well, Nicole," he observes quietly.

"Me?" I repeat, surprised by the assessment. I eye him pointedly as I draw the thread up through his skin. "I'm not the one having an abdominal wound stitched with no pain control in a place teeming with germs."

His brows twitch, lowering slightly. "It is not the first time for me, and I doubt it is the last. But you are not like me."

True enough. And I think I get his point—most normal people wouldn't be able to handle such a high-pressure situation. Most people have never had to. "Well, I do work in the emergency room, and it's not because I'm *bad* under pressure," I mutter.

"You imply that being a nurse is the reason you are acting unusually?"

That suspicion is back, only this time it's irritating instead of reassuring. I shake my head. "Scoff all you want, but I've seen a lot."

"Such as?" he challenges, lifting a brow.

Sometimes I love how predictable people are—everyone loves a good medical gore story. "Gunshots, stab wounds, accidents with nail guns and circular saws... I've seen a man with a three-inch piece of glass sticking out of his cheek sit there for an hour because we were too busy to see him right away."

I glance up at him, but he doesn't so much as twitch at that. Okay... going to have to try a little harder to faze him, I guess.

"I've seen a fistfight break out in the waiting room that got someone thrown through a plated glass window before security could break it up."

Still no reaction. Oddly, it starts to excite me—I get to bring out the big guns that I normally hold back.

"People have come in with bones poking through flesh, and organs literally spilling out."

Not even a small flinch.

"I've seen severed limbs—one guy brought in a hand packed in a fishing cooler with a fish still in it. One guy shot his own dick off."

That's the one that finally cracks the stony facade. Dimitri grimaces, as all men do at that story.

"*Mudak*," he mutters.

"I've seen a lot. Okay? Maybe I'm *acting unusually*, but the only way I could do what I do and possibly sleep at night was to learn how to compartmentalize."

He apparently has nothing to say to that.

As I make more slow, careful, methodical stitches, he does his best impression of a hunk of marble, though the effort is drawing a cold sweat to his forehead. I need to distract him again, I think. "So how long are we going to hide out here?"

"We need answers to several questions before we can return to land."

"Like what?"

"We need to know what is in your stomach. If it is drugs, we will dispose of them. You saw the Narcan in here," he adds, nodding down at the bag. "We also need to know if Kyle is alive. I have contacted some people I know, who will notify me if he appears in a hospital or jail or the morgue."

It almost makes me shiver. He knows people who have access to morgue and hospital records? Those are the kinds of resources cops have, but I know he's not talking about law enforcement. "Then what?"

"It depends on whether he is alive."

Bile rises in my throat. If Kyle is dead, he's not a danger to me—I'll just need to figure out how to convince Dimitri to let me go. "What if he's alive? He's going to come after me, right? He wants this back," I point to my stomach. "And I'll bet he's involved in some really dangerous stuff."

When Dimitri doesn't respond, I hazard a glance up. He's staring thoughtfully. "Are you sure you want the answer to that?"

I don't like the implications of his question, so my response is a knee-jerk, "Not really." I sigh. "But I already know some things, so I might as well have the complete story."

"Some things," he repeats, an implied question.

"I know you didn't want to go to the police when most normal people would. I know that the shooting was probably related to *Bratvas*," I add as an afterthought. I'm not sure if I'm helping or hindering my cause, but I have to hope that if I show him I can keep quiet about stuff, that will help. Right?

"What do you know about the *Bratva*?" he asks, voice sharp.

"Only what the internet tells me," I sniff defensively. "And that my third cousin might have just married into one, if the guest list at that wedding is any indication."

He says nothing to that, but makes a grunting noise that could be anything from an acknowledgment to a pain response to gas. "You cannot un-know things, Nicole. Are you certain you wish to know?" he presses.

"No. Fuck," I curse, turning my head. "Just... tell me one thing. Is there a chance we make it out of this and I don't have to look over my shoulder for Russian guys with guns for the rest of my life?"

He keeps doing that—looking at me with that strange expression. I can see him in my periphery. "*Da*."

"*Da*. Okay. Then I can hold on to that, and it can be enough for now." Even though I still want to know what the hell is going on, I let it drop so I can focus all my attention on the task at hand. I make the extra effort to be sure my stitches are no bigger than necessary and perfectly parallel.

"Done," I announce finally, my breath whooshing out as I straighten. I crack both sides of my neck, work a small stretch through my back and shoulders, then collect the bloody gauze and needle and pile everything into a double-thick bag from the kit for medical waste. The second I stand, my gloves come off, and I rub my closed eyes under the lenses of my glasses.

He's sitting up when I turn back around, examining the stitches with his head tilted to the side. He looks impressed, and it makes my face feel warm.

But that sense of pride melts back into the now-familiar unease as he stands. I fall back a step. Somehow, I forgot how huge he was when he was prostrate. Even with his head tilted forward, he's a full head taller than me—that's never not going to be weird for me. My heart kicks me in the ribs.

He stoops, wincing a little at the pulling on his side, and grabs the shirt from where he placed it next to him on the bed. We both stare at the ruined state of what was once a very nice button-down, and I can't hold back an amused exhale through my nose.

"Shame. Looks tailored," I tsk, taking in the red-brown stain and large hole.

"It was," he agrees.

"You'll never get dried blood out of silk. Believe me, I've tried," I say, my eyes dropping to the wound.

A stirring at the lower edge of my vision catches my attention, and my mouth goes dry as I realize where it's coming from. His sweatpants have plenty of give and room, and I can see a sizable bulge forming and growing.

My eyes widen, then fly up to meet his as my pulse races. He's... he's getting hard? Now? After the pain I just inflicted on him? Medically, I know people can't always control their body's reactions, but personally... a guy I'm insanely attracted to is getting hard right in front of me.

Oh my God, what do I—

The corner of his mouth twitches, like my obvious panic amuses him. "Thank you for this, my med."

Oh, we're doing cute nicknames based on our occupations? What am I supposed to call him, killer? The possessive pronoun makes my heart leap, but... it's good, right? Who would want to hurt *their* medic?

"You're welcome," I manage.

"You should go take a shower. Do not use too much water—it is all we have until we can stop to refill the tank. There are clothes here in this closet that should be sufficient."

I don't need another excuse. I tuck tail and run.

11

DIMITRI

I like games.

"As far as I can tell, the murder and the shooting are the only things the authorities are interested in. No leads in either crime. And no reports of assault by anyone matching your description. That doesn't mean those three twats didn't say anything, just that they haven't involved the police. As far as I can tell, none of them are part of the *Bratva.* So, I'd say you were proper lucky on this one, Dimitri."

My jaw grinds. I hate being lucky. I would much rather be smart.

"James, did you ask Felix what he was doing at the wedding?"

"Yup. He said, and I quote, 'none of your fuckin' biz,' and stopped responding. So, that's helpful. I sent Wes a list of his known aliases, so we can try to find him."

My hand curls into a fist. I would not expect Felix—a man who pretended to be a bartender in order to study me covertly—to be forthcoming about his intentions. "What about this Kyle? Did you discover anything about him?"

"Found a good shot of his face from your cam. Kyle Whittaker, aka Volkevich on his mother's side." As he speaks, I can hear Wesley chewing and typing.

It used to irritate me because I always believed that people should focus when discussing important matters. It did not take long to discover that Wesley does not know how to single-task; he often focuses on the important tasks at hand better while simultaneously managing his servers or responding to online messages. Now it feels commonplace—a soothing background noise for most of our interactions.

"Volkevich? No shit." James whistles.

"I'm still digging, but it appears that he grew up outside the family business and only started going by his mother's maiden name a few years ago. He's definitely the one you saw talking to Felix?"

"Yes." I narrow my eyes, staring into the horizon at a far-off shape that might be a boat. "They were at the bar, speaking casually. Unclear if they knew each other—I was not close enough to overhear their conversation."

"You know Felix better than we do, Mac. What do you think?" Wesley asks.

"I think... Felix is a decent guy, but he's also a cagey fuck. I've never known him not to have an angle. I don't like that he was cozying up to a Volkevich, even if they were talking weather. We need to assume for now that they're doing business."

Silently, I agree.

"I'll keep looking into it then, see what I can uncover. Try another angle with Felix, if you haven't burned that bridge yet."

"I'll give it a go. How's the witness, D?" James asks. "Knowing what she swallowed is gonna be key."

"I will take care of it," I reply, purposefully vague. I have not yet decided on the best path forward. I lift a hand to my side, feeling the tender area around the neat, even stitches. They are excellent work—far superior to anything I would have managed, and better even than what James has done for me in the past with his emergency medical training and steady hands.

"Understood. Let us know if you need backup," he offers.

I disconnect. It was a productive call—Wesley has already checked all the emergency rooms in the city and will begin on the jails and morgues. James is following Viktor Volkevich. As a result of his efforts, we now know where the *Pakhan* lives. It will make completing our hit a simple matter that we can carry out as soon as this nonsense with Kyle Volkevich is resolved.

I hear that the shower is running as I climb back down into the cabin and perform a cursory check of the equipment. We are anchored in a suitable spot, protected from the winds. I saw a fisherman hours ago, but have seen no one since.

A strange feeling mounts as I grab one of my books from the shelf above the lounge and settle my long legs in front of me. Normally, I enjoy solitude and privacy—this boat is small, designed for one man. I have never had to share so much of so little personal space with another person. I know very few things about Nicole, and one of them is simply how much I want her.

The idea of not being able to create space between us if I become *overstimulated* is not entirely pleasant.

When the water shuts off, my heart beats too hard in my chest for me to follow the words on the page. She will come out soon. She will start talking to me. What do I say?

Images flash in my head—Nicole laughing in the moonlight, and smiling up at me, and holding my arm as we walk through a garden. But she was not laughing and smiling only at me. I had helpers in my ears.

I do not know how to be *normal* around a woman. Not one I do not plan to kill.

The seconds tick by, stretching into minutes, and she does not emerge from the bathroom. After half an hour, I slam the book shut with an exasperated noise. There is no escape route through the bathroom—it is underwater.

What is she doing in there?

I wait a few more minutes, then stand and move down into the lower cabin. I notice immediately that the first-aid kit is gone. When I strain my hearing, I am just able to make out tiny hisses of discomfort over the sound of the fan.

"Nicole?" I call, and the parallels to earlier, after she just woke up, are not lost on me. Sharing a bathroom will be an exercise in patience.

She hisses, "Fuck," under her breath and calls, "Yeah?"

"What are you doing?" I demand.

"Um, I'm dealing with some cuts and stuff. My feet."

Guilt rises swiftly, and I rest my forehead gently against the door so it does not make a sound. "You... want help?"

"No," she rushes to reply. "No, that's okay. I can manage. Thanks!"

Her tone is too bright, too forced. I do not like it. "One good turn deserves another, *da*?" I remind her, though the phrase feels foreign in my mouth. It is not a creed by which I would live my life, but I can acknowledge its place in hers.

She laughs once, but it is a self-deprecating noise as she mutters to herself, "Should have seen that one coming." Louder, she calls, "It's really fine, Dimitri. Thank you, but I can put ointment on my own feet."

Irritation prickles.

Why? Because she will not let me assist her? Ridiculous. Why should I care? As if I *want* to tend to her?

No, I offered to return a favor, so there are no debts between us. Her refusal changes nothing.

I return to my seat, but the words drift together as I pretend to read. After what must be hours—possibly days—of waiting, the door opens and Nicole steps up into the navigation area.

I nearly groan aloud. She is wearing my clothes.

The way her breasts strain against a too-tight T-shirt, how the pants stretch over her hips... Her body is so different from mine—seeing her in something that I have worn is sending waves of hot, urgent desire through me. It is as if how she covers her body is something in my control, at my whim, like she belongs to me as much as the clothes I allow her.

The black clothing contrasts well with her golden skin and hair, though white would be better, and I would be able to see more of her...

"This place is... um... cozy. Not really made for company, huh?" she adds, a small joke that not even she laughs at. A wave rocks the boat more than she is expecting, and she nearly falls. I tense, about to lurch to my feet to help, but she catches herself, scrambling to find purchase on the counter. "What is there to do?"

I glance around, trying to see the room through her eyes. Things to do? What do I usually do when I come here? What does anyone do on a boat? I sleep, eat, fish, read... "There are books?"

She squints at the shelf. "In Russian?"

Not all of them. Not the one I am holding. "Do you want a Russian lesson?"

She laughs once. "Do you want to teach me Russian?"

Yes. My pride will not let that be my response to her disbelieving laughter. Besides, I would not make a good teacher in this subject. "No."

As she moves slowly towards the counter on bandaged feet, my eyes are glued to her rear. My lips part, breath quickening. It is a handful and then some. Would her muscles bulge between my fingers if I gripped it hard enough? Would it jiggle as I slapped it? Would the skin rise like gooseflesh against my lips and the bristles of my stubbled cheeks?

My cock jumps in my pants, demanding and heavy. I adjust my seated position so she might not see her own effect on my body.

"Are you hungry?" I blurt, partly to distract myself.

She makes a face, and her hand goes to her stomach. "I'm actually a little seasick, I think."

"There is Dramamine."

"Yeah, I found it already. I took some, thanks."

There is a heavy pause, and my eyes drop back to the incongruous shapes on the page that I can no longer make sense of. Another lurch of the boat tosses her into the edge of the counter, and she exhales a soft *oof*. "How long will it take for me to get my sea legs? That's the term, right?"

"It varies."

"Okay... give me an average?"

"A few days."

"Oh." She sounds disappointed.

I force myself to make sense of the letters...

"Is that a chessboard?" she asks, pointing to the box on the shelf next to the books. It has a picture on the side of the pieces of the game, so I know she knows the answer. "Do you like games?"

"So many questions," I huff, shaking my head and adjusting the book in my lap. When she drops her eyes and presses her lips together in chagrin, I feel like an ass.

"Sorry... I'll um... I'll go back—"

I snap the book closed, set it aside, and stand to grab the box from the shelf. "Do you know how to play chess?"

Last night in the car, I was distracted, tired and losing blood. Now patched up and temporarily at peace, there are things we need to discuss. It would not be such a bad idea to play with her—it may act as a useful way to split her attention and lower her guard. I must know about her involvement with Kyle and the likelihood that she will cause a problem for me in the future—since, apparently, I have no plans to kill her.

Nicole looks almost excited as she nods, and it digs away at my misgivings about her trustworthiness. "It's been a while, but I used to play with my friends on an app. I like games."

I set the board on the table and begin placing the pieces on the tiles as she slides into the other side of the seat where my feet were propped. "I propose we add a rule. For every piece you take, you may ask a question of me. For every piece I take, I will ask a question of you."

That way, it will not seem like an interrogation.

Her eyes drop to the board, and I watch her visually do the math. 16 possible questions that I will answer for her. Unfortunately, her calculations are missing a variable—my skill level. She will get eight at most.

"Is there a grand prize for whoever wins?" she asks, a teasing smile playing at the edges of her lips.

"Yes," I growl, fixated on her mouth. "If I win, I get you. However I want."

She gasps, her eyes rounding. But though this answer has clearly shocked her, there is no rejection of the idea in her expression or body language. Her face is a canvas of interest and desire, though masked by indignation. Her nipples have hardened under the shirt and are poking and creating tiny bumps under the cotton.

The silence becomes a standoff as she searches for the truth, wearing a slight frown. I am expecting her to retreat, but she licks her lips, and I follow the movement hungrily. I can tell she is conflicted about wanting me, and I do not blame her for it.

"You're messing with me," she decides, though she does not sound certain.

In truth, I want these to be the terms of our game very badly. But I know this will create too much tension to get the answers I need, so I incline my head, allowing her to believe—for now—that it was the joke she wishes to think it was.

She nods, then spins the board, so she controls the white pieces to go first, which I allow. The only lingering sign of her desire is how she presses her thighs together when she sits.

"If I win, you show me how to throw one of those knives."

Clever girl, bartering and taking whatever advantage that she can, but no one is permitted to touch my knives. There is no real reason for me to play along, other than that the idea of seeing her wield one of my instruments of death makes my body tighten in a hot, frenzied way.

"If I win, you will be learning how to fish instead."

It is a challenge not to smile when she makes a face of disgust.

I sit. She moves a center pawn—a very common first move. I move one of my pawns into her attack zone to see what kind of player she is. She takes it. She is aggressive and prioritizes early game. Very common in western schools of chess.

"Why do you have a chessboard if you come here alone?" she asks, weighing the painted stone piece. "I'm surprised they're even staying on the board with how the boat is rocking."

Interesting. An aggressive player, but she has wasted her first question. "The pieces are heavy enough. It is sentimental; I brought it with me from Russia."

"You played with someone there?"

"That is two questions."

She rolls her eyes at me. "They're related—I wouldn't have asked if you weren't so stingy with the details. And I'll warn you now that turnabout is fair play," she adds loftily. "If you want good answers to the questions you ask, you should do the same for me."

My jaw ticks. She is correct, and her question is innocuous enough. "Yes, my father. We played often when I was a boy until he died."

"I'm sorry for your loss," she says, sounding very sincere. "I'm a member of the dead dads club, too."

"Why would you join a club for something so morose?"

Her laugh is more of an exhale through the nose and a hum of amusement. "It's not really a club; it's more like a thing people say... a way to express understanding. Everyone's trauma around a parent dying is different, but there's a certain bond you have with others just by living through the experience."

I feel my brows lift, and she notes my surprise with confusion. "What?"

"That was a very good explanation," I offer, thinking of how others often react to the language barrier with poorly concealed condescension. "I understand your meaning and do not feel as if you spoke down to me."

"You mean I didn't talk down to you?"

I scoff. "That is what I said. It is a ridiculous saying anyway. Who could talk down to me? I am too tall."

"That's a good point." She rolls her lips inward to hide a smile. "Your turn, I think."

Oh, yes. The game. I reach down and move another pawn. We go back and forth, expanding into the middle of the board for a few turns, and I take the next piece.

"Why were you at the wedding?"

Her eyes stay locked on the board as she answers. "I think I told you that Jenny's a distant cousin. I was honestly surprised when she asked me to be in the wedding. I guess her friend had to have surgery, and she ran out of other options."

So, it is not a close family tie—this is likely why she was attacked. If Kyle had tried to assault someone more important to the bride, he would have faced terrible repercussions. But not with Nicole. He thought she would be without the extended *Bratva* protection. She was alone and vulnerable, and not one of the powerful, rich guests.

I place the piece in my hand on the edge of the table so I will not damage it in the fist that forms. "And Kyle was your date? Did you know him well?"

A shake of her head brings her hair into her face. "Met him at the rehearsal dinner. Wasn't impressed."

This pleases me, despite how much more difficult it makes it to discover details about him and his potential connection to Felix. "Your turn."

We continue moving pieces. I take the next. "Why were you in the garden when we met?"

"I told you then. I was avoiding Kyle. He'd..." she trails off, searching for the description she wants, and I study her as she does. Does she search for a lie or a euphemism? "He'd somehow managed to hit on me and make me feel terrible about myself at the same time. Though... I guess he wasn't really hitting on me, he was trying to..." She trails off, swallows thickly, and shakes her head. "I was just getting air and running from confrontation."

Before I can ask a follow-up, she takes a piece of mine and smiles at me. "Why were *you* in the garden when we met?"

"I was also running from confrontation."

"What happened?"

"That is a bigger question," I say, shaking my head. "You must earn it by taking another piece."

She huffs a frustrated sigh, then repeats the question when she is next to take a piece. I glance at the board for a moment, ensuring that my plan is still valid despite her somewhat erratic playing style.

"You noticed the guards and security?"

She nods.

"They noticed me, too," I say. The line between her brows deepens at that, and I hold a hand up in a conciliatory gesture. She clearly will not suffer incomplete answers. "I was being followed."

"Why? Wait, let me guess. That's a bigger question."

I lift a brow, and she grins.

"So..." her eyes narrow, but they dance in amusement. "You saw me sitting there, and you thought I'd save you from the big, bad security guard?"

That one nearly gets me. I almost smile at her joke. "You did," I reply simply. "It was very convenient. We appeared to be lovers meeting. I believe this ruse is why he left me alone."

Her demeanor shifts, eyes dropping to her lap and her spine straightening. "The ruse. Right. Okay, your turn."

I am left scowling, with a curious sense of loss. Did I ruin that moment? What did I say?

We trade a few more moves without casualties, and I put her queen into retreat to regain power on the board. She tries to take back some of her positioning in the middle, and I narrow my eyes at the placement of the pieces—she has made a move that makes no sense—sacrificing a knight to take a pawn?

Her smile is half self-satisfaction and half childish glee. "Earlier you said that you have some people helping you?"

I know this is not her question, but a request for clarification, so I will give her this one. "*Da*. My team."

"A team. What is it you do with your team?"

She has decided, then, that she wants to know. It is not exactly disappointment that fills me, but it is close—I had hoped to keep her from this. My voice lowers. "No longer asking the simple questions, I see."

"I had to up the stakes eventually," she returns, the mirth slowly dissolving in her expression at the serious tone of my voice.

"We do bad things to bad people."

Her eyes drop back to the board, but this time I can see that she is retreating from the truth instead of plotting her next move. "I think I knew that," she confesses softly after she processes the information. "What you said could mean a lot of different things, but... I think I know."

I nod. "I also think you know."

She inhales sharply, letting it blow out slowly. I observe her face, looking for signs of panic or fear. Because she will not meet my eye, it is difficult to tell how she is taking this information, so I lean forward and sacrifice part of my plan in order to take her knight now. "What would you say if I told you I was at the wedding to kill someone?"

"Kyle?" she asks softly.

"Someone worse. Someone with infinitely more innocent blood on his hands." Even more than my own, perhaps.

Her eyes finally lift to meet mine, but it is not fear that I see. It is fire. Fury and guilt. "I would say... okay." She huffs a laugh. "Maybe even good riddance."

The cold intensity, the quiet fortitude, the reserved rage... it is so unexpected. And it sets off a chain of conflicting physical reactions. My body goes stiff and still, then a blast of heat pulses through me. I want to reach for her, to grab her and hold on, and I want her to fight me. I want to absorb that powerful reaction into myself and give it back even stronger.

I barely dare to breathe. "Do you think some people deserve to die, Nicole?"

"I mean..." She looks away. The intensity of the moment is perhaps a bit too overwhelming. "Yeah... but... in a decidedly more Kevorkian way than I think you mean it. Or at least I thought I did."

"Explain."

"Kevorkian was a doctor who believed in a patient's right to choose their own end of life." She blows out a long breath, fixing her stare into the middle distance. "Do I think the late-stage cancer patient, whose every breath is a fight through pain and whose body has become a cage, deserves to die? Yeah, especially if he has faith in some kind of heaven or afterlife. He deserves the release, the freedom from the pain, if that's what he wants."

I say nothing to this because I have nothing to add. This is... not what I was expecting. I know I did not misspeak, but she has twisted my meaning in a way that is fascinating instead of irritating.

"Do I think that the man who shows no remorse after raping and murdering his wife deserves to die? Not really. It's almost... too easy, you know?"

"Easy?" I ask. I wish she would look at me. I want to watch her expressive eyes as she confesses these thoughts she believes are so dark.

"A quick death is… I don't know—an easy out, somehow. He deserves to… suffer, I guess. You can't suffer if you're dead."

This is not where I thought this conversation would lead. I merely wanted to understand what she would do if her problems disappeared suddenly, along with the man causing them.

Now I am very pleased that I asked.

My dick thickens, filling with need as my heart pounds out a dark call for her. Such a macabre conversation and such a grotesque response, but this unexpected bloodthirstiness in someone who seems so gentle and giving… it is like an aphrodisiac to me. Perhaps she will not shy away from what I do after all. She is like the winter-toughened women of my home country, in a soft, beautiful package.

"You cannot suffer if you are dead," I echo.

With a musical, emotional noise, she reaches under the lenses of her glasses with both hands to press on her eyelids. "It's all hypothetical, though. I'm the one with the bandages, not the weapons. What I do is help the people who come to me for help. I don't judge. What I think someone deserves doesn't matter, because it isn't for me to decide."

"A hypothetical question, then. What if Kyle came to you near death and you had the power to determine his fate with no repercussions? What would you do?" I press.

It is one thing to rejoice in the death of an enemy; it is quite another to picture yourself holding the smoking gun.

She thinks about it for a moment and sighs. "I honestly don't know. I want to think I would… actually, I don't even know that. This is kind of blowing my mind. I feel like I just realized I don't know who I am."

"You will find it," I assure her. "And you will be stronger for it. I can tell."

The moment hangs between us—tense and heavy with unvoiced possibilities—and her golden stare bores into me. If she makes even half a movement towards me, it is over. I will sweep the board to the floor and have her right on the table.

Not immune to the weight of the moment, she swallows. Her eyes flick down, and she takes my rook. It is not even a legal move; she just takes it off the board. "Why did you do what you did in the maze? Why did you attack him?"

Because he hurt you. The answer is right there, but I hold it back because it gives her all the power. She already has it, but she does not yet realize. Once she knows I cannot and will not harm her, she might become unpredictable. She may refuse to cooperate, and I still need answers from her.

And the old *Bratva* man in me—the one who craved control and relished in subjugation—will not allow me to hand over my power so easily.

"Because I *do* believe that some people deserve to die," I reply.

I hold out my hand, palm up, and she stares at it for a second before handing the rook back to me. I place it back on its square with fingers that shake. I need to get out of here before I do or say something I should not.

What has happened to that tightly held control I consider such a point of pride?

"I need to move the boat before the wind picks up. We can finish our game later."

12

NICOLE

There's no gentleness to him, but a gentle man has never gotten my heart racing.

As Dimitri moves us to another location, I have to go below deck where the rocking is less intense. A particularly large wave tilts the boat, and I can hear the chess set hitting the floor above me while I ride it out with my head between my legs. Well, I guess that game is finished.

My stomach is so unsettled. I don't think water travel is for me.

After he anchors us, I spend the rest of the day on the deck, reading the only book on the boat in English—*Anna Karenina*, of all things—and sunning myself.

The sunset is spectacular, and Dimitri joins me for some of it, sitting quietly near me. We watch the fading pastels settling into the horizon together in silence. Then he leaves me a tidy pile of jerky and protein bars like the gym bro fairy and goes back inside to change batteries and mess with the water pump or something else I didn't quite listen to.

Maybe it's cowardly of me, but I'm grateful for the distance.

I thought talking to him would help pass the time, but I severely underestimated the effect he has on me.

I'd be an idiot to try to pretend like I didn't realize how attracted I was—*am,* still am—to him. Even once he dropped the charming villain act and showed me the man he is under the suit and blood, it didn't make a difference to my throbbing pulse.

There's no gentleness to him, but a gentle man has never gotten my heart racing like this.

And while I'm not completely immune to those flashes of sour nervousness and anxiety from being at the receiving end of that fierce, icy gaze, they just get mixed up with the other emotions I feel under the weight of it.

When I talk, he's so zeroed in that it's like the world around us doesn't exist. I found myself voicing thoughts I normally wouldn't share—like all that stuff about people deserving death that makes me cringe now, remembering how unguarded I was—just so he would stay so locked in. The way he gives me every ounce of his focus makes me feel... important, and interesting, and *heated*.

In fact, I'm burning.

And it's only partly because of his... unexpected physical reaction while I was examining him. It's happened before—people with penises sometimes experience difficulty controlling what is genuinely a very natural response to being touched.

And if I'm letting myself be a little less clinical about it... Lord, he's big. Everywhere. I don't need to see his penis face to face to know that. But I've thought about it. *A lot.*

After I've dutifully choked down a chalky protein bar, I head in for the night and stake my territory on the bed, buzzing with nervousness and excitement as I wait for him to join me. Long moments pass, and I hear him shuffling around in the top part of the cabin. Eventually, he turns off the remaining lights, and darkness blankets me.

He's not coming down?

As quietly as I can, I sneak off the mattress and poke my head up the stairs. He's sitting upright on the built-in couch where we played chess, arms crossed and chin tucked against his chest.

I balk. What happened to *my safe house, my bed*? Disappointment rises in my chest, swift and hot, but I try to tell myself I'm being ridiculous.

Briefly, I consider waking him and offering to switch places, then decide to be selfish for once so I can starfish. Maybe we can trade off nights.

The next morning, we choreograph a careful dance of avoidance. He studies a map while I eat a breakfast of more protein that turns my stomach even more sour than it was. I wash it down with as much water as I can manage. Between the anti-nausea drugs, the lack of fiber and all the stress, my digestion is all out of whack. I'm trying not to think too much about whatever is still making its way out of my body, because worrying doesn't accomplish much more than adding to the stomach ache. If it's drugs, we've got it covered. If it's something else... we'll see, I guess.

I grab my bleak Russian book while he fiddles with the radio, tuning it to various frequencies and listening intently to what mostly sounds like static to me. I try to read, but I'm so hyperaware of him looming in the tiny cabin next to me, I can't concentrate.

Just as I've had enough and stand to head out onto the deck, the tiny tapping noises start—drizzle against windows.

Guess the weather isn't going to let me be a coward about this.

With a sigh, I close the book and set it down on the table. He ignores me.

"We should start over. Start a new game," I add, rushing to clarify when his head comes up. I gesture to the box still sitting out on the table, like it's waiting for us to finish our confrontation. "Lower stakes. Something friendlier."

"You do not want to answer my questions?" he asks, lifting an eyebrow at me.

There it is. That's the reminder. We're just two people on the run from danger, who hardly know or trust each other.

"No, I will. But maybe we can try to keep it a little more lighthearted?" I suggest with an encouraging smile.

He spins the dial on the radio so the noise cuts out with a little click, regarding me with what I assume is interest, based on his tone. "How do you propose we lower the stakes?"

I shrug. "Maybe we can pass on answers we don't want to give, and there's no, like, grand prize for winning. Just bragging rights. I really don't want to learn how to fish, even though I'm bored. I don't think it's possible for me to *be* bored enough to want to learn how to fish."

My silly little joke doesn't land how I hoped it would, but his eyes flash with interest all the same. "Very well. I accept your terms."

I take the same seat as yesterday, watching as he takes his. "You want to go first this time?" I offer in the spirit of a fresh start.

"You need the advantage," he counters, almost playfully.

I chuckle. "Hey, if you want to give it up, far be it for me to turn it down."

I move my first pawn. He repeats his move from yesterday, and I take his first pawn again.

"When's your birthday?"

He grimaces. "Pass."

Whoa. I figured that one was an easy one. I thought I was starting us off gently. "What?" I ask. The question slips out, and I can't control the accompanying smile until he scowls at me. I tuck my lips in and tamp down until the urge passes, then ask, "Okay, then at least tell me why. Is it for safety—because it can be used to identify you or something?"

Without responding, he moves another piece. For a few long seconds I think he isn't going to respond at all, and disappointment swells—this isn't starting out well at all—but then he says, "It is not important. You Americans are so eager to celebrate things."

"You don't tell people your birthday because you don't want a birthday party?"

"Is that not a preferable outcome to telling people and expecting a celebration that never comes?"

My smile dries up. I doubt he'll expand on that, but now I won't be able to stop wondering if he keeps his birthday a secret because he doesn't think people want to celebrate him. I suppose, depending on the people in his life, that could be true. If his team is full of big, scary guys like him, they might not be the type to blow up balloons for a friend.

He takes the next piece. "Tell me about the life you will return to—your job and your family. Do you have friends? A lover?"

A lover? Who calls them that?

If I tell him I have a lover, will he back off?

Do I want him to?

"Well, actually, I'm new to the area. I'm a travel nurse, so I move around a lot. I started at St. Luke's earlier in the week, and I just moved into my new place. I don't really have any local friends yet." My stomach twists as I speak. Should I even be saying this? Should I be revealing just how alone I really am?

"And your family?"

"Obviously a lot of them were at the wedding, but that was mostly extended family that I only see for the big three—weddings, reunions and funerals. My immediate family situation is... a little complicated."

"Complicated how?"

"We're just not very close."

"You said your father was dead. Did something happen?" His voice lowers, and his hand stills. A deep line forms between his brows.

My stomach flips. I know it's probably not how he means it, but he almost sounds like he's ready to go to battle on my behalf. It's so damn endearing.

I shrug and grab the black pawn I took and run my fingertips over the smooth edges because I don't think I can look at him when I talk about this. It isn't light and breezy, but in Dimitri's defense, he didn't know he was picking at old scabs.

I know I could skip the question, but I won't, just to prove that it's not that big of a deal.

"It wasn't some big single trauma or anything, more like a lifetime of small, additive cuts."

Normally, I gloss over this shit. It's third-date conversation material at best, and most guys let it go there—either because they don't really care, or they sense I don't want to talk about it so they let me off the hook. Not Dimitri.

"This does not answer my question. If you want good answers from me, you should give them as well."

"You love turning my words against me!" I exclaim, a little frustrated with the experience.

He's not deterred. "Explain."

I sigh. If he wants it, he can have the sob story. "My dad was a doctor, and my mom fell in love with the idea of him, and then immediately out of love with the reality of his ego and narcissism. They divorced when I was little. My dad was around—in the picture for weekends and holidays—but then he died of liver disease when I was 13. After the divorce, Mom dated around for a while, met another guy, started another family, and prioritized her new life. Meanwhile, I put myself through school and moved away. We're not close."

"It is not right to discard one family for another," he says, shaking his head.

Secretly, deep down in my heart of hearts, my inner child agrees. But I'm not allowed to agree; I don't let myself. "I don't hold it against her; I know she deserves to be happy, too." I've said it so many times—mostly to myself and my therapist—that it's true for me now. So why does it feel more like a lie when I say it this time? "I'm not bitter or anything; we're just... not close. Like I said."

He cocks his head, brow furrowed as he evaluates my story. "You see this situation with remarkable clarity."

"Yeah, well," I blow out a breath, "I've had some therapy about it."

I move my bishop out into the middle of the board, and he squints at it, then at me, like he can't believe I did that—I only realize why when he takes it with his own. I didn't see that countermove at all, and it makes me want to drop my face into my hands. I maneuvered myself right into another question when all I want to do is shut up for a little while.

"Why did you choose to be a nurse instead of a doctor?" he asks.

I scoff, immediately put off and maybe still a bit raw from the last one. I feel flayed, on display for him to poke at all my half-healed emotional wounds.

"Pick a ruder question, why don't you?"

"Why is it rude?"

"It implies that everyone should want to be a doctor, like they're more important. Nurses are just as crucial."

He holds up his hands in surrender, my white bishop still tucked against his palm. "I meant no disrespect. I asked only because you mentioned your father was a doctor. This is something that people do exactly as their parents do. At least, in my country."

If I had detected even a hint of attitude, I wouldn't have believed him, but he sounds sincere. "Oh. Okay, yeah, people follow in their parents' footsteps here, too. Sorry, I guess you found a sore spot. I get that question all the time, but people always mean it like, 'why would you take the job cleaning out bedpans instead of cutting open bodies' and it's really demeaning. It's not better to be a doctor just because you don't have to do some of the grunt work."

"Cleaning up messes is an important part of a job," he agrees with a nod. "A person is not made better by removing the responsibility; it sometimes makes them more thoughtless of the consequences."

I eye him, frowning slightly because I know he's not talking about the healthcare industry, but it feels like he is. I've watched doctors prescribe medications that keep patients up all night or give them diarrhea, when an alternative existed that wouldn't. But doctors like that don't think about it because they don't have to deal with the day-to-day patient care and the side effects that only impact those of us who do.

"Do I want to know what kind of messes you're talking about?" I ask hesitantly.

"Probably not," he allows.

"Well, then, I'll answer the question I think you were trying to ask. Which is 'why go into nursing?'"

He nods.

I sit back, dropping my hands into my lap. "I guess the idea did ultimately come from my dad—he definitely believed healthcare is the noblest profession. Nursing seemed like a better fit for me in a lot of ways. I graduated sooner, with less debt. It offered a better work-life balance and had excellent opportunities, like travel nursing. That one was a no-brainer. I didn't really have ties anywhere, the pay was better, and I got to see new places and then leave after a few months when my contract was up."

"You prefer this life of moving from place to place?"

"I mean, traveling was exciting, especially at first—I got to try out new cities to see where I'd fit," I shrug. "But it's getting old. I've lived in nine cities in as many years."

His brows shoot up. "So many places. Are you running from something or looking for something?"

I blow out an amused breath. "Both, probably. It was always part of the plan to put down roots eventually. I've just been waiting for somewhere to feel *right*—somewhere to call home, somewhere to buy a house and get a permanent position and join a gym and make friends... This was supposed to be the last move," I mutter. "Guess it won't be."

"Why?" he demands.

"Um... was that a serious question?" I narrow my eyes at him, but his neutral expression gives nothing away. "Maybe because there's a guy in the mafia after me? Because I've potentially got drugs in my stomach? Because I don't know what I'm up against? I think even if Kyle is dead, I'll be looking over my shoulder forever. It's honestly easier just to pick up and move far away. I'm good at it by now, and I have nothing holding me here."

His jaw flexes, giving him a distinctly angry look, and he nods once, curtly.

I know his next move is meant to bait my queen into taking the piece, but I don't see a better move, so I make it. "What about your family? Did you grow up in Russia?"

Dimitri crosses his arms and leans back in his seat, regarding me with a shuttered gaze. "I grew up in a very small village. My father was a soldier in the Chechen war, and my mother was…" he pauses, and the corners of his mouth twitch, "a nurse."

"Really?" I ask brightly. I love that.

"Yes."

"What did your father do after the war?"

He sighs. "This is not something I share with people."

My happy heart deflates, and I nod, understanding. Of the two of us, he has way more secrets to guard. "That's o—"

"When I was a boy, my father owned a bar where the locals would come after work," he begins ominously, like he's gearing up.

My heart bangs around wildly. He wasn't refusing to answer; he was warning me, trusting me with an untold story.

"One night the bar was robbed. Some men beat him and burned down the building. Knowing what I know now, I believe he was approached by a *Bratva* and offered protection, which he turned down."

I tuck my hands under my thighs, warming them. "Protection?"

His smile is wry—no mirth at all, just a baring of his teeth—as he scrubs at his short hair with his knuckles. "A *Bratva* has the unique position of acting as shield and sword. They offer protection from dangers for which they are responsible. They take tributes from local businesses to mark or expand their 'territory,' and in return these businesses receive protection. If they are attacked, the *Bratva* they pay tribute to will respond on their behalf. Of course, they are only attacked for being part of that territory to begin with."

"Sounds like the business owners get the raw end of that deal."

"My father believed so, but after the fire, he wished to protect my mother and me. Because he had experience as a soldier from the war, the *Pakhan*—the leader—of a neighboring *Bratva* hired him to be an enforcer. That is how he got involved in organized crime. When it was obvious that I would grow to a similar size as my father, I was also recruited."

I don't want to know, but I ask, "How old were you?"

He's quiet as he rasps, "Not old. Too young. The *Pakhan* told me he saw my potential early. When I was a boy, it filled me with pride; and so, to keep his favor, I became what the *Pakhan* told me I was—strong, ruthless, and loyal—an ideal soldier. As a man, I understand it had little to do with me; it was a thing he did to keep my father in his grasp. Aleksandr was a clever man, one who knew how to control those around him. Son to control father, then later, after my father died in a fight over territory, mother to control son. He took my mother as a mistress when he sensed I was pulling away. She died some years later, but it was exactly the right thing to do to keep me in his fist at 16."

The information alone feels like an assault; I can't imagine living it. What Dimitri is describing is the worst kind of stolen childhood. His anger wraps around him like a shield, even now, though he delivers the words with a kind of resigned detachment, like the memories are more inconvenient than horrific.

I want to reach out to him, but I tuck my hands more firmly under my legs. My heart aches for him.

"You weren't part of what happened at the wedding. You're not in a *Bratva*," I realize suddenly. All this time, I've kind of been assuming that he knew what was going on that night because he was in on it, to some extent. But after what he just told me, I find it hard to believe he'd willingly involve himself with that kind of organization.

"No. And I never will be again," he declares, voice low in a repeated promise he's clearly made to himself.

Hope swells. Maybe he really is just trying to help me.

He makes a move that I didn't see coming, and I take another pawn. I finger it, assessing his posture and the look on his face. He's so stoic, he hardly ever gives anything away, but I recognize the rawness in his expression now because I was just wearing the same one.

Time to shift gears and do what I promised—make this a bit more lighthearted.

"How old are you?"

"Pass."

Fair enough. If he won't tell me his birthday, I guess it makes sense he'd keep this one to himself, too. "What's your middle name?"

"Pass."

"Oh, come on. Okay, what's your favorite food?"

He makes a face. "How does one answer this question? Why must I prefer one above the millions of other options?"

I roll my eyes. "How did you get that scar on your face?"

"Pass."

0 for 4.

"Well... okay..." My gaze falls into my lap for my next question. "You told me about your family, but what about *your* friends and job and... um, lovers?"

When I dare to peek, he's staring. I'm pinned in place by shards of ice that somehow burn like the hottest part of a flame. "I have no lover,

Nicole," he tells me, blatantly ignoring the rest of the question and answering the only part that matters.

Nee-cole. My cheeks are suddenly really hot.

He leans forward, and I swear I am not in control of myself when I mirror his action, expecting to find our faces pressed close. Instead, his eyes drop, and he moves his queen and takes mine. "What is your opinion of law and order?"

And suddenly, I'm reeling from... fuck, I don't know what I thought was going to happen.

Yes, I do. I'm just mortified because it didn't.

I clear my throat and sit back as far as the wall allows. The blood is still pounding in my head, but the intense, almost sharp expectations have fizzled into hot embarrassment. Thankfully, he's letting me save face and keeping his eyes down.

I reach for my bottle of water to give myself a moment for my brain to come back online. "Law and order? Um... I assume you don't mean the TV show."

"You assume correctly."

Shaking off the lingering awkwardness, I square my shoulders. I want to give my answer carefully, because I've actually been considering it a fair amount since our last game. Clearly, Dimitri doesn't exactly operate within the confines of the law. "I think... it's easy to confuse right and wrong with lawful and unlawful, but they're not exactly the same."

His eyes flash, and he demands, "Explain."

"I think the intention of the systems in place can be good, and the execution can be bad. Murderers and rapists walk; innocent people are put to death; the more money someone has the more untouchable they are... It's not pretty, but it's what we have."

"You do not like it," he surmises, and I nod in agreement. "And what is your part in it?"

"In what, the system?" I laugh once at the idea. "I don't know; I don't think I'm really part of it. I don't do much other than vote... and I had jury duty once."

"Everyone is part of the system in which they live," he counters. "Every action has a consequence and touches the life of someone else. In my profession and yours."

I frown, considering that. I can't decide whether I think it's a surprising statement, coming from a man who does *bad things to bad people.* Does that mean he's aware that it's wrong and does it anyway, or that he doesn't think it's wrong?

"Working in emergency rooms has put me in a unique position to help work around some of the systems I hate, like the quality of health care depending on the income of the person who needs it. But at the end of the day, I'm still part of a for-profit hospital, and I still take my paycheck and use it to buy stupid shit made in China on the internet.

"I enjoy being a nurse and helping people. I'm not romantic enough to think I'm changing the world one person at a time, but I'd like to think that the majority of the people whose lives I touch are better for it. That's enough for me."

"Even if it's as part of a corrupt system that takes from the majority in order to serve a few?"

I blow out a heavy breath. "Geez, are you going to ask me if I've read the Communist Manifesto next?"

"Have you?" he challenges.

This took a heavy turn. I'm not sure exactly how we got here—politics, morality, society and social order... But now that we are, a deep, usually dormant part of me thrills in it.

"No," I chuckle. "And I'm not arguing that the system isn't corrupt, but... it's not all bad, either. And I think if I let myself feel like it was *my* responsibility to correct the world's sins, or fight the man, I'd never get anything done. I do what I can—what I think is right—and I live my life in pursuit of my own happiness. Just like most people do."

There's a beat of silence following that, and I want to suck the words back in. The familiar jeers and criticisms echo like a lost memory too prickly to be forgotten.

You're so serious, Nicole. Lighten up.

I meant what I said—I almost always do—but I have a tendency to get too introspective and let it leak out into a conversation where someone actually wanted a lighthearted answer or was making a joke. But his lips quirk up, and I have the distinct impression that, despite the somewhat unsatisfying conclusion, I gave him what he was looking for.

"You are very serious and thoughtful, Nicole. And well-spoken as well."

A very unserious response nearly springs to my lips. *Back atcha, big guy.*

"Thank you."

Warmth blooms on my face and deep in my soul. Whether or not I'd meant to, I'd bared something to him. I showed him the real me—the one who thrives in deep conversation and answers questions seriously, thoughtfully—and he's not turning away. He complimented me for it. He leaned in.

I move my king backwards, seeing his queen is closing in.

"Someone tried to kill me," he says, gesturing to the scar on his face as he puts my king in check. It takes me a second to realize he's *answering* my earlier question instead of asking another. "And they were very bad at it."

It should probably freak me out. And it's not funny—it really isn't—but a laugh bursts out of my mouth that I can't help because his delivery was just as dry as it was when he told me he didn't want a birthday party.

His eyebrows shoot up, but he's otherwise unmoved by my inappropriate reaction. I settle, tipping my king over to signal my defeat. "I'm sorry; it's not funny. It's just... I'm glad they were bad at it."

He smiles, and for a second, I can't breathe. I'm completely caught off guard by how it transforms his face. It's not an altogether happy, light look—the smile deepens the pull of the scar bisecting his cheek, giving him an even more sinister appearance—but it suits him almost as much as the serious stoicism.

"I am glad you think so."

13

DIMITRI

I do not save things; I break them.

Damn leak. Damn bilge pump. Damn houseboat.

It is very late when I finish repairing the hole, and Nicole is already deeply asleep in the bed. On her back, in the middle.

Instead of trying to fit into the space next to her, I hover and watch. Her breasts strain against the tightly pulled shirt. Her stomach expands underneath the hand resting there. Her eyelashes flutter against golden skin as her eyes rapidly move back and forth beneath the lids.

Exhausted as I am, I believe I could watch her for the rest of the night. Watch over her. The idea stirs me, gripping me tightly and refusing to be shaken away—a fantasy where I am her protector, where the blunt instrument of my size and skill is sharpened with a single purpose. A better purpose.

The temptation to stand watch or to lie down next to her is becoming too great. I turn away, moving towards the stairs, when a high-pitched whimper freezes my blood. "*No.*"

I spin, heart thumping hard, and see her shifting restlessly. Her brow is furrowed, and her head thrashes. A broken breath chokes her, nearly waking her, but it shudders out of her lungs with a fearful cry.

A nightmare.

When she rolls onto her side facing the wall and tucks into a shaking fetal position, I do not allow myself another second of debate. I settle behind her, moving closer until there is no space between us.

Almost instantly, the shaking stops. Her whimpers of fear level out into shallow, even breaths, and a deep, primal satisfaction rockets around inside of me.

I place my fingers on her hip, testing, and she shifts backwards until our bodies are nested perfectly. I barely dare to breathe as I reach over her waist and fill my hand with her softness. In response, she makes a musical humming noise and draws her legs up, curling around my touch and lacing her fingers through mine.

My heart thuds an unsettled rhythm for her. I tuck my legs into the space behind hers, unwilling to relinquish even an inch of contact. Her hair tickles my nose, and her even, deep breathing falls in sync with the gentle rocking of the boat. She smells exactly as a woman should—faintly floral and clean, sweaty and musky, just a little sweet.

As my cock stirs, I hate myself for how dirty it feels to be getting hard now.

My presence has never calmed anyone before.

I bring her comfort.

Me.

The night we met, I killed a man—possibly two—and I harbor no remorse. My face alone convinces women to leave me alone and men to tread with caution. I am ugly, scarred, often angry, and unpleasant. I have smiled at her only once.

And what is more, she is strong. Capable. Brave. A healer. She knows her place in the world and does not need me for anything. She would soothe herself without me. She would have gotten herself to safety, perhaps even fought off Kyle, if I had not been there.

But she needs me now. And that makes me feel... powerful. Indomitable.

There is something intoxicating about being needed by a woman who needs no one.

I tighten my arm around her, and she sighs softly in her sleep.

I must fall asleep for some small amount of time, because Nicole's golden eyes haunt my amber-tinted dreams. They gaze up at me, hazy with lust. They dilate in excitement and not fear as I place my hands on her strong, thick body. They roll back in ecstasy as she clenches around me, time and time again.

When I wake, she is *right there,* and I am uncertain whether I am still dreaming. I have her exactly where I want, trapped against the wall; her body is loose and pliable in sleep, and her shirt—*my shirt*—has bunched around her waist, revealing an expanse of smooth skin and a rounded, supple stomach.

She is the rounding my sharp edges need.

It would be nothing to pull down the top band of both of our pants just enough to place my cock in the valley between her legs. I might not even fuck her at first, and she could simply keep it warm.

I woke hard, but become impossibly harder at the images my mind conjures—of fucking her over and over, filling her up, then holding her closely enough that I would not slip out. She would fight me, but she would take it, and then she would want it desperately. I would make her crave me as much as I crave her. I want her body as much as I need her understanding expressions and molten gaze.

Such is my need that my fingers twitch against her stomach, sliding down to the waistband of her pants, slipping inside, and beginning to move it out of my way.

And then my phone buzzes.

My personal line is the only one that makes any sound at all, so I know it must be James or Wesley, checking in. I go rigid, remembering suddenly where I am and what is at stake.

Reclaiming control is a battle, and it takes every scrap of my hard-won resolve to leave her warmth. Slowly and quietly, so I do not wake her, I untangle my arm from around her and rise from the bed.

Moving out onto the deck, I appraise the clouds that look heavy with rain as I unlock my phone. The message from Wesley is unimportant—an update that is the absence of progress—but I am grateful for it. The interruption, the distance now… It is the slap in the face I needed.

I scrub my scar and run an agitated hand through my hair, scraping the wrong way against the growth.

This is disconcerting. The way I want her is *disconcerting*. I might actually have fucked her in her sleep. In the past, it was my way to take a soft, willing body next to me when I woke wanting. Back when I let Aleksandr convince me that everything was mine for taking.

But Nicole is not a *Bratva* whore to be passed around, ignored, or overpowered. And those women… they were powerless. A fucking tragedy. Any man who puts a woman in that position deserves castration and a painful death.

Morning is just breaking over the water, but the wind is shifting. When I check the weather application on my phone, I see the clouds moving on the radar and curse to myself. Not just rain, then—a storm is coming. And the damn battery-powered mechanical winch for the anchor is acting up, so this means I must pull it using the crank on the front of the deck.

I am so consumed by my thoughts that I lose my balance briefly when a large wave rocks the boat aggressively. I fall into the handle of the lever, and hiss as a sharp pull of pain lances my side. I right myself, then check, and curse again roundly. One of my stitches has pulled through the skin, and there is fresh blood welling from the broken scab.

Grumbling, I finish pulling up the anchor and move into my captain's chair to find a better location for us to wait out the storm. I will not return to the marina, but there are several coves nearby that offer better protection than our current location.

As I start the engine, I hear Nicole shut the bathroom door, and my foul mood sinks even lower.

Nicole.

Nicole, who is so easy to talk to that I use more words than I have in a decade.

Nicole, who looks so good in my clothes.

Nicole, who listened to the sorry tale of my youth with compassion and kindness and did not make me feel pitied.

Nicole, who is so curious and thoughtful.

Nicole, whose husky voice passes right through skin and muscle to vibrate deep around my bones. It thickens my blood and stiffens my cock.

Nicole, who is pleased that I was not killed.

Nicole... who will leave Ulysses to protect herself.

I have been lying to myself, thinking perhaps there was some outcome of this *clusterfuck*—as James would say—that meant I could have her. But she is not for me. She will return to her small, safe, civilian life. She will leave Ulysses and all its dangers behind.

She wants to settle down somewhere. She wants a life without looking over her shoulder for men with guns coming after her for whatever mess Kyle involved her in.

Looking over my shoulder for men with guns *is* my life.

After an hour's journey north and back west towards shore, I find the protected area I was searching for. It is private, but not privately owned. The water here is deep enough that we will hit nothing and shallow enough that the current should not toss us about too badly.

After manually lowering the anchor, I am too preoccupied to read, so I grab the large dartboard from the storage container on the deck, hang it on its hook against the cab, get into place, and palm two of my knives.

I warm up with a few easy throws, feeling out the soreness in my side, then begin challenging myself. One eye closed. Both eyes closed. Poorly gripped handle. From behind on a spin. From crouching. From one leg, balancing on a rocking boat.

Center of the bull's eye every time.

I know the instant I am not alone, and not just due to how the wood creaks underfoot and the boat dips slightly from the shifting of weight. I am so aware of her. My subconscious seeks her through layers of wood and glass and water.

She has come to the open window of the cabin and watches from the safety inside. So smart. So careful. She would not be so foolish as to approach and risk startling a man holding and throwing a knife. Her eyes are wide, and the sunlight glinting through heavy, dark clouds glitters off the water and reflects in them, even through the salt-streaked plexiglass.

"You are," she swallows, glancing between me and the target about two meters away, "so good at that."

When I throw another, I tell myself it is to empty my hand and not to show off. *"Da."*

"The noise it makes is very... unexpected. Kind of violent. I guess all of it is, but in a graceful way. Like a dance, almost."

Violent.

I turn the word over in my head again and again until it becomes meaningless, effortlessly tossing another knife into the bullseye, this time with my left hand.

Violent.

An observation and a judgment—cautious and respectful with an undercurrent of fear.

But I cannot blame her. It has been some time since I saw them as anything other than an extension of myself, but I suppose to someone like her, knives have inherent violence to them. Throwing them is an act of *violence*. Being good at it makes me a *violent* person.

"Well, I won't bother you when you're training, but I wanted to show you this," she says, holding something small and metallic between her thumb and forefinger. "It's... um... it's what Kyle made me swallow."

I squint at it, but give up after a few seconds. It is too small to see from here. So, I collect my knives, sheathe them, and climb down into the cabin.

Still gripping it daintily, she places it in the center of my open palm. I squint again. "It is…"

"A USB drive," she remarks with a little confused laugh. "Been a while since I've used one of those. There's usually a whole bin of 'em in some forgotten drawer of the nurse's station. Everyone uses cloud-based storage these days, but no one wants to be the person who threw away something that might be useful in some obsolete way."

Nothing on the boat can read a USB drive, and even if there were something that could, I would want Wesley to look it over before I did anything with it. It might contain anything, and he is the only person I know equipped to handle this variety of *anything*.

"What do you think it is?" she asks as I slide it into my pocket.

"A USB drive."

She rolls her eyes. "What do you think is *on* it?"

"I could not begin to guess."

My eyes cut to her as she moves back across the cabin and settles onto the couch, unwrapping one of our last protein bars. "Well, I, for one, would love to—" She freezes with it halfway lifted to her mouth. "Are you bleeding?"

I glance down, following her eyes, and see a small droplet of red against the white cotton. Fuck. I had forgotten. I should have changed so she would not see it.

"It is nothing."

Setting down the bar, her brows snap together. "What happened?"

Her ire takes me aback enough that I admit, "Just a ripped stitch. Do not concern yourself."

"Let me see," she orders in the tone of someone who expects no disagreement. She stands, wiping her hands on her pants, and moves towards me.

I glare at her and cross my arms. Who does she think she is? She will not order me about this way.

Her demeanor shifts in response to my defiance. "May I see?" she corrects herself, slowly reaching for the hem of my shirt.

My jaw clicks as I grind it down, suddenly angry for small, inane reasons—like why it was such a simple matter for her to pivot and ask nicely. She must have no pride to swallow.

Refusing her now feels childish, so I jerk the shirt out of the way, not wishing to put myself through feeling the brush of her fingers against my stomach. I am strung too tightly.

Her frown deepens as she hunches down. "Jesus, what have you been doing? You're supposed to be taking it easy, but you've got one ripped and another almost pulled through."

"My life cannot stop to coddle an injury."

She huffs an irritated breath and glances up. "Yeah, well, if you rip another stitch, I'm going to be pissed."

"They are my stitches to rip," I grumble, letting my shirt fall and backing away a step.

"Actually," she counters archly, planting her hands on her hips, "they're *my* stitches. And they're an aid, not a fix. They help while your body heals itself; they aren't armor that means you get to do whatever you want. Show the work I did a little more respect than that, please."

In spite of myself, my lips twitch in concert with my cock. Her defiance sets my pulse racing. The way she casually expects control makes me want to back her against the wall, silence her with my lips, force a finger deep inside what I am certain is a pretty little pink-brown cunt, and change that attitude for her. I want to wrap a thick hand around her smooth throat until the only words that escape her lips are "yes" and "Dimitri."

Fuck.

I scrub at my hair, leaning into the harsh motion and scratching at my scar.

"Will you let me fix the deeper one?" she asks.

"Very well," I sigh, preceding her down into the lower cabin.

Though I busy myself with removing my shirt and getting into a comfortable position, resting back on my hands, my eyes remain locked on her as she retrieves the kit. She seems irritated now, and I wonder if it is in response to my own irritation.

She pulls on some latex gloves and moves to sit next to me. "Lay back."

"No."

This earns me another irritated noise. "Fine," she says through a baring of teeth that is not a smile. She stands, spins, and digs an elbow into the mattress to lower herself. Her breast brushes my knee before I understand what she means to do. She grabs my thigh to catch herself.

Instantly, my cock is hard again, throbbing and straining against my pants. All that building tension and desire from when I woke slams back into me at once. The angle... seeing her like this, on her knees before me... "Do not—" I choke out.

She pauses in the act of kneeling, one foot still flat on the floor. Her eyes are round with surprise at my barked order. "What? Why, what's wrong?"

"Do not get on your knees," I grind out, shifting away so she will not get between my spread legs.

"Why?" she repeats, truly confused. She puts her other knee down, and I scowl at her.

Infuriating, obstinate woman, testing my self-control! Does she have no sense of self-preservation after all?

The picture she paints is one I recognize from my dreams. She is wearing far more clothing now, but the raging fire of desire this position creates is no less urgent.

I grip the blanket and sheets so hard that I hear a small tearing noise. "Because I am barely holding back, my *med*."

"H-holding back... from what?" she squeaks.

"What do you think?" I growl. My hips buck, just a little, drawing her attention to the bulge in my pants. It swells a little more, as if the weight of her eyes is a physicality equal to the touch of her hand.

She sits back on her feet, digesting that, then shivers. When her eyes meet mine again, they are shining with need through dilated pupils. Suddenly, there is nothing clinical in how she gazes up at me through her lashes. It is subservient, and torturous, and powerful and sexual and... right. She presses her thighs tighter together, and I can see her nipples pebble against tight, abrasive cotton.

"So don't," she whispers. "Don't hold back."

Desire rages around the tentative flash of hope. She wants it. She wants me.

Perhaps... perhaps this can be enough. One encounter. One release. One brief moment of heat to hold in my chest and revisit when the night is cold and lonely.

I reach for her chin, gripping it firmly between my thumb and index finger. She allows me to lift her head a fraction, and her mouth falls open as her brows slant up in a pleading expression. My nerves are singing, my pulse is pounding, and there is a roaring in my ears.

The temptation of such an invitation is too great. My hand cups along her cheek towards the corner of her mouth. Dipping just inside, I rest the pad of my thumb on the point of her bottom canine tooth and pull her lower jaw down. I open her, testing her, seeing what she will let me do. She touches the tip of my thumb with her tongue, tasting me, and a guttural noise escapes my throat.

My chest is heaving as if I were running at full speed. I pull my thumb from her mouth and slide my hand down to circle the front of her throat. She goes rigid in my grip, then her chin lifts, stretching her neck, making more room for a palm that looks massive against the fragile column of her throat. Her pulse races under my fingertips. Her eyes beg me—a hungry, wild expression—though it is unclear exactly what for.

I tighten my grip. She whimpers, and the sound snaps me out of my obsessive focus. A noise of surprise, of trepidation, of desire, and of torment. It is perfect. She is perfect—she would be. I can tell.

She would give, would allow me to take, would take *me* so well...

And then how would I ever be able to stop at just one night?

I shake my head, stopping myself and pulling away. "I will not. I cannot," I say, and my voice is raw and raspy.

Her sharp inhale is a shard of ice through my stomach. "Why?" she whispers, as if a louder acknowledgment might injure her pride.

The question makes me angry because I am asking myself the exact same thing. She sits there still on her knees, blithe to my suffering. I grab my shirt and stand, momentarily forgetting where I am. I hit my head on the low ceiling. Her expression of sympathy is like a rude, cold splash of water.

I am a *murderer*. I do not need her sympathy. I do not need a soft woman to care for me. Soft things do not last long in my hard world.

"You want to know why?" I hiss, and I can hear that my voice has become fierce.

She shifts back, sitting hard on her plush ass in response to my tone, eyes wide. The edge of her apprehension is sharp against my heart, re-opening the stitches there that she did not know she sewed.

My hands curl into fists that shake. "Because I am a violent man, Nicole. I will not make love to you. I will not have sex with you. I will fuck you, and I will take everything. I will ruin you. Do you understand? The way I want you is violent. *I* am violent."

I see it again—the flash of fear. She is aroused, yes, but she is afraid of me. Good. She should be. Satisfaction twists with shame until I cannot tell which I feel and who it is directed at, me or her.

"I am not a good person. I do not save things like you do; I break them."

I turn away, then I hear her shaky voice. "You saved *me*."

She is not listening. I need to leave before I...

"I'm not afraid of you, Dimitri."

I send her a disdainful look. Seconds ago, I saw her fear. "You are a liar."

Shock and hurt weave through her features, but she schools them.

I need to leave.

"I will tend to my own wound," I growl, jerking the gauze from her hands, shooting up the stairs, and slamming the door closed after me.

14

NICOLE

Ruin me?

Another terrified tear slips from beneath my squeezed-shut eyelids as the boat lurches in a massive wave, tossing me against the paneled wall behind the tub. I thought the bathroom would feel safer—the presence of the toilet was an added bonus when I lost my lunch—but it's starting to feel hopelessly claustrophobic in here.

Every time I open my eyes, I see everything swaying in the flickering lantern light, and it makes my stomach roil. Every time I close my eyes, I have visions of water spilling in from under the door, and it makes my chest tighten in panic. The skin of my knuckles is stretched white and bloodless as I hold on to the handlebar in the wall and the sink counter for dear life. Even anchored like that, I still feel like I'm being thrown around—the sea is the cat and I'm the dead bird it's playing with.

Something heavy falls above me, making me flinch. The boards around me creak ominously, and every beat of a wave against the side has me on terrified edge, thinking that will be the one that makes the wood buckle from the force.

I'm going to drown.

Why did I let him take me on a boat? I *told* him I'm not a strong swimmer!

Where the hell are those life jackets he promised me? I need one, but I'm not sure I have the willpower to leave the bathroom. And I'll be damned if I call out to *him* for help.

Those cold, cold eyes haunt me just as much as the terrified, helpless, intrusive thoughts of drowning.

Now is not the time to relive that breathtaking, heart-wrenching moment of being on the sharpest precipice of desire and having him yank it all away. When he put his thumb in my mouth and his hand around my throat, I almost melted on the spot. I was like a lit firework of need, ready to explode at any second.

Every part of my body ached for him, and he just... turned away.

It doesn't matter how badly we both seemed to want it, how the air crackled around us with electricity. He decided for both of us. He won't let us find out.

Why? Because he's violent. Because, according to him, he'd ruin me.

Ruin me.

Ruin me? What does that even mean?

What would it be like to be ruined by that man? I'm not sure I don't want to find out.

The boat heaves, shaking as it comes back to center, and I bite my lip to contain the whimper. Fuck this bathroom. I'm not drowning next to a toilet. Maybe the life jackets are in the space above the clothes in the closet.

I shoot out of my seat and grab the door and wall, making my way out into the bedroom area. I try to keep my center of gravity low and keep ahold of sturdy things as I cross the room, but there's another sharp tilt and I go flying onto the bed. It's mostly a soft landing, but my forehead crashes into the wall and the contents of the shelf above my head come flying off. A pile of books blankets me, bruising and poking, and I cry out.

What starts as a simple pain response morphs into something greater, and soon I'm choking on heavy, wet, fearful sobs. I curl into a ball, hugging my knees as best I can around my stomach and rubbing the spot of impact above my brow.

Some of it's about the storm, sure, but it's also been a horrible couple of days. First with Kyle and being threatened with a gun—an event my subconscious likes to replay, sending me nightmares where I can't outrun his shadow—then being forced onto this wood-and-brass death trap, then being cooped up with someone who makes me feel like I'm on fire...

The door opens. "Nicole? I heard..." Dimitri stops himself, taking in the scene.

I don't dare open my eyes—I don't want to see the expression on his face when his voice is so even and gruff. I don't want to see him at all.

"What happened?" he demands. "Are you all right?"

"I'm fine," I bite out, trying to curl into a ball small enough that he won't see me. Like *that's* possible.

"You are... crying. Because you are hurt?" There's a heavy pause, and I can picture him scanning the horizontal length of my body. "Or... frightened?"

I don't bother answering, but I crack an eyelid. There he is, a dark shape in the dim light, a hunched but massive presence. His hair and clothes look wet, like he's been out there in the rain. At least, I hope... so far it has stayed blissfully dry in the cabin down here, but I don't think I can handle the implications of taking on water.

"This storm is not so bad," he says, keeping his balance as the boat tilts suddenly by snapping his arm out and gripping the doorjamb. He makes staying upright look effortless. I hate him a little for it. "We will probably not capsize, Nicole."

I would laugh if I were sure that the sound that came out of my mouth wouldn't be another sob. "Probably?" I repeat through gritted teeth. Not helpful.

"This boat is well-built, and we are anchored in an ideal location. You do not need to be afraid," he continues, infuriatingly calm and reasonable.

"I don't? Cool. Oh, wow, look at that—I'm not afraid anymore."

"Nicole—"

"Just go away, Dimitri," I plead, hating how small and scared I sound when Dimitri might as well be discussing... well, the weather.

I don't think this is the kind of weather the saying is referring to.

With a sniffle, I wipe away another scalding tear with the back of my hand. I don't need someone who runs hotter and colder than a fever mocking me. I don't need a violent man making me feel even more like a coward. I don't need *this person* witnessing how helpless I feel.

I hear his long exhale, and I slam my eyes closed again, impossibly more ashamed by his judgment.

"Sit up. You were sick once already; it will help to be vertical, especially if you feel dizzy from the rocking."

I nod, accepting his advice as the pearl of wisdom it is, and uncurl my legs. I expect him to disappear back upstairs, now that he's convinced there's nothing actually wrong with me, but instead he sits on the edge of the bed and settles back against the wall, shoving fallen books out of his way.

"Come here."

The room tilts and I fall back against the wall as my noodle arms give out, but Dimitri remains stable in his seated position, flexing his legs to keep himself in place. "What?" I squawk, gaping at him.

He confirms that he actually said what I thought he did by opening his arms like he's asking for a hug. "Just get over here, med."

I bristle at the nickname—I don't love being reduced to my profession, but now's not the time to request a do-over. "Why?"

He tsks. "Must you always know why, Nicole? You are in pain, and I am offering comfort—you can relate to this, *da*? Take what I offer. Let me soothe you."

My arms shake as I push myself up into a sitting position, and then I lurch towards him with the motion of the boat before I've even made up my mind. I catch myself against his leg and my face heats, so I avoid looking at him as I crawl to his side of the bed.

Yeah, I definitely played that one cool. Ego *totally* intact.

I aim for the space he left next to the wall, but he grasps my upper arm and pulls me towards him. As I arrange my legs over his lap, stopping short of sitting on it the way he clearly expects me to, his arm comes around my back. Holding me in place, he rests his other palm between my breasts, against my sternum. It's a warm, heavy weight that centers me and draws my focus. I freeze, instantly anchored, and locked in.

My eyes drop, and the way his palm spans my chest makes my breath sharply exit my lungs. His hands are... fuck me, they're huge. I'm used to men with delicate hands in my work. You need good dexterity to place an IV or use a scalpel, and fingers with pointed, elegant fingertips, balanced with soft, rounded palms are kind of the norm.

Not him. Like everything else about him, they're enormous. Square, blunt-tipped, and covered in calluses and scars, his hand is strong with neatly trimmed fingernails and thick cuticles. Utilitarian is the word that comes to mind.

Dear God, what would those huge, blunt fingers feel like inside of me?

"Look at me," he says. His tone is a gentle rumble that I feel all the way down to my toes. "Breathe."

My breath expands automatically under his hand, breaking a staccato rhythm in the back of my throat.

"Good girl. Again."

My stomach flops and my pussy spasms at the unintentionally sexual praise.

I grip his wrist with both hands and make deliberate eye contact as I take a deeper breath this time. I know what he's doing, and instead of feeling infantilizing, it feels like a lifeline. I'm not having a panic attack, but he clearly knows what to do when someone is.

Is this what my patients feel like when I try to calm them down? Am I as good at it as he is?

"Good," he murmurs. His eyes drop to my lips, but only for an instant. "One more."

When I complete the next breath, his hand slides down to curl around my waist, skimming my breast in a way that might or might not have been intentional. Succumbing to the calming pressure of being enveloped in a warm, delicious-smelling hug, I lean in and press my cheek against his hard chest. I can feel the texture of his chest hair through his shirt, and I almost rub my face against him like a cat.

"You're wet," I observe, not moving away. The moisture and heat that rolls off him makes the air swampy and humid, but I don't care.

He tightens his arms around me, holding me steady as another wave slams into the boat and makes a loud crashing noise. His legs shift under mine, and he angles towards me more.

"It is raining," he returns in that dry tone.

It's such an absurd response that I have to laugh, even if it sounds a little weak. His head comes down on the top of my hair, and I think I can feel his cheek round, like he's smiling too. As the minutes tick by and we sway together, my heart rate calms. The adrenaline dissipates. The panic in my stomach uncoils. I feel my body relax against him.

"So mnoy ty v bezopasnosti. YA vsegda budu tebya zashchishchat'. Tebe bol'she nikogda nichego ne pridetsya boyat'sya."

The low tones of his voice are so soothing, and the cadence of the unfamiliar language lulls me once I stop straining to understand. My fists uncurl, and I press my hand flat against his hard skin, pretending to myself that I'm just seeking more comfort, not feeling him up. The vibrations of his chest fill my palm.

"It sounds so pretty. What does it mean?" I ask the cotton of his shirt.

"It means do not be afraid," he replies. His voice is more hoarse in English.

He definitely said more than that, unless Russian uses, like, six words for every one in English. I doubt it.

I will fuck you, and I will take everything.

The way I want you is violent.

I *am violent.*

The memory of the fury in his eyes when he said that makes me shiver against him. As soon as I do, the hand on my hip disappears, and he leans us both to the side while he reaches for something. A second later, he's draping a blanket around my shoulders, covering as much of me as he can.

My heart bangs against my ribs, and there's a telltale prickling behind my eyes.

Why does this simple gesture *hurt* so badly? Because it's kind and I'm an emotional mess? Because it makes me want to demand why he thinks he's so savage? How could someone as brutal as he wants me to think he is also be so considerate?

Is he doing this to shut me up because I was crying? Or out of guilt for some unfathomable reason? Does he care, or is he just pretending to?

Every muscle in my body is exhausted, wobbly without the tension keeping me stiff. I don't know what time it is, but I know it's late. "I'm going to fall asleep like this," I warn him, tucking my face back against his chest and hoping he doesn't hear the longing making my tone thick.

He doesn't reply, but I feel the nod against the top of my head.

"Don't you have bilge anchors or water winches or something to check on? Something you should be doing instead of"—taking care of me—"this?"

"I am doing what I should be doing."

Tears well in my eyes again.

Regardless of what he says, he is capable of being tender. He's being so gentle with me. But regardless of what his actions show, what he thinks about himself is true because he believes it is.

When someone comes into the emergency room and I ask for their history, I have to take them at their word. When someone tells me that an entire zucchini got up their own ass because they sat on it, I raise an eyebrow, but I make a note in the chart. It's part of my job. No judgment. I take what people say at face value, but with a grain of salt. I also watch their behavior.

People lie all the time, and often they don't even mean to, or don't realize that's what they're doing.

Dimitri is gruff and standoffish. He's the byproduct of a country where people have hardened to match the bitterness of the cold. And even by those standards, he had it tough—introduced to organized crime before most kids get their license to drive. He doesn't laugh. He barely smiles.

But his eyes do.

Still, I'm in no position to assume I know him better than he knows himself—when he tells me he's dangerous, the smart thing to do is listen. No matter how badly I wish I could have *this*. Us.

But for now, anyway, he's pulling me close instead of pushing me away, and it's making me feel even warmer than this blanket is.

"Thank you. I'm okay now. You can..." I close my eyes, forcing myself to say it, "let me go."

His arms go slack, but when I pull back, I discover I can't go far. I'm locked in a cage of flesh and bone. I lift my chin and find him staring, locked on my lips.

My heart kicks out a faster rhythm. My brain goes quiet. Everything stills. All there is, is him and me—our shared breath, the shadow of desire, the weight of the moment.

Achingly slowly, he dips his head, the movement so slight I could almost convince myself it didn't happen. Just as slowly, saturated with doubt and a longing so sharp I could cut myself on it, I mirror his movements.

Is this...? Are we...? This isn't like before, when I misread the moment...

Eventually, we're too close, and I have to close my eyes because they're crossing. I feel the slightest whisper of a touch across my lips. His hand sweeps up my back and tangles in the hair at the base of my skull, tilting my head back a fraction—controlling, forceful, greedy.

The fabric of his shirt bunches in my grip. Blood pounds between my legs, hot and demanding.

I want to scream at him to touch me. I want to pull away so he'll give chase. I want to feel his hand tighten in my hair and the weight of his heavy palm against my throat again.

The second time his mouth touches mine, it's less uncertain but still exploratory—like he's trying to figure out how much he wants to take, or how much I'll let him. He makes a noise deep in his chest when I try to use my hold on his shirt to pull him closer.

"What are you doing to me?" he murmurs, agonized. Every consonant brings his lips close enough to brush against mine.

I have no answer to that. I don't know what to say. But whatever it is, he's doing the same damn thing to me.

It's the storm that makes the suspended decision for us. A sharp jerk of the boat knocks me into him. Our faces collide, cushioned only by lips pursed to do something else. Our teeth clack together, but his hold in my hair keeps it from causing injury.

The momentum fuses us together for an instant too brief to provide relief, before swinging the other way. We're wrenched apart and I'm left wild-eyed and unfulfilled, heaving huge breaths and wishing I'd opened my mouth for a taste.

In his eyes... No one has ever looked at me the way he does—like I'm damnation and salvation, condemnation and forgiveness, the source of his pain and the only thing that can soothe it.

"Dimitri, please," I hear myself whisper. What am I asking for?

He shakes his head, then presses his forehead to mine. It's almost unbelievably intimate, and I close my eyes against the onslaught of strain and tenderness.

"No, my med. Not here. Not now."

This time his "no" feels much more like hitting pause than stopping it altogether. It's not a rejection—it's a promise.

With an air of finality, he tucks me back against his chest. I can't be sure how or when it happens, but eventually the movements of the boat smooth out. The rocking becomes the tranquil rhythm that has eased me to sleep for the past few nights. My eyes get heavy, and I fall asleep in his arms.

15

NICOLE

I can't believe I backed the wrong fucking horse.

I'm lying down now. The bed is cold, so he's gone. There's some light streaming into the cabin from the door left slightly ajar. I close my eyes again.

"What?!"

The urgent tone grabs my attention, pulling me from that liminal space between sleep and waking. Something about this feels wrong. The door clicks closed, like Dimitri shut it for privacy, and I sit up, craning to hear the soft words.

It's no use; I can't hear him anymore.

Silently, I slip out of the bed—not even really sure why I'm sneaking—and creep over to the door and press my ear to it. Dimitri's low voice is muffled, but audible.

"You are certain it's him? How did he... *fuck!* I must have punctured a bowel with my knife. Usually, it takes days to die from that."

My blood goes cold, and my heart thumps in my throat. Is he talking about Kyle? Is Kyle dead? A punctured bowel would be consistent with where Dimitri's knife went in. And sepsis can set in quickly.

There is a long pause while he is listening. "No. I know. That is... very inconvenient. Fuck."

His agitation is spiking my anxiety. My palms are sweaty, and my knees feel like jelly.

"You know we cannot leave witnesses," he growls. "I will take care of it."

I cover my mouth in time to stifle the gasp. Take care of—*murder*—the witness—*me*? No, I must be jumping to conclusions. Taking care of things has multiple meanings, and I'm sure I'm not the only witness he knows. Or the only one who knows Kyle...

Yeah, that's a Venn diagram that's just a circle. Me.

Fuck.

"*Da*, I have it. It is a USB drive; it could contain anything." There's a long pause. "She knows nothing. I agree. I will finish up here and bring it."

I'm going to be sick.

Dimitri got what he wanted. It's always been about that fucking USB. Now that it's out, he doesn't need me anymore. I'm the only witness to his crime, and he's going to *take care of me*.

He starts moving around, grumbling into the phone too low for me to make out most of the words. Bile rises in my throat from a roiling stomach.

I need to get out of here. I need to get away from him...

Even if I'm wrong—even if what he's saying doesn't mean exactly what I think it does—he's still a murderer. Kyle is dead.

I scramble back towards the bed and start feeling around for the phone I hid under the corner of the mattress. It powers up so slowly that my hands tremble as I clutch my only lifeline.

Fuck. No service. *Fuck*. Low battery.

I curse myself for not charging it before I left for the wedding.

My thumb presses nine, then hovers over the one. I know I'll be able to make an emergency call regardless of the service issue, but I can't exactly tell them where I am. They'd probably ask me to stay on the line while they pinpoint my location, but what if the battery craps out before they can find me, and he moves the boat?

I didn't realize quite how screwed I was until this exact moment.

Fighting back would be stupid—I'm so outmatched, it's laughable.

I don't know where I am. I know nothing about this boat—does it even belong to Dimitri? I know nothing about Dimitri. Is his name Dimitri, or is it Lev, like he originally told me? What if he catches me making the call? What if he figures out that I heard him or that I have a phone stashed away?

Dumb doesn't begin to cover it. I've been life-threateningly stupid.

The urge to cry hits me like a freight train. So many horrible, sour emotions are swirling around that I might throw up. Among the fear and self-loathing is an inescapable kind of sadness and disappointment. It's the literal least of my worries, but I can't help mourning the fact that last night was a lie.

I can't believe I trusted him. I can't believe I backed the wrong fucking horse.

I don't know why I wanted to believe he would help me so badly. Just because I'm attracted to him? Of all the terrible, piss-poor evolutionary impulses... Attractive people are not innately more trustworthy, though we, as a species, tend to think they are.

Okay, trying to make myself feel worse about what I've done isn't going to help. I did what I thought was best in the moment; it just ended up being the wrong thing to do. I won't make that mistake again.

Dimitri's moving around in the upper cabin. When the engine starts up, I feel the anxiety creep up my neck. Battery at 4%. I shut off the phone so I'll have enough juice to make that call once we stop moving.

But what the fuck do I do about him in the meantime?

16

DIMITRI

Something is wrong

The two men in charge of digital security the night of the wedding have gone missing, and Wesley suspects they were interrogated and killed for "losing" all the camera footage. The police continue to search for the murderer of Ivan Minnov, the *bratok* I killed, and now suspect his murderer is also responsible for the gunfire. No one was shot, but three people were hospitalized after being trampled in the panic that ensued.

Felix is also missing. Though, in his case at least, it is possible he is only temporarily unreachable—lying low, as I am.

And Kyle is dead. The family is keeping it quiet, but a report from the coroner's office confirmed it.

My chest constricts as I consider the implications, and find only questions with perplexing possible answers.

Were Kyle and Felix working together, or did I come across an innocent conversation? My instinct is that theirs was not a chance meeting. I have not survived this long by ignoring my instincts.

Assuming they were working together, did Kyle have time to speak to Felix before he died? Does he know I was the one who threw that knife? Will there be repercussions for killing a man in his employ?

Does Felix know about this USB? If they were working together, it is logical to assume that he knows about it and that he wants it. Perhaps it is the reason he was at the wedding to begin with. Whatever it is, it is important enough that Kyle planned to smuggle it out in the dead body of his date. But does anyone else know Nicole has it?

To whom is this USB important—only Kyle himself? Felix? Volkevich? Someone else at the wedding? We cannot know until we find out what it contains. I must return to shore and let Wesley look.

Until we know what is on this USB, Nicole is not safe. Remaining on this boat would be far safer for her than anywhere on land, but she is terrified of the water, and I cannot leave her alone and adrift while I drive to Ulysses and back. It is storm season, and every atom of my being refuses to allow her to weather another without me.

Something about that storm seems to have fixed the electrical connections, so I lift the anchor with the flip of a switch, plug our destination into the automatic navigation system, and make my way back down the stairs.

My stomach tightens, seeing Nicole on her side, facing away from the door, still asleep.

It was a difficult 24 hours for her. The storm began sometime around midnight, and the sun only parted the clouds around mid-afternoon. Hours of sustained fear make you exhausted, and she did not fall asleep until mid-morning.

I want to return to her and live for a while longer without responsibilities or impending danger, but frustration is making me too antsy to sit still, and things are different after last night. I do not believe I have the self-control to contain myself anymore.

When I close my eyes, I feel her weight, her soft warmth. I see her naked desire. I relive her shivering against me in cold, then heat.

If I put my hands on her again, I will not be able to stop myself this time; I promised myself last night that I would be a better man than I have been in the past. The kind of man who could deserve her.

I will have her, but it will be on a proper bed, where I can take my time, and her cheeks do not taste of salty fear.

I go to the closet and change into some new clothes. She continues to rest, and I move about the cabin as quietly as I can so I do not disturb her, readying things so that we can leave—collecting laundry and trash, righting things that have fallen over, cleaning the bathroom. It will take hours to arrive at the second marina, and then several more to return to Ulysses.

We should be home just before morning breaks.

We. She is coming with me. It strikes me with deep satisfaction, right in the center of my chest.

It should feel more like the wrong decision to bring her to the mansion. How will I explain this to James and Wesley?

I will simply have to... make them understand. I cannot trust that she is safe unless she is with me, but I need the expertise of my team to sort this mess out. She ought to be the least of their worries, anyway—we have a *Pakhan* to kill and a *Bratva* to destroy.

I continue to move through the lower cabin, performing the small tasks to prepare the boat to be shut down for some time. The hours pass, and eventually I hear the musical dinging that notifies me we have arrived at my selected destination. The auto-nav system is not good for areas with many other boats, so I have to manually navigate the last portion. Before I make my way back up, I sit on the edge of the bed. Her breathing changes, so I know she is awake. She has slept the day away.

"We are almost to the dock," I tell her, lifting a hand and reaching for her hair. I leave it suspended for a second, deciding, then lower it against the strands that are such a curious texture—smooth, yet rough.

She flinches.

With a small frown, I pull back. "Nicole?"

"The dock? Are you... um, can I go home?"

My chest tightens at the tentative hope in her voice. I do not want to rob her of that, nor can I confirm it. "Until we know what is on the USB, it is safer for you to"—stay with me—"avoid places where you could be easily found. You understand this?"

"Yeah," she whispers.

"Nicole, are you—"

"How far?" she asks, ignoring the note of concern in my voice and remaining in her protective curled position.

I understand her question is not one of distance. Only Americans ask about distance but expect an answer in time units. "You have 30 minutes to ready yourself. When we reach land, we will go to another safe house."

"Where?"

One corner of my lip quirks. Always so many questions. "A safe house is only safe if no one knows where it is," I remind her.

A breath puffs out of her, nearly a laugh. "Of course," she whispers.

My hand flexes, and I tighten it into a fist so I do not turn her around. I want to see her face. I do not like this distant tone. "Nicole—"

"I'll be ready, thanks. Is there enough water left for a shower?"

"A short one," I allow, mollified. She wants some personal time before facing me. She is feeling vulnerable, perhaps. "I will see you up on deck."

There is a strange hollow feeling in my chest as I sit in the captain's chair and take over navigating. I find myself splitting my attention—driving with half my mind and completely attuned to her as she showers and moves through the lower cabin with the other half. The hollow feeling digs deeper when she does not come up to speak to me or keep me company for the final stretch as I dock the boat among the four others. I have grown used to having her nearby. She... eases me.

Perhaps she is still upset. Perhaps I should not have spoken so harshly to her, or kissed her. Perhaps she regrets letting me kiss her.

That thought twists my brow.

I will convince her to explain herself to me in the car.

This marina is much smaller. It is privately owned by a man living in a trailer nearby, to whom I pay cash for the rental of my space. Using the spotlight to illuminate the shore, I tie us off at the portion of broken cement with nailed-in tires that is mine, and the boat bounces around as the wake I created catches us, lapping at the shore. I hear Nicole stumble and fall against something, and I nearly climb back into the boat to check on her, but then she appears on the top deck.

She looks very unwell, and her arms and legs shake as she climbs down the stairs, refusing my offered hand.

"No more boats," I say, hoping she will feel some comfort in knowing that.

Her silent nod is emphatic enough to convince me that this is the source of her discomfort.

All she carries is what she had with her when she arrived—a stained golden dress and a small purse, gripped tightly. I can see that she has changed into a fresh set of my sweatpants and T-shirt. A pair of my thick socks serve to protect her feet from the ground of washed away gravel and sand, which I know is littered with bottle caps and broken glass and other unpleasant things that it is far too dark to see.

"Do you want me to carry you to the car?"

Her head whips up, and she appears alarmed by the offer instead of pleased. "What?"

I believe she heard me, so I just wait for her to catch up with what I said.

She shakes her head. "Y-you can't. I'm too heavy."

My lips purse. "I assure you, Nicole, you are not."

She winces. I frown. She sees it and drops her gaze.

Wrong. Something is wrong. She seems so on edge.

"No, thanks. I'm... I'll be fine. I'd rather walk and get used to being back on land again for a minute."

"Very well," I say, keeping my eyes on her.

We will have plenty of time to talk while we drive, and perhaps once I explain everything, she will... well, it will not calm her, but it may help continue to build the bridge of trust between us. I hold out my arm to indicate she should go first, and steer us towards an old sedan parked half into the tall, weedy grass that encroaches on the cleared parking area.

It is an old car, covered in a fine layer of dust and salt. One tire appears flat from the divot I dug underneath, and the rust and faded, flaking tan paint make it appear abandoned. The shape is boxy, common in older cars, and I much prefer it to the newer models. The key fob battery died long ago, so I must physically insert the key into the trunk to pop it. Once it is open, I toss my bag inside.

I keep her in my periphery, aware of every shaky breath and jerk of her head as she responds to the sounds of the night around us.

So jumpy. So anxious.

Wrong.

"Nicole—"

I hear it then. A police siren a few miles away. That in itself would not be so odd, but it is the dead of night, and this area is very remote. There is only one other car in the parking lot.

But when I meet her wide, teary eyes, I see it. Terror. Guilt. Without meaning to, she displays a tell when she clutches her small purse more tightly.

"What did you do?" I roar.

She is shaking as I jerk the purse from her grip. It rips open, and the contents spill out onto the ground. The phone lands face up in the sandy dirt, the screen illuminated with an active phone call. Faintly, I hear the emergency dispatcher. "Ma'am? Are you all right? If you can hear me, please remain calm; units are already on their way to your location..."

For a suspended moment, I am frozen in a whirl of betrayal and fury. She called the police? She had a phone all this time? They are coming for her? Why? Why would she do this? Why would she—

I am unable to continue processing what is happening because she darts away, sensing her freedom is imminent. The sirens grow louder.

I curse and reach for her, but she slips through my grip.

"Stop!" I growl. I pause for precious seconds to grab the phone off the ground and end the call. In that time, she makes it to the edge of the parking lot.

The beast inside of me that is always waiting to be let out urges me forward—*hunt, catch, claim*—and I close the distance between us in just a handful of long strides. She is in an unfamiliar place, not wearing shoes, being pursued by a monster made and honed through violence, and she thinks she can *run* from me?

I grab the back of her shirt and some of her hair, jerking her back into me. Her head snaps forward and comes back from the momentum, and she hits the wall of my body with a low-pitched *oof*. There is a small metallic noise, like something has fallen, but I cannot stop to worry about it.

"Nicole, stop!" I growl. "Why are you—"

"You think I'm just going to let you *take care of me*?"

Her limbs are flying, kicking back at me and trying to find something soft or unprotected. She is a captive wild animal, clawing and biting for freedom. "Nicole, stop!"

"Help! Help!!"

With a hiss, I cover her mouth with my hand, and it muffles her voice. "You are—"

Fire. Fire in my side explodes under my skin, stealing my breath and momentarily blinding me in a shower of white-hot sparks. Her elbow found the healing gunshot wound.

Enough of this.

With a growl of rage, I grab her arm, spin her, and stoop low enough to force my shoulder into her stomach. With a grunt, I straighten and take on her full weight. A terrified noise escapes her, ending in a choke as air is forced out of her lungs from the pressure on her diaphragm. As I trot back to the car, she cannot suck in a full enough breath to scream.

I lean forward over the lip of the trunk and drop her in among the duffel bags and laundry. My lower stomach burns as my stitches pull, protesting this movement. I think at least one rips the skin, but I ignore it. She hits the floor of the trunk with a weighty sound, and I take advantage of her stunned state to push her torso down into the space, fold her legs in and slam the trunk closed.

The banging and screaming start instantly—as soon as she catches her breath. With a mighty roar to let out all the fury, I toss the phone as hard as I can towards the ocean. A faint splash tells me I hit my laughably large mark.

I cannot leave the boat. It has our prints, our hairs and fibers, our fluids. They could never trace it back to me without much more significant resources than most police departments possess, but Nicole lives her life out in the open. She has involved the police.

I retrieve the gun from the glove compartment and the bullets from underneath the back seat. With a deep sigh, I fire off an entire clip into the gasoline reserves at the back of several boats, including mine.

The force of the explosions nearly knocks me on my ass and rattles the world around me. The tenor of Nicole's muffled screams shifts to true terror, though she cannot see the flaming shrapnel launching into adjacent boats, dry grass on the shore, and out into the water. Some of the dead weeds at the edge of the shoreline catch fire, and it spreads before my eyes.

Doubtlessly shaken awake, lights come on in the trailer park nearby as people hurry to see what happened.

Time to leave.

Flames lick at the dark sky in my rearview mirror as the screaming sirens wail louder, closing in. I wish I knew how many, or from which direction, but I do know some of these back roads very well, so I take a chance that the police will not be on them.

Fuck.

Fuck!

Nicole, what have you done?

17

NICOLE

At least fish in a barrel can see where they're fucking swimming.

Kidnapping.

The word echoes around in my head as realization sets in slowly enough that it's probably concerning. I'm being kidnapped. This is a kidnapping.

I'm being kidnapped?!

No. No way. This isn't supposed to be a thing I have to worry about—I'm a big girl. I am simply too large to be thrown into a trunk and taken against my will. I even joked about it once on an online date. He said he only dated women who weighed less than him as a personal rule, and I said, "Well, at least I won't get kidnapped," and knocked his drink into his lap on purpose.

Doesn't feel like much of a joke now.

My body shifts and tosses with every turn and bump, banging into the corners and sides inside the trunk. The only way I can keep from turning into a pinball is by wedging myself against the side in a deeply uncomfortable position, facing the door, with my head jammed into the corner. I'm too tall for this shit, so my legs are bent at the knee, and my shins are pressing into the trunk door. Though the bottom of the space is lined with something, it feels hard as a rock pressing into my hipbone and shoulder.

The road noise drowns out the sound of my own labored breathing, cutting straight through layers of metal and padding to fill this small, dark space. The vibrations through the floor rattle my whole body, making my teeth chatter together. I scream and bang on the roof, but I doubt anyone could hear it over the roar of the engine. I give up when my hands and arms feel bruised.

Okay, I'm officially freaking out. It's pitch black, and I'm locked in, stuck in this position. I'm not claustrophobic, and there's plenty of air in here, but having a body still flooded with adrenaline wedged into a small, enclosed space where I can barely move is not a great feeling.

A frustrated, terrified tear slides down my face sideways, drawing a path across the bridge of my nose and through my temple. I feel panic closing in on me, so I shut my eyes—that way, the darkness is my choice. And it's not like I could see anyway, even if it weren't dark. When Dimitri jerked me back, I lost my glasses. He probably ran over them.

At least it's evidence.

I breathe deeply, then I scream again, putting all of my fear and rage and despair into it.

It actually helps a tiny bit. It calms me a little anyway, which is what I need. I know this elevated pulse and rapid breathing is an adrenaline-fueled response. If I can slow my racing brain, it should help give me some clarity.

Think, Nicole.

I don't have my phone anymore, but at least the police will be looking for me. I can't hear any more sirens, but they were on their way to the marina. Unless those gunshots and that explosion was...

No. I refuse to consider the possibility.

I gave the dispatcher my full name and told her I was being held against my will by a man named Dimitri or Lev. They'll find his boat. They'll find my hair and DNA everywhere—his, too. They'll figure out who he is and track him down.

Fuck. If I know this, so does he.

He's going to *take care* of me. I made myself into a problem he can easily solve.

A fresh wave of fear washes over me, and I bang on the lid of the trunk again.

"Help!" I scream.

But it's the dead of night. I don't know where we are, but I didn't see a single light from a house or business through the pines and marshy areas by that dock. Even if anyone were awake and it were possible to hear me over the noise of the muffled engine, I'm not sure there's anyone *to* hear it.

I know when we get on the highway because I can actually relax and not have to tense and brace myself against every bump and turn. The tradeoff, though, is the cutting cold of the wind whistling through the not-so-airtight cabin.

I use the respite from all the painful, jarring movements to explore my surroundings. There are a few bags in here with me. One has our dirty laundry, one has the trash we accumulated, and one was already in here. That one is too heavy to move. It takes a few tries, since I'm limited without my sense of sight, but I get it unzipped and reach inside to feel around.

I find something like cold metal. It's got a strange texture, and my heart rate spikes in tentative hope as I feel along it and make out the shape. It's... it is! A gun!

I clutch it to my chest, nearly crying with relief.

Maybe I've never shot a gun. Maybe I've never even held one. Maybe the fact that I'm blind as a fucking bat means that I'll never hit my target, even if Dimitri is roughly the size of a grizzly bear.

But I know enough about guns to recognize the power it gives me. My odds for survival just went from 0% to, like, 20%.

As the metal of the gun slowly equalizes to the temperature of my body, I realize that I'm shaking. And not entirely from fear. The wind has been stealing my body heat, which was already hard to regulate because of the adrenaline.

Fuck. I can't go into shock. I need to hold on.

Hours later—I can't tell for sure, but it must be—we stop. Like, not just stopping at a light or a stop sign. The engine turns off, and the car shakes with the movement of a door slamming. I tuck the gun into the waistband of my pants with a silent prayer that it doesn't accidentally go off and shoot me in the leg or something.

My breath catches, and I tense, waiting and ready for the inevitable. Any second, he's going to open that trunk door, and this might be my only chance.

But I'm so, so cold. I could barely feel the gun clutched in my numb fingers.

I try to be ready and spring into action, but when the key scrapes into the lock and the hatch pops like a can, the light blinds me. I try to move, now that I have more room, and I find that I seem to be stuck in this position.

"Fuck. Nicole, I—" There's a tightness that loosens in my chest as I recognize his deep voice, the *Nee-cole* laced with something like pity or regret. "Can you move?"

I'm tempted to make a suggestion for where he can shove that false compassion, but he locks a hand around my ankle, and my pulse spikes in response. He's firm and focused as he helps direct my leg up and out of the car.

Blood floods back into my limbs, bringing the tingling pain, making me wince. With my leg dangling, my torso is half-turned onto my back. My heart pounds into my throat as I watch his blurry face zero in on the bulge in my waistline that doesn't belong there.

We both reach for the gun at the same time, but I get there first because it's literally in my pants. It brings him close, and with a burst of strength from panic, I swing my foot up at him. I catch him square in the middle of his face. He spins away, hitting the corner of the lid, then falls heavily to the ground.

No time to celebrate a lucky shot. I clamber forward and hop out gracelessly, trying and failing to lift my other leg cleanly over the lip of the trunk. My foot catches, and it's too much for legs that feel like jelly. I go down. Just in time, my hand flies out to catch my fall, but my chin bangs on the ground and the impact reverberates through me, making me bite my tongue hard enough to cut through at the tip. I cry out in pain.

But at least I keep a hold of the gun.

Pain blooms in my jaw, but I scramble to my feet. I keep the gun pointed at him as he rolls to his side.

"Stay down," I say, gripping the gun in both hands and pointing it with what I hope is a look menacing enough to make up for the fact that my voice warbled.

"You are not going to shoot me," he challenges, groaning.

Yeah, he's recovering way too quickly, and he's not as afraid of this thing as I assumed he would be.

I wish I knew how to cock it. I wish this weren't the first time I've ever held a gun. It would really add some gravitas when I say, "Don't make me. Stay down and for fuck's sake, Dimitri, just let me go!"

My heart is pounding so hard I can barely think, but I look around as I decide where to go. Everything is blurry, but I can tell that we're in some kind of cavernous garage where four of the eight bays are occupied. There's a van against the opposite wall with some sort of insignia that I can't make out, and a vague door-shape just beyond it that I can only see because it's so big. I back towards that door, keeping my gun pointed directly at him.

Running feels stupid—following me as I grope blindly through unknown territory will be easier for Dimitri than shooting fish in a barrel. At least fish in a barrel can see where they're fucking swimming.

But what else can I do?

When I'm nearly to the door, Dimitri starts making moves, rolling to his knees, calling my bluff.

"Nicole, let me explain."

My time is up.

I push through the door and make a break for it. The same adrenaline that made me strong as I kicked him is making me fast now. Pale, early morning sunlight streams into my eyes as I try to get my bearings while I sprint. To my left is an absolutely enormous house, and the other way has rolling, soft hills of green. Do I chance the house? What if it's just where he lives? And I can see the tips of a gate from where I am, so I don't think I can go that way.

"Nicole!" he roars, and it echoes off the rubber floor and bare walls.

At the sound of his heavy footfalls behind me, I dart towards the backyard.

Fuck. Should have kicked him harder.

18

MAC

I can't wait to bust his balls about this.

"Yo, D! Was that you at the gate?" I call up through the foyer as the massive oak doors swing shut behind me. I place my earbuds back in their case and wipe sweat from my brow.

All good on my run of the perimeter, and I caught the tail end of some old-ass clunker barreling up the drive. Dimitri and his weird obsession with 30-year-old cars. I'll never get it.

"Hey, Mac..." Wes calls from the kitchen. "You're going to want to see this."

I head towards the sound of his voice and see that he's standing in front of the windows by the French doors that lead out to the pool area. I weave around the giant marble island, snag an apple from the fruit bowl that my girl keeps stocked in the center, and join him as I take a juicy, loud crunch.

"'Sup?" I ask around a mouthful of fruit.

"There's a strange woman running around in the garden with a gun."

Well, that's... something. Definitely not what I thought he'd say. I feel my mouth gape and a little rivulet of apple juice spill from the corner before I can recover. I wipe at it and manage, "What?"

He jerks his chin towards the backyard. "It's not every morning that you get a show with your breakfast. Dimitri's been chasing her around the yard for the past..." he checks his watch, "three minutes."

I snort. "Kinky."

I turn and see a tall, tan, curvy woman sprinting across the grass, looking terrified for her life. She doesn't so much as pause to orient herself, running blindly, and nearly falls as she trips over a sprinkler head.

"Nicole Brooks, I take it," Wes remarks dryly, pulling a chip from the bag he's holding and popping it into his mouth.

I reach in and steal a small handful, which makes Wes raise his brow at me. "The witness? Huh. Yeah, looks just like the picture you pulled from her work ID badge," I confirm.

A few seconds later, Dimitri—looking meaner than I've ever seen him, fucking pissed, in fact—bursts through the tree line after her. His longer legs eat up the distance between them as she recovers from her stumble, and he overtakes her in her desperate attempt to escape. We both lean forward, squinting against the too-bright early morning light cresting over the hill in the distance.

"Looks like he took a shot to the nose. You think she did that?"

"Seems likely." I nearly snort. "Dimitri's got some 'splainin' to do."

I can see her mouth open in a scream as she looks over her shoulder and realizes he's gaining, a noise of panic that's only just audible through the distance and glass panes. He tackles her from behind, and they both go down in the grass.

As one, Wes and I crane our necks to keep eyes on the tussle.

"She's holding her own," Wes observes, sounding impressed as Dimitri attempts to pin her and she manages to roll away and scramble back to her feet.

"Should we... help?" I ask, tracking their movements as they grapple and limbs go flying. It's pretty obvious what's going on here—she's trying to get away, and he's trying to stop her. And I know him well enough to see that he's pulling his punches, trying to subdue her, not hurt her.

Wes chuckles. "Who do you propose we help?"

I make a thoughtful noise, shrug, and take another bite of my apple. With a smack of my lips, I throw a glance over my shoulder at the fruit bowl. "Damn, these are good. You should try one."

"I'll stick to my—Ooh!" Wes hisses, a noise of pity. "What a shot! Right in the nose. If it wasn't broken before, it is now."

I whip back around in time to see Dimitri stumbling backwards, clutching his face as a fresh wave of red drips between his fingers, pooling in the valleys. I hoot with surprised laughter. "I missed it! Damn! How did she get the drop on him?"

"He's holding back. Or, he was. Looks like she's finally remembered the gun she's holding. I reckon the kid gloves are off now."

I stiffen, seeing her lift it towards our fearless leader. "It's not loaded?"

He shakes his head. "Dimitri wouldn't chase her like that unless he was sure she wouldn't—or couldn't—shoot."

The black metal flashes in the sunlight that barely crests over the hill, extended in the space between them. I shake my head. She's holding it too far from her body. He'll have it out of her hand in two seconds flat. "Her grip's all wrong."

Even though she's armed, she's clearly inexperienced. Once Dimitri stops messing around, she's done for. It's almost funny to see some of the moves he's been drilling into us for over a year in action like this. It's not like sparring, since the stakes are higher for both of them, but it's nowhere near a fair fight.

He knocks the gun into the grass with a perfectly aimed and lightning-quick blow to her wrist that she doesn't see coming. Disarmed, she falls back a step and pivots, preparing to run again. He feints left; she darts to avoid him, and he catches a handful of the back of her shirt, using it to jerk her into a bear hug, overpowering her.

But she's not done fighting—she throws her head back, clipping him in the chin. It's only then that I realize how tall she must be to be able to even reach his chin. That's about where Wesley falls on him when they stand next to each other. I see him working his jaw, and his arms bulge as he tightens his grip around her.

Struggling, but apparently filled with more annoyance than anger, Dimitri casts exasperated eyes skyward. When they level back out, they fall on us. He stiffens, realizing we're at the window, watching. Wes uses his bag of chips to salute him, and I jerk my hand in a wave, grinning. I see his chest expand as he sighs, probably muttering some obscure Russian curse. My favorite is when he calls us goat testicles. Or penises from the mountains.

As if realizing how this all must look in front of an audience, he loosens his hold and places a hand on each shoulder to turn her. She takes off as soon as she can break free.

"Nearly had her that time... Oh, no! Not that way! She doesn't see the—"

The screams were muffled before, but we can clearly hear the sharp ripping sound and the giant splash as she steps right through the pool cover. In her defense, it looks just like the rest of the patio—it's designed to. It rips down the middle, and she disappears into the murky water beneath it. Dimitri dives right in after her, and the splashes get bigger.

Well, that's not going to be fun for either of them. We've had a cold front sweep in, and nights have been near freezing lately.

I move towards the handle of the French door, ready to step in, but Wes stills me, thumping the back of the hand still holding the bag of chips against my sternum. "I wouldn't get in the middle of that if I were you."

"Middle of what? He clearly needs a hand in subduing her."

He resumes his casual posture with a one-shoulder shrug. "I don't know that I'd insert myself into that particular lover's spat."

"Lover's spat?" I repeat, grinning. "Fuck off. You think they're..." I trail off, slapping my hands together in a suggestive but meaningless gesture.

He chuckles. "I think that's Dimitri's woman."

"No way," I scoff. "She's running away from him. At most, she's his captive—his obviously unwilling captive. A kidnapped witness."

He shrugs again, but I can see he really believes his statement. And Wes is usually such a stickler for not making assumptions. This guy doesn't speak until his little calculator-brain has done its math about the odds and he's sure he's right. But Wes only *acts* like he knows everything. Half the time, I think he's full of shit, just saying things with enough confidence to convince people he knows for a fact what he's only making an educated guess about.

"Mark my words."

I reach in to steal more chips and roll my eyes. "In the almost three years we've known him, have you ever heard him talk about women? Have you ever seen him with anyone? All he does is work, work out, and sulk. I did kind of think he liked her at the wedding, but we both know she was a cover." I take a thoughtful munch. "My theory is that there was some kind of accident and he took one of those knives to the 'nads."

Wes holds out his hand, palm up. "A fiver says he makes some kind of claim on her today. Marks his territory, as it were."

I glance out towards the pool. They're both standing, heads cresting through the rip in the pool cover and up to their waists in gross, old water. She's shivering as she angrily sends a splash his way that hits him right in the face. Her scream this time is not one of terror, but of outrage.

"All right. You're on." I laugh and grab his hand to shake. "What makes you so sure, anyway?"

"Didn't you see his face?"

I look back. They're getting out now, and he's half-carrying, half-dragging her towards the stairs. "Yeah. Same mean mug as usual. What of it?"

Wes shakes his head, clearly feeling pretty certain about this. "It was the same look you had when you brought Eleanor here after you'd been stalking her and trying to keep it from us for weeks."

"Oh?" I grin. Fond memories. "And what look was that?"

"Like she was yours and no one better say otherwise. Like you had something to protect."

"You're sayin' that has a look? Fuck off." I laugh incredulously.

"It does," he nods. "It's like the caveman, animal brain saying *mine.*"

My brows shoot up. Okay... maybe he does know more than I give him credit for. Because I've never said that thought out loud to him, but I sure as shit have to Eleanor. And I don't remember exactly what I was thinking that night I brought her home the first time, but it's safe to say that was part of it. I remember giving the guys an ultimatum, threatening to leave if they decided to throw her out.

"Besides," he continues, "he brought her *here.*"

"Yeah," I grin, taking the last bite of my apple and moving it into a cheek to speak around it, "And after the shit he gave me about Eleanor, I can't wait to bust his balls about this."

"Exactly. You know how Dimitri feels about us doing the job right. And he can't stand eating crow. If he didn't care about her, he never would have brought her here and put our safety at risk. He'd have taken her to the warehouse or the farm or the meat freezer and locked her away for all our sakes."

Well, damn. Wes might actually be right. As per fuckin' usual. I narrow my eyes at him. "Did you just hustle me, Short Round? You know something I don't?"

Wes laughs, balls up the now-empty bag of chips, and tosses it in the trash as he heads through the kitchen towards his office. "I know so many things you don't, it's honestly embarrassing for you, pretty boy."

"Eat me," I retort to his retreating form.

"I got some new tech in if you want to check it out," he calls, nearly all the way back to his office by now.

"Be right in."

I glance out the window again, see that D's ushering her towards the pool house where he set up shop. If I am wrong about the two of them, I'm gonna be pissed. Five bucks is whatever, but a smug Wesley is pretty fucking insufferable, even if he never actually says, "I told you so."

I check the time. Eleanor is going to be awake in the next few hours, so I hope Dimitri and that woman sort out whatever it is that's going on. My girl is sensitive—she feels deeply for other people, even if she doesn't know them—so I'm not totally sure how she'll react to Dimitri having a captive houseguest.

I sigh. Things are about to get a whole lot more interesting around here.

19

NICOLE

Truce.

I'm shaking so hard I can barely keep my arms up. But I need one across my chest to hide the fact that my nipples are so hard from the cold they could cut glass—they've literally never been so hard, it's almost lewd—and the other to hold up the sweatpants that are soaked and retaining so much water they probably weigh 50 pounds. The poor drawstring is about to give out, so it's up to good-old noodle arms to keep me from traipsing around in a stranger's yard with my ass out in a nude shapewear thong.

When he lays a hand on my shoulder, I hiss and drop away from it. Not just because I'm so cold that his regular body temperature feels like it scalded me, but also because it's *his* hand. I refuse to look at his face as he ushers me towards the building on the opposite side of the slate patio that must be a pool house.

"Nicole, I just told you. You are *safe*. I will not hurt you—"

I shake my head, keeping it tilted down, trying to focus on each step so I don't accidentally step through another portal to icy hell. Why was the pool cover the exact fucking same shade as the stone? Who the *fuck* designed that?

"You threw me into the trunk of a car, Dimitri. The *trunk* of a *car*! You kidnapped me!"

"I did not kidnap you—"

"So, I can go?" I ask, voice dripping with more sarcasm than my body and clothes drip with frigid water.

He doesn't miss a beat. "Of course not."

"Then this is a kidnapping!"

"You are in danger!"

"From who, you?" I hiss, a deep shiver slicing through the accusation. "What are you going to do to the only witness who knows you killed Kyle?"

"Fuck," he whispers, scratching at his scalp.

"Yeah. Fuck. Are you going t-to gaslight me now? Tell me I didn't hear w-what I know I heard?" I demand, my harsh tone undercut by how hard my teeth are chattering.

"And what is it you know you heard?" he retorts, stopping us and spinning me to face him. With a hand around each upper arm that sears my freezing flesh, he shakes me a little. "Tell me."

I'm not so nearsighted that I can't see the pain on his face. The lines around his eyes and brows are deeply carved with worry and anguish. And it's not from that wound I know I accidentally clipped with my elbow or his obviously broken nose. His frown is deeper than anger or confusion. He looks... betrayed.

That must be why I open my stupid mouth and say, "That you don't leave witnesses and you'd *t-take care* of me."

His eyes flick back and forth between mine for a second, then he spears me with one of those extra-intense looks meant to intimidate me. I'm not even sure he realizes when he's doing it.

"I did not mean... fuck!"

He releases me, spins away, and walks a few steps. When he turns back around, I'm wracked with a shiver so hard I bite down on my already damaged tongue and whimper.

Seeing that snaps him out of whatever blind rage he seems to be in. "Come inside, Nicole. You are frozen. I will explain to you what I would have told you in the car if you had not called the police and fought me so hard."

Do I dare? The last time I trusted him because I felt like I had no other options, I ended up on a boat with no escape, then shoved into the trunk of a car.

But I'm shivering so hard I might chip a tooth, and I've gone numb to the sensation of cold. It's never a good thing when you're numb to the cold—hypothermia is no joke. If my core temperature drops too low, I'll stop shivering and lose consciousness. I definitely won't be able to escape if I'm unconscious.

"F-fine," I relent.

He pushes open the door to the building and gestures for me to enter first. I do, looking up as he flicks on the lights, and am startled by what I see. Well, the blurry, out-of-focus, vague impressions of what I see, anyway. I may not be able to get most of the finer details, but I know they are fine. This isn't a pool house—it's a whole-ass apartment.

Everything has the sleek, clean lines of expensive shit. It even *smells* expensive—like a room freshener named after ridiculous things that don't even have a smell, like "cashmere and a soft breeze." There's a king-sized bed with crisp white sheets dominating the entire right side of the room, a sitting area with big brown blobs that I assume are a plush, overstuffed leather couch and chair, and the shape of the stuff in the area towards the back makes me think it's a kitchenette. Two doors along the back wall are open, one leading into what's obviously a luxurious bathroom, full of marble tile and a glass-paned walk-in shower, and the other leading to a separate room that seems big enough that it could be an office or a guest room.

A pool house with a guest room? Where the hell am I?

He steers us towards the bed. "Take off your wet clothes and get in," he instructs.

"Get-t out," I counter. If he thinks he gets to sit in here while I get naked and get into his bed, he's crazy.

His arm snakes around my waist. I stiffen in his grip, wanting to pull away but too numb to trust my own body. The places where he's touching me sting like open wounds—the heat of his body turning into pain on mine. "I will get in with you," he says, and I'm not quite sure if it's a promise or a warning. "It will warm you faster."

"N-no! Go aw-way."

He tightens his arm around my waist and lowers his face close to mine to growl, "If you think I am letting you out of my sight after you broke my nose, then you are more foolish than I thought. Get. In."

I'm so sick of being fucking growled at. I don't even care anymore.

"At l-least turn around!"

I wiggle to put enough distance between us, and it's all the tie in my pants can take. It snaps, and the heavy sweatpants hit the tile with a fleshy, wet plop, splashing my legs. Since there's no point in trying to salvage my dignity, I step out of both his pants and over-large socks, pushing against his chest for enough distance to manage the movement. As he turns to give me a modicum of privacy, I discard his shirt with fingers that shake from more than just the cold.

Suddenly, all my justified outrage from a second ago evaporates, and I'm just a nearly naked woman next to a man she's *stupidly* attracted to. I'm exposed—on display—covered only by nude Spanx. And I know he's going to look. My arms move to cover my breasts, but I'm so frozen that I can barely even feel my own skin.

When he hears the shirt hit the floor, he glances over his shoulder.

I fucking *knew* he was going to look. Asshole!

I curl inwards, falling onto my ass on a plush, bouncy mattress as his eyes forge a path down my exposed chest and stomach and legs. "Stop looking," I hiss.

No way am I letting go of my chest to pull back the covers.

My whole body contracts in one giant shake of a shiver. His face tenses, and he strides across the room.

"Get in the bed," he repeats, opening a closet and grabbing a bundle of something. "We need to get you warm."

Free of the paralyzing effect of his stare, I scramble under the covers, pulling the sheet and blanket up to my chin. It's woefully thin, and I nearly say something, but then I see the bundle tucked in his arms. Bigger blankets.

It crosses my mind that I'm covered in disgusting pool water and grime from God knows what. I'd never get into my own bed like this, but I'm too cold and furious to care. Serves him right. A little laundry is the least he can do.

He lays the blankets over me, and I wince a little under their weight. I'm not any warmer yet, but it's best to do this slowly so I don't go into cardiac arrest. The relief will come soon.

When he drops his pants, I get a blurry flash of white ass that embarrasses me enough to make me close my eyes. The bed dips under his weight as he climbs in next to me. I shift away, keeping my arm firmly around my chest, but he drags me towards him. The sheet bunches up between us as he presses the entire length of his body to mine. He's hard everywhere, his body a wall of smooth skin and muscle with the consistency of a rock.

I'm basically naked. In a bed. With Dimitri. And he's totally naked.

This isn't quite how I pictured this happening.

All the fight goes out of me when the heat of his skin hits mine. Hours of uncertainty, terror, rage, frustration, and physical exertion have taken their toll, and I've got a headache from eyestrain. I'm dizzy now and grateful for being horizontal.

My breath cracks and breaks in a shaky in-and-out, and I squeeze my eyes shut as hard as I can. There's a faint whistling wheeze at the apex of each breath from my asthma that feels cartoonish and out of place.

His body heat stings and burns, making me whimper. This is more than an icy, unexpected dip; it's an icy dip after hours in a metal box with no wind insulation.

He tucks me against his chest and lays a soft, soothing hand on the back of my head. "Shh, I know. It hurts. You will warm soon, and it will not hurt. Put your fingers here, under my arm." He flares his top elbow out so I can tuck my icy fingers in between that hard, hot rock wall of his arm and torso.

I don't know how long it takes, but eventually the heat of him bleeds into me. It slowly chases the feeling back into my rigid muscles and frozen nerves. I clutch harder at his body heat as the cold leeches out of my extremities, replaced by pins and needles under every inch of my skin.

I wince. That'll be my nerves waking back up.

This sucks.

"Truce, my med?"

"You want a truce," I repeat flatly. It's muffled by his chest, but I can't seem to move my cheek from the relief this skin-on-skin contact is providing.

"Yes, I want a truce."

I shake my head slightly. "You threatened me."

"You broke my nose."

"You chased me into a frozen pool."

"You ripped open my wound."

I rear back, just so he can see me scowl at him. How dare he have equal and opposite things to be upset about?! "You shoved me into the trunk of a car!"

"You kicked me in the face."

"Trunk of a car," I repeat. "For *hours*. It was freezing in there, and I was panicking, not knowing what was happening or where we were going. I thought you wanted to… I thought you were going to kill me, Dimitri."

He winces. "I acted rashly. You called the police, and I did not have time to explain everything to you. If the police had come..." he trails off.

I stiffen against him because now I can't help mentally finishing that sentence for him. Would he have killed them to defend himself? I know they have guns and receive some combat training, but... frankly, up against Dimitri, I wouldn't put my money on the cops.

I shake my head. "You could have stopped somewhere and let me out."

"You would have run. You *did* run. I could not risk anyone seeing."

A frustratingly fair point.

"I had no intention of hurting you, Nicole. I do not. I will not. Fight me however you like—try to kick me, punch me, or stab me if it makes you feel better... I may restrain you so you do not harm yourself, but I will not return the blows."

Realization slowly sinks in. In our long list of crimes against each other, mine are the only violent offenses. He hasn't retaliated physically against me in any way, and he's acting *concerned* about me. He's trying to warm me.

If I were ready to condemn him over a single overheard conversation, shouldn't I be willing to absolve him after he shows me that I'm mistaken?

"Okay, truce," I agree. "I believe you don't want to hurt me."

He starts stroking my hair again. I almost stop him, anxious about a man's lack of awareness about texture and tangles, but relax when I feel that he's avoiding the knots and not making them worse. It is oddly soothing.

"I'm sorry I attacked you," I tell him after a moment. "I promise I didn't mean to hit your injury."

"Did you mean to break my nose?" There's a hint of laughter in his voice.

"Yes," I confess, taking after his blunt honesty. I'm smiling a little, too, and grateful that he can't see it. "And I'm sorry for that, too."

There's a long pause that feels almost light in contrast to the weight of the situation. It shifts slightly when he sighs, "After last night, I thought we... You believed I would kill you, Nicole?"

I can tell he's hurt, but he's trying not to be obvious about it.

I wish I could be annoyed about that, but I kind of know how he feels. My own emotions are welling just behind my eyelids, and if I cry, he's not allowed to see that, either. With a sigh of my own, I tuck my chin and press my cheek harder to his chest.

"Put yourself in my shoes for a minute—"

"You are not wearing shoes. Or anything, for that matter."

My heart thumps hard twice against my sternum, a pitiful, too-tired-for-arousal response from a too-cold body. "Metaphorical shoes," I correct. "It means try to understand my perspective. I was alone, trapped on a boat, when I can't swim, with a man who can hit a bullseye with a knife while on a rocking surface with his eyes closed. That man, who's told me repeatedly he's not a good person and who tried to rid me of any way to communicate by throwing my phone out the window, sneaks away to have a secret conversation about taking care of witnesses to a murder he committed."

I let that hang in the air between us. He's gone rigid against me.

"So, yes, Dimitri. I was afraid. I didn't want to think you'd kill me, and I knew there was a chance I was misunderstanding. But there was also a chance I was right, so I figured I was definitely safer on my own."

"I see," he says, and his voice has softened. With regret? Apology? "You were being careful. Smart. After what I have said and done and kept from you, you do not trust me."

It's not phrased like a question, but I answer it anyway. "I want to," I whisper through a tight throat. "I want to think of you as the man who comforted me during the storm. But I guess... I didn't know what else to think after you tried so hard to convince me that you're a bad person."

I wince as I finish because it sounds like I'm blaming him. And I guess I am. But this is a consequence of his own actions, right? I shouldn't feel bad.

Except I do. Because he looks torn up about it, and now I feel like that's my fault.

"I understand," he says after a second and rests his chin on top of my head. "I treated you with disrespect."

I start. He... did? He did. He did!

I'm not sure it would have occurred to me to use that word, but it's the perfect word. How he acted was *so* disrespectful. "Yeah," I agree.

"I do not deserve your trust. Not yet. But I will, I promise. I will earn it."

While the blankets and body heat warm me on the outside, what he said warms me on the inside.

Slowly, the stress-tightened muscles in my back relax. The heat makes me languid and loose, and unfortunately, now I'm hyper-aware of every area of my body that hurts. The main issue is that there are so many. The bottoms of my feet that were already torn up, my calves and thighs from running, my hip from bouncing against the floor of the trunk, my arms from pushing and pulling and banging on the hood, my hands from catching my fall, my chin and jaw and tongue from *not* catching my fall... And topping it all off, my head is pounding with what is maybe the worst headache of my life.

I can barely keep my eyes open. He notices.

"Rest, now," he says soothingly, loosening his hold. "You are safe here. No one will disturb you."

"Are you leaving?" An edge of panic worms into my voice, and I start sitting up.

"I need to debrief my team. I will return here shortly, and when I do, we will talk about what happens next."

20

DIMITRI

The Hitman's Halfway House for Kidnapped Girls

Ever since James invited a civilian to live with us, we typically meet in Wesley's office for discussions related to our work. It is several degrees warmer in here than the rest of the house from the mechanical whirring of too many electronics, and smells faintly of burnt plastic and the odors of a body. The signs of Wesley are everywhere, mostly in the form of empty energy drink cans piled together and surfaces covered in electrical projects half-completed.

When I approach, James and Wesley are in the middle of a heated debate about something asinine. I stop to listen for a moment. It is familiar and comfortable, like the feeling of coming home.

"All I'm sayin' is, don't knock it 'til you try it," James says, brandishing a tall glass that is full of ice and a brown liquid sloshing around. "It's a completely different beverage."

Wesley scoffs, sitting back in his mesh desk chair with his fingers laced behind his head. "And what I'm saying is, no self-respecting Brit would, sorry."

"Hot leaf water—'scuse me, *tea*—has its place and all, but nothing beats a good southern sweet tea on a hot day. Just like mama used to make." James turns to me, lifting his drink and shaking it so the ice rattles against the glass. "Back me up here, D."

I lift a brow. I know James is originally from somewhere in the south-eastern US and has a large family still living there, but he does not speak of it often. "It is four degrees Celsius outside."

"It's a figure of speech."

"You know where I am from, and you know the kinds of things I prefer to consume. You think I would choose a cold beverage that is full of sugar?"

Wesley smirks, and James scowls, sitting back in his chair. With a huff of a sigh, he takes a deep sip and places it on the glass top of Wesley's desk. "I dunno, I guess I thought I could always count on Russia and England to be on opposite sides."

"Well, *politically*, we don't really align. Dictator regime and all that," Wesley says, his accent becoming more pronounced as he thinks of his home country. He lifts James's glass and slides a coaster in the shape of an alien underneath.

"I did not vote for him," I shrug.

Wesley laughs, then turns to James and says, "See, it's funny because—"

"I know why it's funny, you condescending asshole," James says, his grin more a baring of teeth than a smile. He turns to me and gestures to the middle of his own face. "Well, you're looking a bit worse for wear, Big D. Nice shiners. Broken?"

I huff a sigh.

He nods towards the outline of the gauze patch I inexpertly affixed while cleaning my wound after the shower. "And how's the gunshot healing?"

The pain is dull and easy to ignore unless I think about it, which is the benefit of having a high pain tolerance and a properly treated wound, even one that has recently taken damage. "Nothing to concern yourself with."

"Missed all the important stuff, then?"

"A graze. Still, I hate to be shot."

James snorts. "Could have been worse. I'll remind you that *you're* the one who won't carry a gun."

James's derision makes some sense, as he would never allow himself to be parted from the long-range rifle he considers to be an extension of himself. The way he cleans it is so obsessive that I cannot help but approve. He confessed to me once that he does not keep track of his kills, only the shots he has missed. That metric can be counted on one hand.

"Nah, I'm with Dimitri on this one. Guns make you a target—well, at close range anyway," Wesley corrects. James is usually too far away to be spotted, let alone shot at.

"Like being the size of a fuckin' house doesn't make him a big enough target already." James laughs once. "Eh, I guess I see your point."

"If they cannot dodge a knife, they do not deserve to carry a gun."

There is a beat, and they both grin, sharing a look. "Add that one to the Google Doc," James says, jerking his chin at Wesley.

"Way ahead of you," he returns smoothly, placing his hands back on the large, rainbow-backlit keyboard and hammering something out.

"What Google Doc?" I ask, lost.

"We've got a shared document called 'Dimitri-isms'—we're writing down all your little pearls of wisdom."

I scowl. He says it as if it is something I should be flattered by, but it does not feel like a compliment. It feels like another joke that they make where I am the subject, but do not share in the humor. "You record the things I say? Why?"

James hides his grin as he grabs for his phone and flicks his thumb across a page of—presumably—the recorded things I have said. "It's good stuff. Like, 'shortcuts are for people who are too lazy to take the time to do something correctly' and 'dull blades are better at weighing down paper than cutting it,' things like that."

"My favorite is, 'planning is pointless if you cannot account for the unaccountable,'" Wesley adds, joined by James's nod of confirmation. "I liked that one—good wordplay."

I lift a brow. "Ah, I see. Things that are true."

"Useful knowledge, poetically put," Wesley says, his tone a singsong recitation.

"To what end?"

James scratches at his jaw, the motion rasping the wrong way against his facial hair. "To... have it? Hey, who knows, maybe the next generation of hitmen-and-women—hit-people?—would benefit from a manual of sorts. Wesley could post it anonymously on one of those forums."

I consider it. The idea of a future generation benefiting from what my own father taught me and what I have taught myself is not such a bad thing. "I suppose, then, it is allowable. But if this is some kind of elaborate joke at my cost, I will be very displeased."

"At your *expense*," Wesley corrects.

"That is what I said."

James lifts two fingers in a mock salute. "Heard, Big D. Promise, no elaborate joke. It's just stuff you've said that we like and want to remember."

I suppose I have no reason not to believe them, other than the fact that they often share in jokes I do not understand. At the very least, they mentioned it to me when they could have remained silent about it, so it is nothing happening behind me.

I check my watch and sigh. We waste so much time.

"James, what updates on Volkevich?"

"Well, I followed Viktor back to his place and added his personal residence to our file. Also put a tracker on his car. He's been lying pretty low, so I followed some of the goons he sent out back to the estate. As soon as the police cleared out, they went in. Tore the place a-fucking-part."

"Looking for something?" I guess.

"Definitely. My hunch is they're looking for that," James jerks his chin at the bowl of rice on the far end of Wesley's desk.

"Well then, let's have a look, shall we?" Wesley nods, reaching for it. He digs in the grains for a few seconds, then produces the small device.

"The first rule of flash drives is never to plug one in if you're uncertain you can trust it. People find them on the street all the time and let their curiosity get the better of them, not realizing how easy it is to program any number of nasty surprises onto one. A clever hacker can steal your personal information and passwords, give your computer a virus, or even," Wesley says, his voice straining as he bends at the waist to fit the device into the USB port of his computer, "send your location to whoever created the program."

"Wes, what the hell!" James shouts, pointing down. "You *just* said—"

"You think a computer *I* built can't overwrite whatever command this was set up with? I thought you thought more of me than that," he says, scoffing indignantly.

James rolls his eyes, sits back in his chair, and kicks his legs out straight while he crosses his arms. "My apologies, genius. Think it'll even work after its impromptu bath?"

"We're about to find out."

I grip the edge of the desk I am leaning against and watch the screen closely. There is nothing except the soft, constant noise of a computer fan for several long seconds, then two windows pop up at once, and James's hoot of triumph matches the tone of my sigh of relief. It is not ruined from being in my pocket when I jumped in after Nicole.

In one of the windows, Wesley types a few things—likely doing exactly what he promised and overwriting the flash drive's protocol—and I focus on the other one as words appear.

"Looks like..." Wesley squints as we all move closer to the screen to see the tiny writing.

"Russian," I finish.

"Shall I run it through a translator, or do you want to do the honors?" Wesley asks, turning his head just far enough to see me in his peripheral vision. "My vocabulary is conversational at best, or things I've picked up from you. I think I know three different ways to call someone a testicle."

"We'll have to compare notes; I've only got two," James pretends to pout.

I scan the text, ignoring their quips. "It is warning against unauthorized use, and it wants a password."

"Of course it does. *Koz'ye yaichko*," James sighs, calling whoever created the flash drive a goat's testicle with a sly grin directed at me. His accent is terrible.

I huff, and Wesley presses his lips together against a laugh.

"Whatever it is, it must be important," Wesley observes.

"That is putting it mildly. Kyle Volkevich tried to smuggle this out of the wedding inside another person. I agree with James—they are searching for this drive." I gesture to the computer, where Wesley is making selections in windows that look completely foreign to me. He types fluently in a language I will never know, and do not particularly care to. Four is plenty.

Wesley nods, pulling up more screens and typing in more indecipherable text. "I'll give the password cracker a crack at it and all the CPU I can spare. Might take a little while, depending on how strong they made it. We're fairly fucked if it's a multi-factor authentication. Meanwhile... looks like I can at least confirm it's Volkevich's. The signal it just tried to cast was to an IP address at one of their office buildings."

"Called it," James all but physically congratulates himself. "I vote we hold off finishing the job until we know what's on it. Might need Double-V for something. Bet he knows the password."

I wish this were wholly good or bad news. It is always useful to have something someone else wants very badly, but the fact that it belongs to Volkevich means Nicole is in serious trouble.

Does Volkevich know about Nicole's involvement? Was Kyle carrying out an order, or was he acting alone?

"We should try to break it on our own first. We need to know if Kyle told Nicole anything that might help narrow down what it is, why he had it, or how to get in," I think aloud. "I will speak with her after she has rested. Wesley, will you set up an alert at her home so we will know if anyone comes looking for it?"

"Can do."

"And hey, speaking of the big ol' elephant in the room, it's time to come clean, big guy," James says, slapping the table lightly with his palm.

"I am clean enough. I changed after my shower," I protest, glancing down and running a hand down my stomach.

"No, like, it's time for you to explain. What the hell was all that, earlier?"

"What do you mean?"

"I believe he's referring to the time when you chased a terrified woman around the garden," Wesley points out, his voice flat. "What do you think this is, the Hitman's Halfway House for Kidnapped Girls?"

James eyes him. "How long have you been working on that one?"

"You don't like it? I was quite proud of it."

"Meh. Not bad." With a shrug, James returns his attention to me. "Anyway, when you said that you were going to *take care of her*, I assumed..." He draws a finger across his throat.

I gnash my teeth. "Why does everyone think that?"

"It's a pretty misleading euphemism in our line of work, you must admit," Wesley argues.

"I had no intention of killing her. She is not a threat, but she is in danger. Now that we know who the USB belongs to, it is obvious they will come after her."

James and Wesley exchange a knowing look, and James shakes his head. "Yeah, if you expect us to just participate in your little Stockholm

Syndrome experiment, you're going to need to give us a little more than that. You could have dumped her in a motel or another safe house. It's clear she's not directly involved, and the USB is protected, so it's not like she'd really know anything if she were caught. And hey, civilian casualties are… regrettable, but it would have been smarter to just let it happen than to compromise us all here. Right?"

Regrettable. The word sets my teeth on edge. It would have been far more than *regrettable* to allow her to fall into Viktor Volkevich's hands.

"I… could not let that happen," I admit begrudgingly, knowing I am echoing the sentiment I disagreed with so furiously all those months ago when James first brought Eleanor here. I can see the self-satisfied smile growing on his face from the corner of my eye, so I try to avoid looking at him directly as I explain, "She is innocent."

"So… let me just rephrase here… what you're saying," James continues, a large, pleased grin now firmly in place, "is that you put a woman you just met before the team. You could've just killed her or let someone else do it. Should've, by your own rules. Isn't that what you wanted *me* to do?"

My hand curls into a fist. I know he speaks hypothetically, that he is just being contrary and joking at my expense, but I dislike the idea of Nicole becoming a victim of this situation, even hypothetically. "Once this business with the Volkevich *Bratva* is sorted, I will ensure that she does not become a problem—"

"I thought it didn't matter if she wouldn't be a problem. That's what *you* said when I brought Eleanor here."

"I owe her a favor," I grind out. In fact, I owe her more than a favor or my protection. "She sewed my wound. You think I should kill someone who helped me?"

James shakes his head with his eyes closed, holding up one finger to silence me. "Shh. Just let me enjoy this."

"So, she's here for her own safety?" Wesley asks.

I nod.

"If that's the case, how come she doesn't seem to want to fuckin' be here?" James cuts in.

"You're not exactly a paragon of eager female compliance, Mac," Wesley cuts in. "I seem to recall that Eleanor was quite shaken when you brought her here."

James waves his hand through the air. "Now, hold on a second. I have done many questionable things in pursuit of that woman, and I would do all of them again. But I've never tackled her. In broad daylight. While she was armed," he pauses, considering, then adds another qualifier, grinning broadly, "without her consent."

"Yes, yes, you're very happy," Wesley sighs. "Must you rub our noses in it?"

Still wearing that smug grin, he shrugs. "My question remains. Why was she running?"

"Because I handled the situation with her poorly," I grind out.

"No shit," he snorts, eyeing my black eyes.

I cast an exasperated look at Wesley, whose lips twitch as he steps in as mediator. "If you're quite finished," he says dryly to James, who gestures with one hand and a self-satisfied expression for him to proceed. "So, she's... staying?"

I sigh instead of answering. Has our conversation so far not implied this clearly? He is asking a question that he already knows the answer to, and I dislike stating the obvious.

"Well, there's plenty of room up in the loft, right, Mac? I suppose she could stay in that spare room next to—"

"No. She stays with me." It is out of my mouth before I can really consider the suggestion. They do not know her like I do; they will not be prepared for her fire or fight. Besides, I have just made some progress in repairing the broken bond between us, and I will not let anything or anyone take her from me now.

James jumps in. "Yeah, but isn't she a flight risk? More security in the big house. Plus, she'd probably be more comfortable with a womanly presence—"

"She is staying with me," I repeat, enunciating each word and glaring at their twin owlish expressions. I feel as though I am being baited, though I could not say why.

"All right, then. I've got one of my spiders looking into the case file from her call to emergency services. We should have a better idea of how they intend to respond to her self-reported kidnapping within the day."

"Good. If that is all we have to discuss?"

"All on my end," Wesley confirms, sending James a smile that is clearly as meaningful to him as it is indecipherable to me.

"I lost her glasses. She will need a replacement pair. And an inhaler, I believe. Can you access her medical files?" I ask Wesley, rubbing at my heavy eyes.

"Sure. I'll have what she needs sent here today."

Something deep inside twists that I am not the one who can provide this for her, but I nod my thanks, grateful that someone can.

As I turn to leave, I hear Wesley pointedly clear his throat. Looking smug as anything, he holds out his hand towards James, who sighs dramatically and digs into his pants for his wallet. He selects a bill and slaps it into Wesley's waiting palm.

I do not want to know what that is about, so I continue on my path, but their voices follow me down the hall.

"You were leading the witness," James grumbles.

"We never defined terms," Wesley replies lightly. "And *you* were the one who brought it up."

There is a pause while James considers, then I can hear the smile in his voice when he concedes, "Worth it for the 'I told you so.'"

I heave a sigh and scrub at my short hair. My scar aches from being wet too many times, because it makes the skin tight. The headache from the broken nose is a persistent, pounding pressure in my sinuses that reminds me of its presence with sharp pains through the brain like a migraine.

In the pool house, Nicole is asleep. Her deep, even breathing comforts me as I collect the ibuprofen from the bathroom cabinet and shake six into my hand. I can sleep through pain, but I do not wish to wake up so swollen that I cannot see. When I emerge into my room once again, I glance at the couch, then at Nicole in my bed.

She is afraid of me. She ran from me, called the police, and thought I might kill her.

I am the kind of man she should fear. I want people to fear me—need it, to do my job effectively.

But I do not want her fear. I do not want her to look at me like the monster I am. If she wakes and finds me near her, will she react with panic, or would my presence soothe her, as it did on the boat?

Fuck, she looks so good there.

I am too tired and in too much pain to become aroused, but if anything were going to do it, it would be the sight of Nicole's tan, bare shoulder and her hair spilling back across the white cotton like spun gold.

Ever since I saw so much of her before she climbed into my bed—even tinged with blue from the cold—I have not known peace. Every inch of her is soft in a way that would welcome a touch as it welcomes the eye. Wide hips, a deep V between her legs covered with curls darker than the ones on her head that I could see through nearly transparent material, a supple stomach, and large breasts. She is a goddess. A curved, golden goddess.

A better man might give her some space and let her sleep. A better man would take the couch. And though I know I must be a better man for her—one who could one day deserve her—I refuse to accomplish this by sleeping apart from her.

She fears me, but only because I gave her a reason to. Because I told her to.

I know this because she had a phone the entire time we were on the water. For days, she could have called for help. And yet she used it only once, when she felt she had no other choice.

Perhaps it is foolish, but I believe that means that I have not ruined this irreparably.

I strip off my shirt so I am just in sweatpants, pull back the covers, and relish in the sight of the long lines of her naked back. I would look my fill, but she shivers in her sleep, so I slide in behind her.

It is a perfect fit, of course. The dip of her waist and flare of her hip are like a space designed for my arm. Her shoulder blades press into the flattest part of my pecs, allowing our bodies to meet along the entire length of our torsos. Back to front. Her round ass carves a space in my lap, and my bent knees nest perfectly in hers.

She sighs, wriggling back a little, seeking warmth, and I respond by tightening my grip around her. I close my eyes with a small smile on my lips, and my last thoughts before losing consciousness are ones of happy satisfaction.

29

NICOLE

—◆—

You are a loose end, and a Bratva does not leave those to unravel.

My first thought is that my whole body kind of hurts, and my second is that I'm comfortable despite that. I inhale deeply through my nose, and fill my lungs with the scents of... him—a strong scent memory, buried under unfamiliar ones that makes the blood pound between my legs. Clean laundry and spit. Soap and cum. It's aggressively masculine with an undercurrent of something so fresh that it's almost sterile.

Damn. That really shouldn't get me going the way it does.

It's so pervasive, there's no way he's not right under my nose. Am I sleeping on his chest?

I felt him when he lay down behind me. I was mostly asleep, but it's hard not to notice your body being jostled by almost 300 pounds of man meat, no matter how gentle he's trying to be. It honestly didn't occur to me to be upset by his utter lack of boundaries because he was so solid and warm, and it just felt... nice.

My eyes pop open, and I find myself alone, just surrounded by covers and pillows that have absorbed enough of his essence to fool me. I sit up, wincing at the muscle pain and deep bruises littered across my skin. My body feels battered. Almost... used. Like we fought hard, and I lost. I guess that technically is what happened... I just wish all the sensations were swapped—there's, like, *one* part of me that isn't sore, and I sorely wish it were the only part of me that was.

God, this is so messed up. I can't believe I could still want him like this after everything he did to me. And how could he want me after everything I did to him? Our list of sins against each other reads like the criminal charges of one of those *Bratva* guys—assault, battery, aggravated assault, assault with a deadly weapon...

I sigh and scrub my face. My sleep schedule is all out of whack. It's mid-morning, so at this point, I've been here for a little more than 24 hours, and I've been asleep for most of it. I also showered and ate a really delicious sandwich Dimitri must have left for me, but that's about it. Between the trauma and the headache and not being able to see and the terror at imagining who or *what* might be waiting for me in that big house...

Yeah, I hid. Not ashamed to admit it.

Just as I'm about to swing my legs around and get out of bed, I catch sight of something on the bedside table next to me. I reach for the little packages that seem very familiar...

"Contacts!" I cry, squinting and seeing the prescription is mine. My heart flips around in my chest. It's a stupidly small thing, but I can't help how it makes my heart soar. He got me contacts.

Excited, I grab both boxes and race into the bathroom, barely stopping to tuck the towel back around myself that I donned after my shower. After washing my hands, I put the contacts in and sigh in relief as the world comes back into focus. The slight headache that steadily grew from the pointless efforts of straining to focus abates immediately.

There's a noise at the door, and Dimitri appears in the opening, looking down at his phone. He hasn't seen me, so I use his distracted state to stare openly. I... forgot what he looked like. I forgot how good he looked when I could see all of him, all at once, from more than five feet away and not hunched in a rocking boat, or blurry and out of focus.

My mouth goes a little dry at the sight of sweat beading on his face and upper arms. He's always buff, but he clearly just worked out and looks particularly swollen and veiny. When he kicks the door closed behind him, chills erupt over my body. He's wearing gray sweatpants. I can see the thick outline of his...

I gulp like a cartoon character. Damn, is that thing always on display like that?

He lifts the bottom of his shirt to wipe sweat from his face. I want to lick the rolls of his abs and feel out the divots with my tongue.

I hear myself make a helpless little noise. He drops the fabric and looks right up at me, like he knew exactly where I've been standing the whole time. Like his sweaty little pause was just for me, so I could look all I wanted.

His eyes drop, widening with interest and lingering, and I realize with a start that I'm still basically nude. I adjust the towel under my pits, face hot.

"Hello, Nicole."

Nee-cole.

I swallow, pressing my legs tighter together against a sudden, dull throbbing. "Hello, Dimitri. Thank you for the contacts," I say, gesturing to my face, like he wouldn't know where they go. *Yes, thank you for supplying me with what I need to ogle you.*

He just nods his acceptance of my thanks, so I breeze past it so it's not awkward. "Did you go back to my place?"

"No, it would not be safe to return to your apartment." He cocks his head, looking back and forth between my eyes like he can tell that he's in focus now. "Contacts are more easily obtained. You will receive a new pair of glasses later today."

I straighten in surprise. "What? You got me... You didn't have to do that."

He makes a face. "I am responsible for their loss, so I am also responsible for their replacement."

All I can do is duck my head and marvel at the reach required for someone to find my prescription without my authorization. Someone knows how to work around a system, or has unfathomable connections.

"Well, thanks. That was nice of you. You look like you came here to shower," I say, offering a casual-conversation olive branch.

"I did."

"You also look like you've been hit by a truck," I continue.

Black eyes are an unfortunate cosmetic side effect of a broken nose, and the purple of his bruises looks particularly dark against his pale skin.

"*Da*," he allows, a slight teasing edge to his tone. "A small, angry one with surprisingly good aim, even without glasses."

Well, he's clearly not still mad about the broken nose. That's good to know...

Wait.

"Small?" I repeat, snorting as I chew on my lower lip so he won't see my ridiculous smile. "I was almost six feet tall when I started high school. I've been getting things off the top shelf for people in the grocery store since I was in middle school. I've never been small. I'm not small."

"In an absolute sense, perhaps not. But you are smaller than me," he says, almost dismissively, totally ignorant of how being called small for the literal first time in my life is completely rocking my world.

He crosses the room towards the kitchenette and grabs a waiting shaker bottle, draining the protein in one shot. When he's done, he rinses the cup, speaking to me over his shoulder. "I am pleased you are awake and that you look well. I think perhaps my wound should be examined."

My eyes drop down to its approximate area on his torso, and I see that there's a strip of flesh still visible because his shirt didn't fall back all the way into place. My mouth goes dry. "You're probably right. If you want to take a shower and give it a gentle cleaning, I can come take a look when you're done."

"Good." He points. "In there is a closet. Feel free to select something to wear."

For some reason, that makes my cheeks heat. "Okay, thanks."

Like it is about half the time, his only answer is a nod, and then he disappears into the bathroom. I hear the water come on and then turn off five minutes later, barely enough time for me to snoop. Everything is neat, minimal, and organized, and my stomach does a flip as I think about how similarly we occupy our personal spaces. I've never needed or wanted a lot of stuff, and clearly, Dimitri is the same. Everything he owns is intentional, purposeful.

I wait a little bit to give him time to dry off and dress, then I knock.

"Come in."

When I enter the bathroom, our eyes meet in the mirror, and I can see that he's carefully patting the line of stitches dry with some sterile gauze.

Then I balk. My timing was off. He's still got a towel wrapped around his waist.

"Want me to come back?"

We both glance down at the terrycloth. It's knotted, and probably not going anywhere, but for some reason, having just a towel between us feels different, even though this is the same amount of skin that's been on display before. Pants are just so much more... solid.

He lifts a brow. "Does this make you uncomfortable, my med?"

"No, it's fine," I huff, peeved at the nickname, since the intentional use feels almost like he's mocking me.

I'm a *medical* professional. A nurse. I see naked bodies all the time.

He spins and leans against the counter while I grab tweezers and some gloves from the kit. I bend forward, wincing at the state of the inflamed skin.

"How does it look?"

"It was better before, obviously. How's the pain?"

"Not bad. Sore."

"It'll probably be another week or two until you're back to normal, but it doesn't look infected, so that's good. Sorry again about hitting it."

"Do not be sorry—you were defending yourself, and it is always smart to go for your opponent's weakest point. The only reason it has healed this well so far is because I have been in the care of a trained professional," he acknowledges, dipping his chin.

I turn my head, focusing down instead of reacting to the praise. "I'm going to take some of the stitches out and replace them with butterfly strips. But you're still... you're a little wet," I say, nodding at the water that clings to his smattering of chest hair. He reaches for another towel, and I hold out my hand for it. "I'll get it."

With a look that's all liquid heat, he slowly hands me the towel.

Do I have to do this? Nope. But I'm a woman possessed—mesmerized by the sight of his scarred, scary, powerful body. He goes still as I start gently patting him dry, starting around his collarbones where water has pooled in deep divots. His chest rises and falls, expanding under my hand. I feel my breath sync with his as I draw the towel down across his pecs, over the peaks and valleys created by muscle and scar tissue alike.

"Nicole," he says, and it's such a deep rasp that it scrapes against my spine and draws a wave of goosebumps across my arms and chest. The tingling settles around my nipples, which suddenly, desperately itch for a touch.

I bite my lip, but the motion tugs at the tender skin of my chin. It's an uncomfortable reminder, one that cuts through the sexual tension like dull scissors—slowly, incompletely.

Fuck.

This is not the time. He's got a gaping wound, and I'm covered in bruises.

We need a distraction. Both of us.

I clear my throat and set down the towel. "So... you spoke with your team? I assume you were discussing what happened and making a plan. Anything you care to share?"

"*Da.* I needed to ask you if Kyle said anything to you at the wedding that made you suspect what he had planned."

"No. I only remember... thinly veiled insults, bored answers to my questions, and him propositioning me. You already know how he stole my purse to make me chase him, presumably so he could corner me alone in the maze and kill me without witnesses..." I shiver.

"How did he seem? How was he acting?"

"Erratic. I was pretty sure he was on drugs. Something in his voice. And I could have sworn I saw blood on his shirt, even before I hit him with my shoe."

He nods, eyes darting around as he considers that.

I'm silent as I work on the wound, letting him wrap his brain around my lack of information and how it slots in with his plan. I nearly repeat my request for information when he speaks again.

"Normally, I would not share this with a civilian," he begins, making me tense. I'm not sure why being called a civilian feels so strange. Militant. "But you are inextricably involved. And I promised I would do what I could to prove that you could trust me. Honesty is important for this, *da*?"

"*Da*," I repeat, hiding a smile when his eyes flash.

"Our current problems revolve around this USB. Because we do not know what it contains, we do not know what kind of danger you are in."

"It could be nothing?" I ask, knowing that makes no sense. Kyle wouldn't have done what he did to me if it was nothing.

"More likely, it is very incriminating or valuable—this is my concern. We do not *know* who knows about what Kyle did, or who might be looking for you now, but we have logical assumptions. Kyle was part of a

Bratva family, one of a few that operate out of Ulysses. This USB belongs to them, and they will want it back."

Acid churns in my stomach as the unfairness of the situation starts settling in. It's suffocating, making my eyes sting. I pull back halfway through the act of applying a butterfly bandage so I can read his expression as I ask, "Then can't we give it back? Or, make it seem like someone else has it?"

The shake of his head is full of regret. "Even if we did, if they knew you had it for any amount of time, you are a loose end, and a *Bratva* does not leave those to unravel."

"And we can't go to the police," I guess, just like I did forever ago in that car as we fled the scene of so many crimes.

"No, Nicole—you understand why, *da*? It is likely that the Volkevich family is bribing or blackmailing someone high up in the police force. And even if they are not, the police will be looking for you as a missing person. And, by extension, me. The lives of my teammates, of anyone connected to us, and of any officer involved are also at risk now."

Fuck. Well, I made things a lot worse, didn't I?

"So… what? I have to leave Ulysses, right? It's a big country… I'm sure I could disappear. Everything I own is basically ready to go, already packed up and in a U-Haul."

The words sit heavy in the air, and I kind of wish I hadn't said them. Especially when he stiffens.

"If you want to leave, we can provide a new identity and teach you how to safeguard yourself. But it is not a good life to be alone and on the run. I am not speaking of days or months, but for the rest of your life. Could you start over as someone else? Never speak to your family or friends again? Could you kill to protect yourself?"

"I don't know," I whisper, sinking further into discomfort and fear with each rhetorical question. I hate feeling so helpless.

"Then let me help you." It's a grumbling kind of plea, settling deep around my bones. "Stay here with me. Wesley will install a camera at your rented home to alert us if anyone comes looking for you."

"Okay. Then what? You're going to make it safe for me to leave somehow?"

He nods. "We will find out what is on that USB, and we will make sure the Volkevich *Bratva* will not be a threat to you."

I narrow my eyes at him. He wants to help me. *Why?*

A small, scared part of me isn't ready to face the reality and paralyzing fear of knowing someone dangerous is after me, and I want to sink my nails into his offer for protection. But a much larger part of me is nervous and a little suspicious of it.

I stay here and he protects me, feeds me, clothes me, cleans up *my* mess for me after he saved me from becoming a victim of Kyle's evil plan... It's an odd sort of helplessness. It feels like being given a gift I can't hope to reciprocate. I'm not lucky or pretty or popular or special—no one just gives me things. I earn them. I rely on myself.

Is he making amends? He feels bad for kidnapping me, and he wants to make things right?

"How are you going to do that?"

His jaw works, and he captures my stare with one of icy determination. "However we must. They are bad men who have done many bad things, Nicole. They do not deserve to live or to be mourned."

Gulp. So it's part of the job he's working on, then. Relief mingles with an odd kind of pride that he's willing to literally kill people so I'll be safe, followed closely by guilt for feeling that way.

"You're sure we're safe here in the meantime?"

"There is no safer place," he assures me without a hint of hesitation.

It occurs to me suddenly that though this forthrightness is new—I'm more used to having to pry details from him—Dimitri has never lied to me. He doesn't mince words. He doesn't dress up the truth to make it better, even when it's unflattering. Lies of omission are one thing, and he obviously refuses to answer altogether sometimes, but when he bothers to say something, he says it with his whole chest. There's an easiness to that.

My stomach growls loudly, and I wince. His eyes fall to it, and he frowns a little, like it's his fault I'm hungry or something. "When you are ready, we will go get you breakfast, and I can introduce you to the others."

Worry worms low in my gut. *The others.* "How many people live here?"

"Three. Four, including me."

I nearly melt into a puddle of relief. That's not so bad. Though I'd probably be more nervous about meeting a trio of seasoned killers if I didn't have a big Russian bear at my back.

A big Russian bear who wants to show me that I can trust him. Who's going to do whatever it takes to keep me safe, to get me my life back.

Biting down on a smile, I finish taping around the bandage.

22

NICOLE

—◦—

A charming murderer

The handshake is firm, but warm and polite. "Nice to meet you, James."

"People who don't have giant Russian logs up their asses call me Mac."

Dimitri's brows come down. "It is how you first introduced yourself to me. And you, as Wesley."

The big guy with a model's face and golden retriever energy ignores Dimitri's explanation. "But I'll answer to anything—Jim, Mac, Mackenzie, Kenzo, sharpshooter, hey you—"

"Pretty boy," the other one—Wesley—pipes in.

"Right. Just don't call me late for dinner." He flashes me a grin that feels weird—unexpected, like something meant to put me at ease.

I roll my lips inward to keep my jaw from falling slack. My dad used to make that joke all the time.

"Anyway, would you give me a hand with a jump, D? Battery won't turn over; must have left a light on."

"*Da*, I will assist," Dimitri answers, though his attention is on me. I can tell he's watching for signs that I'm too uncomfortable to be left alone.

Before turning to leave, James reaches out and shakes my hand again. "Glad to meet you, Nicole. I'm a big fan of your work," he says with a cheeky grin and a meaningful glance at Dimitri's twin black eyes, so stark and purple against his pale skin.

I try not to balk or laugh, and I'm caught halfway between both reactions with a disbelieving snort. Wesley joins in with a low chuckle of his own, and my eyes cut over to him.

James may make terrible jokes, and Wesley may have kind of a hot nerd air about him, but I'm trying not to be fooled by it. I know they're all as dangerous as each other. Dimitri's team may lack the overtly sinister air he has, but they aren't regular Joes—I have to remember that.

I just... expected a group of men who "do bad things to bad people" to be more severe—serious, gruff guys who did things like pick their teeth with Bowie knives and show you their kill souvenirs just to watch the blood drain from your face. I didn't expect a heavily tattooed British junk food addict and a Southern boy who looks like he'd take being called earnest as a compliment. I wasn't prepared for how playful their dynamic would be.

"Go ahead." I shrug at Dimitri, feeling his eyes on me, still asking the question. I don't need a babysitter. He trusts his team—he wouldn't leave me if he didn't.

"I will not be gone long."

"I'll make sure she doesn't get too lonely," Wesley offers, winking suggestively at me.

Dimitri scowls at him, crossing his arms and letting the unvoiced threat hang in the air. After a few seconds, Wesley clears his throat awkwardly and holds up his hands in surrender. "I will keep my hands, eyes, and famously sharp wit to myself."

My lips twitch. He's a charming murderer, I'll give him that.

Dimitri closes the distance between us and presses a kiss to the top of my head. I freeze at the casual, open display of affection, and my heart lurches into my throat as my face fills with warmth. He did it so... easily. So intentionally. So... in front of Wesley, almost like staking a claim.

I have to clear my throat to pretend like I'm not filled with fizzy happiness as Dimitri disappears down the long hallway.

I know I'm free to explore the house—might as well start here. I step into what is obviously Wesley's office and look around.

There are parts of the room that feel original to the space, like the bookcases and comfy couch and desks pushed against the walls, but then there are a dozen boxes of various sizes and shapes, blinking and whirring like some kind of alien technology. I know they're all doing something because this room is warmer than anywhere else, and it smells like the ozone off-gassing of massive electricity consumption.

It's enough hardware to give any computer nerd a boner. He's got two curved monitors, and even his keyboard is wild—one of those RGB-lit ergonomic split boards where you have to know the exact location of every letter to be efficient. I'm more of an internet-and-spreadsheets kind of gal, but I still thought I understood all the variations of what a computer could look like. Apparently not.

True to his word, Wesley's not even looking at me, hunched over and focused on his screen.

"So, you're the tech guy, huh?" I ask.

He glances up and gives me a crooked smirk. "That's what they tell me." He shoves another salt and vinegar chip into his mouth and washes it down with his energy drink. I see a recycling bin full to the brim with empty cans by the window behind him.

Huh. A charming, environmentally conscientious murderer.

When my perusal of the room ends with me in a spot where I can see his screen, I can't stop myself from taking an interested glance.

Then I do a double take.

"Is that the coroner's report from Kyle's death?" I ask, squinting at the small typeface and messy handwriting that's as bad as any doctor's scrawl I've ever had the misfortune of trying to translate. But I can make out the name at the top, and I recognize the face from the picture attached, even pasty in death as it is.

"Erm... yes." Like I saw something I wasn't supposed to, he reaches up and tilts the screen away with a careful expression. Maybe he's concerned I'm going to be squeamish about seeing a dead body.

"It's weird that..." I trail off as I realize what I was about to do. I don't think professional assassins would thank me for getting involved in their business. "Never mind."

He pauses, looking at me with brows lifted in surprise. "That's right, you're a nurse. You've seen coroner's reports before, I take it?"

I nod hesitantly.

"Is there something off about this one? Have another look," Wesley encourages, tilting the screen back towards me.

"Well..." I glance at the door. I wish Dimitri were here, bolstering me. Not because I'm particularly unnerved by Wesley, but because I feel like I'm about to cross some kind of line, and I'm more used to interpreting Dimitri's facial expressions. He'd stop me if I were.

Oh well. I sigh and point to the cause of death. "'Stab wound to abdomen'?"

"That's what I thought it said," he nods his agreement. "Either that or... *stud wood a achoo*, but that didn't seem right."

I blow out an amused breath through my nose. "It's just... strange. I suppose that whoever filled this out might be new, though usually the new ones have much better handwriting."

"What makes you say that?"

"It's not the stab wound that kills you—not exactly. It's blood loss or sepsis or shock or damage to an organ, or something else. The stab wound is the cause of the condition that causes death. Most coroner's reports I've seen are more specific about that."

"Hmm. Do you see any other mistakes?"

I narrow my eyes, lean forward, and scan the document. "No."

"Then, perhaps this was a slip-up, or intentionally vague in case anyone checked."

I shrug, feeling in no way qualified enough to make that assessment—especially since I don't know what the implications are.

The look he's giving me is so strange that it makes me take a step back. "Huh," he eventually huffs again, turning back to the computer with a faint, uncertain smile on his lips. "Good catch, Nicole. Cheers."

And that's my cue.

Well, that and a rumbling stomach. There's an incredible smell coming from somewhere, and it's making my mouth water.

Exploring the first floor is an exercise in trying not to fall over because I'm craning my neck so hard to see everything at once. I knew the house was big from how long it took my eyes to scan the back of the building when we stepped outside of the pool house, but it was almost deceptive. Inside, it's somehow bigger.

The ceilings are high, the rooms are large, and the hallways are long. I feel like I'm in some kind of weird, modernist museum curated by someone with boring taste—artwork that's, like, a circle and a line on a canvas; that sort of thing. I know it's expensive, but art is subjective, and I don't like this style at all.

All the cavernous spaces in the house appear to make sound carry well because I can hear two people squabbling. I follow the sound down the hallway towards the kitchen, and I can immediately identify a voice.

"Yes, I am. I am throwing it all away." Dimitri's tone is clipped, angry.

Gee, and I thought I was the only one who got to see his prickly, domineering side.

A flash of something—definitely not jealousy—makes me swallow reflexively when I see that he's arguing with a woman.

"—or you could try not eating something unmarked in the fridge just to see what it tastes like!" she snaps back, hands on hips.

"I told you to label things!"

"And I told you not to eat my yogurt, so sounds like we're both out of luck."

"What did he eat?" I ask, stepping into the soft lighting from a multitude of recessed fixtures.

They both react to my voice, Dimitri spinning all the way around, and the woman he's towering over tilting her head to the side to see around him.

She's pretty—taller than average for a woman, with long legs. She's got gorgeous dark hair, running halfway down her back in waves, and a severe line of bangs that cut her round face in half. Her cheeks are somewhat red from shouting, but she stands up to Dimitri's ire—despite being a full foot shorter—without fear, like they're brother and sister. Or lovers.

She doesn't sound Russian to me, so it's probably the latter. A pang in my stomach has me looking away to regroup. Well, that's... unfortunate.

Maybe I'm not the only girl he wants to ruin. Kind of felt like it was implied.

"Sourdough starter," she replies, picking the jar up from the counter and making a face as she removes the spoon he must have used.

"I thought it was yogurt," he says, spitting into the sink.

The jar has clear walls, so I can see the off-white color. It does kind of look like yogurt, except for the bubbles. I know it can't be too bad since—judging from the name—it goes into sourdough bread, which is edible. But I can't help slipping back into my Nurse Nicole skin.

"What's in that?"

"Well, it's wild yeast growing in raw flour, so it's not the best thing for him to eat, but he'll probably live. Unfortunately," she snipes, and he glares back. "You know, I've been keeping the Yeastie Boys alive for nine years. If you got your mouth germs in it and it grows mold and dies, I'm going to be so pissed at you."

"'Mouth germs'?" he shoots back, sneering.

"'Yeastie Boys'?" I repeat with a faint smile.

Damn it. Now I kind of like her.

She shakes her head and turns back around to the stove, which, I now realize, is actively cooking something. I'm staring, I know, but I'm just so thrown off to find someone who looks so much like... well, like me. She's a big girl—thick, like me. Not as tall as me, but hardly any women I come across are. She's sturdy in a way that makes me feel a kinship to her.

"Nicole, I am going to speak with Wesley for a moment. You will be all right here with Eleanor for—what is that?" he cries in disgust, leaning over her shoulder, where she's stirring something in a cast-iron skillet full of oil. "I said no fried food!"

"They're just a garnish; you don't have to use them," she replies, her tone bored with exaggerated patience. Then she turns back to me and stage-whispers, "He's going to use them."

This time, I don't even try not to smile. After how weird everything has been—meeting James and Wesley, and casually discussing completely insane things like incriminating USB drives and Russian mafia men and coroner's reports and murder—her casually friendly air feels out of place, but in a very welcome way.

With a noise of frustration, Dimitri returns his attention to me. His hard expression doesn't shift. "I will be back."

As he strides away, my stomach lets out an embarrassingly audible growl, and I glance at the woman to see if she noticed.

But she's busy rolling her eyes at Dimitri. "You must be Nicole. I'm Eleanor, Mac's... uh, fiancée. Oh, wow, that's fun to say." She extends her hand to me with a huge smile.

The title shocks me even more than her easygoing demeanor. My eyes flick down to her other hand as we shake and—sure enough—she's got one of those silicone bands around her ring finger that some of my coworkers wear when they don't want to damage their real rings or have the diamonds catch on the latex gloves we put on and take off dozens of times a day.

She's engaged to one of these guys? But she seems so... normal. I let my hand fall with the silence that settles around us, and glance behind her at the pans on the fire. "So you're, like, the cook?" I ask, then I wince because I didn't mean for it to come out sounding so snooty.

But she just smiles brightly. "Mhm. Are you hungry?"

"I am, but I'm a vegetarian," I admit with a bit of regret. I'm just as sure that whatever she's making smells divine as I am that it used to moo. Not that I don't make concessions when I have to—like on a carnivore's houseboat with no other options—but now that I have the luxury of choice back, I'm eager to get back to my normal diet.

"What?" she gasps, turning accusatory eyes on the door where Dimitri exited. "He didn't tell me that when he asked me to make you a sandwich!"

Suddenly, I'm not even a little bit surprised that she's the one who made it for me. It was too good to have been made by someone who seemed just fine with chalky protein bars and pepper-flavored desiccated cow meat. "He didn't know..." I trail off, self-conscious about defending him against this woman who clearly knows him so well. "It's not for religious reasons or anything, just a preference. It started as a texture thing, and then it became a habit."

"Of course. Have a seat. I'll make you a plate and we can chat!" She turns back to the stove, carefully lifting the fried shallots out of the oil with a slotted spoon.

When I say nothing, she continues to fill the silence with her disarming, lighthearted rambling. "Sorry if that came off weird and eager, I'm just drowning in a sea of testosterone, here. I can't wait to talk to someone who isn't going to scratch his balls or pull out a gun to clean it in the middle of a conversation."

I snort, shake my head at how strange my life has become, then turn to take in my surroundings as I move towards the seat she indicated. I look around the room, at the small mess on the island counter, the chairs askew around the dining table, and the pans in the sink. It's clear that despite the grandeur, regular people live here—there's something comforting about that.

My gaze drifts out to the rolling grass visible through the wall of windows. At least it's a nice place to be holed up with mafia men after you.

"Do you eat eggs? Dairy?"

"Yeah." I slide into the seat at the literal-island-sized marble kitchen island so I can watch her cook.

"Hope an omelet is okay. I'll add some meatless protein to our next grocery order, since I guess you might be staying a while."

The thought of someone making me food and going out of her way to make concessions to my dietary restrictions makes me uncomfortable. She doesn't owe me anything. Why would she do that? It feels almost calculated, like her friendliness is supposed to help lower my guard.

Especially when she says, "So you saw Dimitri kill a guy, huh? We should start a club."

Maybe it's the acknowledgement of the elephant in the room, but I'm so shocked I can't speak for several seconds. "He told you that? What else do you know?"

When she replies, her head is in the fridge, so it's muffled at first. "Um... Mac told me. He said there might be some pretty nasty people after you. Something about a USB?" The door closes with a soft snick, and she emerges with several eggs, some half and half, and a block of cheese in her hands.

"I guess that's the gist of my story. I don't really feel like getting into any of the details. It's too... raw."

She sets the things in her arms on the counter, then shoots me a conciliatory look as she cracks eggs into a bowl. "I get that."

"What's your story? Not to be rude, but you seem like a fairly normal person. How is it that you're engaged to a..."

Her eyes snap up to meet mine, and the whisk in her hand stills. "Dangerous man?" she supplies, with a smile that falls short of her eyes. "I'll save you the whole saga, but our stories have similar beginnings—wrong place, wrong time. I was minding my own damn business, and I caught Mac in my apartment with a sniper rifle one night. It all kind of spiraled from there."

It's not what I was expecting her to say, and it's a kick to the stomach. "So, you know how this feels?"

"Yeah, I do." Her voice is so kind, it actually hurts.

"How did you... I mean, you seem very well-adjusted. How did you—"

"Cope?"

"Yeah." My eyes prickle, and I sniff once and look down.

I feel like I've been treading water with weights on my feet. Being able to talk to someone who understands is a comfort I didn't dare let myself hope for, and now that I don't have to just suppress everything, it's dredging up a lot of unpleasant emotions.

She considers it, lifting the back of her hand to brush her bangs out of her eyes. "Well, I definitely spent a lot of time feeling pretty sorry for myself and being mad at Mac for dragging me into all this."

Check and check.

"But eventually I realized that being mad at the person who was actually on my side was kind of silly. He didn't *mean* to involve me, and I definitely wouldn't have gotten through it without him. He helped me find perspective and a strength I didn't see in myself before." She stops, then rolls her eyes. "God, that was so fucking precious. Sorry, I'm prone to serious mushiness. I just... love him, ya know? And Wes and Dimitri, too. They're like my family now."

She chops vegetables, and I watch her silently for a moment, digesting that. "You seem very close with Dimitri."

"More like... he accepts my place here, and I know what lines not to cross. And getting to this point took some time. He's so... um..." She cranes her neck to check for the subject of her gossip, then lowers her voice, "big and mean-looking. But now I think sometimes he's intimidated by *me*," she says, and she looks so pleased with herself that it takes me aback.

I can't remember ever wanting someone to be intimidated by me—it's a word that's been used against me in the past, and never meant as a compliment.

She continues, sliding chopped spinach into a bowl and starting on a pepper. "I also realized he's not really mean; he's just not polite. Does that make sense? He is who he is; he's not going to cater to your feelings. Sometimes he's a giant asshole about it, but it's kind of grown on me."

I nod. That's similar to observations I've made before, and I'm oddly pleased that her assessment agrees with mine.

"But he never really forgave me for taking over the cooking. So, sometimes I give him things to object to so he feels like he contributed." She gestures to the paper towel with fried shallots. "Like I would do with my niece and nephew. 'I don't like peas,'" she mimics the high-pitched tone of a child.

"Wait, you're here and you're with one of them—like, *with* him—and you have a family?"

"Most people have families," she points out with a small smile.

"I meant..."

"I know what you mean," she says, letting me off the hook. "Yes, I have a family. Yes, I worry about them a lot more than I used to before I got involved with Mac. It doesn't change the fact that Mac is the best thing that's ever happened to me, and I wouldn't change my life with him for anything. In case you're considering getting involved with Dimitri," she adds.

I decide to ignore the implications of her sly look.

"Oh, hey, before I forget—he asked me to help get you some shoes. Ya know, before he had a temper tantrum and stormed off."

"Oh, right. Yeah, I guess it's not an option to go back to my place for a little bit." Which is a shame, considering it would be pretty easy to just drive the U-Haul here.

"Been there," she commiserates.

"You wouldn't happen to be a size 12?" I lift my brows, and she shakes her head. Tall girl problems.

"No, but I have an internet connection."

"Okay. I don't have a way to pay you back right now, but as soon as I can, I will."

She cocks her head at me, then digs into her pocket and tosses a heavy plastic rectangle onto the counter between us. It skips across the marble, landing right in front of me. "He gave me his credit card."

"He... what?"

He wants to buy me stuff? Well, he wants me to pick it out, but he wants to pay for it. My heart pounds a little harder in my chest. That's... nice. No, it's too much. Is it? My poor, stupid, emotional little heart latches onto the act, like it's proof that he wants to take care of me.

Her eyes drop meaningfully to the too-tight t-shirt and pants that are pretty clearly his. "Yup. He only specifically said shoes, though. Can't imagine why he'd fail to mention the rest of the clothes you need," she says, like she very much can.

At that, I think I actually do feel my cheeks heat.

"Okay. I say you eat this fabulous omelet, and I go get my phone, then we spend a bunch of Dimitri's money, pop some corn, and watch a Japanese horror movie that Wes downloaded for me. They're super weird; you're either gonna love it or hate it. What do you say?"

Sounds like I have a new friend and much-needed ally.

23

DIMITRI

Of course you're serious; you're always serious.

After days of healing, Nicole finally permits me to return to a course of weightlifting.

The gym is what convinced me to live in this house with my team, instead of moving between motel rooms and safe houses as I had for years. I am calmed by the scent of rubber and iron, and the sight of organized, clean rows of weights and machines. It is a large room, full of equipment I do not use. I am "old school" according to James because I prefer to use the Olympic-style weights. But I did not get strong with guided movements from ropes and pulleys. I got strong by lifting heavy things and putting them down. Repeatedly.

The wound on my side pulls as I complete my final set of six chest presses at 320 with the barbell. Anything over 300 pounds does push my limit, especially when healing, but I am recovering well, and I *need* to push myself. I have been trying to keep myself physically exhausted, since there is very little we can do about our Volkevich issue until the flash drive is cracked. In theory, if I spend my energy here, it will help me control myself when I am around her.

But it is just a theory. In practice, managing my desire has proved to be... difficult.

I do not know how James does it—he controls his urges well enough around all of us. He does not embarrass himself or walk around with an erection, like an untried teenage boy.

Perhaps that is because he is getting true relief with a partner.

I have painted the walls of the shower enough times, but it is a temporary respite, only enough to take the edge off for a little while. An empty orgasm is not what my body truly wants, especially as I lay near her every night, breathing in her scent and filling my hands with her.

I grit my teeth and refocus my attention on the weight hovering above my nose. 10 minutes later, with a final, forceful exhale, I rack the barbell. Sweat pours down my face as I sit back up on the bench and reach for the towel and water bottle on the floor.

There is a shuffling noise over by the doorway, and Wesley strides in for a workout, dressed in loose sweats and a sleeveless shirt, his head down and attention buried in his cell phone. His headphones are on, though only one is covering his ear.

He shoots me a friendly smile as he crosses over to the bench, and I pull my sweatshirt on. "All done over here?" he asks, gesturing to the bench and barbell.

"Yes, let me remove the weight—"

"That's all right, mate, I'll rack it up... Jesus, 320? I would have been your spot."

"You were busy," I say dismissively. In truth, I had not checked if he was free.

He cocks his head at me, and his eyes drop to my waist. "Guess this means you're all healed up, then? Can't imagine our nurse would've cleared you for lifting heavy otherwise."

Our? I suddenly need to clench my fists to keep my arms at my sides, as the urge to strike at Wesley's face rises and falls like a wave through me. "Well enough to begin assisting James with his surveillance duties tonight."

After James located the Volkevich base of operations, the routine of Viktor Volkevich was a simple thing to chart. If we wanted to kill him, James could easily have managed by now with a single shot between the eyes. Viktor is complacent. Careless. So far from the men who call themselves *Pakhan* in my home country.

Wesley pockets the clips from the barbell and slides off one of the circular plates. I do the same on the opposite side to assist. "You're taking nights? How'd he rope you into that one?"

It is no secret that I maintain a rigorous personal routine. It is not just a meticulous course of diet and exercise, but also a regimented sleep schedule. I prefer not to stray from my routine.

In this matter, however, there are many reasons I agreed to assist at night. For one, I am making amends to my team for the critical mistakes I made at the wedding. For another... my will is proving to be much weaker than I expected, and I worry that another night spent next to Nicole will be the final test of it.

She never even fought me about sharing a bed, though every night she constructs a wall of pillows between us that end up on the floor as soon as I join her. I know she still suffers from nightmares from the trauma she endured, but she always calms in my arms.

"I am not made of snow or ice—I will not melt or break from a change in my environment. I can make adjustments to my schedule."

"There was a time I would have argued the *made of ice* point," he chuckles, but it becomes hollow as it echoes around us.

I give my brow a final mop with the towel before tossing it into the hamper by the door of the gym and reach for my water bottle. "Any updates?"

"A few. No word from Felix—I'm assuming he's in the wind, now—and no movement at Nicole's place."

"If they have not gone looking for the USB there, either they know she has not been back, or they do not know she has it."

"Difficult to say which is more likely. I've got an alert up for her picture in the usual online places, in case they hire someone to find her."

I shake my head. "It is not *Bratva* style to hire out that kind of work. Or any, really. That is what soldiers and enforcers are for."

He nods tersely, and I understand his frustration. It is easy for him to find things online, but not everything leaves a digital footprint. And when something does not, he is rendered ineffective.

"I'll keep the alert up, just in case."

"What else?" I ask, sensing he has more to update me on.

"Well, turns out Kyle might actually be alive."

I nearly spit out the water I had just sipped. "You are just saying this now? Why was it not your first statement?"

"I don't know for certain yet," he says carefully, sliding 20-pound plates where my 50s were and replacing the clips to keep them in position on the bar. "Something Nicole said made me look into it, and I finally found something interesting in my digging. Seems the coroner who signed the report is receiving sporadic payments from more than just the county—Kyle might have bought a false report and faked his death."

"Nicole caught this?" I ask, chest swelling with pride.

He nods. "Haven't traced the transactions back all the way, but some of my best spiders are on it. I've also been combing his past reports for more mistakes like the one she spotted to see if there's a pattern to help us determine whose thumb he's under."

Wesley's spiders—his army of anonymous amateur sleuths—have helped us countless times in the past. If he says they can help us find out if Kyle is alive, I believe that.

I move over to stand behind him as he lies down on the bench. I keep a hand poised under the middle of the bar, a safety net for any uncontrolled movements. It is 220 pounds, very respectable. And I note, well above where he began his training last year. "If Kyle is alive, it will change the situation with Nicole drastically," I observe, pleased that I kept her close. "Where are you with the password on the drive?"

I am not a man who can do two things at once effectively. Wesley proves he is. With a grunt, he lifts the bar off its perch and presses it up and down as he continues our conversation effortlessly. "You know I can't answer that. Could take an hour, could take a month. Depends on the complexity."

Though sometimes it is frustrating, I appreciate his unwillingness to speak decisively without proof. I am learning to do the same, though I still leap ahead of the truth occasionally.

I observe the rest of his set, waiting until he finishes the last rep to speak. "Have you shared your suspicions about Kyle with James?"

"I haven't seen him yet today. When he's not on surveillance, he's with Eleanor. They barely come up for air now, since they got engaged."

"They are loud," I agree. "And energetic."

He makes a commiserative expression with his face that might also be a grimace under the strain as he begins a new set. "Is that why you moved to the pool house?"

I moved because after so long living alone, I found it difficult to share a living space.

Not that I seem to have that issue with Nicole. It does not bother me, even when she misses the hamper with her socks and does not wipe the sink after brushing her teeth.

"I enjoy the privacy. Sometimes when they believed no one would hear, they began their sex games before they reached the top of the stairs."

"Is that jealousy I detect, big guy?" he grits out through his teeth, straining under the weight.

I roll my eyes. All these nicknames. More common from James, but Wesley also occasionally decides not to use my real name. I dislike this practice almost as much as I dislike the monikers they have chosen for me. Bear, Big Guy, Beast... they evoke an image of a giant, lumbering unskillfully through the world. I do not need to be constantly reminded of my size.

"I would have thought that you and Nicole—"

"One more," I instruct, seeing that he handles a set of five with enough ease. When he finishes that one, I have him complete one more.

"This is why…" he grunts, completing the final push to get the barbell back onto the rack to rest, "I hate when you're my spot."

"This is why you have put on 30 pounds of muscle since we have been training together," I counter, hitting the top of his shoulder with the back of my hand. "This and nutritional improvements."

He smiles and lays the towel over the back of his neck as he sits up for a rest between sets. "Right," he says, shaking his head.

"Would you like me to stay while you complete your routine?" I ask.

"I'm fine here. I'll text you any updates, as usual."

Scents of the morning waft around me as I cross through the kitchen—coffee, bacon, various perfumes from multiple people having showered using different products. The house is awake. I acknowledge Eleanor as I move to the coffee machine, though my mind is elsewhere.

Armed with a coffee for Nicole, I enter the pool house, and my eyes automatically scan the room for her. I begin at the bed and sweep across until I find her seated in the oversized chair, studying a new article of clothing with a critical eye. Her smile of greeting is enough to put all other thoughts from my mind.

I go to her, hold out the coffee, and drop a kiss onto the top of her head. "Good morning, my *med*."

Her small, sharp inhale brings with it a rush of satisfaction and fresh hunger. "Good morning." She gazes up at me with a tentative expectation that she hides behind a blank expression, as if she is not affected. A pretty act to save face. I know she is aching, just as I am.

Over the past week, I have been trying to do small things to help acclimate her to my touch. She reacts with surprise and delight every time, and it warms my cold soul to see her eager and willing for me. I do not want her to think that my distance means more than what I told her it does—that I am trying to earn her forgiveness and deserve her trust. She will be mine, but she will come to me with no fear between us, and I will not have to hold back in any way.

She takes a sip, hiding a smile behind the rim of the mug. "This has oat milk?" she asks, eyes round. "You... know how I take my coffee?"

I know many more things than that. I know what time she rises in the morning. I know she will not sleep in socks, but keeps a pair close to the bed so she can put them on before traversing the cold tile floor. I know she chews her lower lip when she is concerned. I know how she carefully detangles her curls with her fingers in the shower instead of using combs or brushes. I know she gets along well with Eleanor and the others. I know she does not like the television, but listens to the news. I know she has a small scar on her thumb, just underneath the nail. I know that when her heart races, her pulse is visible in a thrumming vein on the right side of her neck.

I know. I watch. I gather the details greedily and hold them close.

"*Da*. Though I do not understand why it is called a milk. Is it not extracted, more like a juice?"

"Oat juice? Yum," she laughs and takes a sip. "Thank you for noticing and making it how I like."

It seems a small thing to do, but her enjoyment of it warms me. I nod.

Her smile is private, but her eyes feel hot as she sweeps her golden gaze across my body. "So how many times a day do you work out?" she asks, eyeing a particularly veiny section of my forearm.

Unable to help myself, I flex a little, relishing in her grin widening. "As many times as I want," I shrug, heading to the small refrigerator tucked under the kitchenette counter. I pull out a protein drink and begin shaking it vigorously. "I find it difficult to be idle."

"That doesn't surprise me," she observes quietly. "I'm the same."

"And what will you do today?"

Her eyes cut to the bags and boxes piled haphazardly on the couch. "Well, I haven't finished trying on all the new stuff I ordered because I was overwhelmed. I got a bit... carried away." She cringes. "You're sure it's okay that I—"

"Of course," I cut in. "I told you. Buy whatever pleases you—that card has no limit."

My offer is genuine, though I initially harbored some irritation. When I told Eleanor that I wanted Nicole to have some shoes, I thought she would continue to wear *my* pants and shirts. I got over it very quickly when I saw her wearing something skin-tight and made of spandex that gave me a view of so much of her strong legs. Then I insisted she order more.

The laughter that spills from her mouth is startled. "Seriously? Of course you're serious; you're always serious. I mean, no limit at all? What if it pleases me to buy myself expensive jewelry?"

"I do not suspect that you wear much jewelry," I observe calmly, recalling her bare neck the night of the wedding. Her ears are not pierced.

I wonder if she would wear a ring...

I have to clear my throat to continue, "But if you want it, buy it."

When I turn to face her, shaking my drink, her expression is not alight with excitement as another woman's might be at the idea of freedom with a credit card that is not their own. Nicole studies me with a pensive look. "Right. Mansion, garage full of cars, a closet stacked with bespoke suits..."

"Da," I say carefully, trying to assess if her tone holds any reproach. James once confessed to me that the fact that our money is so dirty was a cause for concern to Eleanor. But judging from her shrug, it does not seem to bother Nicole very much.

"Right, okay. Well, thank you, but I think I've got enough stuff for now. So, after I finish trying on all of this, I figure I might as well embrace the vacation mindset. Eleanor and I are going to do a streaming workout class and use the sauna—so cool—then we're going to have brunch, and she wanted help taste-testing new recipes."

"A hardship," I tease.

She grins. "I know. I'm really taking one for the team on that," she chuckles. I love the sound of her laughter. "And then I thought I'd explore that giant library a bit. How many of the books are real, do you think?"

"All of them," I reply confidently.

That takes her aback. "Really? Even the ones at the very top? I figured at least some of them were faux to fill the space. Do you do much reading here?"

"Yes, I like to read."

"Back when we were... um, back on the boat," she corrects, dropping her eyes to her hands. For a second, thick golden spirals of coarse hair fall into her face, obscuring it. Then she looks back up, shaking them away, and her eyes blaze with memory and resolve. Whenever her time on the boat comes up, it is always like this.

It is a breathtaking thing to witness her grapple with her lingering unpleasant emotions and intentionally push them away so she can move past the experience. So *we* can.

She honors me with that—it is a gift I plan to spend our lives repaying.

"There was only that one book in English," she finishes.

I nod. "*Anna Karenina*. It is the book that helped me learn English years ago."

Surprisingly, she smiles—not in jest, or in an attempt to mock, but in true astonishment. "Really? That's so impressive. And it explains the occasionally archaic vocabulary."

"Did you finish it?"

"I got about halfway."

"You did not like it," I guess, based on her tone and the slight curl of her lip. "Many people do not; it is bleak, like a Russian winter. Still, it is one of my favorites."

"*Anna Karenina* is your favorite?" she repeats, brows shooting up. "It's so..."

"Poignant? Thought-provoking? Classic?"

"Russian," she finishes with a laugh.

"True enough," I allow, feeling my own smile tugging at the corners of my mouth. "Though I would hope that simply being Russian is not a cause for dismissal."

She hears the drop in my tone, and her body reacts instantly to the implied meaning of my words. I watch as her nipples harden through the brightly colored spandex, and I upgrade my earlier approval of her new clothes. There is a strip of flesh above her waist visible to me that is a few shades paler than the rest of her skin. It makes me want to peel off all her coverings to find all her tan lines and trace them with my tongue.

"Definitely not," she says, and her eyes drag down the length of my shirt, which suddenly feels too constricting. "I can think of several admirable Russian traits. Your people are... proud, resilient, and have a dry, dark sense of humor."

"Hmm," I muse, watching her chew on her bottom lip. "Then you must have a little Russian in you."

"Oh, fuck off," she cries, turning away and shaking her head at me.

I frown, taken aback by this abrupt change in tone. Perhaps I should not be surprised, since I often make errors in my speech. But when it is with James or Wesley, I never let it concern me very much. "What did I say?" I ask.

She must see that my confusion is genuine, because her smile shifts. "Sorry. I thought you were going to... Sorry. It's just that that's the beginning of a particularly bad sexual innuendo."

"What is?"

"It's like, 'Do you have a little Russian in you? No? Do you want some?' or something like that."

"I do not... oh," I say as understanding dawns. Then, I blow out a breath through my nose in amusement. "I would never say this. My cock is not little."

There is a choked, surprised sound, then she laughs. She flushes a charming shade of dark red, covers her eyes with her hands, and groans. "That one's on me—I dug the hole and jumped right in."

The sound of her laughter wraps around my chest and squeezes. My eyes follow her as she crosses over to the couch and grabs one of the plastic-film bags with something black inside. Giving it a tug, she pulls it apart easily and assesses the pants that unroll in her hands. She glances up when she senses that I am watching.

"This was too generous, I think," she mutters, voice low.

I was caught up memorizing the shape of her body and the curve of her ass when she bent over the couch, so it takes me a few seconds to respond. "It is common in my country for a man to show his respect by dressing his woman and giving her gifts."

I expect a minor rebuff for my statement, but instead her eyes become hazy and her nipples harden against her bra once more. "Well, I suppose if it's a custom from another culture, it would be poor form not to accept," she says, swallowing.

Our eyes catch and we remain locked like that, staring, until she breaks first and adjusts her hold on the new pants in a way that presses her breasts together and emphasizes the deep line of her cleavage.

Vixen. She knows what she does.

I need to leave before the sexual tension becomes so heavy that I fold under it.

But I do not. Because I cannot. Instead, I search for more to say—to keep her engaged and focused on me. I love the feeling of her honey gaze.

"I am pleased that you are filling your days. I have been concerned that you might be bored here, or perhaps homesick," I add, though I regret the words as I speak them. If she is, I do not wish to call attention to it, and if she is not, I do not wish to remind her that she could be.

"Can't be homesick for a place you never called home," she counters with a tight smile. "And as for being bored, no. I admit I miss my phone and the mindless scroll occasionally, but I realized yesterday that this is the first time I've taken a vacation where I wasn't being tugged back into work a hundred times—helping a coworker, answering a question about paperwork, stupid small things that add up and make you feel like you never got all the way away from it. Not being reachable isn't something I've ever let myself be—it's almost peaceful.

"Of course, it would be more relaxing if I didn't have the Russian mafia after me and I weren't a missing person. Speaking of which, has there been any change to my case?"

"The police discovered your glasses at the marina, but the boat was lost to them as evidence. They are following the false trail Wesley created."

She chews on her bottom lip. "How long will that hold them off? Long enough for me to, ya know, get back to my normal life?"

Something twists in my chest, making my breath expel all at once. This happens every time she brings up leaving. "I cannot say, but my promise remains unchanged. Once we crack the drive, we will discuss your return. The police are an unfortunate complication, but I am confident we can find a way to deal with them."

She nods, then so do I.

"I am going to take a shower."

"Okay. And Dimitri? Thank you. Again."

"The clothing is nothing, Nicole. I do not require your gratitude."

"No, I mean..." she blows out a breath. "Well, yeah, the clothes, but I meant for everything. I know I wasn't exactly thrilled to be here at first, but Eleanor's been explaining how it all works to me, and I know that what you're doing is keeping me safe. Alive. So... thank you."

I do not want her thanks for this; I would rather she understand that the alternative is unacceptable.

I stoop to pick up a towel from the ground to include in the laundry, then turn in time to see her eyes lingering on my ass, full of fire and longing. Heat slams through me, chasing out the uncertainty and listlessness. I have been giving her space. I no longer wish to.

"There is another way you can thank me, my *med*," I rasp. "A kiss."

Her eyes widen. I watch her lips part as her eyes dart back and forth between mine.

It takes only three large strides to cross the room. Her head comes up as I prowl into her space, the top of her forehead level with my mouth. Still holding the pants, her arms are caught between us as I wrap mine all the way around her. She becomes loose in my grip.

How I crave her pliant response, her softness, her eager passion.

Moving slowly, I watch her watch me coming. Her eyes are locked on my lips, with a rawness and hunger to them. The way my woman looks at me... fuck. It unravels me.

Her own lips part in anticipation. Something soft hits my foot, and I realize she has dropped the pants she was holding so she can clutch at my sides. I brush my lips against hers, reveling in the whispering exhale against my mouth. I am gentler than I want to be, pressing a soft, brushing kiss to her open, willing, waiting mouth, and pulling away before either of us gets the chance to get lost in it.

Blood pounds in my ears, and my body strains for her. But when she does not reach for me to pull me back, I slide a hand into her hair and angle her head down so I can press my lips more firmly against her forehead before releasing her.

She is not quite ready. She must come to me. Because when I finally take her, I want it to feel like a victory for both of us.

24

NICOLE

*What self-respecting woman asks a man to ruin
her?*

This feels appropriately circular.

I'm sitting alone on a cold bench overlooking a manicured property, shivering in a thin dress, staring up at the moon, waiting for a tall, dark stranger to find me. Last time, I didn't know I was waiting for Dimitri. Now, my hands are clasped tightly in my lap, and every large shadow in my periphery draws my attention.

There are other differences, of course. This bench is wood; that one was stone. It's not the same dress; now I'm wearing a silky nightgown that was calling my name from the sale page where I did most of my shopping. He bought it for me, but he hasn't seen it yet. And it's not the same moon—it's in a different phase of its cycle now.

But there's only one reason I'd be freezing my tits off in a skimpy nightgown.

It's a gesture. One I hope he takes as the seduction attempt it is.

I've never tried to seduce anyone before, and turns out I'm pretty bad at it. In my defense, it's *mortifying* trying to seduce someone. And logistically hard, too, since it feels like we've been on opposite schedules for over a week now. Every day I wake up in the bed alone with nothing but a warm memory of him holding me that feels more like a dream. I know he moves my pillow wall, and I stopped caring ages ago. When he holds me, I don't have the nightmares.

So every night I go to sleep, hoping I'll work up the courage to say something the next day. I've almost told him a dozen times that I'm ready for whatever he wants to do to me. I'm more than ready—I need it. I might even say it exactly that way, desperate wording and all.

But what self-respecting woman *asks* a man to ruin her?

I racked my brain to find a way to *show* him. I came up with and immediately discarded a handful of bad ideas—waiting for him on my knees, letting him hear me masturbate in the shower, going to bed naked, grinding back on him when he curls himself around me in the wee hours of the morning, "accidentally" brushing against that fat cock after his shower or before he changes out of workout clothes...

I mean, I know he wants me. There's been no shortage of yearning in this pool house; I feel like I'm living in a damn Hozier song. I know this frustrating delay has nothing to do with a lack of desire. He's down bad. It's honestly exhilarating.

And for my part, I'm going out of my mind. I want him so badly it hurts sometimes—I'm constantly fantasizing and making myself wet, constantly clenching so hard it makes my inner thighs ache. My poor clit is sore, and my fingers just aren't doing it for me anymore. I need to be properly filled.

So yeah, the idea is to seduce him, but it's not really why I'm out here. If it were just sex, I wouldn't be trying so hard. Just sex is easy. I know how to do that.

No, I'm out here because I... like him.

I actually like him.

I'm so screwed.

If it had just been this crazy attraction, maybe I could deal. Everyone knows nothing kills a fantasy you've built up in your head quite like the mundane realities of actually having sex with another person. No matter how intense the buildup, there's no way to get around the awkward clothing removal, the cold toes, the cramping positions, the slapping sounds...

Even good sex, where I'm actually able to come, is still just a thing you do and then you can move on, in my experience. And maybe I've never been quite this on edge for quite this long, but the higher the pedestal I build for him, the harder he'll hit the ground when he gets knocked off.

So why did he have to be legitimately charming? And funny? And endearing without trying to be? Why did he have to be interesting and attentive and thoughtful and generous? Why did he have to be caring and broken?

It's not fair.

I didn't want to like him. I *shouldn't* like him.

I thought "ruining me" would be violent—powerful and savage, like him. In a good way, of course, but in a thoroughly *physical* sense of the word. I didn't think he meant he'd ruin me with anticipation, or with gifts, or little acts of service like bringing me coffee and washing and folding my clothes for me, or with smoldering looks of masculine appreciation of my body, or with soft little forehead kisses.

Fucking forehead kisses? That's *not fair*.

I wouldn't have thought it was possible to fall in like with my kidnapper, and it's definitely a terrible idea. Because when all of this is over, I'm leaving. Disappearing. It's safer for everyone that way. All this can be is temporary—scratching that purely physical itch.

But now, as I sit here, waiting for him to find me, I'm genuinely worried about what's going to happen when we do have sex. What if it's bad? Worse, what if it's as good as I've imagined? Worst of all, what if it's sort of just *okay*—the kind of sex where you convince yourself it might get better with practice, and you end up dating a loser for months because it's got "such potential."

If there's anything worse than a disappointment, it's a disappointment after you've wasted your time.

A shuffling noise on my left startles me, and I turn. All thoughts and worries disappear as Dimitri settles next to me on the bench and his heat seeps into my body despite several inches of separation. I shift a little closer.

My eyes have adjusted to the darkness, and we're facing the brightest thing in the sky, so I can make out some of his features. Same strong jaw and cheekbones, same down-turned lips, same thick brow and pensive frown. He hardly ever sleeps in, but on the few times I have woken before him, I just... stare.

It's such an interesting face. Strong, powerful features.

"You found me," I say softly, hoping to show my approval.

"You were thinking so hard I could hear you from all the way over there," he says, pointing behind him towards the pool house.

I smile. His humor is *so* dry. "I was starting to think I'd have to make you chase me."

His lips part, and I hear a forceful inhale—his version of a gasp of surprised delight—and he settles into his seat with a low grumbling noise. Interesting. Perhaps my predator likes to be a bit primal.

The bench creaks, straining to support him, but he doesn't seem to notice. "You were waiting for me?"

There's a note of longing, of tentative disbelief that makes me feel oddly powerful and wanted. When his gaze drops to the thin straps of my nightgown, the low cut of the bodice, and the thin, lacy material that's scratching against my nipples and keeping them taut with the sensation, he licks his lips.

I shrug, and it makes the tiny strap fall off my shoulder. His eyes dart to it, following the motion and then lingering on my bare skin, and I have to suppress a smile.

A paid actor, that strap.

"I thought we could start over, in a manner of speaking. Well, not start over, but recreate how it *should* have gone at the wedding."

"How should the night have gone, my med?"

I hum at the nickname, like it drives home my point. If it had gone differently, I never would have ended up on a houseboat, treating a gunshot wound.

"You would have found me on the bench and offered me your coat when I shivered. We would have talked, flirted, exchanged numbers…" I inhale sharply. "Gone home together."

"That is how it should have gone," he agrees quietly. His voice is a rasp.

I tilt my head back, conscious of his eyes on my neck. Heat crawls under my skin with a potent surge of energy. Being the sole subject of his intensity is heady. Powerful.

"*YA revnuyu k lune, potomu chto ty smotrish' na neye,*" he murmurs.

"Hmm?" I ask.

"You were also looking at the moon the night we met."

"I love the moon. I used to pretend there was this tragic love story she had with the sun—they loved each other but were doomed to be in different skies forever. She would disappear once a month, and that was when they could be together, and she'd come back getting fuller and fuller of love, which would start to wane when she missed the sun." I laugh a little, hearing it out loud in my adult ears. "Doesn't make a ton of sense, but I was, like, five."

"It makes sense to me," he says quietly. "My mother told me when I was a boy that the moon was watching me sleep. I remember thinking it was a very large eye, blinking very slowly."

I smile. I like that. I like how he listens. I like how he offers his own details to make mine feel less lonely. It's just so fundamentally human to make up stories about things we don't understand.

"How do you say 'moon' in Russian?"

He turns his head. I can feel his breath against my temple when he says, "*Luna.*"

"Oh," I say, a bit surprised at the familiarity of the word. His boat. "That'll be easy to remember."

"*Da.*"

I can feel his eyes on me, and it's making me hyperaware of the rise and fall of my chest, of the way my lips are slightly parted, of the tiny white puffs collecting around each breath in the cold air. My face is warm, like he's breathing his own heat into me, or like his eyes alone are capable of eliciting a thermal reaction from my skin.

"*Da,*" I repeat faintly.

"You look cold, my med. Let me bring you inside." He stands, not waiting for my response, and holds out his hand to me.

My heart thumps fast and loud, and I swallow the thickness stuck in my throat as I take his hand. This is it. This is the moment where he fulfills his promises, or I find out that I waited for him in the dark, on a cold bench, not wearing any underwear for no damn reason.

He leaves me in suspense as we cross the patio, heading for the pool house, but he wraps his large hand around mine and rubs his thumb lightly across the skin of my knuckles as we walk in silence. I start to get concerned that he meant what he said exactly as he said it—I look cold, he's taking me in to get warm.

When I reach for the door handle, since I'm closer, he drops his hold on me, and disappointment swells.

He's killing me.

It'll be the first documented case of death by *yearning*.

Screw being mortified. Apparently, I have to say something and explain just how badly I need him. I turn to face him, but he fills the space behind me. He doesn't let me pivot away; he steps us both forward through the doorway. I feel his lips on my neck, and my knees turn to jelly. I fall back, leaning against him for support.

"Nicole," he breathes into my skin.

Nee-cole.

My breath is coming in way too slowly to keep up with my racing heart, and my body feels like it's prickling in all the most sensitive places.

I ache. Everywhere. From that deep, clenching emptiness inside my core to the heaviness in my breasts. I'm burning for him.

He kicks the door closed, plunging us into darkness, and I spin against him. His mouth is on mine in a second, and I part my lips immediately to let him in. Our kiss is all desperation. It's sloppy, and open, and hard with the need to get as physically close as we can. I feel surrounded by him in the best possible way—his scent, his taste, his warmth—and I can't wait to know what it feels like to be so full of him that I can't breathe.

I reach up to grab his waist, to pull him even closer. My hands settle against his soft cotton shirt, clenching as I bite his bottom lip. When I give it a tug upwards, he pulls away.

"Take off your dress. Now."

25

NICOLE

I would melt if I wasn't so sure I was on the precipice of combustion.

Thrill at his words, at the command, zings through my stomach. My body snaps to do what he says, peeling my nightgown off before my brain can even catch up. As it slides against my skin and falls to the floor with a soft swish, leaving me completely naked while he's fully clothed, I'm suddenly grateful for the darkness. In the dark, I don't feel like I need to cover my imperfect, dimpled skin, or stretch marks, or moles and divots.

I work hard to love and appreciate my body the way she is—for all the things she does for me, like carrying me through the world—but sensitivity towards the judgments of others is deeply ingrained. I have good days and bad days like everyone, and most of the time I manage a certain amount of ambivalence towards my appearance and trust that sexual attraction is so deeply personal that there's no point questioning it.

Now, though? Even ambivalence is tricky when every damn inch of him is so tight and hard, and it's such a contrast to my own body...

Stop, Nicole. This is what you want, and it's finally happening. Get out of your own damn head.

I wish I could see him better. My pupils are slowly adjusting to the amount of light, and I can make out his dark shape well enough, but the details are coming in slowly—too slowly for this sharp urgency.

"Nicole," he groans, his eyes blazing and roving across my bare skin. It prickles under his gaze, my nipples pebbling as if rising to meet him. I want to run my fingers through his chest hair and drink my fill of the planes and valleys of his muscular form. "You wore only the dress with nothing underneath. You hoped I would do more than just find you out there."

The dark thought is electrifying, and I shiver at the image of him on his knees next to me with his hand disappearing under the skirt of my nightgown while the moon bathes our skin in a milky glow.

"I'll admit it crossed my mind," I confess, emboldened by the rawness in his throat and the hunger on his face. "But tonight, I just want it to be like this—you and me. One day, maybe it can be... you and me and the *luna*."

His head falls back, and he groans out a string of words I don't understand, except for one—med. Me.

"Perfect woman," he says, and I hope it's a translation. "Perfect, wicked woman."

Using the back of his collar, he tugs his shirt over his head and tosses it aside. His pants are next. I realize I've left distance between us in my eagerness to see him naked, too, and that I'm a fool for it. Why just look when I can touch?

I step forward, reaching for him, and we come together in a full-body press. He places one hand around the back of my head, tipping it to slant his mouth across mine, and one hand around my waist, holding me steady. I grip his shoulders, massaging, feeling hard skin and thick scar tissue and rough hair. He drinks from me, and I rise to meet him. My blood pounds everywhere at once, beating a rhythm of our desire into my tender flesh over and over.

Dimitri walks us back towards the bed, grips both of my shoulders, and pushes me down onto the mattress.

Thrown off balance by the unexpected move, I simply fall, weightless, before I hit the padded surface. I bounce onto my back, breasts following the momentum of my body, and he's on top of me before I even lose that momentum.

When his lips come down on mine this time, I try to meet him with equal energy, but he demands control of the kiss. He explores my mouth, forcing my tongue against his, our teeth clicking together. It's wild, consuming, mindless.

Now, as I touch him, I feel free to explore the hardened planes of his back. I rake my nails against his smooth skin, delighting in how it makes the muscles contract underneath like a wave.

I inhale sharply as his knee wedges between my legs, which hang off the bed. The sudden pressure brings a heavy pounding to the forefront of my awareness. I need to be touched so badly. My hips move in small circles of their own volition, trying to get some contact where I ache the most. His quad is so hard, the perfect unyielding surface to get some friction—finally—against my clit.

Realizing what I'm doing, he rears up, breaking the kiss, and presses his leg harder against me, making me whimper. "Needy woman," he says, amusement dripping from his low words. Each roll of my hips makes a soft, wet sound as my sensitive flesh drags across the abrasive hairs on his thigh. "Would you take your pleasure from me this way, or have me give it to you?"

My mind goes fucking blank at the weird phrasing and frank eroticism of that. All I can do is whimper in response. His hands circle my waist, stilling me, pressing me into the mattress so I can't move against him. I make unintelligible noises at the loss of control, maddeningly frustrated and breathlessly aroused.

"Answer the question, Nicole."

He asked me a question? Um... Oh, right! The way he said it was confusing, like something was lost in translation or in the clouded desire of my brain, but I think I got the gist. Enough to demand, "Give it to me," in a half-whisper, half-groan.

He makes a thick noise in his throat and starts moving down my body. "I want to taste you."

The feeling is so *mutual.* But I hesitate. I'm not sure how long I can take the foreplay after weeks of gentle, courting touches that hinted and teased what could be. I really, *really* need to get fucked. Hard. "No, that's okay. We can just—"

"Just my fingers, then."

"No, I meant…" I exhale in frustration. I don't want his mouth or his fingers, I want his cock. "I'm ready. Let's just skip the foreplay."

"We cannot skip the foreplay," he shakes his head.

Wait, a *guy* is suggesting more foreplay? I nearly laugh; it's so absurd when measured against my previous experiences. "It'll be okay. I'm already pretty wet, and once we get going and it feels good, I'm good. Or I can, like, add some spit or something…" I feel my cheeks heat, blushing like a damn virgin. Explaining this feels weird.

"No." He's firm. "I must prepare you for my size."

I choke on my next breath. That's not quite what I was expecting to hear. Where did this concern come from? A second ago, he was throwing me around like a pillow.

I try not to let my sexually fueled frustration seem so obvious as I say, "Um… that's really not necessary. I can… *stretch*. I know you're a big person, but I'm also a big person—I think we'll be okay."

His smile is little more than a quirk of half his mouth. He pulls back. "Yes, I know you are a large, strong woman. This is good. Even so, I will hurt you if I do not do this first."

"Oh, come on, Dimitri," I begin, nearly rolling my eyes as I bend my elbows to prop myself up. The unbelievable audacity of men. "You're *so big* that you—"

The sarcastic remark withers on my tongue as he drops his boxer briefs.

Yes. Yes, he is so big. Even in the near-darkness.

I couldn't begin to guess the length or girth, but it's definitely among the biggest I've ever seen. And I suppose it's proportional to the size of the rest of him, but... I'm a medical professional. I've seen a lot of penises.

None quite like this.

Uncut, it hangs, slightly tipped down from its own goddamn weight. He looks even bigger, too, since he's hard, and veins stand out against his pale skin, weaving up from the thatch of dark hair all the way to a purple-red head, which glistens at the very tip. It's not pretty—show me a cock that is—but it's... raw and powerful, like him.

Urgent heat pounds between my legs, reminding me of just how achingly empty I am. I'm desperate to taste that perfect, pearly drop of his desire.

"Certain positions might be uncomfortable for you," he says, almost chagrined. "You should not be on top, for example. The gravity and full weight of your body may pull you down too much, and it will be too deep and cause pain."

It's difficult, but I manage to look away from the one-eyed monster between his legs. Were it not for the totally grave expression on his face, I would laugh. But he obviously means it, so I clear it from my throat instead. "Yeah, that's not happening. I enjoy being on top. It's easier for me to come."

"In the past, perhaps," he inclines his head. "But I assume that is because it is easier for women to take care of themselves when they are on top. You think I will not take care of you, my med?"

My breath catches. Okay, I need him desperately. Now. However he wants to do it. "Yeah, okay, fingers first," I say, nodding my encouragement. "I don't care, just touch me. I need you."

I scooch back further toward the middle of the mattress and lie back down. Nerves of anticipation flutter around in my stomach as he comes down on the bed.

He fills the space, hovering just over me on his side. Face to face like this, it's almost unbelievably intimate as he strokes my cheek. He traces my lower lip with his thumb, and I rake my teeth against the pad. I feel the rumble of his groan through his chest. His lips twitch.

"Are you wet for me, Nicole?"

The question makes my legs tremble, the implication that my body's responses are *his*, something for him. I nod, though I don't know how to gauge my answer. I get wet, sure—and I think for me I am very wet, but I don't know what he wants or expects. It doesn't, like, drip down my leg or anything. Lube is my friend.

His hand traces a path down my body, leaving goosebumps in its gentle wake, and he guides my legs apart. It opens me up, exposing me to the cool air and making me shiver with the temperature change. Our eyes are locked as his fingertips brush against my clit. I inhale sharply, my face warping with the rush of sensations. Every muscle in my stomach quivers with anticipation.

"Fuck," he growls. A flurry of Russian words spills from his lips. *"Tvoye telo prekrasno, ono gotovitsya ko mne. Ty tak khorosho menya primesh'."*

I ache to know what he's saying, because whatever it is, it sounds *reverent*. Poetry. A prayer. An ode to the silky wetness of my body and the way it feels to him.

And for my part, my pussy clenches around nothing, feeling so deeply empty that I'm half-insane with it. The movement that muscle spasm causes creates friction against the fingers he holds still, but it's not enough, and it's not in the right place. I roll my hips, trying to help him find that spot on my clit where I desperately need him.

"Is that where you like it?" he asks, switching back over to English. "There?"

His blunt fingertips strum against the hard little bump of my clitoris, and my body jerks against his hand. A breathy noise escapes me, mostly blowing out my nose, and I search his gaze as he searches mine. I nod.

"Yes, you like that," he whispers, almost more to himself. The rasp of his skin against the most sensitive part of me is a tactile feast for my nerves.

Those fingers start moving down, exploring further until I have to spread my thighs to make room so he can find the entrance he's looking for. "What about here?"

I whimper and nod again, my head bobbing without a single thought other than *yes, more.*

"Do you want me inside here?" he asks. His stare is hypnotizing.

"So bad," I moan.

I feel one finger swirling around, collecting moisture, before it plunges inside me. His thumb settles against my clit, applying pressure firmly. My hips buck against him as my lower belly spasms.

Of course, he'd touch me like this—confidently and intentionally. I shudder.

When I whine a moan, the pressure of his thumb gentles. "Are you sensitive?"

"Not that sensitive. More," I whisper the demand.

Maybe because I'm not that sensitive, I've always been a girl who likes a little pain with her pleasure—it centers me, helps me focus, works in synchronization with the good feelings to make everything feel more intense.

His hands are so big, with fingers long enough to stroke deeper inside of me than some of my previous partners could have hoped to reach. I make throaty noises as he finds a rhythm, stroking and pumping. The firm pressure on those hypersensitive nerve endings almost hurts because it feels so good, and my eyes drift shut at the pleasure of it.

With so many sensations to focus on, I forget about his other hand until it tightens around a fistful of hair. The slight sting makes me gasp. Fuck, I love a man's hand in my hair almost as much as I love it around my neck. I grasp at his chest, feeling immobilized.

"I want you to look at me, Nicole." His icy blue eyes are colorless in the dark as they rake across my face, collecting and cataloging each of my expressions.

A second finger probes my opening, and I cry out as the first, already inside, strokes a spot that makes electricity shoot outward, through all my limbs. The second finger is a stretch, and he twists them together as he pumps. I feel him pressing against the tight space, exploring and massaging, and I almost come just from the knowledge that he's preparing me to take his giant fucking cock.

When I feel a third finger, a musical whimper blows out of me. I tense and clutch at his shoulders.

"Shhh," he croons. "Relax. You can take another finger."

I moan, thrashing my head. It already feels like so much. Too much.

"You will. You *must*," he says sternly, stroking so deep and filling me so full that I'm about to lose my damn mind. "You cannot take me if you cannot take another finger."

I gasp at that, and it melts into a long noise that's almost a sob as he works that third finger inside me. His thumb stills against my clit as I adjust to the additional pressure, taking in a few shuddering breaths. My fingernails dig into the hardness of his shoulders.

"That's it. Good girl. I knew you could take it."

Good girl? Okay, I love some good, dirty praise, but hearing it in his controlled, deep, accented voice... I would melt if I wasn't so sure I was on the precipice of combustion.

With three of his fingers crammed deep inside me, his chest hair brushing against my hard, sensitive nipples, and his swirling thumb bringing my body higher and higher, my stomach clenches as that familiar, building sensation grips me from inside. I try to move against him, but the fingers in my hair that I forgot about tighten, anchoring me.

"That's it," he rasps. "Are you going to come? Tell me. Speak."

"Yes!" I blurt out at his demand. "Keep doing that, right there. Just like that." There's a desperation to my voice as I chase the orgasm that's hovering just at the edge of my physical awareness.

I'm not sure if it's that he's good at taking direction, or he's just unlike the vast majority of men who hear "right there, just like that" and decide to change the pace or position of their fingers, but he keeps his touch there, and keeps doing just that. All other thoughts fall away as I zero in on the sensations, reducing my world to just the two of us.

It builds and builds, and I'm soaring. "I'm..."

That's all I get out, before the world crashes back down around me in a jumbled mass of color, light, sounds, and sensations that feel conflicting and nonsensical—hard, soft, pointy, flat... I lose myself as my body shakes, tightening and loosening around the intrusion of his touch.

I've barely come back into consciousness when he withdraws his fingers and moves his hips between my thighs. My legs flop to the side to make room.

"I cannot wait any longer," he growls.

"Yes," I moan, still panting as I come down. I tilt up my pelvis for him because I need more, even though I'm still throbbing from my last release.

He rears back, looming over me on his knees in a way that casts his entire face in shadow. I wish he were closer; I want his weight on me, or at the very least, I wish I'd turned on the damn light so I could look at him if he's going to be so far away. Improve my view.

He grips my waist with both hands, adjusting himself between my legs, draping them almost obscenely over his rock-hard thighs. Rough palms, hard grip, fingers digging into soft flesh... his touch locks me in place, and it's nowhere near enough contact. He cups himself to aim the thick, rounded, blunt head at my entrance.

"This is it, Nicole—your only chance to say no before I make you mine. Tell me to stop; I will stop. Now. Or never."

I suck my lower lip into my mouth and resolutely shake my head. "Don't you dare stop."

I want to be taken, to become his, for however brief the moment will be. I know he just means physically, but my heart aches with how much I want it to mean more—scary and ominous and sincere as that is.

"Then relax for me." He works himself through my slit, coating the velvety, smooth length of him in a way that makes me shiver with need, then lines himself up at my entrance. Reclaiming his grip on my waist, he pulls me towards him with both hands and pushes forward at the same time. It's just enough that the tip of him nudges inside.

In spite of all that wetness, in spite of the languid, relaxing feeling left over in my muscles from my first mind-blowing orgasm... it's a fucking stretch.

"Oh my God," I whimper.

"Relax," he repeats, adding more force to his voice through gritted teeth. But his thumbs stroke against the bottom of my ribcage, an un-spoken apology for the harsh tone.

I try, but he's so thick that I can't help but tense against the intrusion. I feel my body resist as he forces me open around him. He was right to use three fingers—I've never been so thoroughly filled. It stings a bit.

But he doesn't push inside me all at once. With the last shred of his control, he holds me still and nudges forward slowly, letting me feel every stretching inch as it parts me.

He's trying to let me adjust, I know, but my muscles have ideas of their own, fluttering around him, and he groans. He pauses, gives me a moment, then shifts his hips back. His first thrust is shallow, slow, and he watches me so carefully that I know he's still not convinced I'm not going to call the whole thing off. I can feel myself molding around him, conforming to every ridge and vein. A perfect fit.

"Fuuuck," I wheeze as the air squeezes from my lungs.

It's a lot. It's almost too much. And I love every damn bit of it. Tears prickle behind my eyes. I cry out as he hits my cervix, and his hip bones touch my inner thighs.

His penetration is so absolute, it feels life-altering.

How can I ever be the same after knowing how full I can be of someone?

26

DIMITRI

That makes her mine entirely, whether she likes it or not.

I have pictured this exact moment, when I would finally take my woman, many times. In the darkness of the top cabin as it rocked gently on calm waters under the stars, I imagined how it would feel to have her under me. In the quiet, soft moments of morning when I woke with her in my arms, I imagined how it would feel to turn her onto her back and settle in between her legs. In the happy moments when I managed to make her laugh, I imagined her on her knees before me, with ruined makeup and a willing mouth.

But I was not imaginative enough to picture the line forming between her scorching golden eyes as her brows come together in pleasured focus, or her lips rounding into an O on a silent cry.

Nothing I imagined could have compared to this. I am glad she did not turn on the light—I do not want her to see me so close and so bare, to remind her I am hard and scarred and ugly, not beautiful and soft like her. But I also hate the darkness of this room for how it deprives me of the finer details. I can feel better than I can see her flushed, heated body, covered in a thin sheen of sweat from what I did to her with my fingers. But the scent of her, the sounds she makes against my lips, the feel of her...

God, the feel of her. Fuck, she's gripping me so hard.

I intended to fuck her slowly, staying up on my knees, too far for her to reach, but it is too much. I fall onto my hands, framing her lovely face, curling around her until she is everywhere. Her heat is scalding. Her staccato breaths spur me on, ghosting across the sweaty skin of my neck. Her hands clutch my sides. Her legs curl around me.

And her pussy drips with need. She craves me, wants my cock more than she knows how to express. It satisfies something deep and jealous inside me. I wish I had more time or self-control to touch and kiss every inch of her.

Next time.

One hand digs into the mattress for balance, and the other curls around the back of her head, weaving between the rough yet silken strands of hair. She is in a cage of my arms and legs and body, pinned by my grip in her hair, but her skin is hot with lust, and the noises that escape her lips encourage, even as they convey overwhelm.

I greedily claim those noises, taking them into my mouth, swiping my tongue along her lips and teeth. Her taste is so unique—strange, and addictive. I press forward, swallowing her mewl of surprise at the invasion.

The width of her hips provides the perfect, smooth cradle for mine, a pillow for my body that absorbs the force of each thrust. I start slowly—controlled and deliberate—giving her the chance to get used to me. But her sweet moans of pleasure are too much, and after a while, I am driving myself crazy with the achingly slow pace. The burning heaviness in my balls and shaky tightness in my legs and abs are distracting. Holding back like this is torture when all I want is to clench, to pound, to release my strength into her open, willing softness.

She squirms underneath me, tilting her hips up for me to urge me on. And even though the apex of each thrust has my cock nudging her insides in a way that rips a small cry from her chest, still this little vixen's golden eyes shine in the low light as she meets mine and hoarsely requests, "Please... please, more."

Faster, she could have said, or harder. But no, *my woman*—my *med*—wants more. She wants all of me.

With a growl, I adjust our positions, grabbing her upper calf and jerking it away from my hip so I can slide my arm underneath. I pull it up, fitting my forearm into the space behind her knee, and she gasps as the angle changes and I sink even deeper.

"No, no, no, no, no," she chants, whining on an exhale, moaning and tossing her head side to side against the sensations. Her brows come together, and her face screws up with the pleasure-pain.

My grip in her hair tightens, halting the movements that tug on her scalp. "Yes, Nicole. You can take it. You *will* take all of me."

Fuck. *Fuck.*

That final inch. That last part of my cock that never seems to fit except in certain, less intimate positions. Inside her. It is a tight fucking fit, like a too-small glove, but we are locked in.

"Fuck, Dimitri," she gasps. "You're so... so deep!"

"Tell me to stop," I order as her voice pinches with pain that bleeds into her tone. I know I told her she already had her last chance to say no, but I grit my teeth and manage to still myself, hovering over her.

She just inhales shakily through her teeth.

"Say it," I growl. If she does not say something, I am going to unleash on her; that final thread holding me back is just about to snap.

"No, don't! Just... No one's ever... It's amazing."

I know now—it is the confirmation I needed. No one has been this deep inside my woman before. And that makes her mine entirely, whether she likes it or not. Any fucker that might have come before—and there will be *none* after—could not take her like this, fill her this way, give her what she really craved. The jealousy feels oddly like triumph, and I want to roar my victory.

"Yes," I croon into her ear, feeling her shiver against my hot breath. "Good. Such a good girl, taking me so deep. I knew you could."

"So big," she whispers, her words like broken music notes of overstimulation. "Ohmygodohmygod."

The primal satisfaction is addling me. My desire burns, and my blood pounds so hard that I can do nothing but increase my speed, finding the rhythm I need. Her whimpers become moans once more, but she denies me her golden gaze, squeezing her lids shut. I will allow it—just this once—because she is pleasing me greatly, her greedy cunt taking me all the way on our first time.

It is only when the pressure disappears that I realize she has been digging her nails into me. Her hand moves from just under my ribcage on my right side and starts working in between our bodies, down towards where we are joined, through the hole created by the crease in her lifted leg.

"No," I growl. I release her knee, feeling it fall without my arm propped against it, to grab her wrist. "I take care of what is mine. I will do it."

She tugs, but I refuse to let go until I know she will not try it again. "I... I just need..."

"Oh, my Nicole," I rumble, gratified by the desperation, the frenzy in her voice. "Tell me what you need."

"M-my clit. Touch it. Please. It feels... it's so much. I need to come."

She is unable to keep her leg where I had it on her own, so I sacrifice that final inch of my cock being buried in her sweet pussy in order to take care of it. I release her hair so I do not pull it too hard, and angle my body back far enough to slip my fingertips against her slick, tight nub. Her whole body seizes as I make that gentle contact. She lets out a long, stuttered moan on an exhale.

I work my cock in and out, nearly losing myself to the exquisite, wet heat and push-pull of delicate skin. When she came all over my hand earlier, I learned what pressure and speed she liked, so I try to maintain an unbroken rhythm for her—and it does not take long.

Her stomach clenches, her legs and arms tensing as she tosses her head as far back as it can go against the pillows. Her release shakes her, shaking me, pulsing against my fingertips, and making her grip my cock even harder.

Fuck. She is spasming tight, then loosening with an unpredictable, uncontrollable pattern. I will not last. The tingling sensation is starting at the base of my spine, and I want to be as deep inside of her as I can be when I come.

With a growl that is part relief and part urgent demand, I stretch her leg back up and slam into her all the way. Still in the throes of her own orgasm, she cries out, but her voice is hoarse and spent. Then she lifts her hips for me, relaxes back against the pillow—her body's signal of permission to me to take what I want.

So, I do. I pound into her hard. I take, and I take, and when she finally returns to consciousness and meets my eyes with a satisfied, sex-drunk stare, that is it for me—all I can take. Muscles bunch along either side of my spine, reacting to the familiar building sensation of my own release. My balls tighten against my body, and my cock jumps inside her.

When it comes, it is quick. Pinpricks of colored light sparkle within the blackness of the inside of my eyelids, and I shake violently, seizing up as the pleasure crests and overtakes my limbs. I lose myself and let loose, filling her with every drop I have. The release is weighty, dragging me down after soaring so high. I fight to fill my lungs completely, pleased that we are exchanging air—to have her inside of me as I am inside of her. After a moment, the pleasure wanes, and the grip of my fingers loosens, and I am much lighter than before.

I shake my head to clear the muffled ringing in my ears and swallow the thickness in the back of my throat. When I begin to let her leg down, she winces, and I press an apologetic kiss to her lips as I withdraw. Then

I roll to the side to give her some room to breathe. I weigh a lot—muscle is heavy—and as much as I like the feel of her underneath me, I can see it is hard for her to take in a whole breath.

She looks up at me, lips parting as her hazy eyes beg me to kiss her again. I swipe aside a sweaty lock of hair plastered to her forehead and trail just the very tips of my fingers down her jaw, tracing the line. She smiles faintly, stretching her neck to give me better access. Needy, greedy girl. So pliant and responsive.

"Hi," she whispers.

"Hello."

The sound of her answering laugh is throaty, and I inhale deeply to fill my lungs with it. "That was…" she blows out, pursing her lips and letting her eyes roll back. "I think I owe you dinner. Maybe my firstborn. Jesus."

My lips twitch at the languid satisfaction in her voice. Pride spears me through the chest, knowing I am the reason for it. "Your gratitude is unnecessary. You were perfect."

Something shifts in her expression, and I fight with the conflicting urges to move away so I can turn on the light to see better and to keep her in my arms like this. "I think I need a shower. Want to join me?" she asks. Her face is open, hopeful, almost innocent as she huffs a laugh. "You did all the work."

"Being with you was not work, Nicole."

I cup her cheek, and her eyes round, staring up at me with misty eagerness. She rolls her lips inward against each other, I think because they are trembling, and hides her face from me against my chest again. "Maybe we just lie here like this for a little bit. The shower can wait."

"The shower can wait," I agree, hugging her closer.

She stretches her neck, and I meet her halfway.

The press of our lips is sweet and soft—a gratitude for what has occurred and a promise of things to come.

27

DIMITRI

———◆———

I refuse to be alone in this.

The door shuts behind me with a soft click, and I head right for the refrigerator. The house is mostly silent, but the light was on in James and Eleanor's apartment at the top, so I must be quick to avoid them.

As always, the shelves are filled with neat stacks of Tupperware, but as I examine the labels, I frown. An entire row seems to be only for Nicole. Eleanor does not usually dictate who eats what, so it surprises me. Perhaps Nicole made a special request.

Armed with a few meals for Nicole and a few from one of the unclaimed rows, two water bottles, and a fresh cup of coffee, I head out to the pool house. I pause before entering, and curse under my breath when I hear the shower.

I suppose I will wake her with my head between her legs another day.

It is all right. We have plenty of time, and now we have enough food and water, so we will not have to leave this room today. I will need to rest at some point so I am ready to relieve James's watch tonight, but other than that, my plans are to keep Nicole naked and satisfied all day.

Last night I held back. I was not as demanding as I wanted to be, as it was our first time.

I will not hold back today.

Today, she will take me as many times as her body can withstand, wherever I want her. She will know what it feels like to have my hand on her throat, covering her mouth, squeezing a breast to the point of pleasure-pain, or buried in her cunt while I lick her to soothe and tease. I am going to explore her golden-brown skin with fingers and tongue and teeth, and I hope she fights me, just a little, because it makes the giving in that much sweeter.

When I told her I would take everything from her, it was because anything less is unacceptable. I could not let her believe that the way I want her is casual or anything less than all-consuming. I am not here to *borrow* her; I am here to have her. She must be mine, because I am hers, completely, and I refuse to be alone in this.

She may not realize it, but last night she claimed me just as fiercely in her own way as I claimed her. My shoulders bear the fingernail scratches, and my lips are bitten and swollen. I am not complaining; I want more.

I place the contents of my arms on the coffee table, remove my clothes, and approach the bathroom. As I walk, my dick begins to swell. Even the thought of her in there, nude, possibly still dripping with my cum... the skin around the head of my cock tightens, throbbing with pinprick pulses of need synced to each beat of my heart.

She left the door open—a clear invitation. The sound of her humming—a light tune I do not recognize—spills out through the doorway and wraps around me as I step into the steam.

Due to the design of the walk-in walls, I cannot see her until I am nearly inside the shower with her. I lean against the marble tile, just beyond the perimeter, and grip my dick in a calloused palm, resenting my hand for its size and roughness because it is not hers.

I watch, mesmerized as the water hits and bounces off her shoulders, sending small rivers down her smooth skin. Her back is to me, and every small movement as she rinses her hair makes her ass jiggle. Knowing how her flesh gives way under my touch makes me want to reach out and squeeze it.

My hand tightens, and I move it faster. There is a distinct flesh-on-flesh sound that it makes, and I know she hears it because her humming falters. She throws me a look over her shoulder, eyes falling first on my cock before dragging up to my face. The way her eyelids lower is sultry, as is her curved smile of feminine satisfaction.

"I had a fantasy about this," she says, letting her eyes drop back down to what I am doing. She licks her lips.

My cock jerks and I nearly fall back against the wall at the unexpected shot of desire. "Of what?" I croak.

"Of you watching me. Wanting. Just out of reach," she half-turns, and I get the profile view of her breast. The tawny nipple pokes outward, begging to be in my mouth.

"Your fantasy is that I want you?" I nearly laugh as the muscles contract in my lower back and I have to restrain myself from pumping my hips. "I have excellent news for you, Nicole."

She does laugh. The happy noise fills the air. "I guess it's an easy one, huh?"

This talk of fantasies will be my undoing—I will spill myself onto the floor or wall, and I refuse to waste it anywhere but inside of or on her body ever again. "Wanting you is constant. As easy as being awake, or breathing."

Her eyes flash, and she spins to face me fully as I cross over the lip of the shower. She takes a half-step back, moving just outside the spray from the showerhead. "My God, Dimitri. The things you say..."

I reach for her, but she shifts back again.

"Not here, not in the shower. The water washes away fluids, and it doesn't feel good for me. You and I..." she trails off, eyeing my cock with some apprehension twisting in the corners of her eyes, "we need the lubrication," she finishes, and my dick jumps like she was talking directly to it.

Maybe she was.

"Then go get on the bed," I order impatiently. "On your knees, facing the pillows, bent forward with your legs spread. Stay like that until I come for you." The thought of watching her waiting, ready, spread and open, quivering with need and anticipation of when I will finally touch her... my dick pounds painfully now, in time with my heartbeat, swelling with thick desire.

She licks her lips, and I watch as her nipples harden her breasts into rounded peaks. She likes that. And I like very much that she likes that.

"Oh my God," she chokes. "That's... oh my God. I will, I promise you I will, but... You have to give me more than eight hours, Dimitri. Maybe not after the next time or the time after, but last night was the *first* time, and our bodies need to get used to each other. I'm... I need a minute. And some Advil. And maybe a pad," she adds with a slight wince.

All I heard was her making plans to fuck me again and again.

"Ah," I say, understanding. I should have anticipated her discomfort, but I do not really care. If she will not take my cock, she will take my tongue and fingers. And I watched her closely last night—it hurt her at times, but she did not care then, either. She liked it. She enjoys some pain with her pleasure.

She is strong, my *med*, like iron and silk.

The smile on my lips shifts. "I will kiss it to make it better. That is the saying, *da*?"

She laughs again, a throaty noise that echoes among the water spray, bouncing off the glass and stone. Tilting her head up so she can catch my eye, she slowly walks towards me and shakes her head from side to side just as her hand closes around my cock. My body tenses in her grip, and my eyes lose focus for an instant. "That's the saying, but I think I want to go first."

My cock pulses, ready for whatever she wants.

I planned to take her mouth at some point. If this blowjob is a consolation, meant to soften her refusal, I do not care. I will gladly accept any reason to have her mouth on me.

At the end of the shower near the entrance, there is a tile bench that I usually avoid because it is so cold against my balls—that does not matter much to me now. I sit facing her, and she reaches for the shelf to steady herself as she lowers to her knees. I halt her with a finger held up, reaching out of the shower to the towel rack. I jerk one down and lay it on the hard floor for her knees. She smiles shyly at the gesture in a way that swells my chest with pride. It is such a small thing, but her gratitude makes me feel like a better man than I am.

I sit back, extending my long legs and making room for her between them. She settles, tucking her feet under her round ass, and slides her hands along the tops of my thighs.

The way she looks at me makes me feel so powerful and desired that I want to honor her like a queen. She is on her knees, but somehow, I am the one fully at her mercy; I would do anything she asked, give her whatever she wanted.

How lucky I am, then, that what she wants is to wrap those plush lips around the head of my cock.

Just before she makes contact, I wind my hand in her wet hair and use my grip on it to tilt her head back. Her fingernails dig into my thighs, and she gasps, pressing her legs tighter together. I make her stay like that for a few seconds, still and waiting, and watch as the water drips down her skin, sparkling in the low light.

From this angle, my cock looks monstrous next to her, sticking up straight so it appears nearly the length of her head. I wonder idly how she will fare—how much of it she will manage to swallow. Does she know how to relax her throat?

After a few seconds under my admiring scrutiny, she squirms.

"Dimitri," she breathes, her chest rising and falling. A single droplet of water beads on the very tip of her nipple, and I press the tip of my finger against it and bring it to my mouth. Her eyes round, watching me, then close on a hissed exhale.

"Yes, Nicole?" I ask. I can be patient. I want to hear her say it.

"Please, I... I want..."

"What do you want?" I challenge. I know now that she struggles to vocalize her desires, but there is no cause for shyness here. She may keep nothing from me, have no barriers to hide behind—not even ones built from language. She will speak to me with the honesty of her body, and she will ask for what she wants without fear of how I will react.

"I want to... um..."

"Suck my cock?"

She nods, as much movement as my hand in her hair will allow. "Yes."

"Then say that. I cannot know what you want if you do not tell me. I want to hear the words from your pretty mouth before I fill it," I tell her, giving her the permission she needs to speak the words.

Her eyes close again, and her legs shift, clenching hard. I know she is desperate for a touch between them, and that if I reached down and checked, I would find her dripping wet from more than just the water of the shower. "I want to suck your cock."

"Good," I praise, relishing in how flushed her cheeks have become, both from the steam and from the heat inside of her body. "Open."

Her mouth pops open as if it had a hinge, and I guide her towards my dick, upright and curving like an invitation. When she is near enough to touch, I relax my arm and let her close the rest of the distance on her own. I gather her hair to hold it out of her way as she moves her right hand from steadying herself on my leg to wrapping around the base of my length. Her thumb and middle finger do not meet, even when she squeezes.

Her lips kiss the crown, then the head of me disappears into her rounded mouth. I feel the warm, silky touch of her tongue against the most sensitive place on my body, and I jerk a little in her mouth. She smiles and makes a humming noise. My abs flex, my body wanting to surge forward with my hips into the feeling of heat and velvet. She pulls back and licks around, leaving a wet trail.

"It's so much easier to suck a small dick," she mutters, like it was not meant for me to hear.

My hand tightens in her hair. "You had better not be thinking about another man while my cock is in your mouth, my *med*." *My med.* Mine.

At the warning in my tone, her eyes flick up. There is a flash of defiance, and eagerness, then submission. As if in apology, she lowers her mouth back around the tip of me and starts to suck. I curse; the exquisite pressure of her mouth is second only to the warm lave of her tongue. Her hand moves at the base, maintaining a firm pressure and working up and down with a circular motion on what remains when her mouth is stuffed too full to continue.

This will not take long.

"Fuck," I hiss. "You are incredible, Nicole. Keep going. Deeper."

She tries, pushing harder and convulsing around the tip in the back of her mouth. I groan—the pleasure is so great it has almost become pain. She finds a rhythm that does not choke her, and I let my head fall back against the tile. I can still watch the view through half-closed eyes.

She bobs her head and twists her hand, and I am lost to the sensations and the sight of her.

"You enjoy this," I realize as her eyes drift shut. "You like sucking my cock."

She hums her response to my question, and my whole body erupts in chills. I know she can feel it happen where our skin makes contact, and I think I detect an excited increase in her pace.

"If I took my fingers and reached down, I bet I know what I would find," I say, watching her reaction. One of her brows quirks up in a look of helpless arousal. I know instantly I have found another thing she likes—the frank, sexual, somewhat degrading talk. "I bet you have made a mess. I bet you are ready for me again, though you say you are not."

She makes another noise, one that might be closer to denial, but her pace increases again. My words are spurring her on.

"I know what you said, but your body tells a different story than your lips. Though now I suppose your lips are too full of cock to say 'fill me with cock,'" I muse.

She snorts, a thick, wet noise around the length in her mouth that makes both of us groan for different reasons. She gags herself on me again, and my legs tense as my body bows towards her.

"Is that what you want, Nicole? Do you want me to fill you? Do you feel empty without me inside you?"

She whimpers, and the vibrations go straight to my balls. They tighten, and my breath quickens. The nerve endings in the rest of my body awaken, readying to send me over the edge of bliss. She rolls her tongue along the rim of my dick's head, and my eyes roll back.

"Yes, like that, *med*. Fuck, you are so good. I am close; you will swallow it all. You can do this, *da*?"

A muffled noise of agreement fills the air. Suddenly, she cups my balls with her other hand, and it is like being electrified. My body goes so rigid, so hard that it snaps, releasing in an instant.

She moans. Lost in the moment, I tighten my hold on her hair, groaning through the pulsing orgasm, seeking more of the warmth in my release. My abs are still lurching, caught up in the intensity of the sensations, when she pulls back against my grip.

With a curse, I release her. She swallows pointedly, wiping the corner of her mouth, and takes a few deep breaths. Through the breathless haze of the release and the swirling steam of the shower, I realize that there is not a drop of my cum anywhere on her. She swallowed it all, and if the self-satisfied look on her face is any indication, she liked it.

My balls tingle. I will be ready to give her more very soon.

"Come here to me," I rasp, grabbing her wrists and standing with her so I can kiss her.

28

NICOLE

Love language: touch.

We shower together, and he refuses to stop touching me, even when I laugh and try to pull away. He wraps me in a towel, trapping my arms, then curls his hand around the side of my neck to hold me in place for a kiss. He's languid now that the edges of his need have dulled, but the feeling of his lips against mine and his tongue sliding in, taking easy, unhurried ownership, revs me right back up.

The pounding between my legs is persistent and urgent, but my stomach growls loudly, and he smirks against my lips. "I was prepared for that," he says, leading me out into the main room.

I fix the towel, tucking it under my arms, and pad along behind him, watching as he takes two containers from a stack of four and places them in the microwave. I gently scrunch my hair as they heat, mindful of his eyes on me, then follow him over to the sitting area while he sets everything out onto the coffee table in front of the couch. I accept a fork and take a seat with a smile of thanks while I reach for the still-steaming container.

Once I'm settled with it, he leans back in his seat and angles himself towards me. I mirror his posture, thankful for the small distance. Maybe I'll actually be able to focus on eating if I can think straight.

"Why are some of these containers labeled with your name?" he says, nodding towards the food. "Is it an allergy?"

"No, it's probably because it's meatless."

Eleanor has been so good to me. And the first bite is bliss. It's got an amazing, flavorful sauce, rice, and perfectly steamed veggies. Bit odd for breakfast, I'll admit, but considering Dimitri's eating chicken and broccoli right now, I know he probably just didn't look at what he grabbed. Plus, I don't mind something a bit more fortifying, since he had a look about him in the shower like we're not going anywhere for a while.

"Is that what those cubes are?" he asks, pointing to one with his fork.

"Yeah, tofu. You've never seen tofu before?"

"Tofu?" he repeats, but it's a scoff, not a request for clarification. "Why would you eat this?"

"I'm a vegetarian. I'm surprised you didn't notice before, considering how observant you are. I guess we haven't really been eating together."

His brows snap together. "You do not eat meat? That is not good. It is very difficult to get your protein requirements from beans."

The number of times I've had almost this exact conversation with people has prepared me for most arguments. "Common misconception. Well, maybe it's hard for someone like you," I allow. If the size of his portion and the shape of his body are any indication, he probably eats a whole chicken every day for the lean protein. "But I'm not trying to maintain anywhere near your muscle mass. And eating meat weighs me down and sometimes hurts my stomach, so it's easier to avoid it."

His eyes narrow at me, and I can tell he wants to argue some more. Instead, he spears a hunk of chicken aggressively and chews noisily. "I do not like this. I will not allow you to become malnourished, my med."

I lift my brows. I pop the vegetable into my mouth and chew a few times before tucking it into my cheek to say, "A significant portion of the world's population subsists on a vegetarian diet and eats tofu daily. Besides, do I look malnourished to you?"

He grumbles something I can't quite make out, so I raise a brow at him. "And what makes you think you have any say in what goes into my mouth?"

The look he gives me is pure, raw lust, and it brings a rush of heat to my face that makes me purse my lips to keep from grinning like a fool. Okay, I'll admit that one was a bit of a tease, but it's like the more contentious my tone, the more it gets him going.

"At least allow me to calculate your nutritional requirements so I can be sure you will stay strong and not become vitamin deficient."

A laugh nearly bubbles up, but he seems so sincere that I swallow it back. I've never had someone show me they care by offering to do math for me. "If it'll make you feel better."

In the silence that falls, I debate asking the question that I imagine is on the tips of both our tongues. *So... what now?* But I don't want reality crashing back in. I want to bask in this easy feeling that he likes me, and I like him.

Unfortunately, there's one way reality won't be ignored, and it really should have been brought up last night. "So... we didn't use a condom," I say, staring down at my container and picking through the rice with my fork.

He throws a look at me and balances his breakfast carefully on his thigh. "We did not. We will not. I had a... *vazektomiya.*"

"Vasectomy?" I guess. The word sounds very similar.

"*Da.* Also, I have not had sex in many years, and you are a nurse, so I know that if you exhibited symptoms of a disease, you would recognize it and treat it immediately."

Relief whooshes out of my chest with all the air. He's right about that. "And I have an IUD. Almost feels like overkill."

He cocks his head. "An... explosive?"

I frown for a second, then chuckle. "That's an IED. An IUD—intrauterine device—is a form of birth control that sits inside the uterus."

"Oh. *Da*, I know you have this." I must make a face of disbelief because his eyes drop to the outline of my legs through the towel. "Nicole, my fingers were deep inside of your pretty little cunt. I could feel this IUD. It has strings."

Heat rises to my cheeks. I don't know why it feels so much dirtier and hotter when he says shit like that, as if he were ordering a pizza. So blunt. So casual. Not a shred of embarrassment. "Yeah. Okay, so… we're good. No STIs, no pregnancy…" just his cum dripping from me before my shower in a way that makes my pulse race at the memory of it…

"Wait, did you just say you haven't had sex in *years*?"

"Years," he confirms, shoving more chicken breast into his mouth.

I nearly gape. I know my own gender, and I've seen how feral they go for a man over six feet—with each increasing inch, the feral-ness grows exponentially. "How is that even possible? Women must try to jump your bones everywhere you go!"

Even he isn't immune to being stunned by a blunt compliment. He huffs what could be a laugh, and it casts vibrations through the padded cushions underneath us. He throws his left arm over the back of the couch, leaving a large open space where I'm pretty sure I'd fit perfectly. It brings his hand within inches of my shoulder, and I shift so he can just brush my skin with his fingertips. He does immediately.

Love language: touch. Got it.

"Perhaps you are the first person I have let close enough to touch me in a very long time. Or perhaps you are the first person brave enough to try."

At the reminder that he is no ordinary man, my eyes drift to his scar, then forge a path downward to his torso, littered with the memories of pain and injury. They catch on the tally mark tattoo on his pec. Most of the lines are old and faded, with stipple marks that make it obvious that they weren't professionally done. But there's a new mark at the end that I don't remember seeing, with crisp lines and a darker shade of ink.

"What are you keeping track of?" I ask, pointing to the tally marks tattoo on his pec.

"What?"

"Oh, um... this tattoo," I say, leaning forward and pointing to the area with a finger. When his eyes immediately drop to my cleavage, I have to lick my lips to speak. "There were 12 tally marks before, when I treated you on the boat. Now there are 13. What are you keeping track of?"

"It is the number of times I have survived being shot."

I balk, feeling my jaw fall. "You... keep track of that? On your body? With a *tattoo*?"

"A man should know how many times he has been shot."

He's been shot a dozen times?! 13 now? "Yeah, it's kind of just more concerning to me that it's happened enough times that you were afraid you'd lose track—and that a tattoo is the best way you could think of to keep that count. What about good old-fashioned pen and paper?"

"In a past life..." he eyes me as he trails off, evidently rethinking telling me the sordid details.

But my curiosity is piqued now.

"Keep going. I want to know," I say, giving him some space to speak by shoving another bite of my breakfast into my mouth.

"In a past *job*, I was supposed to inspire fear, and my boss believed this tattoo was visible proof to show to others that I am difficult to kill. It was meant to be a sign of strength and an intimidation tactic. It was not often visible, but everyone knew your number."

I swallow a bitter thickness that rises in the back of my throat despite the delicious sauce. "When you were in a *Bratva*?" I guess.

He nods. I don't want to know how old he was when the first tally mark was made. It's super faded and wavy, like it stretched as he grew.

"How did you get out of the *Bratva*? You put in for a transfer or something?" My joke feels feeble, but it makes the corners of his mouth twitch, which feels like a win.

"My father used to say that being in a *Bratva* is like a marriage—you are parted only by death." The faraway look shutters in an instant, morphing back to neutral, but not before I catch a glimpse of happy nostalgia. "I promised to earn your trust, so I will not lie to you. I will tell you if you wish, but it is not a nice story. It will not make you think well of me, Nicole."

Yeah, I knew that. But I'm done tiptoeing around it. "I've always thought that the past designs us, but it doesn't define us. What happens to you is the full story, and you get to decide which parts of it you carry with you."

"Useful words, poetically put," he says, with a faint smile, some of the rigid tension leeching from his posture. It sounds almost as if he's reciting something.

I smile, because it feels like praise, but it freezes on my lips as he begins, "I told you of my childhood—of Aleksandr. Do you remember this?"

"I don't think I could forget," I confess. Frankly, I'm haunted by the thought of a man evil enough to put a gun in the hand of a child and use that child's love for his mother to control him.

"I told you that my father worked for him, then upon his death, Aleksandr took my mother for a mistress. I believe I mentioned she died, but I did not tell you that he killed her."

I can't contain a gasp.

"Not with guns or knives. He killed her with words. He killed her spirit and beat her body and stole her light until only darkness remained. It was declared a suicide, but I knew better. Aleksandr killed her. So, I vowed to take everything from him."

He closes his eyes and takes a few deep breaths, and I use the opportunity to wipe away a tear on the back of my arm so he doesn't see me do it. I've seen the effects of domestic abuse firsthand in the emergency room too many times. What he's describing is heartbreaking and far, far too common.

"It took me many years to rise to a position where I was considered a trusted man of the inner circle. Once I was close enough, I made my move. I killed him and every single member of his elite group—a dozen men, maybe more. I remember little of that night, but I woke, stained head to toe with blood. It was a massacre."

A shocked noise slips out of me, and it makes him flinch. But he continues, eyes remaining locked on the other side of the room.

"But every man I killed had sons and brothers, and there is no way for one man to destroy an entire *Bratva*, no matter how motivated by rage. Word spread of what I had done, and I knew it was only a matter of time before someone found me and killed me to avenge their *Pakhan*. I fled Russia. I landed here. Wesley and the man we answer to—our handler—helped me disappear."

I can see why he was hesitant to tell me. He was right; it's not a nice story. Full of murder and death and betrayal.

And even so, I want so badly to comfort him, but I feel like I know him well enough at this point to anticipate his reaction. Sure, he likes touch—welcomes mine, even—but the memory of pain is a solitary experience, and not everyone appreciates a pat on the shoulder while in the throes of emotional turmoil. Dimitri is a deeply pragmatic person, like me, and sympathy only goes so far. It can't change the past.

"So, Aleksandr had you make these marks?" I ask, gesturing to his pec. He nods, and I ask, "Why keep it up?"

"I suppose I think... that it is not possible to erase what made you into the person you are. That man is dead, but his impact persists; they are not good memories, but I carry this with me as a reminder of the things I have done."

Chills climb my arms and torso. "Seems to me you wear your reminders, even without a tattoo," I say, jerking my chin at his collection of scars. "How did this all happen to you?"

His chin comes down, but since I'm staring at his abdomen, I can't tell if he's looking down at me or at the scars littering his skin. "Knife, shank, pistol, shotgun, uh... fireplace poker," he starts rattling off, pointing to each scar.

After a grimace at the last one, I shake my head. "After everything you went through with Aleksandr... I'm surprised you chose this life. You could have started over when you got here—done something else, or been someone else."

His chest expands with a noisy inhale through his nose, and I can hear the rasping of short hairs as he runs his hand across his head. It's his *I'm uncomfortable* tell. "As you said, the past designs us. I was raised in blood. I watched my schoolmates become carpenters or doctors or accountants, but I was always told this was not for me. Killing men is all I have ever known. I am very good at it."

I have no words for that. He doesn't even sound proud of the fact; he sounds like he's reciting a truth he's told himself enough times that his belief in it is unquestionable.

All at once, worry creeps back in, tainting the calm serenity and afterglow of physical and emotional intimacy, and reminding me of how complicated this situation is. I just had the best sex of my life with a man who kills people for a living. The Russian mafia may be after me. The police think I'm a missing person.

Actually, *complicated* doesn't even scratch the surface. The consequences of everything that's happened and the choices we've both made loom on the horizon, growing and shifting and staying too obscure to really be seen or understood. I'm terrified of what happens when they finally catch up with us.

Dimitri stands, taking his empty container to the kitchenette and depositing it in the sink. I pick through some of the rice with my fork, sensing the emotional distance growing. And it doesn't take a genius to understand where it's coming from.

I'm an ass. He bared himself to me, telling me something that obviously makes him uncomfortable, and I'm so in my own head that I turned it around and made it about me.

"You've had a really hard life; I'm sure it's not fun reliving those memories," I say quietly. "And for what it's worth, I'm glad you told me. I... want to know more about you. Anything you're willing to share. I'm happy just to listen."

There's a sharp, tinny noise of cutlery hitting the base of the sink, and Dimitri's head hangs as he clutches the sides. *"Ty zhenshchina, kotoraya smogla ukrotit' monstra."*

"Dimitri?"

"Thank you, Nicole."

I don't know what I said to elicit this kind of response, but when he turns, his dick is pressing against the towel, thickening and straining as it grows. The look he gives me is so hungry, I forget where I am and what I'm doing for a second. My vagina clenches, aching deep inside where he slammed into me again and again. Like a machine. An animal.

Fuck. Last night was... everything.

I'm sore, but I think I could probably stand being a little more sore. Going another round is preferable to this maudlin conversation, that's for sure.

Emboldened, I set aside the rest of my breakfast and unwrap the towel from my torso. As I reveal my nudity to him, he reaches back to steady himself against the counter in a white-knuckled grip.

The intensity of his desire for me is *such* a rush.

"No. Finish your meal," he orders on a rasp. My nipples prickle under the sharp heat of his gaze.

"I'm done."

I part my legs and let my hips shift forward. My breath stutters as his eyes rake down. The towel starts to tent around his groin, but he shakes his head.

"You are not done. You will need your strength today," he promises, reaching down to adjust himself and letting his hand linger to rub his cock through the terrycloth. "But stay just like that until you finish. I wish to watch your body ready itself for me. Drink your water, too."

A thrill zings through my stomach, and I grab for the Tupperware to do as he says, even as my body sends the rush of moisture exactly where he's watching for it.

29

DIMITRI

It's not a last resort; it's a first-round draft pick.

I turn the lock on the door, expecting the sound to echo and reveal my intentions, but it is lost among the squeaking of rubber mats against sneakers as Nicole makes her way across the gym.

This was not my original plan—the plan was to work out. We have been fucking several times every day at this point for over a week, and though it is excellent for cardio and one's core, I must not neglect my strength training program. But Nicole saw me tie on my sneakers and wanted to come with me. And then she came out in those damn tiny shorts and... well, the plan changed. And when I offered to train her, and her eyes flashed with a different kind of interest, it cemented the derailment.

My heart is pounding, and it has nothing to do with the lingering effects of our warm-up. I gesture over to the bench where I normally complete my chest presses. The pleather creaks as she settles onto the seat, and my eyes are glued to the shifting of muscles under golden skin—thighs, abs, shoulders. My cock stirs against my leg.

I remove most of the weight from the bar, setting it on the ground, leaning against the frame to be easily reachable. "This one is simple. Lay back with your head here, place your hands here and here, and push the weight up from your chest."

She does exactly as I instruct. "Like this?"

"Yes, good. Can you hold it up like that for a moment?"

"Yeah," she says, her voice strained.

I adjust the brackets down. "Okay, you may release the bar."

When she eases it down, the bar settles with a clank on the much lower braces. She tilts her chin up as the metal kisses her skin and shoots me a puzzled look.

"One more thing." I move quickly, removing the clips and then adding the heavier weights back to each side.

"Dimitri?" she asks, confused. "I don't think I'm going to be able to lift that."

Once I have finished, I nod. "Correct."

Her sharp inhale is filled with sudden understanding. She is in no danger of the barbell falling on her neck, but she cannot sit up. She is laid flat, immobilized by too much weight for her to lift away.

With a forceful breath out, she pushes against the bar. It rolls forward, then falls back into place with another loud clank. "Dimitri, what... What are you doing? Let me go," she finishes with a laugh.

"I will. When I am ready," I reply casually, moving around to the end of the bench and settling onto my haunches between her splayed legs, which hang off the edge of the bench. I grip her waist with both hands and watch as the skin around her middle dissolves into goosebumps. Her nipples suddenly poke through the bright, stretchy material of her bra.

She has some freedom of movement, and if she really wanted to get away, she could, but she will not. I know she will not. Her grip on the bar has gone from pushing at it to holding onto it for support, and the protests she is making are half-formed, undercut by the dilation of her pupils and slight rolling of her hips in excitement.

I reach out and shove her bra up, revealing her breasts from underneath the blue fabric, then hook my fingers into bike shorts and panties, dragging them down. She wiggles her hips to help me with a soft, needy noise. "What if someone comes in?" she manages as I tug her shorts down around her ass and thighs.

"I locked the door," I reply. I hope the confidence in my tone will convince her to take me at my word. "Lift your legs."

The tight shorts get stuck around her sneakers, but they pull off with some maneuvering. Then she is bared for me, mostly naked, laid out on a weight bench. I swallow, memorizing the erotic sight. I will have to replace this bench—unbolt it from the floor and steal it away—because no one may use it but the two of us now.

Her breasts are heaving, rising and falling with her quick, excited breaths. I kneel next to her, reach down to cup both at once, and she moans loudly. Flicking across her nipples with my thumbs, I admire how eagerly they respond, hardening from the sensations.

"I don't think I—" she cuts herself off, groaning as I bend forward and take one into my mouth. I swirl my tongue around the peak, enjoying the texture of her pebbled skin and the musky, salty flavor of skin and sweat. I take the very tip between my teeth and bite down gently.

"Ah!"

I pull back, blowing cool air, and she groans as it beads even more tightly against the sudden, wet cold. Bending forward, I give her other nipple the same treatment until she is writhing against me, squirming and panting.

"I don't think I want you as my trainer anymore," she manages.

"No?" I ask teasingly, lifting my head. I tweak the one that was just in my mouth, and she jerks against my hand.

"This is very... oh God... unprofessional!"

With a small, dark smile, I rise, only to sink back to my knees at the very end of the bench, finding my place between her legs and staring. The skin glistens, some moisture pooling onto the faux leather under her slit. I place my hands on her hips and tug her just a little closer.

Her head comes up, and she tries to see what is happening without choking herself on the bar. The tone of her false outrage changes into something sharper. "What are you doing? Dimitri, wait."

I pause, eyeing her with something halfway between curiosity and suspicion. "You are too sore or tired?"

"No. I'm..." she trails off and laughs again, though this time it is an entirely self-deprecating noise, like she cannot believe I am going to make her say it out loud. But I am. And I am going to keep making her say things out loud so there can be no confusion and no embarrassment between us. "I got all sweaty on the treadmill, and I probably smell. I need to shower before you—"

"Of course you have a smell," I say, pausing and staring at her naked skin in a way that makes her inner thighs tense, as if she is trying to close her legs. "I like it. Very much. Now, hold still."

"Dimitri—" she begins, even sharper this time with irritation.

"Do it," I command.

Her squirming takes on a new urgency. She is pushing at the bar again, wiggling like she is trying to roll off the bench. I slide my arms under her knees, sandwiching her legs in the crooks of my elbows so she cannot go anywhere and will not hurt herself trying.

"You will not deny me. Your desire smells sweet, my *med*. I cannot wait to have it in my mouth."

"Dimitri!" she cries at the swipe of my tongue. Her hips still, then buck upwards, seeking more of the pressure against her clit.

I will never tire of the sound of my name on her lips. I hum against her heated, soft, wet skin. "Like a sour fruit on my tongue. Not so sweet, but tangy." I wet my lips using her liquids and create a circle around the most sensitive place on her body, and suck gently.

Her nails scratch gently against my scalp as she reaches down to hold my head in both hands. I am pleased she has realized she retains the use of her arms, even if she cannot move from her position on her back easily.

"Fuck," she hisses. "Oh... fuck. You're good at that. Keep going."

Good. She is learning to be more direct and vocal about what she wants. I rumble my approval of her surrender, feeling how it vibrates my mouth against her sensitive skin. The flavor may be hard to describe, but the feeling is not. Her clit is a slick bump, much like the head of my own cock, only much smaller—like the tip of a nose, spongy and stiff, but pliable. It resists under the pressure of my tongue, popping back against my lips every time I release it. A button to press again and again.

Her noises are music to my ears, and I steal away the memory of each gasp and moan. I know now that the true signal of her impending orgasm is when her noises quiet and give way to heavy breaths of concentration. The high-pitched sounds help me find the preferred rhythm and place, but it is the silence afterwards and intense focus that tell me it is correct.

A light layer of sweat builds on the surface of her skin, and her muscles tense. She starts squeezing against me, as if she would press into my ears with her thighs. Her fingers continue to brush against my short hair, massaging my scalp mindlessly for something to do with her hands. My body answers with a shudder of its own, the sensation drawing downwards along either side of my spine. My cock is already hard against my leg, thick with desire for release—both from its prison of fabric, and the all-consuming need to come.

All the while, my tongue follows the pattern her body tells me it likes. If we were in our bed, and I could prop up her hips on a pillow, I would work in a finger or two to ensure she is open and ready for my cock. But the angle has her pelvis tilted down, and it would be too much pressure to work in a single finger. She is slick with her desire for me, but gravity is not working in our favor.

"Oh... my..." she breathes, and I must steady myself, as her excitement instinctively makes me want to move faster. "I'm... gonna..."

Her pussy clenches, tightening around nothing, and I can just see at the top of my field of vision how her stomach rolls and pulses with her release. She jerks, writhes, grabs my head even harder, and rides out the pleasure on my face like this was always her idea. I smile against her, slowing but maintaining contact as she comes down from the high.

As her body relaxes back, her legs falling loose in my arms and her hands folding across her stomach, she laughs and makes a pleased humming noise with an exhale. "That was really hot."

"Da," I agree, blowing some cool air against her clit and making her giggle. My cock is pounding so hard against my leg that it may explode, but there is not enough room to safely fuck her this way. It will be much easier if she gets up first, and I bend her over the bench.

"Da," she repeats, and I can hear the smile. "I'll admit, I wasn't sure where you were going with this bar initially, but lying here and knowing I couldn't sit up but not actually feeling the restraint of it was... I don't know. Fucking incredible. I never thought I was that girl who wanted to be tied up."

"I have no wish to tie you up," I say simply. I lay her legs down one at a time, letting her get used to their weight again, and stand. As I walk around, I commit the sight of her to memory. She has not yet fixed her bra, and her breasts are flushed and covered with the same glistening sweat that is on the rest of her body.

"You don't?" she asks, sounding somewhat disappointed.

"Rope is not in my style. I prefer a more... manual approach." I remove one of the heavy plates and then the other, reaching down to lift the bar out of the way for her so she can roll up. When she turns back to look at me, I can see from her hazy, desire-filled eyes that she likes the distinction I have made. "You like to be handled by a man, *da?*"

She smiles, lifting one leg and bringing it around so she can stand. "You mean manhandled?"

"That is what I said."

She shakes her head. "The words are the same, but the connotation is slightly different. But either way, you're right. I think I do like being manhandled, but only if you're the man doing it."

"Good. Then bend over the bench. Let me show you the proper form for—"

There is a buzzing against my leg. And then another. I curse.

"You want to get that?" she asks, glancing down at my pants.

No. I do not want to get that. I want to fuck her. I want to never stop fucking her. "I should. It is usually important." I have to add the qualifier because sometimes it is very much not, like a picture of James's dinner or a sports match update from Wesley that I do not care about. Whenever they get too off-topic, I leave the group chat.

I reach towards her, and she comes, as if pulled by an invisible force. Wrapping my hand around the back of her neck, I tilt her head and kiss her. The flavor of her, still on my lips, changes as she licks against the seam of my mouth. I pull back and tilt her head down to kiss her forehead, then let her go to dig in my pocket.

As she finds her shorts on the floor and struggles to pull them on over her shoes, I scan the message. "It is... very important. Shit. I must go."

"It's fine," she assures me, smiling. "I'll just finish down here."

Fueled by irritation at the interruption, I take the stairs two at a time. Wesley pauses with his drink halfway to his mouth when he sees me in the doorway of his office. "You look... more pissed off than usual," he begins, glancing up and down with a curious frown. "Did I interrupt your workout?"

"Different kind of exercising, I think, Wes. Didn't you hear them going at it like rabbits down there?" James says from behind me. I spin, moving aside to allow him through the doorway and then following him inside. The smell of coffee wafts behind him, and he salutes me with the mug as he settles into his chair.

I scowl at him. I do not wish for Nicole to be embarrassed that the others heard us. "We were not—"

"Don't bother denying it, Big D. The chandeliers were shakin'," he continues with a wink aimed at me.

Unlikely. They are bolted in. "We were not—"

Wesley groans. "In the gym, Dimitri? The gym we *all* use? Ugh. You'd better sanitize everything."

"Why? Your OCD ass is just going to clean it again," James quips. "And he's far from the first to christen the gym. One time, Eleanor and I—"

"Animals. Both of you."

It is ridiculous to think they might have heard anything through layers of wood and carpet, but I know this teasing is part of male camaraderie. I perch against the side table behind the desk, looking between them with my arms crossed, but I cannot bring myself to admonish them for their childishness. For the first time, I do not feel singled out as different or strange for my behavior. Though the jokes are at my expense, they are meant to include me.

"You said you had news?" I say, adjusting my position. My cock is still half-hard.

"In a rush?" Wesley asks with an insincerity that I would normally find quite grating. This morning, it does not bother me so much. Though cut short, my "workout" with Nicole has put me in a good mood. I can still taste her on my lips.

"Yes. I am training Nicole."

"To do what?" James asks, his double meaning plain as he waggles his eyebrows.

"*Koz'ye yaichko.* What are these important updates?"

Wesley flashes a grin, but chooses not to make whatever humorous comment he is thinking. "A few things. First, I got through the first layer of security on the USB—a fairly simple PIN—but there's another. And it's multifactor. We need Viktor's phone and a password. No way around it."

With those small, simple words, a torrent of emotions is unleashed that is so strong, it is nearly painful. Once the pride in my team dissipates,

I am left with a prickling irritation about this setback, and a cold kind of fear.

I promised her that once we cracked the USB, we would discuss her leaving. This is one step closer to that.

I cannot lose her, not now that I have just had her. There is too much left between us—too much unsaid, too much to explore.

"Snatch and grab, then," James says, interlocking his fingers and resting them on the top of his head. A relaxed, leaned-back posture. He looks to me. "Store him on ice?"

Our faceless corporation owns several properties all over the tri-state area, which are useful to us. The old butcher's shop has a stainless-steel freezer that is soundproof and lockable from the outside, and it is in a quiet enough area that no one is around to see bodies being hauled in or out. It has become the perfect short-term prison, with the added benefit that the threat of frostbite makes people much more willing to cooperate.

"*Da*. We will need to infiltrate his life more closely to determine the points in his routine where he is the most unguarded. What are the other updates?"

"I've got our confirmation about Kyle." Wearing an excited expression, Wesley turns the monitor to show us a grainy picture of the side of Kyle's face through the front window of a car. There is a timestamp at the bottom with a date. "Traffic cam footage caught him leaving the home of our coroner in the wee hours of the morning after the wedding—well past his supposed time of death."

"And *this* is why I drive the speed limit and do not run red lights," I say, vindicated. I have been teased about this relentlessly for years—accused of driving like so many dead grandmothers.

"Yeah, yeah," James rolls his eyes and waves dismissively. "So, he's alive. Do we know where he is?"

"No."

"What about Felix?"

"That's my last update. I had a hit on one of the aliases Mac sent me: Roberto Lomas bought petrol in a Podunk town in western Pennsylvania last night. No way to confirm it was Felix. No cameras."

"Felix would know which places didn't have cameras—could definitely be him," James nods, thoughtfully stroking his chin. "Long way from home. Kinda seems like maybe he's not involved in all this with Kyle and the coroner."

My eyes cut to Wesley, and we both look at James. He has some lingering loyalty towards Felix that I do not quite understand. Perhaps it is an abundance of caution where my woman is concerned, but I would rather treat Felix as a dangerous unknown. I can see that Wesley agrees with me.

"I've been thinking about that. I know we can't be certain they're working together, but if you had to fake your own death, who would you go to?" Wesley asks carefully.

"You."

Wesley smirks at the speed of James's answer, but shakes his head. "If you couldn't come to me."

After a few seconds of grinding his jaw, James sighs. "Felix. It's not like he's got a menu of services or anything, but he's the guy who gets you things—he makes things happen." He sighs, casts his eyes towards the ceiling, and shakes his head. "I just... I dunno. I know we can't set our watches by my gut, but something doesn't feel right about this."

"Explain," I demand.

"It's not like we're pals or drinking buddies or anything, but I know people. I know him. He goes where the money is, but he's real careful and smart. I'm not saying he doesn't occasionally cross paths with a *Bratva*, but they're not subtle. They run guns and drugs. They're on all kinds of FBI lists. You get what I'm sayin'? A guy with a reputation as someone real careful and smart wouldn't get in bed with the likes of them."

Wesley lifts a brow. "You're saying working with a *Bratva* is not his style?"

"Kind of. He'd do a job for them, get himself set up with a fat stack or a favor or two, but he wouldn't work *with* 'em. The distinction is small, but it feels important. If he's involved, he's an independent player. He's got his own agenda—maybe it aligns with theirs, but it's separate. And to a point Big D's made before, Volkevich has everyone he needs to take care of issues in-house. *Bratvas* don't use contractors. So why would he need Felix?"

"Valid points," Wesley admits. "Perhaps Kyle is working outside the family on something."

"That's my guess," James shrugs.

"Well, I'd argue we need to keep Felix in our sights. He's dangerous."

"Fair enough," James acquiesces, though his mouth is tight and his brows are drawn together. "Priority is Viktor and his phone. And Kyle."

They both glance at me for the final word. Realistically, my opinion holds no more weight, but we often default to my decision since I assume the most risk as the man on the ground.

"It is poor form to kill useful, neutral men. James believes he is not directly involved. I would rather avoid violence against Felix for now, and focus on the job we have been paid to do."

James's brows shoot up. "Wow. This from the guy who loves violence," he says, directing it at Wesley. "Usually, it's not a last resort; it's a first-round draft pick."

"Truly baffling," Wesley agrees dryly.

"Must be going soft in his old age."

I roll my eyes. "But if it turns out that he is a threat to Nicole, I will not hesitate," I tack on.

James's smirk tilts to something altogether more bloodthirsty, and I receive a nod of approval from Wesley.

"And James, perhaps you should come down to spar with me if you truly think I am becoming soft, and I will show you that you are wrong," I level the challenge at my sniper.

He laughs in his easy way. "I'll hand you your own ass some other day, when I'm not covering it."

I roll my eyes at his needling. Even if it were true that he could beat me as easily as he implies, it would be a testament to my own abilities as much as his—he has learned much more about hand-to-hand combat under my tutelage than from the US Army.

"You know, I've been charting points scored while sparring. Care to see just how many times you've handed Dimitri his arse in the past six months?" Wesley asks lightly, turning his screen slightly to display a graphic of a circle with two distinct colors.

"I assume it is the very small blue wedge in the much larger red circle," I point to the screen, shamelessly taking immense satisfaction from the visual representation of my skills.

"You made a fuckin' pie chart? Why am I not surprised?" James shakes his head, a small smile at the corners of his lips. "Where's our sparring pie chart, you fuckin' nerd? I've gotta be the bigger slice in that one."

Wesley lifts one shoulder. "By a margin smaller than your ego, that's for sure."

I laugh, and the two of them turn around as if they had coordinated the movement in advance, gaping at me. I look between the two of them, but they just stare. "What?" I ask, scowling. "It was clever."

They exchange a look. James snorts, and Wesley shakes his head and reaches for his mouse.

"I got the joke," I say, still baffled by their reaction. "Normally, people enjoy it when you understand the things they say to be funny, *da*?"

"Yeah. And you laughed at it. You never laugh."

I scoff and push off the desk. "You are both ridiculous. I will finish what I started with Nicole, then return here so we can discuss the plan."

"Have you ever heard him laugh?" Wesley asks James, his question following me as I leave the room. I cannot tell if it is another joke, so I ignore it.

If this is what comes of showing Wesley that I understand his humor, I will save my laughter for someone who does not make me feel ridiculous for it. Like Nicole.

30

NICOLE

—◦—

My dreams were once red with blood

The harsh midday sun hitting my eyelids wakes me, but it's not an abrupt shift from sleep to awareness. I'm gently roused with the growing awareness that Dimitri and I are naked and tangled in each other—ankles stacked, his stomach expanding slowly behind me, his breath warm and even against the back of my neck, blowing at a piece of hair and making it tickle against my cheek.

I'm trying to adapt to his weird sleeping schedule because I love him like this, filling the space behind me. Even though his hand is on my belly, I'm not even self-conscious about it anymore—

That hand is moving. He's not as asleep as I thought.

I remain completely still, though my eyes pop open. His fingers are pressing small circles into my skin, a light massage that's slowly traveling towards my breast. My body wakes instantly with a zinging sensation of awareness and arousal. As I work to control my breathing, I register the rasping quality of his.

His large, warm, rough palm brushes my nipple, which instantly hardens against his hand. He kneads the flesh softly and delicately for a moment, sweeping his thumb across the taut tip. I let out a longer, louder breath, and heat prickles at my skin, pooling between my legs. I feel the telltale throbbing beginning as my sex swells with an excited demand.

I love how he cups and squeezes my breasts and plays with nipples I was taught to be self-conscious of long ago. Not that I'd ever tell him that.

Instead, I take a mental picture of each look of reverence and enthusiasm as proof that boys *do* like big, dark nipples and huge tits.

I work not to squirm against his hand as he starts tracing it down, along the lines of my soft body. I know where he's headed now.

My pulse thrums quicker as my body reacts to being touched with a rush of moisture between my legs—how far is he going to take this? Does he think I'm asleep? Would it change anything for him if I were? My enjoyment is important to him, I know, but the finer details of blanket consent might be lost on him...

So why is it so hot to me that he would touch me, thinking I was asleep? That he wants me so badly, he doesn't want to wait?

"Always so wet for me," he whispers into my ear as his fingers slide around the curve of my stomach, in between my legs. There's no friction, just the silky desire and pulsing, heated skin. When he taps my clit, I can't stop my body's shuddering reaction. I jerk against his hand, and my insides clench around nothing.

The jig is up, so I move my leg out of the way—back and bending my knee towards the ceiling, making a tent of the covers—to make room for his hand. "Always so hard for me," I pant back.

Dimitri's other arm shifts, creating a cradle for my head as I turn my body halfway towards him. "Would you like to have awakened with my cock deep inside of you, my med?"

I shiver, and it has nothing to do with the little frizzles of sparkling heat from his fingers against my nerve endings.

Maybe I was wrong about the blanket consent thing...

I catch sight of his face in the strange, golden light filtering in through the windows, and I suck in a breath at the intensity in his expression. Scratchy black stubble on his chin makes the insides of my thighs prickle with the memory of its texture. He's clenching his jaw, which makes his scar look more pronounced around his temple. There's no trace of sleep in his eyes, though I still feel like I'm wading through the viscosity of drowsiness and arousal, both of which cloud my mind in different ways.

Pinned under his icy stare, all I can do is nod.

I would. I really would. I want to be so full of him that he takes over my subconscious. I want to be dreaming of him so that when I wake in startled confusion, aroused and unsure why, he'll be my first thought long before I register the stretch of him deep inside me. I want to be able to recognize his weight on me, to breathe him into my lungs so he's everywhere at the same time.

His lids lower, softening his stare, and his finger glides across and around my clit. "Do you like it when I take what I want from you?"

"Yes," I breathe, my pulse quickens as his fingers pick up speed. Flames lick the inside of my skin, triggering a wave of goosebumps that prick at my nipples and making me shiver at the heat.

"That is good," he hums, close enough that his warm breath is a puff of air against my ear. "I wake wanting you, Nicole. I go to sleep wanting you. I am filled with wanting."

I whimper, rolling my hips and grinding against his hand as the sensations he's calling forth start to collect and grow. The frankness of his words emboldens me to the same level of bare honesty.

"So am I," I manage. "I want you all the time. It's never been like this before for me."

"I believe I dreamt of you—I think I always do, now. My dreams were once red with blood, but they are now tinted like golden honey. Like your hair..." he nuzzles closer, breathing in like he can't get enough of my scent, "and your skin, and your eyes... my med."

Fuuuuck. The things he says...

I cry out sharply, feeling the pressure in my abdomen build towards the peak. But his hand stills against me, and he swallows my frustrated groan as he turns my neck and fits his mouth over mine. His kiss is lazy, unhurried, self-satisfied, and I clutch at him, trying to draw him down more fully over the top of me. I spread my legs to make room for his body between them.

"I need you," I moan, breaking away and panting. I'm so empty, so painfully empty.

He smirks. "And you will have me. After I prepare you."

An idea strikes through the shroud of helplessness. I don't have to lie here and let him toy with me. My hand around the side of his neck moves down to his sternum, and I shove at him. I'm strong, but he's obviously stronger—so when he shifts back, I know it has to be due mostly to surprise. I use it to my advantage and follow him, coming up on my knees and pinning his back to the mattress with both my hands squarely on his chest.

He watches with a laid-back kind of interest, like he wants to see what I'll do before he decides whether to intervene. I throw a leg over his hip, pressing down on his chest for leverage and to keep him in place. His cock folds upwards against his body, and I position the length of him along the seam of my pussy. Then, I roll my hips forward and grind. And groan.

The look in his eye shifts to one of rapt focus, watching the head of himself disappearing between my legs under my stomach, then reappearing wet and slick with our combined desire.

I watch him watching us, and it only makes me hotter. He's so hard, and I'm so wet; all it takes for him to slide right in is me leaning forward and rocking my hips to find the right angle. Then, it's his turn to groan. I shut my eyes as I slide back and down onto his length. It stretches me deep inside, a brief, fleeting sting that proves my memory a liar. Somehow, he fills me more than I seem to remember, every time.

"See? Isn't this..." my breath shudders as I grind my hips in a circle. There's got to be some sort of pleasure button buried in the deepest part of my vagina. Every time he brushes it with the head of his cock, it sends me into orbit. But now? With the weight of my body on top of his, his tip is *pushing* it. Repeatedly.

"What?" he asks, caressing my hips with his thumbs. His grip there is gentle, instead of a controlling hold meant to spur me on or move me at his pleasure.

"Isn't it nice?" I gasp, letting my head fall forward and my hair curtain my face.

"No. I would not call being inside of you *nice*," he rasps. "It… is… everything."

I still at that, emotions rising in the back of my throat. His hand moves to my face, pushing my hair back and placing his thumb on the edge of my mouth. I move my neck slightly to purse my lips against it in a kiss, then I take it between my teeth. He watches with heat in his eyes, breathing audibly as he locks in on the movement.

I hold that hand to sweep it down my collarbones and rest it on my breast. He takes over from there, massaging the full weight of it, then plucking at just the tip. "You know I mean, isn't it nice with me on top," I counter. It feels like a moot point.

His smile is a ghost of a flicker at the edges of his mouth. "*Da.*" Breaking the intensity of the moment, he stretches back, placing both arms behind his head in a way that both lengthens and displays all the hard planes of his upper body. "Very nice. I enjoy the view."

I nearly laugh, but the cocksure look on his face makes me want to ruin his composure, so I lift up and snap my hips down, tightening at the same time. It makes both of us groan, but it also makes him whip his arms out to grab me again.

"*Zlaya zhenshchina,*" he hisses. "Wicked, wonderful woman."

"Ah, ah," I tsk, knowing from how tightly he holds my waist and how his lower abs tense against me that he's about to flip us. I splay my fingers on his chest, one on each pec, pushing him back against the pillows as I lift myself up and down just a few inches. I want to keep him as deep inside of me as I can while still giving each of us some friction.

Even now, even in this position where I'm supposed to be in control, his power and strength are a coiled spring, ready to be released. I can tell from the look on his face he's not going to let this go on much longer, and it fills me with an illicit kind of heat—half nervous and unsure about what he'll do next, half delirious with desire because I don't know when or how it's going to happen.

Better make the most of this.

I roll my hips, grinding my clit into his pelvic bone and rocking back and forth along his length. I can feel my pussy gripping him, trying so hard not to let him go, just as much as I can feel that dull ache of the stretch when I pull him all the way back in.

His eyes are locked in, staring at where our bodies are joined. I know he's seeing how his own thick, hard length emerges, shining with the moisture of both our bodies, only to disappear into my swollen skin. "You take me so well, my med. You like it deep, *da*?"

Concentrating so I can finish before he takes over, all I can do is nod with my eyes closed. The sum of the sensations is amazing. Even though my hips creak a little, my thighs spread so wide over his that I don't have much leverage, I love being able to move exactly how I like. I love being able to fill my hands with him for once, to tease him with my body as I take what *I* want.

"Deep and hard," he groans.

"Yes... it's so good, Dimitri. I'm... so... close..." I murmur, feeling the tension building deep inside.

That was apparently what he was waiting for. In an instant, I'm off-balance, falling backwards, and he's rolling on top of me. I don't think his cock even slips out as he finds his position between my legs. And then he's kissing me with bruising force, slamming into me and drawing a cry from me that he consumes into his own mouth at the apex of each thrust.

That's how I come, writhing underneath all his power and force, completely at his will, loving every inch and second of it. The build was slow and comfortable, but the release is a crack of lightning—stunning, bright, intense, and quick. I lose myself, my grip on reality, and some of my sanity as my body shudders in its release.

He's right on my heels, so lost that he can't focus on our kiss, dropping his head into the crook of my neck as he groans. I stroke his back with my fingernails, earning little shivers from him and a deep rumbling laugh that makes me wonder if he isn't a tiny bit ticklish.

Ticklish Dimitri? What an almost unbelievably charming thought.

Once he has himself under control, he pulls back and catches my eye. I can't decipher the look on his face, but it's not just the thorough satisfaction of a good sexual release. There's something else in there, buried deep, and it's inherently somber and conflicted. Not wanting to let it intrude on our happy moment, I wrap my arms around his neck and draw his mouth back down on mine.

He tastes like a combination of the two of us and a little bit of bitter morning breath that doesn't even bother me. I melt against him as he deepens the kiss. His tongue sweeps just inside, tangling with mine. The scratch of his regrowth against my lips and chin is uncomfortable, but I lean into it harder. I want to feel him after he's gone, even if it's in the rawness of chafed skin.

Like he senses I need it—or maybe *he* does—he stays with me, making out and taking comfort and pleasure in the closeness, until I pull back first. I sigh to myself as he rolls away and gets to his feet. Reaching for my glasses, I get them on just in time to watch his ass disappear into the bathroom.

I'm dozing when he emerges from the office/closet, fully dressed. I open one eye sleepily, then sit up with a start, wide awake.

Holy fucking fuck. I forgot how good he looked in a suit. How is it possible for him to look better wearing clothes than being naked? My eyes scan zigzags up and down his body, taking in the way the slacks tighten around his hips and his biceps strain against the nice shirt. He's clean, sharp, polished. Between the clothes, the scarred face, and the air of menace, he's like a Bond villain.

"A little fancy for a workout," I remark dryly despite a racing heart. I am *so* going to jump his bones later.

"Viktor Volkevich will be visiting his casino tonight, so we are moving forward with the plan. Wesley, James, and I will spend some time preparing, and we will be back very late."

My brows shoot up, but I don't say anything. Viktor Volkevich. The infamous *Bratva Pakhan,* whose USB I apparently had shoved down my throat. His death means my ultimate release. My return to normalcy.

No wonder that look Dimitri gave me was so conflicted—he's obviously about to do something dangerous. My stomach flips over, suddenly nervous for him.

I take a long gulp of water and bring my knees up into a crisscross seated position. "I'm surprised you can even find nice clothes that fit you," I say, knowing at least this is a safe topic.

He turns and assesses the fit in the mirror on the back of the bathroom door. "No one with shoulders as wide as mine would ever choose to wear a suit," he agrees. "If the jacket is large enough for me to move freely, it is baggy and ill-fitting. I am too large to simply walk into a store; I have to get everything tailored or made."

"Sounds expensive and time-consuming."

He sits on the bed to pull on some silk socks and lace his fancy, uncomfortable-looking leather shoes. "Perhaps, though Helga is an excellent seamstress, even if she insults me under her breath the entire time she is pinning the fabric. And she knows I speak German."

I hide a smile by pressing my lips together. "How many languages do you speak?"

"Four," he shrugs. "German and English are close, so it was not so hard to learn both."

It's a strange thing that this is what cuts through the haze of denial. Seeing him in a suit again—a throwback to the night we met that started with such bright, bubbly happiness, only to melt into panic and fear—and being reminded that he knows more languages than anyone I've ever met is a sort of wake-up call.

I swallow and look down at my hands. "I think I just realized how long the list of things I still don't know about you is."

The bed dips by my feet, and his hand is warm around the side of my neck, tilting my head up towards him. "We have time for these discussions," he says.

I feel the line form between my brows. "Do we?"

I'm filled to the brim with uncomfortable questions that sour my stomach and dissolve any of the lingering happiness from waking up and having Dimitri rearrange my guts.

How long until I can go home? What happens then? Will he still want to... date? Is that what we've been doing? It doesn't feel like it. So how would we even begin to navigate a casual relationship after all this? Should we even try?

I think I prefer being in denial.

"We have time," he repeats.

Don't worry about it, not yet, he seems to say.

I nod.

He pulls me forward, meeting me halfway, and presses a kiss to the middle of my forehead.

He leaves, then, and I fall back against the pillow with a sigh, staring at the beams in the ceiling. *We have time,* he says. Too bad I'm a serial overthinker—it's a skill to be so many steps ahead of myself, truly.

Objectively, it hasn't been that long, but I already have a hard time picturing myself going back to my old life. And I loved my old life, as messy and chaotic as it sometimes was. I miss work. I miss the sterile smells of the hospital, and the camaraderie of bitching about a trouble patient at the nursing station. I miss feeling safe enough to leave the house. I miss the comfort of being surrounded by my own stuff. I miss having full control over every decision I make.

It's not uncomfortable here by any means, but there's a world of difference between waking up and thinking, "what should I do today" and "what *can* I do today."

I jump out of bed and head towards the shower. I need to rinse away the evidence of how Dimitri says good morning, then I need to put on some bike shorts and release some of this nervous energy. Maybe I'll hit something. That sandbag in the gym will do.

31

DIMITRI

*Torturing a man for information is nothing like
bicycling.*

After shaking out my hand from the jarring impact of knuckles against
bone, I crack my neck to release the tension from my right shoulder and
turn back to Viktor Volkevich, who is slumped in the chair. Bright red
falls one droplet at a time from his nose onto his chest, getting lost in
matted hair and older, dried blood.

Drip. Drip. Drip.

He and I have only been at this for two hours, but it is rather cold in
this meat locker. Fluids dry and freeze quicker—that is why it is a favored,
if somewhat stereotypical, place for interrogations such as this. That and
the drain conveniently built into the floor.

My breath puffs out in front of my mouth, almost making me smile.
I have missed the cold. Winter in New Jersey just is not as bitter or as
long as it is in Russia, and the summers here are much too hot. I feel very
energized.

I can taste victory.

In the end, getting Viktor to the butcher shop was a relatively simple
matter. I disposed of his driver, donned my disguise, and picked him up
at the usual time in the usual place outside the casino. He got right into
the car with his guards—men who are now dead, though they are still
sluggishly bleeding out on the floor at our feet. Viktor flinched when I
sliced their throats, but has given their bodies little attention since. Ever

the cold, aloof *Pakhan*, believing his life means so much more than the men who keep it safe.

"This guy's a real piece of fuckin' work. The more Wes finds on his cell, the more I want to get in there and knock a few teeth loose myself," James growls, low and dangerous.

"Drugs, prostitution, gun running... there aren't many illegal pots Viktor isn't sticking his finger in," Wesley adds. *"There's stuff on here about a shipment, too. Encoded. Probably human trafficking, if I had a guess."*

They are both angry and ready to punish him for his crimes, but James will not leave his lookout post to join me in here, and Wesley will continue searching Viktor's devices for information.

We each have our roles.

Mine is delivering retribution using my fists and inspiring fear.

For a man who has ostensibly ordered his men to do much, much worse, Viktor Volkevich is surprisingly weak-willed when it comes to pain. He was sobbing before I even began—all I did was slice his Achilles tendons so he could not run. He is a coward. A coward who preys on those less powerful. A coward who now stinks of fear and piss.

We need that password, but Viktor knows that he will only live long enough to give it to me, and he is stalling. But he will not last much longer. In fact, he will give me what I want after just a few more hits, and then I will end this. I have done this enough times to know when every man will break, though it has been many years since I have been forced to use this particular skill.

What is it the Americans say? It is a thing you never forget, like bicycling? Another senseless idiom. Torturing a man for information is nothing like bicycling.

I examine the knuckles of my right hand. They are bruised and have some small cuts, since I never wear brass knuckles for interrogations—I need information, and men with no teeth find it difficult to enunciate—but overall are faring far better than Viktor's face. I survey the damage to his cosmetically enhanced features as I sink into a low crouch to be in his line of sight.

His nose is not just broken; it is crushed. His orbital bone is cracked in three places, his lip is split, and several of his teeth are loose. Blood spills from his nose and his mouth. Several fingers are broken and missing fingernails. Burn marks litter his bare chest, though his skin has taken on a pallid tone from the cold.

Yes, he will break soon. He really is nothing like the men of his title in Russia. I have been through worse myself.

"Please," he moans, barely lifting his head. One of his eyes has begun to swell shut. "No more."

"The password," I remind him of what will make the pain stop.

He spits blood, aiming for the floor but only managing to spill it into his own lap. "Let me go and I will tell you."

I scratch at the stubble on my jaw, regarding him. The silence stretches for long enough that he chances a look up, almost childlike with hope that I might believe his lie. The expression freezes on his face as I wander back towards the stainless-steel rolling table, where my instruments sit in small pools of blood.

"No!" he hisses.

I lift the pliers from the table.

"No! No more!"

"The password."

"It is of no use to you! Just some documents."

Ever since we began, and I asked for the password, he has been trying to convince me that I do not want it. Even if I knew nothing else, this would convince me that I do. "The password," I repeat calmly.

"Why?" he wails. "Why? It is nothing. Nothing!"

I cross my arms. As the interrogator, it is never a good idea to answer any questions. Information passes only one way; it is not an exchange. I must maintain the upper hand.

"There are no stupid *Pakhans*," I begin, knowing that he will fill in the rest of the phrase. *Only smart* Pakhans *and dead men.* "You are a dead man, Viktor. No one will rescue you. No one knows you are here, and your men are dead. How quickly and painfully you die is the only thing within your power. I can make it last for days. I can draw out your agony until you remember nothing but pain. Or, I can put a bullet in your brain and end your sorry life quickly. Either way, you will die."

Hopelessness twists his features, deepening the lines between his brows and making him appear much older. "There are many others... They will avenge me," he whispers, his teeth stained with red. It is not the first time he has made this threat, but he no longer believes in its power.

"And we will kill them, too. No one will ever find your body."

When a tear slips from beneath his closed eyelid, freezing on its path downward, I know I have succeeded. One final threat should do it. I had better make it a good one.

"Give me the password, or I will skin you. Starting with your cock."

He flinches, trying to draw his thighs together to protect his tiny prick. "Moscow1980, one word, capital M, with an exclamation mark at the end."

The Moscow Olympics? Interesting. Easy enough for a man of his age to remember, I suppose. I do not bother asking if Wesley heard, and a second later, he proves my confidence in him is well earned, as always.

"Checking... Yes. I'm in!"

Relief and triumph surge in my veins, making my hands shake. "Not so stupid, in the end," I approve. I replace the pliers on the table and select one of my favored knives. Even with cold blood moving more slowly, it does not take long for a person to bleed out. We should have plenty of time to dispose of the body before day breaks.

"At least tell me who sent you," he wheezes, eyeing the knife with a glint of resignation and determination in his eye. He will not fight me, but he will meet his end with a modicum of dignity. "I thought at first Gorchev or perhaps Wozniak, but you are no *bratok*."

I spin the knife in my grip, watching him watch the blade flash in the eerie blue-toned fluorescent lights. On a whim, I lie, "Kyle."

All at once, his entire demeanor shifts. Rage boils in his expression. "What?" he hisses, pulling against his ties. "He is alive?! That little... I gave him *everything*! This is how he repays me? I should have known that son of a whore would betray me like this!"

"Guess we know Kyle was acting outside the family business. Sounds like they don't even know he's alive, much less what he took from them. Good one, Big D."

He continues to thrash against his bonds, switching to Russian to curse Kyle and his entire line. Then he begins cursing me, struggling so viciously that his chair nearly tips.

"Whoa," Wesley's voice is so soft I must strain to hear him over the stream of Russian threats. *"There's... a lot on here. I'm going to... erm, need some time to sort it all out."* Wesley is not unshakable, but I have not heard his voice this strained and distinctly uncomfortable in some time.

"What is it? Anything we might still need him alive for?"

He clears his throat, and when he speaks again, his tone has hardened to something nearly unrecognizable. *"No, it's..."* his voice breaks, and he clears it again. *"Little girls. I... this is horrifying. Let's just say that he deserves the most painful death in your repertoire, Dimitri."*

Just as well. I am done asking questions, particularly as Viktor has begun the bartering phase. "Whatever he is paying you, it is nothing compared to what I will pay you. Tell me where he is, tell me where my drive is, help me kill that—"

Generally, I prefer more of a fight, but even under these less-than-satisfying circumstances, there is no greater rush of power than holding another man's life in your hands and deciding to take it. It is sick, perhaps, and made even worse by a lack of remorse. I do not know if James and

Wesley experience the same, or if it is just me. It is not something we discuss.

His hate-filled speech dissolves into screams as I slide the knife into his shoulder in just the spot that severs the carotid artery. Because I am a man of my word, it is the quick death I promised in exchange for the information, though I no longer believe he deserves it. I am splattered with red by the unavoidable spray, and Viktor is unconscious in five seconds, asleep as his life's blood runs a staining river down his chest, to the floor, and creeps towards the drain.

Once he is dead, I feel nothing. The act of killing him arouses nothing more than the satisfaction of successfully completing our mission. He was *Bratva* scum. And one day, if I am killed similarly, my killer should feel no remorse because I am not better than him—just much harder to kill.

By the time I have finished cleaning his blood down the drain and rinsing away the bleach, much of the adrenaline has worn off, allowing every painful sensation in my body to return. My right hand aches fiercely, a dull throb that I cannot shake away, and the area on my abdomen where one of Viktor's guards got in a good hit before I slit his throat is sore and bruised.

I wash away the bloodstains on my bare skin as best I can in the large sink just outside the meat freezer, then discard my clothing in favor of something clean from the go-bag in my trunk for the drive home. Wesley returned to the house to start processing the USB on his larger computer ages ago, and James is disposing of the pieces of the body, so I will be driving myself.

My mind is elsewhere for the entire ride, filled with blood and nauseating concerns that have nothing to do with the life I took tonight.

It is done.

Kyle may be alive, but he was not working with his uncle, so there is no reason to believe that the remaining Volkeviches know anything about

Nicole. We have unlocked the USB. It is only a matter of time before we will unravel its mysteries, and once we do, she can...

What? Leave?

No.

She speaks of her job with longing. She tries to hide her boredom from me. She enjoys the pleasure I give and take, but it is not enough. She needs more.

I wish I could think of a way to be enough. To make her want to stay. I would give her anything—everything—except the only thing she wants.

Freedom.

What if this is our last night?

When I arrive home, I move silently through the house to the back-yard. It is very late, and all the lights are out in the pool house. Nicole must be sleeping—that is good. She sleeps deeply, and I need to shower and clean up the wounds on my hand before she sees me.

I stalk towards the building, feeling wild. Unhinged. My heart beats harder and faster the closer I get, and I want nothing more than to wake her. Take her. Pour myself into her.

Fuck. And she would let me. My generous, passionate, beautiful *med*. She would open her arms and her legs and let me take whatever I wanted from her.

I *need* that. I need her. Too much.

By now, I know how her strength matches my own and how her body opens and fits me so perfectly. Even as out of control as I currently feel, I know that I will not hurt her. But that does not mean she deserves... whatever I want to unleash on her. And if I see her lying in my bed, I may not be able to stop myself. My control hangs by the thinnest thread.

I should return to the house, sleep in my old room. She should not see me like this, or I will scare her.

But I need her. Need her to soften and soothe the hard edges of my terrible, monstrous mind, so full of rage and destruction and triumph.

It is ironic, perhaps, that a man like me—who prides and defines himself by his strength—is too weak to do what I should. I go to the pool house, pulled to her like a rope is tied around my middle.

Hovering at the end of the bed, I watch her sleep. I listen to her even, unworried breaths. My desire builds with each rise and fall of her chest.

I am sick for this. Sick for wanting her now, this way.

It takes enormous effort to drag my eyes away, but eventually I manage, closing myself in the bathroom and retrieving the well-used first aid kit from the drawer in the vanity.

32

NICOLE

❧

Florence Nightingale and the Grim Reaper.

A sharp noise like glass against metal jerks me awake, shaking me abruptly into a strange, confused kind of consciousness. I fumble on the bedside table for a second, then place my glasses on my face and check the red numbers on the clock. 4 AM.

The light in the bathroom spills out in a perfect rectangle from the spaces around the door, and the sound of running water nearly drowns out the voice within. I would recognize that low, fluid speech in a crowded room, even though I have no idea what he's saying. I downloaded Duolingo on the new cell phone he bought me, but I haven't made it very far yet.

I knock. "Dimitri?"

The water cuts, then déjà vu hits me like a train as the door opens, revealing an enormous expanse of bare chest and a stormy expression. Only this time, it clears, shifting into something much softer when he sees me. I wince, turning away from the bright light.

"Nicole," he murmurs with an air of sheepishness. "I did not mean to wake you. Go back to sleep."

When I try to see past him into the bathroom, he shifts to block my view. But I still notice the med kit sitting out, and the new bandage on his right hand. Next to a red-brown smudge on the counter, there's a pair of tiny scissors lying on top of a pad of gauze—clearly, he decided it was time to remove the stitches and butterflies from his weeks-old gunshot wound while he had it out to treat his hand.

My stomach flops. Where was he tonight? How did he get hurt? Obviously, he was trying to keep it from me—to take care of it himself. The knowledge twists up inside me, making me feel awful, like it's my fault he didn't come to me.

Did he not want to wake me, or did he not want me to see and ask questions?

I decide to test that. "You're taking out the rest of your stitches? Want some help?"

When he doesn't answer right away, I return my attention to him and find his eyes glued to the bare skin exposed by my nightgown. I've always liked silky things, and sleeping in pants makes me feel like I'm being strangled. So this thin-strapped, mid-thigh, semi-transparent satin dress has become a favorite.

His chest rises and falls in short bursts, like his breath quickens with a racing heart. Seeing his reaction, my body is instantly awake, tingling and warm between my legs. Our suspended moment of longing ends abruptly as he jerks a nod and turns away.

He settles himself on the counter and leans back towards the mirror. His eyes remain locked on something on the ceiling as I approach and glove up to examine the area.

The stitches can definitely come out. It's silly, since I'm the one who set his healing back, but I'm proud of how well and neatly the wound has closed.

So, when he goes rigid as I gently place my hand on his side, I know it's not because of any pain. The fabric of his pants in his lap shifts, and he covers the area with his free arm, which nearly puts it in my way.

"What happened?" I ask softly.

"I killed Viktor Volkevich tonight."

My stomach flops, and bile rises in the back of my throat, along with a dozen questions. Worry mingles with every other emotion, weaving through them until it saturates every thought. I know it's an unusual reaction, but every discarded curiosity about what happened—who, where, why, when—is second to one horrifying possibility.

What if he's caught?

When I say nothing in response to his revelation, his eyes search my face, desperate and wild. His expression is pinched tight, like he expects judgment, rejection, disgust. But I don't feel... any of that. I feel angry that he was in danger and he didn't tell me, and confused about my own reactions. And for the first time in a while, hopeful.

Hopeful and desperately sad about it.

"The USB?" I ask, breathless. I hate the words as I speak them, but I have to know.

"Wesley is working on it. We should have answers in the morning."

The silence that stretches after that statement feels heavy and sour. He won't meet my eyes, and every line of his body is filled with tension that has nothing to do with the gentle pull of my fingers at a healed wound.

"Are you... okay?"

He exhales sharply, almost a laugh. "I tell you that I have taken a life, and you are concerned about *my* well-being?"

I bristle at his unkind tone. "I already know about what you do, Dimitri. I knew Volkevich was going to die. I'm not upset about that, if that's what you're—"

"I beat a man to death," he interrupts harshly, flexing his bandaged hand. "I killed him with my bare hands. And while I watched the life drain from his eyes, I felt nothing."

My breath catches at the confession. My eyes flick down to his wrapped knuckles, and I itch to redo it for him. Our differences have always been obvious, but they've never felt quite so tangible as they do now.

Florence Nightingale and the Grim Reaper.

"I don't believe you."

His brows snap down. "No? You think there is some tenderness or remorse hidden deep? I am not redeemable. I am not broken. I am destroyed. Broken things can be fixed; there is no hope for things that are destroyed."

"No," I correct myself quickly, realizing his statement was purposefully meant to ruffle my feathers. "I mean, I don't believe you beat him to death because your hand would probably be broken. I think you're capable of it and strong enough to do it. I just don't think you did."

His bark of a laugh surprises both of us. "Clever, Nicole. You are correct. I did beat him, but in the end, I slit his throat and let it drain into the sewers where he belongs, like the rest of them."

I swallow the thick bile suddenly coating the back of my tongue. I don't like this. I don't like how he's talking about death like he hopes it will scare me. This feels like a test somehow—one I'm not supposed to pass. It's like he doesn't want to be the one to push me away, so he's hoping I'll do it myself if he throws something I don't want to hear hard enough in my face.

I never asked to be shielded from what he does, but I don't deserve these shock tactics either.

"If you're trying to make a point, just make it, Dimitri," I say, forcing a neutral tone instead of snapping like I want.

His icy eyes bore into me. "This is the line between us, and it always will be. We will always end up here because I take from the world and you give to it. But just as you cannot change what you are, I cannot change what I am."

"What's that? A hitman?"

"A monster," he decrees, meeting my eyes with a kind of fierceness that makes my stomach flutter, even more than his declaration about killing someone with his bare hands.

The chills that have been hovering just under my skin for this entire conversation spread outward, prickling unpleasantly. I shake my head.

He doesn't really believe that about himself, does he?

Misinterpreting my denial for something else, he catches my hand, and the anger shifts to something else. Something softer, more urgent and pleading. "But a monster has his uses. I would be a good protector for you, Nicole. Say the word and I will be *your* monster. Or tell me no, and I... think I could find a way to let you go."

I realize suddenly what this is really about. The USB. The encroaching reality. Tomorrow, we're going to find out what's been keeping me here, and he's as afraid as I am about what comes next.

Our gazes lock. He sits up straighter so he can reach for my side, landing just below my bottom rib. His thumb rubs against the silky nightdress, a delicate rustle of calluses catching against fabric. The tiny friction goes straight to my core.

He doesn't want to let me go. I can see it in his eyes.

He's trying to convince me to see him how he sees himself and begging me to accept him for it anyway.

I open my mouth to reassure him, but I can't force the words out for some reason. My chest tightens as I realize why this feels so wrong. If I say yes now, he'll think that I want him *in spite of* thinking of him as a monster. I can't let that happen—not when it's so far from how I see him. I don't want him to think of himself in that way.

But what the hell am I supposed to do? How do you tell someone you think that their self-image is fundamentally flawed? What could I possibly say that would be enough to erase years of additive experiences that convince us we are who the world tells us we are?

The world has tried to tell me who to be a hundred times. A thousand, maybe.

Be strong, but be vulnerable. Be independent, but you still need a partner, of course. Be mothering and gentle and put others first. Actually, put yourself first and take time for yourself. But don't be selfish. Be brave. Be nice. Be a badass, but don't intimidate anyone. Be smaller. Be different. Be less.

There's no right way to be a woman, or to be me. And I'm willing to bet it's similar for him—the things he's been told about himself are just very different.

All I can do for him is what I've done for myself—to varying degrees of efficacy—which is to remind him that *he* gets to decide who he is.

"On the boat, you told me you were dangerous and violent, and then you took care of me when I was freaking out. You kidnapped me, but you... gave me space and earned back my trust. You try to warm me whenever I shiver. You know how I like my coffee, you bought me clothes, you always check to make sure my toes are covered by the blankets, you clean my glasses for me—"

"How do you know that?" he interrupts. "You are always asleep."

"Sometimes the nose piece is still wet," I chuckle.

He huffs a breath through his nose. "I have seen you clean them on your shirt. You will scratch the lenses."

I bite down on the smile that forms because he's kind of making my point. "Do you *want* me to think of you as a monster?"

"I do not want to lie to you about what I am, but... no," he admits, like I'm pulling it out of him through his teeth. "I do not want you to think of me in that way. I would not care if everyone in the world feared me... as long as you did not."

"Good. I don't," I assure him. "And I don't want you to think of yourself that way, either."

To make my point, I let my hands glide up, trailing over the raised white skin of old scars, and rest them on his chest. His skin is so firm, so hard under my touch. I resist the sudden urge—intrusive thought, really—to thread my fingers through his curly chest hair and give it a sharp tug, just to hear him cry out a surprised protest.

When he inhales against my touch, his chest expands, and it draws my attention to his tally mark tattoo. I trace the lines with the tip of my finger, recalling when he explained why he continues to add to it.

"I know this is a piece of your past, and it means something to you, but I think you're holding on to the wrong thing. You should rewrite the narrative. You should keep track of the lives that you've saved instead of the gunshots you've survived. And that," I say, tapping on the tattoo with the tip of my finger twice, "makes two of those tally marks mine."

He covers my hand with his much larger one, dwarfing it. We're so close—there's an almost palpable anticipation in the air. His lids lower as his eyes drop to my lips, which part under the weight of his stare. Can he feel my pulse racing against his fingertips? Can he see how fast my breath goes in and out, or the outline of my nipples that have gone painfully hard under my nightgown?

Need pulses across my skin, making my breasts feel heavy and zinging to my lower stomach.

"*Vse, chem ya yavlyayus', prinadlezhit tebe, i ty dlya menya vse,*" he says hoarsely. "I will never let harm come to you, my med. Never."

He hops off the counter and grabs me in a movement so fluid and fast that I hardly see it coming. In an instant, I'm in his arms, and his lips are on mine.

He circles my waist with his hands, dragging me against him, and slides them around to cup my ass. I moan as he squeezes, kneading the flesh so close to where I'm dripping and pounding with need. Suddenly, I feel him lift me, and then the cold, unyielding stone countertop against my warm skin.

I jolt, making a surprised noise that he swallows as he refuses to let me break away. He steps between my legs, rubbing his bulge against my extra-sensitive flesh. I probably shouldn't have gone for that second orgasm with the showerhead before bed, but I couldn't help it. He's turning *me* into a monster. An orgasm-hungry one.

His fingers replace that bulge, shoving aside panties and then tearing them apart at the delicate seam. The urgency and aggression in the ripping sound go straight to my core, just as his fingers make contact. They slide through my slick skin, and I cry out as the rough pads of his index and middle fingers make abrasive contact with my clit. It's a sharp kind of pleasure—at once too much and not enough.

"Fuck! I need you inside me, Dimitri."

A desperate, pleased noise sounds from his throat, and I let go of his shoulders to lean back onto my arms to tilt my hips. Height-wise, we're well-aligned on the counter, but my abs simply aren't strong enough to keep my legs lifted around him if I'm not leaning back.

His pants drop, sliding off his dick and leaving a shiny trail of precum that stuck to his skin instead of the cloth.

Eyes locked on my pussy, he spits, and I gasp. The harsh noise, the sudden wet impact on my lower lips, the cheek-burning, squirmy feeling of the slightly degrading act... Heat explodes under my skin, turning the burn of desire into an inferno. It's worse, too, when he slides two thick fingers through it—our combined fluids—and pushes it inside of me. My head falls back as a throaty moan reverberates off the tile and glass.

"Nicole," he snaps, withdrawing his fingers and getting into place.

My head comes up so fast, I barely have time to breathe.

"Eyes on me. I want"—I gasp as he interrupts his own order with a powerful thrust that fills me in one smooth motion and curls my toes—"to watch you"—another hard, controlled, deep push of his body into mine—"come apart for me."

I do as he asks, and there's an exponential jump in the intimacy of the moment. Tears prickle behind my eyes. I cry out as he grits his teeth and homes his hips against me.

"Holy fuck, you're so deep. Fuck, Dimitri."

He grunts, and it might have even been a laugh, but it cuts short as he rears back and slams forward again.

Full. I'm so full. The stretch is a delicate pain, a rasp of pleasure. My pelvis is tilted at the perfect angle for me to see as he seats himself fully inside, and it's driving me out of my mind.

I adjust my grip on the sink, wishing I could hold on to him, and wiggle my hips slightly to encourage him to move faster. As he picks up speed, I can sense that this is the rhythm he likes by how his expression changes and his breath drags through his teeth. We move together, and a chorus of heavy breathing, moans, and skin slapping fills the air.

I'm mindless to anything but the pleasure. He fills my senses, completely surrounding me, making it impossible not to focus on here, now, what he's doing to me. Each inward stroke is a pinch, followed by a wave of bliss to soothe it. His pelvic area rubs my clit, the abrasion of his hair a maddening brush on such a sensitive area.

He thrusts harder, beginning to chase his own release now that I've opened up for him. In an instant, I know that he's going to finish before I can, unless I do something about it for myself. I barely care. It feels so good, even if I don't come.

I shift my weight to one side, trying to lift my hand and get my fingers where I need them, but he pauses and grabs my wrist. "I take care of what is mine," he reminds me emphatically.

It's some sort of witchcraft, the way he's able to maintain his pace to thoroughly fuck me and strum his fingers against my clit. The combination of sensations is almost too much, so this time the build of the orgasm is not gentle or nice. It's a whirlwind of aggressive intensity that leaves me gasping for air.

"Dimitri!"

When I come, he's right there, mashing his lips down on mine and giving me a much-needed outlet for the feeling. My whole body convulses against his, and a second later, he joins me. He grunts once, twice, then his hips slow and stop altogether.

The silence between us as we both try to catch our breath isn't content or comfortable. There's an air of expectation that I can't shake.

But then he pulls back, and his eyes are smiling at me as he rests his forehead against mine, and I'm boneless, brainless, and I can't think of a single thing to say.

33

NICOLE

Hitman Witness Protection

Last night changed something. I'm not sure I even realized there were still walls up between us until they were torn down.

After we cleaned up, we went to bed. Just as I was almost asleep, he slid his cock between my legs and took me from behind while we lay on our sides. With relentlessness and urgency, he stroked me to another mind-numbing orgasm. He was still inside me as I fell asleep.

And I loved it.

Sex with him is so... uncomplicated—I want him, he wants me; we act on it. It's never easier for us to communicate than when we do it with our bodies. And because it's easier, I've been completely focused on the temporary gratification, avoiding what happens *next*. So, I'm totally unprepared for its inevitability. Something is going to happen. Something *did* happen. Dimitri was gone by the time I woke, and he's been holed up with James and Wesley in that office all morning.

Initially, I assumed there was no decision to be made—that we were oil and water; there was no way for us to mix except temporarily—and all roads ended with me leaving. I assumed it was what we both thought was for the best. I assumed it was what we both wanted. But after last night, I don't think it's what either of us wants.

Say the word, and I will be your monster.

The memory of those words makes me shiver and brings a faint smile to my lips, even now. So, I think I owe it to myself to find a way to stay. And to do that, I need to gather information.

I find Eleanor covered in flour and engrossed in a project. The kitchen smells like fresh bread and tomato sauce today, and my mouth waters the second I open the sliding door.

"Hey," I greet her.

She straightens in the act of shutting the oven, a mitt on each hand, and flour streaked across her face. "Hey, Nicole! Want some pizza? I'm experimenting."

I glance over where she gestures with her elbow and burst out laughing. Half of the enormous island is covered in flatbreads of various shapes, sizes, and colors on cooling racks and cutting boards, and the other half is a mess of bowls and floured surfaces and dirty pizza paddles. "Love some," I say, taking a seat at the island.

"Excellent. Okay, so you're not going to want the prosciutto or the sausage ones, but..." she mutters to herself, looking over the various pies with her hands on her hips. Selecting a few meatless options, she cuts me some slices, places them on a plate, and hands it to me.

She watches me take my first bite with a keyed-up expression. "It's great," I say around a mouthful of hot cheese.

"Oh, yay! Okay..." she trails off, searching the notes she made on a legal pad covered in flour and red sauce, "that one had the sourdough crust and an overnight proof. I thought the sourness would play off the umami of the mushrooms and the hint of sweet caramelized onions and goat cheese."

I nod, eagerly taking another bite. "I'll eat pizza in most forms, but I'd ask for this one specifically."

She beams, and her enthusiasm to please people with her food is as endearing as it is fortunate for me, the recipient. "Really? How's the ratio of toppings to crust? Good? Okay, yay. I can add that one to the list as a vegetarian option. Lactose-free, too," she adds, sounding proud of herself.

"So, Eleanor," I begin slowly, hoping by the time I finish her name, I'll know how to start this conversation with her. "Do you like living here?"

"Love it," she replies, distracted as she writes something down.

"Do you miss anything from your life *before*?"

She taps the end of the pencil against the paper. "Hmm... I guess I miss the freedom of, like, leaving my apartment and getting to go anywhere I want. Not so much the apartment itself, but the concept of just getting up and leaving, of doing whatever I want to do, whenever I want to do it."

"You can't do that? You can't just get up and leave if you want to go shopping or something?" I ask. I feel like I've seen her come and go way more than anyone else, but it's not like I've quizzed her on where she was and what she was doing.

"Not really. I mean, it's not like I'm stuck here; I can leave. Mac prefers I don't, but I'd go crazy stuck here all the time, and he knows that. There are just some stipulations."

I feel my brows come together. "You have to ask permission to leave?"

"No!" she shakes her head, hopping up into the chair next to mine and taking a bite of her own slice. "No, not permission. It's not like I ask and he says no—well, I guess one time he said no, but that was because he was worried about an active shooter in the area that I didn't know about. We just decide together on the specifics, like how long I'll be gone. It's more like sharing a car than asking for permission, if that makes sense. You have to consider what the other person needs. There are... stipulations, like I said."

"Like what?"

She ticks them off on her fingers. "Well, there's a tracker in my car and my phone and my purse. And in something I wear, because he's paranoid and overprotective. We can't leave together, and we can't have routines like Wednesday date night or something. We do go out, but it has to be somewhere we won't be seen, or most people won't recognize either of us. It's not like a normal relationship."

"But you don't care," I guess, observing the faraway, dreamy look in her eye.

"Nope," she says brightly, taking a bite of a different slice on her plate. Her eyes widen, and she drops her jaw to breathe emphatically around the bite. "Fuck. Hot."

"So, you have to be careful about being seen together?"

She nods, fanning her open mouth, then chews and swallows quickly. After washing it down with a few gulps of her Diet Coke, she continues, but her voice is a little strained. "When you're in love with a dangerous man, sometimes you have to take it on faith that he's doing what it takes to keep you safe. Plenty of people want Mac dead, or they'd try to hurt him by hurting me. Took me a while to come to terms with that, honestly, but here I am. At terms. Again, it's just part of what you sign up for."

"And the other stipulations are designed to keep this place a secret, right? So, no one can link this location to those guys."

"Yup. If I had friends, I wouldn't be able to invite them over—"

I straighten in my seat. "Wait. You don't have friends? You *can't* have friends?"

"I mean..." she grimaces. "I probably could if there were someone important to me I really wanted to go see. But truth be told, I've always been kind of a loner. My sister lives in Pittsburgh, so we always had more of a phone-based relationship. I drifted apart from my friend Harrison, I suppose, but he got a girlfriend, and it probably would have happened anyway. He and Mac didn't get along—bad first impressions on both sides," she confesses.

"So, you moved in, you left all your friends behind, and you quit your job? All to live here and be with him?" I ask. I know I sound judgmental, but I never realized any of this. Even knowing about the dangers, what she's describing sounds more like being in a cult than being under someone's protection.

If I lived here, I couldn't have friends at work? I couldn't have my own space or adventurous hobbies or leave whenever I felt like it?

In the name of safety, sure, but... I'm a nomad. I've lived on my own since I was 18. I value my freedom. I know I told Dimitri that the goal was always to settle down, but I never thought twice about having the autonomy to choose where that was and move if I wanted to. I've built my life intentionally, depending on no one but myself.

Living the way she's describing seems stifling. Even the thought of sharing a car with someone is making me itch, and that was just the metaphor she used.

She winces, correctly interpreting my tone. "Well... yes, but not in the way you're implying. I didn't just drop everything to be with him because he made me or something. He's a controlling asshole sometimes, don't get me wrong, but he doesn't *make* me do things I don't want to.

"I didn't mind quitting my job—I hated that place. Same thing with my apartment. It was tiny and crappy, and I was stoked to move out. Mac's the one that encouraged me to start my business. Living here honestly feels like a dream sometimes; this place is, like, a million times better than anywhere I would ever have been able to afford. He didn't take my independence either. I chose to be with him, and we work around the limitations the way you would in any relationship. The limitations are just... different, because the stakes are higher."

I turn that over in my head, trying to see how the pieces of my own life compare against the broken remnants of what hers used to be. "Could you have kept your job and your apartment if you wanted to?"

"Um..." she scratches underneath her bangs, leaving them in disarray. "Maybe? I'm not sure. It's not something we had to talk about."

I drop my eyes to my plate and grab another slice, but I don't lift it to my mouth. I'm not sure I'd be able to taste it right now.

"Why?" she asks, eyeing me and taking a bite. "You thinking about moving in?"

"Maybe," I admit.

She gasps and immediately begins choking on what was in her mouth. "Oh my"—cough—"God! That's"—cough—"so amazing!" She dissolves into a fit that ends with her running to the sink and pouring a glass of water.

I watch her to ensure she's not going to actually choke, alert and ready to administer back blows or abdominal thrusts. She's probably fine because if you can cough, you can breathe, but it never hurts to be ready. "You okay?"

Having gotten herself mostly back under control, she wipes some tears from under her eyes and joins me back at the island. "Yes, fine," she sputters. "But oh my God, what?! You're going to live here?! *Yay!*"

"No, no... It's not like that," I object, grimacing because I've gotten so far ahead of myself that I'm all the way moved into the pool house without an invitation. "I was just... um, thinking about what happens next for me and Dimitri. Logistics and stuff. Obviously, it makes sense for me to stay here while they deal with the bad guys, but I don't know what happens after. Like a transition back to reality."

She nods, goes to take a bite of her pizza, then eyes it like it offended her and sets it back down. "It's a tough situation, for sure," she says. "It's definitely easier living here than anywhere else."

"I guess it's a moot point until I'm out of Hitman Witness Protection, anyway."

"Right. Yeah, until then it's definitely more... um..."

"Suffocating?"

"I was going to say *confining*, but sure. Don't worry, though—those three are the best at what they do. You won't have to be in lockdown forever."

"Right," I agree, chewing on my lower lip.

"Nicole? Could you come into the study? There is something I think you will want to see," Dimitri's deep voice cuts through the swirling storm of worried thoughts.

We both turn, finding him in the doorway to the kitchen, eyes on me, and hand outstretched. I glance at Eleanor, who gives me a blank smile, so I know she didn't hear the strain in his voice or see the slight pinch in his brow. Not as attuned to him, obviously.

"The USB?"

He nods.

I inhale sharply. "Time to find out what someone was willing to kill me for. It's kind of like knowing what my life is worth."

Eleanor reaches over and squeezes my forearm encouragingly. Heart racing, I hop off my stool and make my way down the hallway, pausing only briefly to take Dimitri's hand and accept the kiss he places in the center of my forehead.

34

DIMITRI

The nicest wedding present ever

What her life is worth.

I do not like the idea that she would think of her life this way—in terms of some arbitrary numerical value—but she deserves to know what is on the drive, after what she has gone through because of it.

Mid-planning session, Wesley's scanning program reported something unusual in the drive, and he grew increasingly excited and agitated, clicking around and typing faster than James and I could follow. Knowing he was close, I left to retrieve Nicole.

As we enter, James stands and offers her his chair—and while there is a flash of irritation that he thinks to give my woman this comfort, no man who would call himself a gentleman should sit while a woman has no seat. Excluding Wesley, of course, who must sit while he does his important work.

"Ready? Among all the..." Wesley trails off, eyes darting to Nicole quickly, and clears his throat, "other *nasty* bits on the drive, we have..."

"My breath is fucking bated," James drawls.

With a flourish, Wesley hits a few keys and angles his screen so we can all see.

"I'm seeing... that's a lot of numbers," James frowns. "Enough dramatics, Short Round. The hell am I lookin' at?"

"Bitcoin wallets," Wesley replies as if the answer were obvious.

"Okay..." James says, scratching at the stubble across his jaw.

There is some silence between us, and Wesley looks around, his excitement slowly dying at our blank expressions. "A series of public and private keys for transaction ledgers that are untraceable."

"I have a confession," Nicole says, glancing at me, then directing it at Wesley. "I don't really know what Bitcoin is... I only know enough to sound good, so guys wouldn't try to explain it to me on dates. You're saying this is money, right?"

James looks at me, relief plain on his face. Nicole saved him from having to ask. I have a rough understanding—enough to know that Wesley has found what basically amounts to an illegal gold mine. Or a platinum mine. Perhaps a diamond mine. Or all three combined, depending on how Volkevich managed his fortune.

"Lots of money. Things only have value—money, gold, whatever—because years ago we decided it did, right? Well, Bitcoin is like that. These codes are 2000-bit numbers that represent a blockchain, which is like a documented proof of historical ownership. Every transaction adds to the blockchain, changing it slightly. Having one of these private keys allows you to sign a transaction to add to the Bitcoin ledger, proving your ownership. Think of it like a code with a signature."

As he speaks, he types one of the keys into a website that shows the value of the coin. "Having the private key means you have proof that this *public* key is something you own. This is a public key from the flash drive," he says, pointing to the numbers he has typed into a search engine within the site.

"So, my life is worth..." she leans forward, finding the figure on the screen, then blows out a breath. "Half a million dollars. Okay... that's... something. It's more than an insurance payout might be, I suppose."

Wesley shakes his head. "No, Nicole. That's just one of the wallets on here. There are thousands of them."

She goes pale. "Th-thousands of... I'm sorry, you're saying I had thousands of millions of dollars in my stomach?"

"Sometimes called *billions*," James observes with a laugh.

I cut him a sharp look. If he makes some kind of joke about how she defecated money, he will lose some of his teeth.

"It's unlikely each micro-transaction is the same size, but I'd lowball the value of this drive in the hundreds of millions, all said," Wesley continues.

She sucks in a noise of shock, and I watch her reaction curiously. The going rate for a hit these days is close to eight million, depending on the target. More, when the target is difficult—dangerous or high profile. It does not seem like so much to me anymore, but I suppose it would be to most of the people in this country, who will never see one million, let alone 100.

"You think it was the nicest wedding present ever?" James asks me.

I shake my head. "No, it was thousands of payments made for years of dirty business dealings. I think it is Volkevich's safest bank account—the one with no central governing entity."

"Bitcoin has become the preferred method of payment of the under-world—better even than cash, in some situations, because it's safer and as anonymous as you want it to be," Wesley adds.

"*Da,* and weddings are excellent places to strike up business deals—everyone is in a good mood and no one brings their gun—so I imagine that is why they had it."

"A smart, careful man would only have one copy," Wesley nods. "And we know Kyle wasn't working with Viktor, so he must have stolen it from him that night."

James laughs, rubbing his hands together. "I love a heist! Okay, so Douchebag Kyle knows his uncle is going to do some business, so he gets in there and steals it. But if anyone finds it on him, he's a dead man, so he plants it in Nicole before he leaves the scene of the crime, planning to circle back to her for it later. Maybe he even starts the gunfight on his way out to cover his tracks."

I have to admit, that seems very likely. Particularly as it aligns with Nicole's description of Kyle from that night—on edge, covered in blood, manic.

"But wasn't that risky?" she asks. "I mean, I got away, and he lost the money."

"Obviously, he didn't consider that. But even if you'd found it, you never would have known what you had. The wallets weren't exactly easily accessible, hidden behind several layers of passwords and a two-step authentication that required Viktor's personal cellphone," Wesley explains. "Kyle likely didn't even realize that was the case, since he didn't steal the phone."

Understanding lights her expression, and she exchanges a look with me. I wonder if she is aligning this story with the bandage on my hand and my strange state of mind last night. "Okay, sure. But even if it was inaccessible with passcodes and all that, why let it out of your sight? Why me?"

"They were checking the men," I remember. "They were patting us down for weapons, checking our pockets. You were in the wedding party, very distantly related to the bride, above suspicion. And you were the only one without a date."

She lifts a brow at me, and I respond with a smirk. She arrived without a man, but she did not leave alone.

She shakes her head. "Still. If I had my hands on that much money, I would never let it out of my sight."

"She has a point," I say.

"A damn fine point," Wesley adds.

"That hundreds of millions of dollars isn't just something you give to a stranger and *hope* you catch up to them later? Of course I have a point... did that not occur to you guys?" She stops herself, and her eyes flick around, as if she is seeing the grandeur of the house again for the first time. "How much money do you *have*?"

"Hundreds of millions more than we did yesterday," James chuckles. "Well, you do."

"Me?" she squeaks. "People want to kill me for that, and I don't even really get how it works. I don't want it!"

Her reaction is not a surprise; still, it is always nice to know that your woman values the right things—her life over money, for instance.

Her round, frightened eyes meet mine. "He's not being serious, is he? We're not keeping that money. That would be insane."

I can feel my teammates' eyes weighing heavily on me. "James and Wesley and I will discuss the best path forward. Our first priority is always to ensure the safety of everyone involved. When we form a plan, usually the right option or opportunity presents itself."

"Even having it is making me nervous," she says softly. "It's like I'm doing something actively illegal, just knowing about it. I know Viktor is dead, but... Hundreds of millions of dollars went missing from a crime family. I can't imagine they're going to just let it go."

"Probably not."

I can see her mind spinning, and I take a half-step towards her, made uncomfortable by the look of such doubt and concern on her face.

"So how do we get out of this? Can we give the money back?"

Wesley takes this one, his voice gentle. "We could, though I doubt it's the right call. Volkevich has been in business in this area for a few decades; in that time, they've bought and sold everything from automatic weapons to drugs to people."

She pales.

"You said you got a job at St. Luke's, right?" James continues. "That's *Bratva* territory. On any night, you were probably treating overdoses, gunshot victims, trafficked women... all part of Volkevich's legacy. That money is how they stay in business. Right now, they're cut off, and they can't make payments to their suppliers. It'll run them into the ground and get 'em all killed, eventually. But if you give them that USB back, they'll pick right back up where they left off."

She winces and her shoulders round under the weight of the knowledge. "Okay, so we're definitely not giving it back. But it's evidence... not to be the one that suggests involving the authorities again, but they're already up my ass anyway, right? Can we just turn it in?"

I stroke my thumb down her arm. "The gears of the machine of bureaucracy move slowly, and there are no guarantees the evidence would be admissible, or that it could be linked back to Volkevich."

"Building a case against organized crime is no simple task, and bitcoin is secure against identification—it's why they use it," Wesley adds.

"But their leader is dead. He was the one with the passwords and everything, right?"

"*Da*, Viktor is dead, but there are many more beneath him, and they will spend the rest of their lives looking for this money. Remember how I said Volkevich has men in the police department? They would use those men and whatever resources they had left to track us down and kill us in retribution for stealing everything from them."

I can see the vein in her neck thrumming as her heart jumps, picking up in rhythm. "So, we can't give it back. We can't turn it in. We're not going to use it ourselves for the same reason—they'd know a transaction had occurred, and the money was gone, right? We're not going to give it away because we'd make a target out of anyone who received it."

She looks to me for confirmation, and I nod.

"So... what do we do?"

I cannot take that look in her eyes, so I pull her in. She is rigid against me, but melts a little at the reassuring kiss on her temple. "James and Wesley and I still need to discuss. We will figure it out, trust me."

She blows out a breath, shaking both of us with the motion. After a second in my embrace, tight and meant to calm, she nods. "Okay. I... um... I'll leave you to it, then."

Instead of letting her turn away, I place my palm on the side of her neck and tilt her head up towards me. "I will always keep you safe," I remind her, leaning forward to brush my lips against hers.

"I know," she whispers back, offering a weak smile before stepping away and disappearing out of the study.

"She's freaking out, D," James observes, staring at the closed door.

"*Da*. I will need to calm her, I think. I would prefer to do this with a valid plan. We need to eliminate the rest of the Volkevich clan and draw Kyle out of hiding."

Wesley chuckles, lacing his fingers across his abdomen and sitting back in his office chair. "Well... we've got the entire Volkevich fortune at our fingertips, so I'm thinking the plan kind of writes itself on this one."

35

NICOLE

Too rigid to bend, he'd break instead

I move to the pool house like I'm in a trance, going through the motions of putting on workout clothes for lack of anything better to do. I guess a workout would help ground me, and I desperately need that right now because I feel like a light breeze would knock me over.

Hundreds of millions of dollars.

That's so much money. It's too much money. It's frankly a stupid amount of money.

It doesn't feel real. And maybe it's not, in the tangible sense of the word, but neither is money in a bank by that reasoning. It terrifies me. The guys were pretty blasé about it, so I'm guessing it's not as big a sum of money to someone in their world as it is to me, but that's... hitting the lottery. It's being set up for the rest of the lives of everyone in your family. It's never worrying about anything again.

It's money to kill for—to *be* killed for.

I had a dozen guesses about what was on that flash drive, and money was one of them. But I'm not really sure where this leaves us. As long as we have it, or someone thinks I do, I'll always be a target.

I will always keep you safe.

He's said it before, and he said it again last night. At the time, it left me breathless with a delirious kind of happiness because the sincerity in that promise is so deep, I can't touch the bottom. But in the light of day, it just feels daunting.

In his world, safety often comes at the cost of another life. In this case... every Volkevich out there? Viktor is one thing, and I'm sure he's got guys in his inner circle who are just as bad, but where does it end? What about their families? What if innocents die, caught in the crossfire? What if Dimitri can't get to everyone?

He'll take care of me; I know that much. He's told me over and over that he will.

And while I definitely couldn't do this alone, being taken care of doesn't... *fit* me. It doesn't sit quite right. It makes me feel like a burden, something weak that needs protection.

The deeply independent part of me bristles. In *my* world, I don't need protection. I'm fine alone. I look out for myself—I have since my mother gave me a key to the front door at eleven years old and I started using my babysitting money to refill the pantry so I didn't go to sleep hungry—and there's a fierce kind of pride in that. But in his world, I'm smart enough to recognize my own shortcomings.

He's willing to be my protector. My monster.

For now.

And then what? How long does that last? As long as the sex stays hot? What if things don't work out and he ends up feeling tied to me for a promise he didn't mean to make? Am I out on my ass, or would he soldier through and slowly resent me more and more? I know what that does; I watched my parents spiral downwards to a divorce borne of resentment.

I don't think I could stand losing him bit by bit, with stupid arguments no one meant to start, and unkind words that go without an apology, and festering silence.

And what if the dangers of his job catch up with him? Am I collateral damage, or a burden to be passed on to the next member of his team?

I can't do it. I can't.

But I don't want to leave him.

What if... what if he came with me, or we figured out some kind of back-and-forth arrangement?

I try to picture him waking up next to me in my bed, and I just draw a blank. I'm not sure if there's enough room in my rental bedroom for a king, and he probably wouldn't even fit in the tiny shower I sighed at during my walk-through.

I could move. That's no big deal. But... would he want to sleep over, outside this center of operations? Would he risk being followed to my place? Would he come late at night, covered in blood, rushing in so my neighbors wouldn't see? Would we go out to dinner, or to the movies, or play mini golf? Would he come to Thanksgiving and meet my stepfamily? Would he fix a broken window for me, or drink wine on the couch and pretend not to like reality TV, or keep a toothbrush next to mine, or fold laundry with me... or any of the hundreds of small, banal things that comprise sharing a life with someone?

I can't see it. We're like a melody played in the wrong key—beautiful, but discordant.

He just doesn't fit in my life, as I've built it. Being a hitman is all he has, and he told me he's not flexible enough to be anything else—too rigid to bend, he'd break instead. He wouldn't like my life the way I've built it. I couldn't ask him to change for me.

After speaking to Eleanor, I'm not sure I can handle staying here. I mean, I haven't felt especially trapped, but... what if I do? What if I want to leave?

Do I want to leave?

I drop my face into my hands. I don't know. I don't know! Yes, in some ways; no, in others.

Why does this feel like such an either/or? A fork in the road, and each direction is a one-way street with no return. One way is freedom; the other is confinement. One way is lonely; one is with the man that I lov—

Whoa.

Fucking *whoa*.

No. Absolutely not. I can't... there's no way. I'm not going there.

36

DIMITRI

◆

I am no more than a convenient monster.

"All right, it is settled. We set our trap, plug in the flash drive, let the signal send out, and—in theory—we will draw everyone who is after it to the warehouse," I summarize.

"Or at the very least, most of the heaviest hitters. Kyle too, if we're lucky," James finishes.

"We've got our falcon," Wesley nods at the two of us.

"Is that what you Brits call a flash drive?" James interjects.

Wesley frowns. "No..."

James frowns back. "Why'd you call it a falcon? Is that the brand or something?"

"It's not—" Wesley cuts himself off with a frustrated noise. "It's not called a falcon. It's *our* falcon. As in *The Maltese Falcon*?"

I do not have to be looking at James to know that we are wearing twin expressions of blank confusion. Wesley has also lost me with this reference.

"The extremely famous film noir? *The Maltese Falcon*?" He throws his hands up. "Fine, we have *the thing everyone wants*."

"Why didn't you just say that?" James asks.

"Didn't think I needed to explain. Uncultured swine," he grumbles, cracking the top of one of his disgusting, fruity cans of energy drink. By now, I can control my facial expressions, but they smell so bad to me.

"Hey, let us know how Nicole's doing after you talk to her, okay, D?" James asks, switching topics and assuming a more somber tone.

My brow quirks. "Why?"

He cuts me a look. "I dunno. Maybe because I'm a decent person, and she seemed upset. Made me feel like a deer in headlights, like seeing one of my sisters crying." He shivers.

"I second that. Feels like she's part of our dysfunctional little family."

It pleases me to hear them say that. So much so that I confess, "I plan to ask her to move in."

Wesley grins as James leaps up and claps me on the shoulder. "Hey, congrats, man!"

"What happened to 'women are a distraction'?" Wesley jokes.

"They are," I sigh, though even as I say it, I know the word falls short of describing Nicole. Calling her a distraction is putting it lightly, and the implication that it is an unwelcome one is incorrect. "But perhaps some distractions are worth the problems they create."

"The most romantic guy in the world, over here. Women: a worthwhile problem," James chuckles, throwing an arm over my shoulders and waving his free hand through the air like he is reading from a sign.

I do not turn to him because I know it would put our faces closer together than I would prefer them to be, but he gets the message of my displeasure as I cross my arms. "Get your head back in the job—this is not over yet, but I would like to finish it as soon as possible. We rarely have the luxury of control over the environment and plenty of time to prepare."

"Agreed," Wesley chimes in. "Best take full advantage. If we can get everything in order tomorrow, we should be able to finish this tomorrow evening."

James releases my shoulders, turning the move into one that stretches his back, which makes a cracking noise as he does it. "Sounds like we've got an early start, then. I'm turning in. See you both at 0500?"

Though James is the one to end the meeting, I am first out the door. Planning sessions take hours, and we had much to discuss, so it is fairly late. Still, I need to speak more with Nicole, so I am pleased to see the lights still on in the pool house.

She is standing by the edge of our bed, wrapped in a large robe that splits around her propped-up leg. As she rubs something into the soft skin of her muscular legs, it leaves a sheen that smells warm and floral. My cock stirs at the sight, hungry still from this morning. She seems lost in the motion, not looking over as the door closes.

I step behind her and curl my arm around her waist, blindly searching for the tie. The warmth that radiates from her body is slightly damp, creating a friction against my touch. As I undo the tie and the robe falls apart, she shudders against me.

"What are you thinking about?" I murmur as I press a kiss against her neck.

She grabs my wrist as my hand reaches up towards one of her full breasts, and I smile against her skin. But there is a sharp tug and, in an instant, I realize that she is not holding on; she is stopping me. So, I still.

When she pulls away, there is not much room between where we stand and the edge of the bed, so she steps to the side. I watch, perplexed, as she reties her robe.

She is... refusing me? Not in the mood? Still upset?

"I was thinking about the end," she says softly, eyes downcast.

"The end?" I repeat, heart thudding. "Of... the threat to your life?"

She nods, and some of the weight is lifted from my chest. "On how it ends, I suppose. I knew I'd have to eventually, and I think I put it off because..." I watch her throat work on a swallow. "This was so nice, despite how it began. I wanted to live in these moments with you."

A spark of hope ignites, tempered by confusion. Her words do not match her tone or her careful physical distance. "We can live in these moments," I promise.

Her smile is soft and odd, like this information brings more than just happiness. "Did you guys decide what you were going to do with the money?"

I nod. After her reaction to the contents of the drive, we agreed I should not give her all the details. Still, it is her life, and she deserves to know about what will happen next. I sit on the bed, resting my elbows on my thighs. "We will transfer it to a secure new location so it can no longer be accessed with the information on the USB. Same money with a different lock and a different key that only we will know. Then we are going to use the tracking feature built into the drive to draw anyone who wants it out to a place of our choosing."

"And then you'll kill them?"

I search her face for any hint that this is the source of her concern. We have spoken of death many times, and she knows of its inevitability—its place in both our lives. "*Da*."

"And then I'll be free."

I feel the blood drain from my face. "Free?" I repeat. Surely, I misunderstand her meaning.

"To leave."

No. Without thinking, I spring to my feet and reach for her wrist, as if she plans on running and I must hold her in place. I can feel the echo of the action from weeks ago—the other times she has run from me for one reason or another.

She pulls back, but I tighten my grip.

"We both knew this was coming," she says quietly, brows tilted up in the middle as she watches the shock and denial play across my face.

"I disagree. You want to leave?" I ask. I sound stupid. I feel stupid. It is like trying to think through a haze of drugs—every thought is difficult to catch and hold. All the contentment I felt in her approval and acceptance last night has been abruptly snatched away, and my head is spinning.

"I thought... I thought after last night..." I break off, clearing my throat of the emotions making it thick. This is not who I am—some imbecile that cries when a woman turns away from him. I am rational. I am like stone. "I thought you would stay here. I thought you would want to."

She begins saying several words at once, snapping her mouth closed when the noise that emerges is unintelligible. Glancing down, she tucks the edges of the robe in around herself more tightly. "We've been avoiding having this conversation. And I think we both know why. I have to go. It's what we talked about, right? Back when I first got here, you promised to help me. You said as soon as we knew what was on the USB drive and we understood the extent of the danger, you'd get me a new identity and help me start over."

"No," I deny. I remember saying this, but I did not expect to hear my own words used against me this way. "You cannot leave. The danger is too great. I am the one who can keep you alive and safe, my *med*."

I know I am blindly reaching for any damn reason, but her hopeless expression is digging into my gut and laying me bare. This is what I can do for her—keep her safe.

And it is all I have to give.

She shakes her head and offers a smile that makes her bottom lip wobble. "Viktor's dead. And the rest of them... they don't care about me, not really. They want the money, and your plan will make it clear that I don't have it, right? If I go far enough away and I have nothing to do with this money, there's no reason to think—"

"No," I repeat, more angrily.

Her inhale breaks in her throat, and she shoots me a look full of apology and sadness. "I don't want to do this without you, but I can't stay here," she says, and her voice cracks. I watch with a morbid, detached sort of curiosity as the bead of a tear forms underneath her closed eyelid.

"Why?" I fall back a step, resisting the urge to lift a hand to my chest to ensure my sternum is still intact. It feels as if there is a hole blown through it.

"I can't be imprisoned. I need a place of my own, and a job that's fulfilling, and friends, and hobbies—"

"You would not be a prisoner here," I interject. "You could live like Eleanor, who comes and goes. You could have a job, you could—"

She interrupts me this time. "In Ulysses, I'm a missing person who had hundreds of millions of dollars of Mafia money in my possession. There's no scenario where I'm free to live how I want here—not safely. I can't be looking over my shoulder for Russian guys with guns for the rest of my life."

The words echo around me, recalling a memory of a conversation we had over a month ago. This has always been her concern. "You told me you were searching for a place to call home. Why not here? You like Eleanor and James and Wesley. You like this house. And *I* am here." The second I say it, it makes me grit my teeth. I feel like a fool. I believed we were aligned, that I would not have to argue with her or fight for my place in her life. "Unless it was... Was it meaningless to you?"

"No!" she gasps, but the denial feels too little, too late. "I don't want to leave you, but... We barely know each other, Dimitri—we haven't talked about the important stuff. And there are things I want in life. Things you can't give me, that I can't have if I'm forced to live here."

Forced.

"Like what?" I snap, hearing my voice harden.

"Normalcy," she says simply. It is not a challenge; it is a fact. "A life where I'm not stitching you up in the bathroom at 3 AM and worried you're out there adding another tally to your tattoo. I'm not equipped to handle that life. It's better to just leave now."

"You do not even want to try?" I take a step back, away from the steely, heartbroken resolve written all over her face.

"I can't. There is no trying. If I stay with you, there's no way I'm not falling for you. And if I fall for you, you're going to break my heart. So, I think it's best to end things now. Before either of us gets... too attached."

My body goes cold and still.

I have already fallen. I am already attached.

But obviously, I am alone in this.

"I just... don't see another option—I can't be here, and I can't ask you to leave your team to come with me to start over. Like you said, this is who you are. I don't want to take that from you."

My jaw clicks as I grind it. Admittedly, when thinking about our future life together, I never considered the possibility of leaving my current life behind. Was that selfish of me? To assume she would give up everything for me?

Even if it were... what use could I be to her in the small, normal life she wants? I cannot hold a real job or go out freely without concern of being recognized by the wrong person. I could end up getting her hurt or killed.

The weight is back on my chest, and it has brought a rush of conflicting, horrible emotions like guilt, hurt, frustration, and vindication. I always knew the truth, though I let myself believe she thought differently—I am no more than a convenient monster. I will shield her from the dangers and fuck her when she wants as a temporary distraction, but she would not choose a life with me.

Deep down, I always knew. I knew she would never want someone like me.

I knew I was not worthy.

"So that is it, then? You have decided? You chose for us both?" I ask. I hear the hurt-laced venom in my voice, but I am past trying to control it.

Her eyes are downcast, shielded. "From the moment we met, you've been making decisions for me. Running in the maze, getting on that boat, putting me in the trunk of the car, coming here... I don't regret it," she adds quickly, "but it's... not how I want to be with someone. It's not sustainable. I don't have it in me to meekly follow orders or sit at home while someone kills people on my behalf.

"I need to be able to make my own choices. Don't take that from me again. Don't take this choice from me."

I reel as if she physically struck me. In fact, I have to turn away, so she will not see how her words have destroyed me.

"I have to go. You have to let me go, Dimitri." It is so soft, it is nearly a whisper.

My heartbeat thuds so hard and loudly, it is the only noise I can hear for several long seconds of tense silence. I keep waiting for her to take it back—to realize she makes this decision too rashly, too rooted in fear. But her expression haunts me. She is resolute. Almost calm, if slightly broken-looking.

"Very well," I say tightly. "I will have Wesley falsify some documentation for you. It will take a few hours."

She has the grace to thank me, but it makes me flinch. I am halfway to the door, refusing to look back over my shoulder when I hear her soft sniffle. Cringing at the sound, I pause. "In the morning... you can go."

$$37$$

NICOLE

Take that, unhealed trauma

"I'm sorry," Eleanor blurts into the uncomfortable silence, surprising me. She squeezes the steering wheel in both her hands, glancing in her rearview as she changes lanes. "After we talked, I saw that you were struggling, but I wasn't sure what to do. I realized I might have made it seem like you shouldn't want to stay with us, or like the arrangement you figured out with Dimitri had to be like mine with Mac, or—"

"Eleanor, stop," I say, holding up a hand. "It's not your fault I'm leaving. You told me what I needed to know and gave me some perspective so I could wrap my mind around what was really going to happen. I'm glad I talked to you."

"Well, I'm not," she grumbles. "You say it's not my fault, but I feel like it is."

"Trust me, it's not."

She blows out a long breath, sending long sideways looks at me. "You're really not going to tell me what happened?"

What's to tell? I cried myself to sleep. And when I woke up...

I swallow and glance down at the heavy, thick mailer envelope in my lap.

When I woke up, this was waiting for me, sitting on top of a duffel bag already containing all my things—everything he'd bought me, rolled tightly in neat layers. I'm not sure how he managed it without waking me, but while I slept, Dimitri neatly packed away everything I had to make it as easy as possible for me to leave. To get me out of there. To erase any sign that I'd ever slept, eaten, bathed, fucked... or lived in that pool house with him.

I know it's my own damn fault, but it still stabbed me in the heart.

And then I found the house empty except for Eleanor. That was like the final twist of the dagger. I'm bleeding out emotionally. I'm trying to stem it, telling myself this is what's best for everyone and that the guys must be kind of mad at me for hurting Dimitri the way I did. But I had to.

Still, he left without saying goodbye. They all did.

I mean... I know I'm the one that's actually leaving, and they had important, time-sensitive things to do, but I thought I'd at least be able to see everyone one last time. To tell Wesley about a recent study I read about energy drinks contributing to concerning blood conditions, and to look at the mole on James's back for him, like I promised I would. And to say goodbye, too, I suppose.

That's why I haven't opened the big envelope yet. I'm kind of afraid of what I'll find, but I'm more afraid of what it signifies—the end. The last piece of them. Final. Finite.

"Thanks for driving me to the bus station, Eleanor." I look out the window, noting the signs as we pass them on the highway.

She hmmphs and rolls her eyes. "Fine, point taken—I'll drop it. I'm happy to drive you... happy for the distraction, anyway. I'm usually a mess when Mac goes to work."

Even though it hurts to think about him, I can't help wanting to know if Dimitri will be okay. Of course she's worried about James, but... from what I understand, Dimitri's the one taking the most risk, out on the front lines, as it were. He's the one in more danger.

"He's—they're going to be fine, right?" I ask, gauging the faraway look in her eye.

"Yeah. Yeah," she says, the first time for me, the second time softer, a private reassurance. "They're careful, and they have each other's backs."

"But you're still afraid for them. For Mac," I confirm.

Her eyes dart over to my side. "I don't think I ever won't be afraid for him. In fact... want to know something awful?" she asks, signaling to get off at the next exit.

Not really, but I nod, grateful for any and every distraction. I want to soak up these final moments with this woman I've become so attached to.

"I joined an online support group for the partners of people in the armed forces. This feeling I get—the helplessness, the worry, all that—it's similar in some ways to how a lot of people feel when their partner is deployed. It's been... really helpful to get other people's insight."

I sit back in my seat. "I don't think that's awful. Knowing you're not alone is a comfort, I'm sure."

"It is. And it's been really nice having you around. I know the circumstances weren't ideal, but it's been nice to have someone to talk to who knows what it's like *and* the truth about what they do."

It's hard not to be warmed by her gratitude and vulnerability. It's not just endearing, it's admirable—she talks about her feelings so freely... like she's not even afraid that talking about them will make it hurt worse. "I have your number. Once this is all settled, maybe I can reach out. You could... visit me when it's safe."

"I'd like that. You probably can't come to me," she hedges. "Can I ask one thing? Just one."

"Sure."

"Do I need to start spitting in Dimitri's food?"

It startles a laugh from me that's hard to stop once I get going. It feels like an outpouring of every emotion. I wipe the corner of my eye. "No. It's definitely not his fault."

"Fine. But text me if you change your mind, because I totally will." She sounds a bit relieved now that she's made me laugh. "What's in that envelope, anyway?"

"Stuff to help me leave and start over, I think."

"Might as well open it and see. We're here."

As she pulls into a parking spot in the small lot, I turn the mailer over in my hands a few times, feeling at the bulk in the center, and rip open the seal at the top. When I reach in, there are a few loose pieces of paper that come out easily. I unfold and scan the first one.

Sorry for the rush job—not my best work, I swear. When you're settled, drop me a line and I'll send you a better one. Good luck, Nicole. - W

There's more underneath it.

Eleanor tilts her head, trying to read over my shoulder. "That's Mac's handwriting," she points to the cramped scrawl at the bottom. "What did he say?"

"Um... 'Nice knowing you. Stay safe,'" I read.

She rolls her eyes. "*Nice knowing you?* That's the best he can do? Ugh. You know, he talked about how good Dimitri's stitches looked nonstop for days. He said, and I quote, 'It'll be real nice having a medical professional around here,' more than once. He told me you had a calming, grounding effect on everyone. He liked having you around, Nicole. He's going to miss you." She sniffles. "Me too."

There's an uncomfortable burning sensation in the center of my chest, like emotional indigestion. I reach across the center console to squeeze her hand. "I'll call you."

Her answering smile is watery and perfunctory. "Yeah, sure."

So, Wesley and James both said their goodbyes after all, and they were short and sweet. That leaves the longer note on the second page with big, round handwriting. Dimitri. It must be from him. Immediately, I have to fight a smile at how his script fits him.

But I can't read it yet. I'm not ready.

I set the papers aside to save them, and reach into the bag, extracting a thick, heavy stack that's bound together with a few rubber bands. On top is a new, freshly printed ID that names me Jenna Jones from Iowa. I squint. "Did Wesley give me a porn name?" I ask, flashing Eleanor the ID, hoping to lighten the mood that has been spiraling down since she put the car in park.

Her smile is half-hearted at best. "Sounds like a thing he'd do."

Under that is a tri-folded resume that I'll need to study later, and under that is...

"Whoa," Eleanor croaks, echoing my thoughts exactly.

It's a two-inch thick stack of 20s. Thousands of dollars in cash. I've never held thousands of dollars in cash before. "What the..."

"Whoa," she repeats, placing a hand across mine and lowering them into my lap as she looks furtively around. "Let's not go flashing that shit around... This isn't the nicest area. Jesus, how much is that?"

"Enough to be hush money," I say, my voice sounding hollow.

Her face twists at that. "Or... maybe he's trying to take care of you the only way he thinks you'll let him," she suggests.

I chew on my lip and tuck the money back into the envelope. Heart racing, I reach for the note.

Leave everything behind. It will be repossessed and sold off, and create a paper trail that leads away from you. Do not use your name or identifying factors again. Use cash to leave town, take the bus to a city that is walkable, or try to find an old used car that someone will let you pay for in cash without a title transfer. You may need to go to a chop shop. Medium-sized cities in rural states are best—you can get lost in crowds, but organized crime is unlikely to have a significant presence.

Take self-defense lessons and buy a gun at a trade show so there is no paper trail. Do not start looking for a job until Wesley sends you some new identification. The cash should last you several months. Get an apartment somewhere with excellent security and be friendly with the guards because they will protect you better if they like you. ~~Avoid Russian Men~~ *Stay away from any businesses run by Russians.*

~~Stays~~

~~Bes~~

~~Goodb~~

Ты забираешь мое сердце с собой.

- Dimitri

"Do you have a translation app on your phone?" I croak.

She hands me her device, open to Russian-to-English, and I hover the camera over the unfamiliar letters. Then, I shut my eyes.

You take my heart with you.

I thought I was all cried out. I'm practically dehydrated from it. At the very least, I assumed that I'd gotten it out of my system and I was safe from my emotions leaking out onto my face. Apparently not.

It's not the fact that his final message to me reads like a laundry list of advice for how to be on the run. It's not the fact that for the most part, it's practical, factual, and unemotional. It's not even those final words. None of that is what pushes me over the edge.

It's that I'm never going to hear him call me *Nee-cole* again.

A tear drops onto the page, pulling the ink up into its droplet and making it swirl around. I brush it away with trembling fingers, streaking and smudging some of the other words. Frowning, I wipe my cheeks so another doesn't fall.

I can't ruin this. It's all I have of him. I'll need to laminate it or something if I want to keep it forever.

Ugh. What is the matter with me? I'm supposed to be moving on, not planning on how to save and keep the broken pieces of this brief time in my life.

My facial expressions must display my internal torment, because Eleanor's brows come together in concern. "Nicole, you're scaring me. Please tell me what happened," she begs.

"Nothing happened," I say, hearing the unsteady rhythm of my voice. "I just can't stay. I can't live like this."

"I didn't realize you were so unhappy here," she says softly after a moment.

"I'm..." I trail off, glancing up out the front window of the car, watching as a few people board one of the buses.

Idly, I wonder where that bus is going, but not with the same kind of squirmy thrill I normally would. It strikes me that I've never been sad like this, leaving a place. I've been excited, maybe a bit nervous, but generally in a positive state of mind. I normally love a fresh start. But this time... I can't help thinking about how lonely I'm going to be. Again. And this time, I won't have anyone to blame but myself.

"I'm not," I realize. "But I will be. This life isn't for me. I can't do it."

She frowns. "You don't think Dimitri could make you happy?"

He definitely could.

She can see the answer on my face; I don't have to say it out loud. "Then you don't think he *would*? You don't think he cares about you enough to make sure you're happy?"

I shake my head. "He would, I'm sure, but what if it's not enough? I'd end up feeling bad because he was unhappy that I was unhappy... It's a cycle. I can break it before it even starts. It's the kinder thing to do, for both of us."

Her frown deepens, and she shifts in her seat so she can face me more fully, a look of accusation written plainly on her face. "I'm sorry, but I *cannot* have understood you right. Are you telling me you're leaving because you're worried that at *some point* in the future you *might* be unhappy?"

"I know myself," I say defensively. "And in my experience, it's best to get ahead of these things."

I'm not sure how I expected her to react, but it's not with a high-pitched, mocking, childish comeback. "Oh boo-hoo, *I'm running away from my sex god boyfriend who would burn down the world to keep me safe because I'm not 100% sure we'll live happily ever after."* She rolls her eyes. "That's you. That's what you sound like."

I cut her a look, and a pretty pink blush colors her cheeks. "Eleanor—"

"I'm sorry, but that's just fucked up."

"Don't judge me," I hiss. "You don't know me, Eleanor. You don't know what I've been through."

She sighs, and her shoulders drop. "Sorry... got a bit caught up. It's just... the possibility of being unhappy is *life*, Nicole. What you're describing is life. You can't control every aspect so you're never unhappy. That's not how it works."

"It's worked for me all these years."

Her face softens. "Okay, look, Nicole. Lord knows we've all got our demons, but I'm not letting you leave thinking you're doing the hard thing and making some huge sacrifice when in reality you're just running away. You love him," she accuses. "And he loves you. You're scared. And there's nothing wrong with being scared, but—"

"I'm not," I defend. "I just refuse to live like a prisoner."

She squints at me. "So don't," she says, shrugging. "I told you—you don't have to do this like how Mac and I do. There are other ways. Don't you want to be with him?"

I scoff. "It's not that simple! The cops are looking for me, and an entire Russian mafia knows I had millions of dollars of their money. They're always going to keep coming after me."

"So? Nicole, those three have a combined IQ of, like, 600. They could easily figure out another way—you don't have to leave. Of course there are other ways. I reject that reason. Try again."

"He doesn't really want me to stay," I confess, feeling my chest cave, pulling down my shoulders in a protective curl.

I thought after the night he killed the Volkevich leader that he agreed we were worth fighting for. I hoped last night he'd at least *try* to talk me out of it. But... seeing that duffle this morning, and realizing how easy it was for him to let me go... He's a fighter—it's what he does; it's *all* he does—and he didn't fight for me. No one ever has.

It hurts so much.

"What makes you think that?" she demands incredulously.

My nose is starting to drip, but it feels too undignified to sniffle at this exact moment. "Because if he wanted me to stay, he would have... said something, or done something so I'd understand. I was honest with him about my reasons for wanting to leave—why couldn't he have told me that we'd find another way? I feel like he didn't even try to convince me."

She lifts both hands and covers her eyes, rubbing harshly. It makes me bristle, even before she groans, "The two of you are going to give me an ulcer. You're so stubborn." She levels her index finger at my face. "That is a total cop-out."

"What? Why?"

"Girl, be so fucking for real—that man is repressed. They all are. They *kill people* for a living. You don't get into that business because you're in touch with your emotions. Take Mac, for example. He didn't reason with me to get me to live with him, he—" she cuts off abruptly, cheeks flushing. "Never mind, bad example."

"He what?"

Her cheeks stain redder. "Let's just say it wasn't a calm, pleasant, um... *face-to-face* conversation. But anyway, my point is, of course Dimitri wants you to stay. I've never seen him like he is with you. He loves you," she repeats, louder, as if volume was the reason it didn't land the last time she said it. "Don't you love him?"

I sigh.

Again, she sees the answer on my face. "Nicole, what are you doing?!" she cries.

"Why didn't he say it?" I insist. "I explained my concerns last night; he could've—"

I stop.

So that is it, then? You have decided? You chose for us both?

I didn't explain my concerns. He came in, and I told him what I'd already decided. He didn't suggest alternatives because I didn't let him. He even pointed it out to me. Why would he confess his love when I was pushing him away?

That's what I do; I push people away. Moments ago, I was lamenting how lonely I was going to be, like it's not *always* my fault. It totally is. I'm always the one that moves. I'm always the one who leaves. It's a pattern of behavior.

The blood drains from my face. Oh no. And I did exactly what I accused him of doing. I decided, and I just expected him to go along with my decision. I assumed that if he had a strong enough alternate point of view, he'd push.

But instead, I hurt him. I made him think *I* didn't care enough to find a way to stay with *him*.

"Fuck," I curse slowly. "I'm an idiot."

"Yeah," she agrees without hesitation.

"But... he's usually so confident and forceful and *blunt*! He's always saying exactly what he thinks."

My uncomfortable revelations seem to have calmed her somewhat, because she considers my question and all the anger is gone from her voice when she tells me, "I think it's easy to assume that someone who says what they think without sugarcoating it is going to be a good communicator, but there's more to it than that."

I chew on my lip, turning that one over. "I guess it *is* pretty hard for him to understand subtext sometimes," I agree, thinking back on all the missed jokes, and *that is what I said.*

She nods. "There's a difference between being blunt and being emotionally intelligent. Dimitri says what he thinks, not what he feels. He may not have the tools to understand or express how he feels. Most people don't. You clearly don't, even though you're in, like, the top five smartest people I know."

My lower lip pops out from between my teeth as my jaw falls slack, and I stare at her, feeling especially prickly and raw from being read like a fucking book. "Whoa. What the hell, Eleanor?"

She shrugs, totally unrepentant as she senses her imminent victory.

I huff a sigh. "Are you some kind of secret therapist or something?"

Her smile is a little rueful this time. "Did you know that they've done studies that show that people who read a lot are more empathetic? I was kind of a loner growing up—I read a lot; still do."

I flash her a half-smile and sit back in my seat. My leg jiggles as I turn over what she's said. "So, I would have to do all the emotional labor for us?"

"Maybe, or maybe just this time you do. You could try *letting him know* that you need him to be more open about his feelings—you're allowed to ask for that, you know—and if he cares, he'll try to do it for you. And I think we both know he cares," she winks. "Sometimes you have to learn together how to communicate."

I stew on that. She's right.

And that means I owe Dimitri one hell of an apology.

I groan. "I can't believe what I said to him. I can't believe I... We have to go back."

She hoots triumphantly, happy tears shining in her eyes. "Yeah, we do! Take that, unhealed trauma—today, love wins!"

My mind is racing. I know we have hours until they return from their mission, and I have plenty of time to plan what I'll say, but I'm anxious to start. I may even write myself a little script.

"Oh my God, I'm so pumped. I'm trying not to be a total dweeb about this, but I'm so happy you're staying. Anything you want to do while we're outside the fence? I know you haven't left the mansion in a few weeks. I could go for an ice cream cone," she says, almost to herself as she starts the car back up.

I smile. "Ice cream sounds nice. I think I was a kid the last time I had an actual cone. It's one of the few good memories I have of my dad—we'd always get an ice cream cone before he dropped me back at my mom's after his weekend."

She smiles. "That's nice."

"Yeah. I don't have a lot of nice memories, but..." I frown. "Hey... actually... any chance we could stop at my place real quick?"

The look she gives me is wide-eyed. "What?"

"Only for a minute. In his note, Dimitri said that my stuff is going to be repossessed. I don't care," I hurry to add when she grimaces, "but there's a photo album from when I was little, and it's the only pictures I have of my dad. Stuff is stuff, but if staying with Dimitri ends up meaning that I have to stay a missing person, memories are the only thing I care about losing." And then, because she doesn't quite look convinced, I add, "It'll seriously take five minutes. I know exactly which box it's in and exactly where the box is in the U-Haul."

She chews on the inside of her cheek. "Let me text Mac and see if he thinks it's safe enough."

"Sure. Just... um... don't tell him I'm staying, or ask him not to tell Dimitri. I don't want to distract him from the job, and I have some serious groveling to do."

Her thumbs make a soft clacking noise against the screen as she types out her question, and she holds it, staring at the open message chain. He responds instantly. "He says it's okay to stop there. They've cast the signal on the flash drive thingy, so chances are low that anyone is still watching. And he knows it's broad daylight, on a fairly busy street. That next message is for me..." she blushes, angling the phone away from me so I won't see whatever private words he sent. "And then he's reminding me how to circle the block and keep an eye out for plainclothes officers. Okay. Mac stamp of approval. Let's go get that album."

She pulls out of the parking lot, and I watch the bus station disappear into the background with a buzzing sort of excitement. As she navigates across the city to my barely lived-in rental, our chatter is lighthearted, full of the first deep bonds of sisterhood.

"I can't wait to see the look on his face when he realizes you didn't leave," she says, giggling. "He's gonna be all, 'this pleases me greatly,' which is like Dimitri for, 'I've never been happier.'"

I laugh at her terrible accent. "You sound like the Count from Sesame Street." We grin at one another, and after a beat, I tell her, "Mac is really lucky."

"Because of how good I am at impressions?"

"Because you're amazing. So insightful."

"I know," she says gravely. "Everyone's always so surprised by it. Do you think my bangs make me look younger than I am or something? I've been thinking about growing them out."

I laugh as she lifts a hand and parts them in the middle to show me how much more serious and adult she looks when I can see her forehead.

We arrive at the top of my street, and the mood in the car immediately shifts. Eleanor's eyes dart around, up and down, and in every car window as she circles the block. I try to help, but I don't really know what to look for.

"Okay, I think we're good. I'm going to park in that spot over there," she points. "In and out, five minutes, right? Pull up the hood of your sweatshirt just in case."

I do just that and pop out of the car.

Luckily, the front door opens with a code, and the U-Haul key is still hanging on the little key hook that the previous tenant left screwed into the wall. Heart racing from adrenaline like I'm actively being chased, I snatch the orange keychain and scurry down the short driveway in front of the row home towards the back of the truck with the recognizable orange branding. I jiggle the key in the lock when the door won't roll up automatically, and curse to myself as it catches halfway. Piece of shit... it smelled like cigarettes in the front cab, too, which I now remember gave me a wicked headache for most of the 10-hour drive.

I climb up into the back and start rearranging boxes to get to the row near the front. It doesn't take too long, since I'm organized and methodical, and I know I'm looking for the one labeled "Mementos and Misc Office."

Just as I get my fingernail under the clear packing tape, I hear the grinding of metal against metal and spin around in time to see the rolling door close. My heart leaps into my throat, and I shoot towards the disappearing opening, but before I make it two full steps, I hear the resounding metallic click echoing in the dark chamber around me, locking me inside.

38

DIMITRI

For her, I will beg.

"Anything yet?"

"Negative. That car just turned on the next road, and they're not looping back. Whatcha got, Big D?"

"Nothing on the ground."

I am in the back of our warehouse, where we set off the USB, waiting in the shadows. I can see the area behind the warehouse up to the line of trees about a mile away. Though I do not have James's eagle eyes, I would be able to detect movement. There is only one road, and farms for miles. Wesley's van is parked behind a barbed wire fence and has been made to look derelict. That van is my exit strategy if things get out of hand and I need a quick escape.

The warehouse was a good choice for our setup. It is remote, defensible, and it looks abandoned. Volkevich's men will approach with caution, and assume they are being watched; but there is no way for them to spot James up in a crow's nest, nearly a kilometer away, or me hiding behind so much concrete. And if we are overwhelmed by their numbers, well... that is what the backup plan is for.

If anyone ever fucking shows. We sent the signal hours ago.

"So... I know I said I wouldn't pry, but since we're all sitting here with our dicks in our hands..."

Wesley is the one who makes a knowing noise. *"You're a dog with a bone."*

"Don't tell me you're not curious, Wes."

"I was trying to give him some space. Not all of us have such shite impulse control."

"Whatever—tell that to my five total career missed shots. Anyway, what gives, D? One minute you're ready to ask her to move in, and the next you're having Wes put together a getaway package and telling us to fuck off when we ask about it? It's bullshit. Like Wes said, she's part of our dysfunctional family. Don't make me a child of divorce."

I am an expert at pushing emotions down or away—unpleasant or otherwise. But now, something rises in the back of my throat at the memory of last night. It took me hours to collect and pack her belongings because I could not stop staring at her curled form in the furthest corner of the bed.

"Mudak," I curse at him. "This is not about you. It is about her. And she... deserves to have the life she wants. She wants to find her home. To have her freedom."

"So, you told her to go?" Wesley asks, aghast, voice full of poorly concealed condemnation.

"She wanted to leave. I let her."

Quiet on the line follows my declaration, and I am horribly shamed by it. I can feel their judgments mounting, finding me as wanting as I do. But I know I am doing the right thing, honoring her wishes.

Right?

Unsurprisingly, James is the one to break the silence. *"Wait a minute. You're just... giving up?"*

"You didn't give up when she broke your fucking nose," Wesley adds wryly.

"This is what she wants."

"It is?" Wesley repeats in a tone of disbelief.

"I cannot give her the life she wants. She said as much."

"And what life is that?"

"A better one. One without me. She deserves better than a ruined man who will probably be killed violently one day."

"Whoa, that's what she said?" James sounds offended on my behalf. *"Doesn't sound like her."*

I grit my teeth. "Not in so many words. She did not need to. After I killed Viktor... that night..." a sharp pain lances my chest, and I rub the area. "She knows I am a monster. How could this ever work between us?"

"She makes you feel like a monster?" James presses.

"Well..." She did everything she could to convince me that she did not fear me that night. "No..."

"We call that one 'projecting,' my guy. Besides, ain't you ever heard of Beauty and the Beast? *Chicks love a monster."*

"I think what Mac's trying to say is that relationships are never going to be easy for us—I'm sure Eleanor would agree—so it won't work if you don't make it work. Sounds to me like you both got scared. She pulled away, then you did, and now you're both twiddling your thumbs, pretending not to see how monumentally stupid you've been."

"What would you have me do?" I growl.

"Bring her back," Wesley says, emphasizing each word. At the same time, James laughs and shouts, *"Go after her!"*

"She wants to leave," I repeat dumbly. "She does not want me."

"Oh, please. You guys are just really shitty communicators."

"Everyone can see how mad about each other you are. Maybe we're wrong," Wesley says. *"Well, I'm not familiar with the experience, so Mac will have to explain what it's like so I can be sure—"*

"Eat me, Short Round."

"—but don't you want to at least try to talk it out? To know?"

"Talk it out, Wes? What is this, Dr. fucking Phil? Take it from me, Big D—women like it best when you use your tongue for something other than

talking, you feel me? You gotta go up to her, get on your knees, and apologize. Then do it again, in case it doesn't stick the first time."

It would be sound advice, if not for one thing: I cannot get on my knees for her because I have been on them since the moment I saw her.

The man I have always been has never begged anyone for anything before—would never beg someone to want him.

But to keep her, I must not be that man. For her, I will beg.

Fuck this. One fight cannot ruin what we have. I will not allow it.

Wesley is correct—we were both afraid. She is scared, but not of me, as *I* feared. She is scared of... truths, and pain that she cannot heal herself, with stitches and bandages. In fact, the more I consider this, the more obvious it seems. She told me of her nomadic lifestyle, of her search for home and belonging. I should have expected that running is her preferred method of dealing with issues—she avoids them instead of facing them.

I was too wounded by her rejection to think rationally. I allowed my pride to dictate my response. Never again.

When it comes to her... I must have no pride.

I am nearly in the doorway leading out to the back entrance and the van when the swish of my tactical pants and the weight of the knives in my palms remind me of where I am.

Fuck!

After. I will find her... after. If she follows my advice, she will be untraceable until she makes contact, but once she does, I will find her. I will remind her that she is mine and that sometimes, taking care of her means forcing her to confront her own fears. I can help. It will be easier to do together.

I nearly jump at the sound of James in my ear again. *"Hey darlin'. You get what you needed from... whoa, whoa, whoa, slow down. Eleanor, slow down..."*

In an instant, my blood turns to ice, and I know. It is Nicole.

"Wes, I'm switching the line, patch her through?"

There is a dial tone in my ear on James's side, then I can hear Eleanor's panicked voice, *"—just closed her right in and I didn't know what to do, but I—"*

"What happened?" I growl. Kyle found her, somehow.

"Dimitri? Oh my God," Eleanor sobs. *"I'm so sorry! Before I knew what was happening, they were driving away... this is all my fault."*

"Breathe, darlin'," James coaches, and I want to wring his neck for suggesting it. She does not need to breathe; she needs to tell us where to find Nicole!

"We were stopping for five minutes at her place to get something from the U-Haul before we went back home—"

"Home?" I repeat. Surely that was a misspoken word... still, hope weaves around my heart, winding through the confusion and panic. "You mean to the bus station?"

"No, I... fuck it, that promise is so unimportant now. Nicole was coming home with me, Dimitri. She decided not to leave."

Something unnamed slams into my chest, stealing all the oxygen from my lungs.

"They must have been there watching, waiting for her to show. She was only in the back of the van for three minutes; I timed it. Some guy with his hood up snuck right up to the truck and locked her in the back, then got into the driver's seat and drove away! She's still in the back!"

I mute myself to scream my rage. It burns my throat and makes me feel out of control for one brief, sharp moment, but that leeches away with the air in my lungs, leaving only steely resolve. I tuck away my knives and sprint out to the van.

Kyle obviously is not coming here. We need to find him.

My *med...*

Fuck!

We will find him. And we will make him pay.

"Where is she? Where are you?" I growl. The sliding door slams against the end of the track, jolting the entire Bugs-B-Gon van and revealing Wesley, hunched over his laptop and scowling. I throw my bag into the back, and follow it in to watch Wesley's screens.

"I'm following the truck!" I can hear the rapid, whimpering breaths she is taking in. She is clearly terrified.

"You activate that tracker on your watch?" James asks, his voice calming and gentle—soft for her as ever.

"Shit! I forgot. Okay, hold on, we're coming to a stop... Okay... there. Sorry! It all happened so quickly!"

"You did good, darlin', your quick thinking probably saved her life. Now, take a deep breath for me—atta girl—and one more. Are you all right?"

"Not really," she laughs, but there is no humor in it as she sniffles. *"I just watched my friend get locked into the back of a van, and I'm following the bastards that did it to God knows where. My hands are sh-shaking and I feel like I'm going to throw up."*

"I know, baby," James says, *"but you're doing great. You've got this. Wes, you got her tracking info?"*

"Looks like... south on Vine?"

"Yeah," she confirms. *"What's going on? Who was that guy? What do they want with Nicole? Know what? Never mind. Just tell me you're coming to get her."* There is censure and warning in her tone.

Fierce little creature. It nearly makes me smile, though I am far too angry. "Every man who touches her will die."

There is a beat of silence. Wesley glances my way, lifting a brow.

"That's what I'm fuckin' talking about," James approves. *"All right, D. How do you want to play this?"*

I check the location where Eleanor has stopped, feeling triumph bleeding into the edges of my panic. They are heading towards a run-down part of the city, currently undergoing a wave of gentrification.

"Scorched earth."

"Uh..." with one word, James puts both Wesley and me on high alert. Gone is the breezy excitement, replaced with a tightness meant to hide panic. *"Hey, baby, I'm gonna mute myself for a sec, but I'm right here, and I can still hear you, okay?"*

"Okay."

"Code fucking red. I've got three SUVs heading your way."

"Fuck!" Wesley curses, shaking his head. His fingers fly across the screen, and he moves back and forth between windows fast enough to make my head spin. One of the views is of an intersection a few kilometers away, and I can see the cars James flagged. Three identical, clean, shiny black cars with tinted windows driving in a line. They certainly give off the impression of *Bratva* men coming to collect.

"We do not have time to wait for them to arrive," I decide. We have to move. Every second Nicole spends with Kyle is a second her life is at risk. She is still in transit, but we are a long way from Eleanor's tracking dot. They will certainly arrive at their destination long before we do.

"I do. I'm already in place here. You and Wes go, I'll stay. They'll never see me coming, and I'll be long gone before they even realize where I am. I may not get 'em all, but I'll make as many of them pay as I fucking can. Now, go get our girls."

39

NICOLE

—◆—

People really need to stop kidnapping me.

When I wake, I know instantly I am somewhere different.

Calm.

I have to stay calm.

In the U-Haul, once my brain caught up with what was happening and I felt the rumbling under my feet, I tried bracing myself, but that first abrupt shift from reverse to forward launched me face-first against the side of the truck. I hit my head against the hard metal, and it was lights out.

My head is pounding, and I can tell I'm sitting upright. A small, exploratory tensing of my arms confirms the sinking suspicion I got from the pressure at my wrists. Whatever is holding me in place wraps around my arms and my chest, and my ankles are bound together.

A whimper escapes my mouth when I crack an eyelid enough to see that I'm duct-taped to a chair in the middle of a half-finished hardwood floor near a stack of paint cans and dirty bins with brushes. The drywall is bare, and the spacious room is empty of furniture and decorations.

On the far side of the cavernous room, there's a wall of windows displaying the tops of several nearby buildings and an awful lot of sky.

If I had to guess, I'd say I'm in a half-finished penthouse in a new construction apartment building. And since I'm not gagged, presumably no one is close enough to hear me scream.

I hear two men speaking in low tones, the indecipherable words flowing quickly. Spanish, I'm pretty sure. I look over and see a large, buff guy with his back to me, perched on a bar stool, facing another man who leans against the cavity where the fridge will go in the unfinished kitchen. I know almost instantly he's the one in charge, though I'm not sure why. Maybe because he exudes a quiet kind of danger and authority. Maybe because he looks totally unbothered, listening to the man's report while taking large bites of something beige from his hand.

No imminent danger there, so I continue glancing around furtively, trying to get my bearings.

It's not just the three of us in here. Behind a closed door on the other side of the open space, there's someone in the bedroom. I can hear a telltale, rapid, rhythmic squeaking noise and soft crying whimpers that sound feminine, but not the kind borne of pleasure. I wince, feeling utterly helpless, and shudder as bile climbs up the back of my throat.

This must be Kyle's handiwork. I don't see him, but there's no other explanation. I'm not sure what kind of operation he's running with Mexican guys, but no one else would have any reason to kidnap me. Those two definitely don't—I've never seen them before in my life.

For a second, that sets in. I've been kidnapped. A-fucking-gain.

For fuck's sake. People really need to stop kidnapping me. This is getting ridiculous.

"Oi, she's awake."

My head whips around, and I find both Hispanic men looking at me. The one eating stares, unblinking, chewing slowly with an unnerving smile growing on his lips. He nods to the other guy and pushes off from his leaning position, stalking towards me like a lion.

"That's quite a bump," he says, his voice deep and lightly accented, smoothing over consonants and lengthening the vowels. He holds up his hand, splaying his index and middle fingers. "How many fingers?"

"Enough to fuck yourself with," I hiss.

Now that it doesn't matter if they hear me, I jerk viciously against the tape on my wrists, twisting in the bonds. It doesn't give an inch. How are a few thin layers of something so damn strong? The chair rolls backwards from my struggling, startling me into stillness with its movement. I look down and do a double-take, realizing both that I'm in an office chair—and that it's *my* fucking office chair.

"She's got claws." He laughs, though whether it's at my feisty joke or in mockery of my failed escape, I couldn't say. He closes the distance between us, goes down onto his haunches, and holds out the last bite of his food. "Want some tamale?"

I turn my head, and he laughs.

He pops the rest into his mouth and talks around it. "Sorry for the dramatics with the duct tape. I've been through this before, *sabes*? You say you're not gonna run, I turn my back, you run the first chance you get, I have to shoot you..." he shakes his head, and I grimace at the lack of emotion in what feels very much like a promise. "No one wants that shit. It'd be a damn waste."

I already let the headache get the best of me once—I really shouldn't have cursed him out, considering my position. I'm not rising to whatever bait he's trying to catch me with.

"Stroke of genius with this wheely chair, don't you think?" he asks, gripping the armrest and tugging it rapidly back and forth, jerking me around. When he smiles, it reveals a flash of gold in the back of his mouth, like one of his teeth has been capped. "Couldn't carry you, found this in the truck, and wheeled you right on up."

I press my lips together, feeling my face heat in rage and a shame that I hate so much I burn with it. I really don't want to let this fucker make me feel bad about myself, of all things, but my lower lip trembles like I have no control over it.

"Hey, hey, hey, hey," he holds up a finger, frowning at my grimacing reaction. "None of that. I wasn't saying nothing about it like that. In fact, I like 'em with something to grab onto, *sabes*?"

His eyes flash with naked interest as they rake down my torso. It makes bile churn in my stomach, but suddenly I realize that though this position is very precarious, they didn't restrain me with intent to rape. Someone would have to cut through layers of tape, and once they did, I'd have the chance to fight back until they got me back under control. Hope sparks in my chest. This guy is taller than me, and his muscular form makes it a daunting proposition, but he probably wouldn't be as desperate as I am. Desperation makes you strong.

He continues, not really waiting for a response. "I'll tell ya, it's a damn shame you got caught up in this, *mamacita*. If we'd met under any other circumstances, I would've been begging you to use those claws on me."

Is that supposed to make me feel better? Should I feel honored my piece of shit kidnapper wants to fuck me instead of just killing me? I grind my jaw and lift my eyes to meet his. They're a warm brown, with deep smile lines at the edges. "Other circumstances? Ones where you don't work for Kyle?"

He grins. "'Work for Kyle.' Sure. Let's call it that. Does that mean you know why you're here?" He leans forward, getting into my space. "Because if you act nice and tell us where the money is, I bet I can convince *my boss* to let me keep you instead of throwing you to the bottom of the Atlantic."

I swallow around a dry throat, and a cold fear creeps into my extremities. "I don't—"

"Found a stray, Felix," announces another deep, accented voice. "She was obvious as fuck, following us home."

The man and I both turn to the source, and a sound of pure panic escapes my throat, seeing Eleanor being forced forward, struggling against this goon's grip. Her wide eyes meet mine, flashing with relief, concern, terror, and rage, all at once. My heart bangs around in my chest in answer, even as a spark of hope ignites. Suddenly, I've got an ally. I hate that she's here, too, but we have a better chance together than I did on my own.

Unlike me, she's got tape over her mouth. Otherwise, she looks unharmed. God, the panic she must have felt... wait a minute, if she's here, does that mean she tailed the U-Haul here? That spark of hope catches into a small, controlled fire. Eleanor told me that Mac makes her wear trackers whenever she leaves the house.

They'll find us. Dimitri will find me.

The man—Felix—looks between us. "I take it you two know each other. She your rescue attempt?" he asks, grinning. He turns to the goon holding her. "Grab that folding chair. Jose, grab the tape. Looks like we've got another witness to question."

I watch in mute horror as the two guys manhandle her into the chair, wincing when she puts up too good of a fight and one of them slaps her. Since her hands are already taped, she gets the around-the-torso treatment and nearly clips him in the face with her knee when he tries to get her legs. When he stands, fists clenched and wearing a murderous expression, I rage. But Felix shakes his head.

"We talked about this, Leo. No marks on the merch."

Fuck. Merchandise? What the fuck does that mean?!

"Eleanor!" I whisper as soon as the men turn away from us. "Are you okay?"

As she's nodding, Felix's head whips around. "Eleanor?" he repeats sharply, eyes snapping back to her. They narrow, like he's studying her much more closely. "James MacKenzie's Eleanor?"

The recognition in his tone is so unexpected that I nearly nod, automatically assuming that if he knows James, it's a good thing. Eleanor—who has presumably been trained more extensively for this kind of scenario—doesn't say anything. She doesn't move. Her eyes stay fixed on him as the color slowly drains from her face.

That's apparently enough of an answer. "Oh, fuckin' hell. Fuck!"

While his two goons look on in confusion, Felix spins and strides away, shoulders hunched with agitation. Leaning close to the windows, he peers out, looking back and forth rapidly, as though checking for something, and mutters to himself in Spanish.

He rubs his eyes with one hand, spinning back to face us. "Fuck."

When he shifts his focus to me, I go rigid. This emotional swing doesn't feel particularly safe. There's no heat or anger or violence of any kind in his assessment, but I do catch a flash of recognition and well-hidden fear.

He crosses, uncrosses, then recrosses his arms, poking his tongue into his cheek and sighing. "I take it that means the Russian guy that stabbed Kyle is... Dimitri?"

He knows Dimitri? I guess if he knows James, it's not that big of a leap, but... what the hell is going on?

"And... let me guess. You're Dimitri's woman."

The act of looking at Eleanor for guidance is all the confirmation he needs. He heaves another huge sigh. "This payout was gonna be so fuckin' good. Fuck. All right. Go get the car. I'll meet you down there in five," he instructs his men.

"Boss?"

"Do it," he replies, not lifting his voice but hardening it.

The two of them look at each other, then hustle towards the elevator. While it dings its way down to the lobby, he moves across the room to the chair where Eleanor is tied. Grabbing something from his pocket, he squats next to her. I hear a mechanical snap, then a sawing noise like he's cutting through the tape. It takes a few long seconds, then he rises and lays a heavy hand on Eleanor's shoulder that makes her flinch away from the contact. "Up you go, babydoll. You're coming with me."

I open my mouth to ask what the fuck is going on, but there's a loud shout from behind the closed door of the bedroom. "Ah! What the fuck?! You fucking bitch! You cunt!"

Bang! Bang!

My heart leaps into my throat.

"Yup, time to go," Felix grinds out, lifting Eleanor from the chair with a firm grip under her armpit.

Locking eyes filled with tears on me, she struggles against him as he pulls her towards the elevator. I open my mouth to urge her to go, to save herself.

At that exact moment, Kyle emerges from the bedroom, face red and jerking at the buttons on his shirt with one free hand. The other has a gun. He tears off the fabric and throws it furiously onto the ground. "Fucking cunt," he growls, wiping at a spot on his bare stomach where I recognize the color and consistency of vomit. "Fucking *cunt*! Fuck!"

I flinch at his scream.

He sees me, pauses, then glances around until he finds Felix, before turning his attention back to me.

I know, then; this is real evil. Felix may have an air of malice, but Kyle is insane. One look and I know he tortured animals when he was a kid.

I'd hoped to go my entire life without ever seeing his horrible face again. My stomach is in knots. I might vomit all over him next.

"You found the cunt. Turns out you're not totally useless, eh, *amigo*?" Kyle asks, butchering the pronunciation of the last word so badly that it sounds like a hate crime. His eyes fall on Eleanor, and he frowns. "Who the fuck is that? Another hostage?"

"Boys thought I'd like to play with her," Felix replies, sounding bored. Just then, the elevator dings and opens behind him. I think I see him flinch.

Kyle scowls. "Where the fuck are you going?"

Felix rocks on his heels, considering the other man. After a beat, he tosses Eleanor towards the open elevator and steps into the doorway, preventing the doors from closing without him. She hits the back wall and nearly goes down, but recovers.

"That *cabrón* who had you shitting out a bag for four weeks… Did he have a big fuckin' scar all down his face like this?" He gestures, miming a curved line with the side of his hand.

"Maybe. It was dark," Kyle shrugs. "What does that have to do with anything?"

Felix nods a few times, mostly to himself. Then he straightens. "I'm out. Keep the money."

This is obviously not what Kyle was expecting to hear. He clenches his fist around the gun, staring at Felix with bewilderment that quickly shifts into anger. "What? You're backing out now? You're the one who told me that signal was a trap! And my backup is nearly here—"

"Ain't no amount of backup that's gonna save your white ass."

Felix's eyes flick to me, and Kyle follows the movement, frowning. "What the fuck are you talking about?"

"You know how people like to say you're playing with fire? Well, you're not playing with fire; you're playing with fucking napalm. That shit's gonna burn down *everything*," Felix says, expression a bit unhinged, like he kind of wants to watch it happen. "Smartest thing you can do now is leave her here and run for your sorry little life. He'll still catch you, but maybe he'll kill you quick."

"You're telling me you're running away? You're afraid of some—" Kyle begins, his voice pitching higher in outrage and taunt.

Felix cuts through it with a chuckle. "Yup. Yeah. I am."

"Pussy," Kyle shakes his head and returns the laugh, though his is far more bitter. "Whatever, man, don't come crying to me later. Deal's off. I don't owe you a dime."

As he presses the button in the elevator, Felix moves half behind the wall, ushering Eleanor over to the side and blocking her from my sight. Is he... protecting her?

"There are those finely tuned instincts that are gonna get you so far," Felix taunts. "Piece of advice. Maybe take a couple seconds and ask yourself *why* I would walk away from a payout this big." He taps his temple twice. "Think about it."

The doors close.

Kyle turns back to me, jaw slack, eyes burning with blame and a whole mess of things I don't even want to try to name. He stares for a few seconds, shakes his head, and strides past me to the kitchen island. Once there, he leans down over the quartz and makes a heavy, thick snorting noise.

Did he just do a line of cocaine? I slip into my Nurse Nicole skin and make my observations as discreetly as I can from here. Judging from how unsteady he is on his feet, that probably wasn't his first hit. He's having trouble with visual focus, his fine motor skills appear to be compromised, he's unhinged, and his emotional state while he spoke with Felix seemed to shift quickly and unpredictably.

He falls back, making a groaning noise of relief, and goes slack in the low-backed chair.

Heart racing so fast I'm sick to my stomach with it, I grapple for something—anything—that might be helpful while I have a few seconds to think.

I know how to handle several different types of crises; I just have to try to remember my training—there had to have been one about how to handle an unstable, dangerous person with a gun. Active shooter trainings advise running and hiding, but I know I took a seminar about dealing with patients with suspected psychosis. And, sure, calling the doctor or security isn't an option here, but there has to be something buried in my brain that I've learned about calming people down when they're having a mental break.

That could be what's happening here, or he could just be really high. The same tactics wouldn't work on someone who was really high.

Okay, Nicole. Think.

If I play my cards right, I might be able to stall long enough to… I don't know. I don't know!

It feels reckless not to make a plan of my own and just hope for Dimitri to come for me, but I'm *so* out of my depth. How is he going to get up here without being noticed? Will he come in time?

The only thing I'm really sure of is that antagonizing Kyle is a bad idea. He might just shoot me for fun or by accident because he's worked up. I have to be careful and use what I know about him to my advantage.

What do I know about him?

He's entitled. He's self-important. He thinks he's smarter than he is. He thinks he's more charming than he is. He's a shitty dancer… Okay, that's not immediately relevant… But there's a theme here—he's obviously got a huge ego.

So, though I want to rage at him, to taunt him, to scream obscenities and warn him that my big, scary boyfriend is going to come rescue me, I can't. I have to pretend to be docile so he feels like he's in control.

I might be able to confuse him or create some paranoia. I might be able to fool him. He obviously wants the USB and the money, though he hasn't even asked about it yet. Felix knew I knew about it anyway. Something tells me it won't go well for me if he realizes I don't have it—or worse, that the money was transferred away and I have no idea where it is.

Every second that ticks by digs the pit in my stomach a little deeper. At least Eleanor got out. I hope she manages to fight off Felix, or holds out for long enough that Mac comes to get her…

Kyle groans again and shuffles to his feet, leaving the gun on the counter.

"What the fuck was Felix's problem?" he asks, and I'm not totally sure if it's directed at me. I stay silent in case it's not.

He moves towards the windows, then remembers his gun is still on the counter. When he picks it up and tucks it into his waistband, my stomach sinks. Fuck. I'd really been hoping he would forget about it. As if he can't decide where he wants to keep it, he slides the weapon back out of his pants, fingers the trigger, and taps it against the outside of his leg. Then, he turns, pointing the barrel right at me.

I flinch, nearly losing control of my bladder. Holy fuck, it is terrifying being on the wrong end of a gun. Staring down the barrel is bad enough—it steals rational thoughts—but feeling like the person holding it is unpredictable makes it so much worse.

My time for planning has just run out.

"Who's the fucker with the scar and why is Felix pissing himself about him?"

"I don't know," I whisper the lie, hoping he'll accept it because he wants to. "I don't know what he was talking about."

He makes a noise of satisfaction, dropping his arm.

Tears in my eyes, I decide to try pleading, "Why are you doing this, Kyle?"

He rolls his eyes. "A fuck-ton of money. Fucking obviously."

"Okay, fine... everyone wants to be rich. But you're not a bad guy, right? You don't have to do it this way. You don't want blood on your hands like this, right?"

The look he levels at me proves just how futile my plea was—apparently, appealing to his (nonexistent) good side was the wrong gamble. "I've got so much blood on my hands, spilling yours doesn't make a difference. I'm a Volkevich, you stupid bitch," he spits. "*Bratva.* Family first. I've killed for my family, did everything my uncle told me to..." he trails off, his voice lowering like he's no longer speaking to me. "Matt agrees to marry some ugly cunt, and suddenly I'm not good enough anymore? It was supposed to be mine. *My* money. *My* legacy. *Mine.*"

Okay. Motive. He stole the money because he clearly felt cheated out of his future. I can work with that. "And that's not fair that they took that from you," I say, trying to be gentle and sound sincere when the thought of his entitlement is turning my stomach. "I'd be pissed, too."

"It was supposed to be me!" he roars.

He swings the gun around, finger pressed against the trigger, landing with it pointed at his own head. I hold my breath, hoping this issue is about to sort itself out, but he just scratches his scalp with the silenced end of the barrel.

I swallow my disappointment and try again. "Are you sure this is the best plan, Kyle? Have you really thought this through?" I ask as he crosses the room back towards the kitchen and the other lines of coke waiting for him on the quartz countertop.

He doesn't answer for a few long seconds, staring longingly at the white lines on the counter.

"Whoever freaked that guy Felix out is probably on his way. Maybe it would be a good idea to—"

"Enough!" he screams, making me flinch.

He pulls out his phone and presses it to his ear. When the person on the other side picks up, he starts speaking rapidly in Russian, glancing at me periodically. I tense, waiting, trying to pick up on a single word in the unfamiliar language. His tone brightens, and it makes my stomach sink further and further. He's happier now, and I can't imagine that means good things for me.

He hangs up, closes his eyes, breathes deeply in through his nose, and focuses back on me. That edge of mania in his eyes has shifted to something that looks a hell of a lot more like triumph. Oh fuuuuck.

"Time to talk, bitch. Where's my money?" he asks. It's the most lucid and calm he's sounded yet.

I wish I'd bothered to come up with an answer before now—a lie that might sound true. "I... I don't have it on me," I whisper.

"Fucking obviously! Where is it?! Where is my fucking money?"

He takes a few steps towards me, lifting the gun. When he's within arm's length, I turn my head, and he presses the tip into my cheek.

I'm shaking so hard it's making the chair vibrate. "I don't know, but I can bring you to the people who do." My throat tries to close around the words several times as I attempt not to dissolve into sobs. If I can stall, or hold out, or get him to take me somewhere out of here where he has to stow that gun...

"I don't believe you, cunt. Sounds like you need to be taught what happens when you lie to a Volkevich."

40

DIMITRI

Be strong, Nicole. I am coming.

The apartment complex is not yet open to the public, so it was laughably easy to discern that Kyle is occupying the penthouse—it is the only floor with lights on in the fading daylight. Once we tucked the van in an alley of two adjacent buildings, Wesley pulled up the building plans so we could determine how I will get in.

"It's actually a pretty smart location—highly defensible up at the top. He's got a good visual, potential rooftop surveillance, looks like those windows are reinforced glass, and I'm sure there are alarms. Limited egress, but likely hidden escape routes through service elevators or maintenance tunnels."

As he speaks, I follow the movement of Wesley's finger across the screen, pointing to various spots on the blueprints of the unfinished high-rise.

"Penthouse floor has its own elevator. If you use another one that stops just below, you might be able to switch over and climb up the shaft the rest of the way—" Wesley cuts himself short, squinting at the video feed from the back entrance. "Wait... Is that... Is that Eleanor? And *Felix?*"

Without a second thought, I am out of the van. I can hear Eleanor crying, begging to be released, an instant before they come into view.

And what a sight it is—a familiar tall, handsome man with a death wish, holding a sniper's woman by the wrist, dragging her towards a waiting car, and struggling with her while he tries to get the door open. If James were here, Felix would already be dead. James is going to be very upset that he was not here and that he cut the line moments ago to focus.

"Felix!" I roar. It is not to get his attention; it is to let Eleanor know I am coming.

Felix spots me as I lift the knife in my hand. "Whoa!" he calls, taking a half step behind Eleanor.

What a coward, using a woman for a shield.

For her part, Eleanor understands what is happening and renews her struggle. In a move that leaves me nearly breathless with pride because I recognize my own maneuver, she twists, spinning under his arm, breaking his grip, and shooting away before he can grab her again. The instant she sees me, she sprints in my direction.

I meet her halfway, tucking her behind me and adjusting my grip on the knife, hiding it in my palm when I hear a car drive past the alley.

We are alone back here, but it is still bright enough to be seen and not so late that I can be sure no one is watching.

Felix holds up his hands in surrender. "Whoa, whoa, whoa. Whoa there, Ghost."

The man in the driver's seat gets out and points a gun at me. My vision sharpens, and I tighten my grip on my knife, but Felix cuts his man a look, which causes him to lower his weapon.

"Hold on. Look, *ese*. We can do this dance as long as you want, but you're wasting time you don't have. Time *she* doesn't have. You shoot us, we shoot you. All the while, she's up there alone with Kyle," he jerks a thumb behind him at the building, "and I promise you, he's pissed. And he's got reinforcements on the way."

"He's right," Eleanor cries, tugging at my arm. "You've got to go get Nicole!"

I do not lower my arm. This may be my only opportunity to kill Felix before he disappears, as he did before.

"What's it gonna be, Ghost? Her or me?"

The choice is easy. "Get the fuck out of my sight," I demand, voice low.

"Wise decision," he nods, wrenching open the car door and disappearing into the back behind tinted windows and bulletproof glass. The car peels away.

I turn, and Eleanor envelops me in a hug. She is sobbing, shaking us both. "Thank you. Thank you. Please go save her!"

"Wesley's van is over there." I jerk my chin in that direction and watch the steel form behind deep blue eyes. It was the same when I came for her at the restaurant many months ago—I believed she would crumble under the pressure of danger and panic, but she is tougher than she looks.

She nods, scampering away, and I assess the maintenance entrance in front of me. Luckily, it appears to be secured with a physical deadbolt instead of a keycard reader. I can pick that.

"Eleanor's secure."

"Good. I need all cameras off and alarms disabled."

"Give me 30 seconds."

Crouched, I wait for Wesley to cut the power to the building so the alarm will not go off when I pick the lock. Once I see the entire block go dark, I get to work. It is a simple lock—even in the dwindling light, it takes no time to pick. The door opens into a maintenance stairwell that I know from the blueprints will bring me to the 11th floor, one below the penthouse. I take the stairs three at a time, picking up speed. My woman is close.

Be strong, Nicole. I am coming.

The door opens into a U-shaped hallway that smells like wet paint, with a carpet that is completely devoid of stains. I hug the wall until I reach the elevators, then pry open the doors of the one marked *P.* Then, I curse. The floor of the elevator is blocking the shaft. Even if I could get inside the car, I would still need to force open the doors to enter the penthouse, which would alert Kyle. I could have Wesley create some kind of distraction to draw him out, perhaps, or I could keep going up until I got through to the ceiling and drop into the apartment somewhere, though that also bears the risk of—

"Dimitri, you've got company. Oh, fuck—you've got a lot of company."

"How many?"

"Six, and they're headed straight for the front doors. Looks like... yeah, they've got a key fob. Must be Kyle's reinforcements that Felix was talking about."

"Fuck," I whisper.

I am so close. Nicole is just a floor away, in pain and terrified for her life, and hoping I will come... but now I must go down and deal with a different threat instead of continuing up. Every second I leave her with that fucker is another second she is in an unacceptable state of fear and anguish. But I must go.

I will carve her retribution into his body when I am done.

Running down stairs is an awkward waste of time, so when I get to the top of the staircase, I grab hold of the railing and leap over. I land a story down on soft knees, though the impact still rattles my bones. Going back and forth between leaping down the stairs and controlling my fall down a story at a time, I arrive at the ground level in mere seconds.

"Any weapons?"

"Two with guns drawn. They're waiting for the elevator, crowding around it."

I quickly calculate the best approach. The odds of six on one are not favorable, and they likely all have guns. I will need to surprise them. I will need to time this perfectly. "I will get into place around the corner. Tell me when the last man moves into the elevator—I will only have seconds before those doors close."

"Fish in a barrel, I like it. Roger that."

Silently, I creep into the hallway, using the corner as cover. In the silence, I hear a gruff Russian voice order, "Milo, you will stay here to stand guard. Boris, we leave you on the last floor before the top."

If Milo will not be getting into the elevator, I need to drop him first.

"Okay, they're getting in."

I peer around the corner, heart thumping. Am I going to lose my chance? Milo's back is to me, and he is standing between me and the closing brass doors. In a fluid motion, I toss a knife at the back of Milo's head.

Yet another instance of a knife's superiority to a gun. He dies instantly and nearly silently.

In the time it takes his body to hit the floor and for anyone to realize he has fallen, I have palmed another knife and made it down the hallway to the elevator. The doors are closing, but stop as I throw my boot in the way.

In the dim elevator lighting, five surprised faces greet me. I punch the one closest to me, feeling his nose crunch under my hand. With my left hand braced on his shoulder, I lift my leg and kick back towards the next closest man, who is wearing a red tie, sending him into the side of the elevator car. He hits the wall, cracking his head against the mirror, splintering it, and the other three respond as one, each reaching for a gun in his waistband as I step inside.

I shove the man with the broken nose towards the two in the corner, and they all fall like bowling pins. My knife goes into the last man standing as he reaches for his gun, sliding through the bones in his hand and straight into his stomach, halting the removal of the weapon from his pants. He screams, and my left arm comes up to slash his throat.

Four to go.

As the doors to the elevator close, the man with the red tie recovers and tackles me from behind. We go careening into the wall, and he delivers a few good punches to my kidneys that have me wheezing and breathless with the sharp pain of it. I throw back my head, connecting hard skull to soft cartilage, and his newly broken nose throws him off balance. I spin with my armed hand outstretched and catch his stomach in a long, deep slash that makes him choke and stumble backwards.

Three left.

Movement in the broken mirror catches my eye, and I turn back in time to see one of the men on the floor—the smallest of the group by far—in the corner raising his gun. A hard kick knocks it from his grasp, just as one of the others gets his feet under him enough to charge at me. His long ponytail smacks me in the face as his shoulder in my stomach knocks the breath from me long enough to drive us towards the wall. I hear glass shatter behind my head as the man with a ponytail delivers poorly supported blows to my torso.

If I were unarmed, this would be a terrible position for me, but I am not, and his entire spine is unprotected. I switch the knife to my hand with more freedom of movement and jam it down into the ridge in the middle of his shirt. With the significant downward force, the thin blade of my knife slides right between two vertebrae, and he goes down like a stone thrown into the river.

Only two now.

I kick the ponytail man's body away, forward at one of the remaining men coming towards me—the very thin one. He knocks the body of his comrade aside and points his gun at me. I am a large target in an enclosed space, but that also means he is too close to recover quickly when I duck down and spring towards the other man. I bring my knife down into the thin man's leg above the kneecap with one arm and grab behind his hip to swing him down and around to cover myself just as the last man fires his silenced weapon. It hits my bony meat shield in the back, jerking his whole body and making my ears ring with the noise. Silencers do not make guns completely silent.

One man remains. The largest of them.

My position is less than optimal. I am on one knee, the last man has a gun, and there is a body between us. My angle is terrible, so when I throw the last knife I am holding, it clips the side of his face when I was aiming for its center. But it is enough to make him turn his head, and that gives me the second of distraction I need. A blow to the solar plexus, one to the throat, and a kick to the knee, then he is down and cannot get up or take in a breath. I pull a knife from one of the other bodies where I left it, find another on the ground a few feet away, and use that one to slice his throat for a quicker death.

During the heat of the moment, fights like this feel like they take hours. In reality, it is done before the elevator reaches the top. Seconds, perhaps a minute at most. My chest is heaving as I try to take in enough air, but I can barely feel anything through the rush of adrenaline. I am a creature of instinct and survival, halfway between a cornered animal and a predator on the hunt.

The elevator comes to a smooth stop, makes a cheerful dinging noise, and I can hear a muffled voice through the doors, "And here they are." At the sound of his voice, I squeeze the handles of my knives so hard my arms shake.

I settle into a soft-kneed position. I am ready.

The doors part.

49

NICOLE

A couple that stabs together

One time in New York, I got clipped in the eyebrow by a patient's elbow when he was fighting being sedated. I remember the crack of pain—how the sound registers long before the feeling of the impact—and how my vision swam. Even a glancing blow makes your ears ring, blinds you, and makes it hard to think through the agony.

Before today, that's the closest I've come to being intentionally hit in the face.

I'm not ashamed to admit that I started crying as soon as I could get a full breath in after his first blow landed on my cheek. The pain was white-hot. Unreal. Even now, moments later, it throbs and burns, too sharp to ignore. I can feel blood trickling down my cheek from where he broke the skin with the butt of his gun. The cocaine seems to be making Kyle strong, but wobbly and imprecise—while painful, he didn't break more than just skin.

The second blow to my stomach didn't hurt quite as bad, but it did knock the wind out of me and cause panic to set in when I couldn't draw a complete breath for several long seconds. The fear that instilled hasn't dulled. My heart is going to explode out of my chest.

I don't want to die.

Luckily, that was as far as he got into his interrogation before the elevator dinged. Unfortunately, it doesn't seem like I'm going to like who I find behind that door.

"And here they are," Kyle announces to me with a horrible, smug smile as the penthouse elevator arrives at the top floor. "My backup. You're not going to like these guys. They know exactly how to make a bitch like you—"

I never gave much thought to what the Grim Reaper would look like. They sell you on this idea of a hooded figure—a skeleton, usually, with a scythe—but after everything I've seen in the ER and years of trauma cases and the messy, awful sides of humanity, that image always felt a bit too *clean*. And now I know why. Any personification of Death that I'd believe in would have to be... bloodier.

The elevator chimes and the doors part, revealing a single, enormous figure in shades of darkness and violence; a man, wearing black, covered in blood. His skin is streaked with crimson, his face is splattered, and still more blood is dripping from the tips of two sharp knives—one in each hand—pointed down at the ground. He's surrounded by a ring of bodies on the floor, slowly and fatally leaking their insides into pools of ruby red.

He's the Angel of Death. Justice with a blade. The reckoning of... Kyle.

God, that would have sounded so much cooler if the bad guy wasn't named Kyle.

I know it's Dimitri before I recognize him through all the gore. My soul sees him. My heart soars, and I nearly cry as relief swells and rushes out of me, taking all the ugliest feelings with it.

Dimitri barely waits for the doors to open all the way before he strikes, and the way he moves melts my brain. He bends the laws of physics, I'm pretty sure, because momentum and energy conservation and gravity... they just don't seem to work the way I think they do anymore.

He takes a running leap that lands him almost all the way across the room, within reach of Kyle. He drops to the ground and kicks out his leg with a spin, knocking Kyle off his feet before the man can even react to what's happening. As Kyle falls, Dimitri pops back up just far enough to drive one of his knives into Kyle's stomach and smash him into the floor with it.

Kyle's head slams back against the floor, and he screams in pain, but Dimitri doesn't stop. He takes Kyle's arm and stabs him through the hand, driving his knife into the hardwood through flesh and bone. He does the same thing to the other as Kyle writhes and curses and cries.

"Stay," Dimitri growls as he rises to his feet.

If I weren't taped to a chair, I'd probably be picking my jaw up off the floor. Did I just witness a real-life superhero in action? No one should be able to move like that.

He approaches me, chest heaving, eyes wild, fury still written into his features, and his face still dripping with the blood of I don't know how many people...

Not the superhero. The supervillain.

In that instant, I'm afraid. He doesn't look real, or human, or sane. He stalks towards me, and my body wants to shrink away. My stomach drops.

And then, when he's within a foot of me, he falls to his knees. "Nicole," he whispers, broken, hands hovering like he doesn't know where to touch in case he hurts me.

It's all I can take. I dissolve into tears, and he disappears in a blur of color behind the water. I want to reach for him, but my arms are tied. I want to scream his name, but I can't speak through the choked noises my mouth is making.

Dimitri carefully slides his knife under the layers of tape. With a series of short, loud rips, I'm free, and I fall from the chair right into his arms, sobbing. Heavy, ugly, loud sounds escape me that I do nothing to try to control. He wraps his arms around me, hugging me tightly, and I melt against him. From the way his body shakes, I think he might be crying, too.

"You came," I sob.

"I will always come for you," he promises, the words coming out muffled in my hair.

"I knew you'd come," I say, over and over, clutching at him in an effort to get as close to him as possible.

We find each other's lips and pour ourselves into the union. My cheek is pounding, my head aches, and my stomach feels like one giant bruise, but right now I don't care. I wrap my arms around his neck, and he cups a hand behind my head. I want to stay here like this always, melding with him, connected and safe. I resent needing air.

Eventually, he pulls back, and his hand comes around to cup my jaw, thumb ghosting beneath what is probably a nasty cut and bump from the butt of Kyle's gun.

"I was so scared," I confess, eyes filling back up with tears.

"I know," he croons. "I told you. I take care of what is mine. That means I will always come for you. You are safe. He cannot harm you or anyone else."

That phrase snaps me out of it, making my whole body tense with an urgent memory. I scramble to my feet, out of Dimitri's lap, and he rises smoothly next to me. He opens his arms to receive me, but I shoot past him towards the other room.

"Nicole?" he says softly, confused as he follows.

The door of the bedroom slams against the wall, denting it, and I make a horrified noise. Just as I feared, there's a dead body on the bed—a mostly naked woman with a bullet hole in her forehead, lying next to a small puddle of vomit. Kyle killed her for daring to throw up on him.

I sob again and feel Dimitri spin me and tuck me against his chest to protect me from what I can't unsee.

I've seen death before. I've even seen violent death before, but this was... cruel, and senseless. I'm reminded of my conversation with Dimitri on the boat, which feels like years ago. I didn't realize how much I believed what I said until this exact moment.

Not everyone deserves to die. Some people deserve to suffer.

I lean back against the arm bracing my back. "Give me your knife."

Without so much as a questioning look, he takes a clean one from a holster in his belt and offers it up, letting it dangle by the circle cutout at the end of the handle. I grab it, careful of the sharp blade, and step around Dimitri. Kyle is still moving on the floor, though it's clearly painful and taking a lot of effort. He's bleeding freely from the stab wound in his stomach, and he can't do anything about it with his hands skewered like that.

I feel a little thrill seeing the fear in Kyle's eyes as I come into view.

"Will it kill him, where your knife went in?" I ask Dimitri, gesturing to the wound in Kyle's stomach. I could check for myself, but I don't want to get that close yet.

"Fuck you both!" Kyle screams. "I'm going to fucking kill you—my family will kill you and everyone you love! Let me go and fight me like a real fucking man—"

I can feel Dimitri's presence at my back. "Eventually," he says softly. Surprisingly, it's easy to hear him despite Kyle's screams. "I wanted his death to be slow and painful."

The words make me shiver, but there's no horror in my body's response to the remorseless malice. I look at Kyle and feel only hatred. I tune out his vitriol as I approach and nearly smile when he shrinks away.

"Do not straddle his leg," Dimitri coaches from behind me. "Do not hesitate, just strike—and use more force than you think you have to."

I swallow, gripping the handle. My hand trembles. I want to stab him so badly. I want him to sit in the fear he inflicted on me. I want him to suffer the same helplessness and hopelessness he made me feel using violence and sexual threats.

Kyle curls in on himself, even as he shouts obscenities at me from the floor. I find my target, adjust my grip so the slippery, bloody handle of the knife won't cause a problem, and strike. I use more force than I think I have to, and I'm met with a sickening resistance that gives way to a satisfying yielding of muscle and skin. His screams ramp up, higher and more fearful than they've been yet, then the noise cuts out. He's passed out.

"Yes. She stabbed him in the cock," I hear Dimitri say, and I know he's not talking to me. There's a deep chuckle, a surprisingly happy sound amid this macabre scene. "Wesley says that because we are a couple that stabs together, we should stay together. I like it."

In my shock at the realities of how it felt to stab someone—the force, the smell of his blood, the sound of skin splitting—I released the handle of the knife. Now, I reach for it, jerk it upwards, and stare down at the spreading stain of blood in the crotch of his pants for an instant.

"We need to get out of here," Dimitri says, laying a heavy, warm hand on my shoulder. Despite the blood soaking him, I can still smell his true scent. It stings my nose and feels like home. "What about Kyle?"

We stare down at Kyle. His chest is rising and falling, barely, and the blood has started soaking into the hardwood. I consider what Dimitri asked.

What about Kyle?

Will he die on his own? Should we leave him? I know Dimitri's question is partially an offer to handle the situation for me. He might as well have asked, *What part do* you *want to play, Nicole?*

Well... what do I want to do?

I look up at my man. His eyes meet mine, fierce and proud, dipping to my swollen cheek and hardening in anger. That one brief look speaks volumes and lights me on fire from the inside.

I'm done with this shit—Kyle, the USB, all of it. I think I'd even like to kill him, but he might still have some value to us. Though I'm not sure it's strictly necessary for him to be alive for this next idea...

"Let's frame him for my kidnapping."

His brows shoot up. "What?"

"We can... plant the drive on him. Anyone in his family that's still alive will assume he took it, and it'll be in police lockup before they realize the money was transferred away anyway, right? And that way, I have an excuse for where I've been all this time that has nothing to do with you. It's a good idea, right? It protects all of you." And maybe one day I can even rejoin the real world here in Ulysses.

He lifts his hand, rubbing the backs of his knuckles against my un-marred cheek. "Are you certain, Nicole? It will not be easy. Lying to the police is not simple, and you will have to face them alone—"

I reach for his hand and hug it to my chest. "It'll be worth it to stay with you."

42

NICOLE

This time it's me taking care of what's mine.

I'm in the middle of the bench-style front seat of a rusted-out exterminator van. Dimitri's leg is pressed against the length of mine, and his hand is tucked between my thighs, his thumb stroking circles against my pants as a comfort to both of us. Eleanor slumps against me on my other side, hugging me around the middle, careful of the area where I told her I was hit. The ride back is silent, and it feels excruciatingly slow, and when I look over at the speedometer, I can see why—Dimitri is driving exactly the speed limit. It makes me smile for some reason, despite the strangely tense, somber mood.

I know we won, but I'm too battered and tired and worried to feel only happy about it.

It takes much longer than it should to get back, since Dimitri takes every back road he can. We're pulling into the driveway of the mansion before it occurs to me to ask, "What do we do about the... um... the bodies?"

"After Mac gets back to check on Eleanor, we're going to stage it so it aligns with the story we give you for the police," Wesley says.

"Okay," I agree, because what else am I going to do? This is so... way over my head. It's so beyond what I ever care to worry about ever again.

Dimitri helps Eleanor and then me out of the passenger seat, and we head inside. It's a blur. I'm in a daze, and the next thing I know, Dimitri and I are in the bathroom and he's gently peeling my sweatshirt over my head.

"Are you hurt anywhere?" I ask, realizing how much blood he's wearing as I rest my hand on his sticky shoulder when he encourages me to step out of my jeans.

"No," he replies too quickly.

"I don't believe you," I say softly, and I do mean it, but I don't really have the energy to fight him.

He ignores me to start the shower, then resumes his perusal of my naked body. There's no heat in his eyes, just an almost clinical concern as he checks me for injuries beyond the ones I already told him about. I have a few cuts and bruises, but I'm otherwise unscathed. Somehow.

"Take off your clothes," I insist. "Let me make sure you're okay, too."

More ignoring. He bends over and retrieves the first-aid kit from one of the bottom drawers in the vanity and sets it on the counter, then takes my hand and ushers me into the shower under the spray.

I wipe the wet hair from my eyes. "Get in here with me. You're covered in blood."

I think he's going to protest, or ignore me again, but he lifts his shirt over his head with a grip on the back of his collar, and lets it fall. It makes a wet plopping noise on the tile, heavy with viscous fluids. His pants fall next, and he slides off his boots, so it all comes off in a big pile that he kicks aside, leaving a streak of red against the tile.

When he joins me in the shower, my instinct is to wrap my arms around him, but then I see the outline of a bruise on his ribs. I reach for it, but he catches my wrist. "I am fine, Nicole," he says.

"I don't believe you," I repeat, this time more forcefully. "Let me take care of you, too."

"You do not need to. Not while you are... not like this."

He steps into the spray and scrubs roughly at his skin. I suck in a breath, turning a gasp into a sharp inhale through the nose when I see the tiny cuts and more bruising on the pale skin of his back. That broken mirror on the elevator…

When the water runs clear from his efforts, he moves me back under the stream and starts gently soaping me up. I don't have nearly as much blood to wash off, but I appreciate the warmth, even if the water stings against the cut on my cheek. When I wince and gently prod at the swollen area on my cheekbone, he watches the movement with a frown.

"Will it scar?" I ask.

He reaches for my cheek, replacing my fingers with his own. "No," he says with an unexpected, faint smile around the corners of his mouth.

I'm simultaneously relieved and disappointed. It might have been nice to have a battle scar—and I'd even kind of match Dimitri, with it on my face—but I know I wouldn't want to look in the mirror and be reminded of the worst night of my life. I realize with a start that that must be how Dimitri feels. It didn't occur to me that a scar could be more than just marred skin and a ruined self-image. It's a memory of whatever he was feeling, of the bone-deep fear and helplessness.

My heart aches.

I reach up and curl my hand as far as it will go around the outside of his. His thumb stops its gentle path along my cheekbone, and he pulls back, spinning his palm to grab mine and draw my hand towards him. He presses his lips against the back of my hand, squeezing his eyes closed. My pulse thumps, spiking at the tender contact.

"Dimitri, talk to me," I plead.

He nods, as if he's agreeing to do as I'm asking, but he says nothing. Instead, he rinses me, reaches around me to turn off the water, and guides me gently from the shower. I have half a mind to take a stand and refuse to do anything else he wants until he talks to me, but I'm chilly outside of the steam, so I let him tie my big, fluffy robe around my waist.

He roughly towel-dries himself, tosses it on the floor, and takes my hand to lead me back out. Though I get to watch his round ass as he walks towards the couch, I'm almost too distracted to appreciate it.

I'm starting to think he's still upset with me after yesterday, but when he sits, he pulls me on top of him by the tie of the robe. With his dick stretched up between us, I straddle his lap, a leg on each side, and settle against his chest. What's normally an eight-inch height disparity in his favor is turned on its head as he has to tilt his head up to meet my eye.

His fingers curl around my waist, his grip a little too tight to be comfortable, but I don't care. I place my hands on his shoulders, and we stare into each other's eyes.

He nods at me again, and it's a different one this time. I don't know how I know that, but I do. This one means he's ready to talk.

"Are you okay?" I whisper.

His fingers tighten around me. *"Da."*

"Are you sure? No internal bleeding? Your vision is okay, no unexplained pain anywhere? I'm pretty sure I don't have a concussion, so I'm fully capable of treating any symptoms you have. I just need you to tell me what hurts."

He's silent for a moment, breathing noisily through his nose. "Everything."

My brows come together in concern. "Dimitri—"

"I hurt everywhere, my med. I nearly lost you. I feel like I cannot breathe."

"What do you need?"

"I need... to know that you are all right, Nicole," he says. I gently take his face in my hands, and he closes his eyes, his voice breaking around an unsteady inhale and exhale. "I need to... Fuck, I do not know. My med. I need to hold you, to know you are here with me, that you are staying with me..."

I swallow, watching him grapple for words. Seeing it breaks my heart. It's even worse—more alarming—as tears leak out from the corners of his closed eyes. Words in Russian spill from his mouth, too fast and urgent and pained to be filled with anything but horrible emotions.

"You need me to show you," I realize.

It's time for me to take care of what's mine.

Not waiting for him to even stop murmuring what must be apologies, I lean forward and take his mouth, still framed in my grip. I stroke his lips with my tongue, tangle it with his, hold his jaw tighter when he slides his arms around my back to pull me closer against him. He moans, and I steal his breath into me.

I feel his cock against my belly, hardening and stretching into the area between us to match my energy. He unties my robe, and our arms get tangled as I spit in my hand and reach down and rub it across his tip. I let him take control of aiming his own dick, and lift up as much as I can on my knee to one side. Then, I sit on him. I take him all the way, all at once, and swallow his groan of satisfaction into my mouth with another kiss.

With as tightly as we're holding each other, I can't move very much, but I rock against him, small and unsatisfactory movements that leave him so deeply inside of me that there's no respite from the twinge of pain of the head of his cock against my cervix. I don't care. I want it. Because after experiencing so much intentional brutality tonight, this pain feels almost sweet—it's not the kind that wants to hurt. It means he's in me, with me, feeling me.

"Nicole," he murmurs.

Nee-cole. I close my eyes and breathe the word. How is it possible to miss something you've only gone hours without hearing?

"Dimitri," I answer the unvoiced question with one of my own.

No, he's not okay.

No, I'm not okay.

But *we* will be.

His hands find their way under the flaps of the robe, and he uses a firm grip on my hips to help us find the friction we both need. I ride him, taking and giving, feeling the sweat building on my skin and my heart racing from exertion. The raw physicality of it shuts out the outside world and shuts down the internal monologue. All I am—all I can be—is the way my nerves fire under my skin, the way his hard body feels under my fingertips, and the rasp of his smooth shaft in and out and in and out.

"Tell me," he demands on a gasp. "Say the words. Tell me you are staying with me."

"I am. I'm staying. Dimitri, I'm so sorry—"

"No," he cuts through my apology, slashing it to pieces. "No. Not sorry. I do not care about sorry. Tell me. Tell me what you want. Tell me about this life you want. I will give you anything—everything—just tell me what to do so you will never leave me again."

A million apologies are on the tip of my tongue, but I swallow them back. "I, uh... I want to travel." I sniffle, wiping the wetness from the edge of my jaw onto the fluffy fabric covering my shoulder.

His lips find my throat, like I bared it to him for just that. "I will take you wherever you wish to go, my med."

I groan, rolling my hips up.

"What else?" he demands.

Feeling silly, and impossibly inadequate and undeserving of his adoration, I tighten around his cock with my pelvic floor muscles and greedily watch his face crumble. I feel so powerful in his arms.

"I want stupid hobbies that I have to leave the house for, like rock climbing and pickleball."

"Pickle..." he repeats, panting, then shakes his head. "Fine. Whatever you wish. I will climb rocks and make pickles into balls with you."

I laugh, but it turns into a wet moan as his cock hits that spot deep inside. "I want a dog."

"I do not like small animals, but we can discuss. Perhaps a large breed would be acceptable."

"Yeah," I whisper, realizing that I'm much more of a Great Dane kind of girl, anyway.

"More," he demands, clutching my hips and tugging me down on him.

"I want a house of my own. I'm not living in a pool house."

He drags in a rough breath through his teeth. His cock jerks inside of me. "I will build you one."

"I want a baby."

That makes him stop, eyes wide as he looks up at me. Heat rises to my cheeks, but I refuse to break eye contact. He needs to know. We need to talk about this. He's the one who asked, and it's something I want.

"Now?" he croaks, looking down at my stomach like I'm already pregnant.

"Eventually," I reply softly, running my fingertip along his lower lip.

For a brief second, I think I've managed to scare him. Then he groans, grabbing my wrist to move my hand aside so he can slam his lips on mine and pull me down onto his length.

"Yes. Fuck. Yes." His hips jolt underneath mine, frantic now. The pace of his thrusting increases, and I'm crying out as he croons in my ear, "You will carry my baby. Our baby. A baby. Yes, my med."

The fire in his eyes makes my stomach flip, and the intensity of his desire for it—for me, for a baby, for forever—brings a fresh wave of tears to my eyes. Emotions eventually give way to real arousal, with the building pleasure of having his cock deep inside, stretching me. I break our kiss so I can rock my hips more easily and get some more friction. The scratch of his hair and pubic bone against my clit only feels good when he's so deep that I can barely breathe. It touches me on the inside of my lungs, forcing an exhale and a whimper on each downward stroke.

He comes, shouting and burying his head into my shoulder. His cock pulses inside me, jerking as his body shakes, and I slow my motions. My thighs are burning, and my hips are creaking, and this position is so not ideal for bigger bodies.

For now, though, I don't care. I didn't come, and I don't want to anymore. That kind of release isn't what matters, because I already feel so... full.

Dimitri frowns as I still in his lap, and his hand moves down, fingers ready to finish me off. I shake my head and lean backwards so I can see him better. "Don't. That was perfect."

His frown deepens. "You have not... I have not satisfied you—"

"You did. You let me take care of you. Sex isn't always just about finishing," I tell him, cupping his jaw. "Sometimes, it's about intimacy. I don't just want the orgasm; I wanted the closeness. That was what I needed. That was what you gave me."

His eyes rake across my face, darting to catch every shift in my facial expression. After a few seconds, he decides to believe me, and he moves his hand back to its resting place on my hip.

I'm sweating under the robe, so I let it fall from my shoulders, pooling at his feet, and I settle against him on his lap while he's still inside me. I rest my head in the crook of his neck, and he strokes my hair.

"I'm sorry," I whisper, worried he'll stop me again if I say it any louder. "I wish I could take back everything I said."

"You deserve freedom, Nicole. I would not keep you from—"

"No. I was wrong. I was..." I trail off, trying to put words to it. "When I was a kid, everyone left. People have always left me. Somewhere along the line, I decided it was easier if I did the leaving—that's why I moved around so much. I don't let myself really like things because it makes it harder to leave them. I'm... bad at being vulnerable. I'm bad at knowing what I want and asking for it. I need to be better. You make me want to be better."

He's silent for a moment, letting that sink in. "Never be afraid of telling me what you want. If you want to leave, I will follow you anywhere, my med. You will always have me. As long as you want me, you will have me. And frankly, even if you decide you do not want me, you will have me still."

I make a soft, amused humming noise.

"Promise you will come to me if you ever feel trapped or in danger."

It nearly makes me wince, but I deserve much more than that gentle reprimand. "I will. I promise to be honest with you from now on. I promise not to push you away without explaining what's going on in my head ever again."

"And I promise to fight *for* you—for us—and not against you."

I smile at that and pull back to meet his stare. "I never want to fight with you if it means that I might not get the chance to make up with you."

It's only as I'm saying it that I realize just how true it is. I've been through a lot tonight, but one of the lowest points of the night was when I really thought I was going to die—and on the list of regrets that everyone runs through when faced with their own mortality, dying on bad terms with Dimitri was the very top.

He nods solemnly, kisses me again, and I sigh in relief. An emotional weight is lifted with his forgiveness. I lean against him again, content to let him lazily stroke my back. For once, I'm not worried about being too heavy or about reciprocating the calming gesture.

"I should never have let you go."

"It doesn't matter now. I'm done running. I'm done making up reasons that my life can't start. I've been looking for home all this time, and I assumed it was a place."

He quirks a brow.

"Turns out it's a person. *You're* home, Dimitri."

His eyes are shining. The grip on my hips tightens, and I swear I feel a stirring of the semi-soft cock inside me.

"I want *you*. I want everything with you. Man, monster, partner... everything. I love you, Dimitri," I say, nearly sighing in relief when it feels more right than I could have hoped.

"*Ya tebya lyublyu,*" he replies softly. "I love you, my Nicole."

This time, his kiss is gentle. His movements are slow and deliberate as he lowers me onto my back and makes *love* to me for the first time. Each movement of his hips against mine is a purposeful promise of more to come and a reminder of declarations that don't need any more words tonight. When I reach down to finish myself so we can come together, he cups his hand around mine, letting me drive but still needing to be part of it in his own way.

43

DIMITRI

Fun Dimitri

I rub the healing skin of my chest tattoo to stop it from itching. Fresh tally marks for saving Nicole have now taken the place of the three oldest lines. Every time she sees it, she smiles, which far outweighs any temporary irritation.

"So, what the fuck are we gonna do about Felix?" James asks, placing a glass of vodka in front of me and taking a swig of his beer. He sits in the chair in the corner, leaning back and crossing his long legs at the ankle, accidentally jostling the table with his foot, shaking Wesley's champagne.

"Oi," Wesley complains, snatching up the top-heavy glass before it can fall over. Very little spills in a house of men with such quick reflexes.

"Sorry," James replies instantly.

"First, we must find him," I point out.

James was angry for days, inconsolable to anyone but Eleanor, and barely released her from his sight. Though I wanted very much to treat Nicole the same, I had to let her go long enough to submit herself and her story to the police. Wesley is keeping a close eye on the investigation, and Nicole is a person of interest, but between finding Kyle dead in a pool of his own blood full of cocaine, a sexually assaulted dead prostitute, and the bodies in the elevator, they are leaning towards organized crime. If it goes to court, she will not be testifying, but we will have access to all the information we need to track down everyone who remains of the Volkevich clan.

It terrifies me every time she must leave to go down to the station, but Wesley watches from hacked cameras inside, and I watch from the shadows of nearby buildings. She also wears twice as many trackers as Eleanor.

"At least now I have a photo to use," Wesley says, sipping his drink. "That's one step closer to finding him. He can't hide forever."

I nod thoughtfully, taking another deep sip from my vodka. It burns the back of my mouth, but slides smoothly down the throat just as good alcohol should. I think of my woman, off with Eleanor somewhere in this house. Then I steal a look at both of my teammates, my *brothers*, and consider my life in a way I never have before—with hope and direction. Disregarding the future was purely self-preservation, to ignore what I believed would be an inevitable violent death. But Nicole... my *med*... she is the catalyst for a new kind of thinking, though I am uncertain exactly how to transition from a hitman who lives day to day and expects to be killed in the line of the job, to someone who has a reason to keep himself alive.

I study the glass in my hands as I announce, "I am old for a hitman."

James chokes on a sip of his beer. "Oh? And how old is that, exactly?"

"Fuck off. Suffice it to say, most hitmen do not make it to my age. Particularly the ones who are on the ground, as I am."

"Yeah, and?" Wesley asks, sending a meaningful look at James as he places his glass on the table. It makes a faint, high-pitched tinkling noise.

"I am saying that we will finish this business with the Volkevich *Bratva*, we will track down Felix so I may have my revenge, and then... I do not know what the future will hold. Perhaps Nicole will be content to live here for a time, but... I do not know what happens next."

A baby. The word echoes in my head and chest, making my heart race. It inspires fear and hope in equal measure. All I know is that once there is a child, everything will be different. To take risks for myself is one thing, but when there is another person, born of my blood... that is no longer an acceptable recourse.

James claps me on the shoulder. "You'll figure it out."

In the silence that follows, the sloshing liquid in James's bottle is the loudest sound. He exchanges a look I cannot decipher with Wesley. After a moment of trading more incomprehensible looks back and forth, he asks, "But until that happens, we can count on you, right, Big D?"

I incline my head. These are concerns for another time, far from now. "Of course. I enjoy this work, and both of you require me to keep you in a line. You will not be rid of me so easily."

Wesley clears his throat as James rolls his eyes. "In that case, we got an email from the General earlier. Maybe we should move this into my office?"

"This is a celebration," I observe with a scowl. "At a celebration, we drink; we do not discuss work."

James gapes at me, and even Wesley is a bit taken aback. "What is happening right now? You don't want to discuss work? You're the guy who always kicks off our meetings."

"You also leave the instant the discussion of work is done," Wesley chimes in, and I roll my eyes. "And you leave the group chat whenever we get off topic."

"What is this, some kind of new Dimitri?" James continues, grinning ear to ear at my obvious annoyance. "*Fun* Dimitri?"

"I would not say that," I object. "But perhaps I am... experiencing a shift in my perspective. The past designs us, but it does not define us."

"Google doc," Wesley sings.

"Actually, this is something Nicole said," I inform him, pouring myself another drink.

James groans as he shifts forward to reach into his pocket and retrieve his phone. "Now there's two of them? Fuckin' Christ."

I chuckle. "She is clever."

"I think allowances can be made for *Dimitri-isms* to include the words of his equally wise and poetic lady." Wesley smirks at me. "And I really do have something I want to show you in my office. Bring your drink; we can keep celebrating in there."

I do not bother with another round of protests because his insistence is beginning to feel suspicious. Instead, I grab the unmarked bottle of homemade potato vodka and grip the ring of my glass in my other hand, and follow them down the hallway. The door to his office is closed as usual, but the usually unoccupied library across the hall has light shining from within.

"Lights are on," James observes. "Weird."

They approach the library instead of the study, and I follow in confusion. When I get to the doorway, I pause, impossibly more puzzled by the sight before me.

"Surprise!" three people chorus, in varying depths and tones of excitement.

"What is this?" I demand, gesturing to the decorations with my index finger lifted from the rim of my glass. Vodka sloshes, hitting my palm.

The first things I notice are the small, inflated cows littering the floor. About the size of cats, they cover the rug and occupy the couch, and James kicks one aside as he moves towards a tray of food set up on the low table. Next, I notice a string of metallic balloons hanging from the curtain rod over the windows, spelling out *Holy Cow, D is 40 now!*

"We didn't know when your birthday actually is," Eleanor begins.

"Nor will you," I interject, then nod my head as if to say, *go on*.

Eleanor grins at me. "So, we randomly picked today. Happy 40th, Dimitri!"

"It was the girls' idea. Unless you like it, in which case, happy birthday from all of us, big guy," Wesley says, spreading his arms wide.

I frown at the balloon words as Eleanor approaches me with a tray of appetizers, nearly tripping over one of the cows. I assume now that there are 40 of them.

"They didn't have enough I's to spell your whole name," she confesses, watching me take a dumpling on a toothpick.

I place the pelmeni into my mouth and make a noise of approval. She has refined her recipe, and they are excellent now—even better tasting than those from the nostalgic memories from my youth. I glance around, but I do not need to see it to confirm that there is someone very important missing. "Where is Nicole?"

Eleanor winces. "Bathroom. She's gonna be so pissed. I feel bad. I'm the one who told her just to go."

"So, you're 40?" James whistles before popping a pelmeni.

I am not, but I will be sooner than I care to admit.

"And what if I am?" I ask as Wesley hits a button and some light music fills the room—a good backdrop for chatter.

James's smile is all charm. "Nothing, it's just that most 40-year-olds I know need a plan for getting up off the floor. I think it's safe to say you're subverting the expectations for your age group."

"I only need a plan to get up off the floor when you are in the way because I have just wiped the sparring mat with your body."

James is already throwing his head back and laughing when Wesley says, voice full of real admiration, "That was almost such a good joke, Dimitri. The raw material is there, but the execution needs refining."

"Shit! I leave for 30 seconds to use the bathroom, and I miss the surprise? Guys!" Nicole's deep voice behind me makes me turn, but her eyes are on James and Wesley, and her expression is full of censure. "I can't believe you did it without me!"

I turn towards the door and see her long, bare legs first. My mouth goes dry at the sight of so much skin revealed by the frilly, flowery skirt.

There is something about a leggy woman in a dress, particularly when she is my woman.

Her look is apologetic, like it is her fault she was not here, as she comes over and fits herself against me for a hug. "Surprise," she breathes.

"I am not 40," I say, lifting a brow as I tilt my head down to look at her.

She grins. "I know. But the cows made me laugh."

"And it is not my birthday."

She shrugs. "It's not really about getting older, and I know you don't want to be celebrated—but I wanted an excuse to celebrate you, and to try to convince you birthdays aren't so bad. It's the one day you're allowed to make all about you."

"That is a very American way to look at it."

"Well, unless you're going to tell me when your actual birthday is—"

"I will not."

"Then it's today from now on."

It is very far from the correct date, but I have no intention of ever telling anyone. I do not need to be celebrated, but since this one appears to be little more than a family dinner and a few blow-up cows, I do not mind. And I like the idea of being reborn after Nicole, by her will.

I lift a hand, and she tilts her head to make room for it at the base of her neck and shoulder—a synchronized call and response our bodies make to each other. "I will allow this—for you."

"Good, because birthdays aren't all bad. I got you a present," she murmurs, eyes locked on my lips.

"Oh?"

"I'm wearing it," she whispers, brushing her breasts against my chest. Her breath ghosts across my lips, and the blood in my body rushes downward.

Perhaps birthdays have more merit than I thought. "I want to open it now."

She grins and runs the tips of her fingernails along the line of her cleavage, tugging down the center of her dress and flashing a hint of red lace. "It's not really something you open. It's more something you... remove."

The blood that rushed south starts to pound insistently. She is going to have me hard in front of my teammates. Wicked woman. I shift my hand so it is less caressing and more circling her throat. Her breath catches, and I watch a wave of goosebumps rise and fall on her skin. "We are leaving."

She grabs my wrist and pulls so she can shake her head. "Eleanor and I blew up, like, 60 balloons. We're staying, at least until the food is gone."

I bend my head down, and she rises on her toes to meet me. Just before our lips touch, she smiles, knowing she has won—that I would do far more for her than delay my raging desire and stay at a silly party, just to know she was pleased.

"As you wish, my *med*."

44

NICOLE

It's sort of a term of endearment

"Okay, so, do they have code names for each other? Like, is James *Eagle Eyes* or something?" I ask in a low, conspiratorial voice.

Next to me on the couch, a tipsy Eleanor huffs a laugh as she takes another gulp of her champagne. Her cheeks are flushed with it, and I keep catching James looking over with a funny expression on his face. It warms me that he keeps an eye on her, even though it makes me feel like I'm witnessing something private when his gaze shutters as she purposefully ignores him to pour herself another glass.

He's pissed, and she's egging him on. This is going to blow up. Soon.

"It's so funny to me that you call him James. It takes me half a second to realize who you mean every time."

"Sorry," I laugh. "I guess it's hard wrapping my mind around the nicknames since Dimitri never uses them. Except for me, I guess."

"Really? You have a nickname?" Eleanor asks, swiping her bangs out of her eyes with the back of the hand clutching the flute. "Not that you don't deserve one or anything, it's just... out of character, I guess?"

"That's what I thought," I admit.

"What's out of character?" Wesley asks, taking the seat on Eleanor's other side and refilling her champagne glass before his own.

"Dimitri gave Nicole a nickname," she tells him.

"Should I feel flattered?" I ask, rolling with the vibe.

"Dimitri gave Nicole a nickname?" James repeats, only a few steps behind Wesley. He reaches down and swipes Eleanor's glass and drains it for her while she scowls up at him. He turns and throws Dimitri a look over his shoulder. "You gave Nicole a nickname?"

"No."

I narrow my eyes at him. Was I not supposed to talk about this? It's not like he hasn't used it in front of them... Wait, has he not? "What do you mean?"

"What do *you* mean?" he counters with a quizzical frown. He closes the distance between us and pulls me up off the couch. There's only one seat left, so he settles back down and brings me onto his lap. My face heats as I fall into the space between his leg and the arm of the couch, leaving my thighs draped over him.

I feel my face flush, but mine isn't from champagne. "Um... You call me your 'med.'" His lips purse, and I feel even more confused. Am I giving away some kind of secret? "Because I'm like your personal medic. Right?"

At the sound of a muffled laugh, I glance over in time to see Wesley grin and James raise taunting eyebrows at Dimitri. For his part, Dimitri scowls at them, like he's daring them to say something. He drapes an arm over my legs, curling a possessive hand around my knee.

"What? What did I miss?"

"It's sort of a nickname, but it's sort of a term of endearment, too," Wesley explains. "He's not referring to your profession; *med* means honey in Russian."

Eleanor gasps, "Aw!"

I feel my body tense as chills erupt all over me and tears prickle behind my eyes. He slides his hand to that spot on my neck—it's a practiced motion now—and I tilt my head up to meet his eyes before he can even put enough pressure in the right spots to do it for me. I grab his wrist. The rest of the party falls away, and it's just the two of us.

All this time, I thought he was calling me "nurse" or making a teasing joke about how we first connected when I sewed him up. And sure, it felt a little reductive at first, but then it felt like something secret we shared, like a nickname born of an inside joke.

"It is your coloring," he murmurs, low. His gaze sweeps across my face, pausing on my cheeks, my lips, my brows, then settling back into the intense eye contact. "You are like golden honey. My sweet *med*."

I try not to gape. He wasn't calling me "med," he was saying *med*.

All this time, he was being affectionate. All this time, he was being open about how he felt, but I was too stubborn to see it, and he was too oblivious to realize he needed to explain it. It makes me want to laugh because if that isn't just the perfect metaphor for our relationship so far, I don't know what is.

I laugh, and he cocks a brow at me, but smiles in response.

"I love you, too, honey."

EPILOGUE I

Wesley

The sounds of the lamest birthday party I've ever been to follow me out of the library. It's not even Dimitri's actual birthday... not that I'd ever call him out on what he clearly wants to keep quiet. Plus, everyone is having a good time, and moments like these are bright spots in an otherwise dark existence.

I can hear the conversations echo across the hallway, the intermingling of four distinct voices and accents. As I shut the door of my study, muffling the sounds of two couples and their easy camaraderie, I have to swallow down a rush of sharp, uncomfortable emotions. I'm not really jealous—they all deserve whatever fleeting happiness they can get in this life—but it feels a hell of a lot like it.

It never occurred to me before Mac brought Eleanor back home one night that any of us might pursue a romantic relationship while doing what we do. Most women wouldn't fit into this life of death and violence, nor would they want to. I assumed Dimitri felt the same way I did, but then he found Nicole and forced that square peg into a round hole, as is his way.

And I've come to think of both those women as an extension to this strange little family we've built, but... it's not a good life. Just because Eleanor turned out to be nearly as crazy as Mac, and Nicole puts up with it for now, that doesn't mean any other woman would. Or should. It's dangerous—Eleanor was nearly shot, Nicole was kidnapped—and it forces you to leave behind who you were before.

I never let myself imagine having what they all have. A woman. A partner in the house, here with me. Someone to soften the edges that this job hones. Someone to give myself to, to lean on, to support, to tell anything...

Right. I don't tell *anyone* everything. Not even the men I kill people with—and I willingly put my life in their hands every day.

I sit at my desk and reopen the various windows I obsessively close every time I leave the room. The last requires a tertiary password and brings up the few bugs I secretly installed within the house. I know it's a gross invasion of privacy, but they're focused solely on my own hallway, and I only use them to ensure that I won't be interrupted. It's far less conspicuous than a locked door. And in a house where we're all on top of each other, someone will assume I'm having a wank and I'll never hear the end of it.

Once I'm certain, I unlock the middle desk drawer with the unmarked key on my chain and pull out the battered, black Moleskine notebook. The page I want opens automatically from the overworked crease.

Jacob Rossi, arms dealer

Kevin Anderson, corrupt—involved? maybe looking the other way?

Dr. Oliver Pinsk—running synthetic drug lab?

Julia Dennison—counterfeit ring? forgery/elite/lone wolf possibly

Wearing a grim expression, I place a single strike through the next line.

Viktor Volkevich, Russian Mob

There are a few more names, but surrounded by question marks, doubtful notes, and erasure.

Felix Cruz—cleaner? Motives? Well-connected, possible source

John Mariano—Italians... lost turf war with Russians, hobbled but not out?

Alfano Cartel—drugs, distribution... coyotes? Smuggling? Human trafficking? No sophistication, doesn't fit

Adrian Chekhov—up and coming Bratva, too young/on the radar yet? VIP gambling probably, small ops

That's the end of the list. Every other name is crossed out with a single neat line, scratched out in anger or frustration, or erased. I flip through the familiar pages that follow, taking care with the paper that's worn down from all the handling.

I skim the disjointed, scribbled notes that contain dozens of unanswered questions, like: Why Ulysses? What's the connection? What is the growth source and potential? How did they evade notice for so long? Someone on the inside?

With a long exhale, I amble over to the mini-fridge I installed and crack open a new can of energy. There's a message blinking on the screen when I settle back at my desk.

> mermaidav: I was just sitting here thinking today felt incomplete. Then I realized I hadn't talked to you yet.

A grin forms on my face before I even finish reading the greeting. My fingers are on the keys in an instant, typing out my response to *her*—my favorite spider, and quickly becoming my favorite *person*. Full stop.

> SpyderMan: Good thing the night is young.

Epilogue II

Mac

"It was so nice seeing you again, Eleanor. You too, Jake. Enjoy your night."

I grab the edge of Eleanor's chair, dragging her to my side so she won't see my eyes narrow at her hero, Red Elephant's head chef. The fucker keeps "forgetting" my name, and it's starting to feel real intentional. His face is blank, expressionless, but his unwavering stare feels challenging, and it's all I can do not to bare my teeth at him.

He's the luckiest fucker alive that Eleanor loves his food so damn much. It's, like, the one thing I can't do for her.

"Jesus, Mac, you going to pee on me next time?" she huffs, but I can hear the rawness underneath the exasperation. I know my girl likes it when I go all caveman on her.

"Maybe," I grumble.

"He's not interested like that. We talk food. There's nothing remotely sexual about our conversations."

I level her with my most unimpressed look. "Okay, first of all, he *is* interested. Second, you talk about food the way some people talk about sex," I point out. "Don't you dare try to tell me otherwise, darlin'."

She shifts on her seat, rolling her eyes. "Fine, but it's not like whatever is going on is my fault, right? I'm not flirting, I'm... sharing a passion with someone. I'm trying to learn how to improve from someone better than me."

I can't hide the grin. "*Better* is debatable. And you know it's not you I'm worried about, baby," I add, catching her hand and placing a small kiss on the tip of each of her fingers. When she responds with a sultry smile, my cock swells under the table.

I pay special attention to her left ring finger. I make her replace that ugly silicone placeholder with the big-ass diamonds every time she leaves the house. She tried to get me to swap it for something smaller, but I know she secretly loves how huge it is when it catches the light.

"Because I'm your good girl?" she whispers, eyes entranced by what I'm doing.

I take her thumb between my teeth and grin at her sharp inhale. "Damn right."

"Well, isn't this romantic? I'm almost sorry to interrupt," announces a deep voice.

We both look up as the chair on the other side of the table is pulled out, and a tall, thick, Hispanic man folds himself into it. He takes up every inch of space, dominating it and showing his utter lack of concern for the danger he's in. Eleanor squeaks, recognizing him immediately.

Felix.

My heart leaps into my throat as he reaches for the empty bread basket. Seeing nothing but crumbs, he frowns and sits back, like he doesn't have a care in the world save an empty stomach.

I recover, but it's damn slow. How is he here? How did he know where I was? Fuck... Eleanor... I can see the piece in its holster under his jacket, though he hasn't drawn it. This restaurant is quiet, winding down for the night. There aren't enough witnesses for him to concern himself, and he's a professional cleaner.

This is bad.

"Darlin', why don't you go to the—" I begin.

"Eleanor, stay right where you are," Felix counters, leveling those dark eyes on my girl.

When she makes a fearful noise, I bare my teeth at him, feeling a primal kind of anger that only seems to rise up in her defense.

"I'll fucking kill you with my bare hands if you look at her again. You don't look at her," I snarl. "This is between you and me."

Eleanor's hands are shaking as she lowers them into her lap. I leave mine on the table where he can see them, to put him at ease, just in case he's feeling brave or stupid. I can see it out of the corner of my eye when Eleanor presses the panic button built into the underside of the watch she wears whenever she leaves the house. Wes's design. It sends an SOS and a GPS coordinate to the group chat when pressed for five seconds. Wes or Dimitri will respond, and when they get no answer, they'll rally their asses on over.

Good girl.

"Hey, hey," Felix says, lifting empty palms in mock surrender. "It doesn't have to be like that, Mac. We're old buddies. I come in... well, not peace, but I come to settle our debt. Eleanor here can just be our witness, eh, *mama*?" he winks and flashes her a smile.

"Hey," I growl.

He grins wider.

"You left Nicole to die," Eleanor hisses, sounding more ferocious than I'd expect, considering her hummingbird heartbeat.

"I gave her her best chance. And look, I know shoulda-woulda-coulda means jack shit, but for what it's worth, I was gonna go back for her. But when we got down there, Dimitri was already there, looking ready to rip my dick off, and I realized I didn't have to go back. My best move was to split," he says, jerking his thumb over his shoulder, "with my dick intact."

"The fuck do you want, Felix? Because from where I stand, not killing you after you kidnapped one of us settles our debt just fine." He doesn't need to know that killing him is very much the plan.

"I didn't kidnap her. I didn't know who she was, okay? And everything's fine now, right? No harm, no foul."

"Fuck. That."

He hums, sucking on his teeth and regarding me with a quiet that's unsettling in its calm. "I thought you might say that. So, I came prepared." He reaches into his lapel, and both of us tense, but he just tosses a piece of paper onto the table.

I reach for it, scanning, frowning at the printed email. "What am I looking at?"

"How well do you know this *cabrón*? The General? Your patron, or… handler. That's what you lot call it, right?"

Blood freezes in my veins. Felix knows about the General?

I have no way to verify, but the email feels eerily similar to the ones we receive with information about our hits. I scan the text, pulse picking up when I see the time, date, and place of the Volkevich wedding, and the words *USB drive*. And a ridiculous sum of money.

My boss hired Felix to steal Volkevich's USB? And us, to kill Volkevich at the same time? And he never bothered to mention anything about how the job would likely cause us to cross paths with a dangerous man that I'm pretty sure he knows I have a history with?

What the fuck.

He watches realization slowly dawn, and a smile spreads across his face. This time, there's no mirth, only knowing eagerness and a twisted kind of pride, like he figured it all out.

"Yeah, he never told you that, huh?" he shakes his head, like I've just confirmed his suspicions. "The second I realized who that lady was and what she meant to your Russian, I knew you guys were involved and that some real shady shit was going down. Whatever game this General is playing, we're just pawns."

There's no proof, but his words arouse a series of long-standing, unanswered questions. It's hard to trust a man you've never seen, and the General is an enigma. By design. Obviously, he's got an agenda, but I haven't given it that much thought beyond how it aligns with our own fucked-up moral compass.

"So?" I challenge.

"So... you owe me one in exchange for that intel you bought from me months ago—a cleaning job, wasn't it? Right here in this fine, fuckin' fancy-ass establishment, if memory serves," he says, making it clear his memory serves him just fine.

I swallow, and the word carries a bit less weight this time as the blood starts draining from my face. "So?"

"So, I'm not a fucking pawn. Are you? I'm calling in my favor—we're gonna find the General and kill him."

Acknowledgements

The first, biggest thanks to *you*, dear reader (again, always), for picking up my book.

Thank you so much to my supportive family and friends, especially Ben. This was a tough one and it would probably be sitting in a file called rev26Imgonnaripmyhairout, if not for you. I'm still going to talk to myself in a Russian accent forever, though. That's your life, now.

Dana, as always, thanks for doing your thing. Your enthusiasm makes me so happy. And after all those months of waiting, and listening to story lines that never panned out... you helped me find this story and I'm so grateful to you for that.

Sammie! I'm so glad we found each other. Thank you so so much for all you did to make me better and help this book look so good! We're gonna have to gild that fine-toothed comb, girl. You find all the squicky parts.

Bri—my first true book bestie, and the kind every writer needs in her life. You are so supportive and amazing, and I'll never forget what you did for Dimitri and the end of this book, even though we both know where your heart truly lies.

You can't change my mind, so I'll say it again: every ARC reviewer is a rockstar. You're so important to me. Thank you, thank you, thank you.

ABOUT THE AUTHOR

L.M. Whiteley writes dark, steamy romance with morally gray male main characters, relatable female main characters, obsessive love and hard-won happily-ever-afters.

When she's not writing, she can be found cooking, gardening, gaming, playing outside with her friends or letting book boyfriends written by other fantastic indie authors ruin her.

Blog posts, signed copies of the books, and links to all socials can be found on her website: http://lmwhiteley.com

<u>Loved the book?</u>

The best way to support indie authors is by leaving a review!

Please consider rating and reviewing Kept in the Dark on **Amazon** and **Goodreads**. Scan the codes below!

Kept in the Dark on Amazon

Kept in the Dark on GoodReads

<u>Stay Obsessed</u>

Join the newsletter on my website for exclusive content, sneak peeks, and bonus scenes:

Website: [http://lmwhiteley.com]

Follow L.M. Whiteley on social media:

Instagram [@LMWhiteleyauthor]|

TikTok [@LM.Whiteley]|

Facebook [@LMWhiteleyauthor]